LIPO QUEEN

LIPO QUEEN

a novel

Suzanne Edmonds

ISBN-13: 9780692713563
ISBN-10: 0692713565
Library of Congress Control Number: 2016911012
Lipo Queen, Beverly Hills, CA

Cover art by Helen Trott and Tomi Monstre

For Adam

and for Linda

Foreword

When I learned that Suzanne, my good friend and colleague, had written a novel about a young plastic surgeon whose life takes a detour through the insane world of reality TV, I knew I had to read it immediately. I had no idea that she was as talented a writer as she is a surgeon. So, although I intended to sleep on my last flight from L.A. to São Paulo, I couldn't put *Lipo Queen* down and finished the whole thing before we landed—and was left wanting more!

I did not realize that Suzanne had finished writing *Lipo Queen* way back in 2011. I am shocked that it has been read by *so many* people over the past five years, and yet it is *just* being published *now*! Not only is this brilliant book long overdue, but there's something in it for *everyone*: behind-the-scenes plastic surgery, reality TV, the conflicting joys—and pains—of success, the tragic comedy of a dysfunctional adult family with a "crazy" mother…even a fairy-tale romance for our heroine, Rachel.

This story is especially personal to me, as it parallels my own struggle of trying to reconcile my public persona with my professional world, and all of the criticism that I received from my colleagues. Suzanne captures so well with honesty and authenticity some of the conflict that *I* faced when creativity and opportunity clashed with the traditional—and sometimes outdated—standards of our field.

Like Suzanne's heroine Rachel, I experienced prejudice from my colleagues for doing something "out of the box." *A TV SHOW*! *How dare I?* But *Dr. 90210* ultimately brought awareness of the benefits of plastic surgery to millions of people around the world who otherwise never would have known about it.

I was immediately engaged by Rachel's voice, and related to her both as a surgeon and as a person navigating the world of television while trying to navigate her "real" life. The book flows with a rhythm and writing style that compels you to keep reading, to find out what is going to happen to these fascinating characters that absolutely jump off the page at you. They are people that you would follow anywhere—you want to be right there *with* them!

I laughed out loud throughout much of this book (getting looks from the passengers seated nearby like, "Oh, there's that crazy Dr. Rey!"), loving the deft yet often beautiful prose of Suzanne's writing. *But!* I did not miss the relevant questions posed within it regarding our modern-day perceptions of beauty and—to put it bluntly—the examination of how our appearance so markedly affects our greater human experience. This is not just an L.A. thing. It's not something that is talked about, but I travel and work around the world and see it *everywhere*.

Even more so, woven skillfully throughout the storyline within this addictively entertaining "beach read," are heartbreaking issues that are too often misunderstood and harshly judged by society; major topics of concern that we all deal with, yet are "taboo" to discuss. We all have secrets. But if we are suffering, if we share them with each other, we will discover that most of us have the same secrets, and that we can help each other instead of hiding our true selves.

So, in the same vein as *Doctor 90210*, *Lipo Queen* tackles serious subject matter while totally succeeding as the ultimate delicious guilty pleasure. It too will capture an audience of millions. And actually, I have to admit, the title is even catchier.

Dr. Robert Rey

"A normal life is boring, but super stardom's close to post mortem"

—Eminem, "Lose Yourself"

1

Everyone on the road is my enemy. The black SUV with the water polo sticker straight ahead, the faded brown sedan with its old, sharp edges to my left. Even the beautiful baby blue convertible Bentley catty-corner to the sedan. Come to think of it, what was a *Bentley* doing in this part of town anyway?

Everyone's in the way and they're all against me, keeping me from my destination. At least that's how it feels when you're driving anywhere in Los Angeles and you're late.

Not only was I late, but I was in trouble. No question. And not *because* I was late. I knew Donarski had a soft spot for me, but no way would he ever call me into his office for a friendly chat.

The digital clock on my dashboard said 12:52. If it had been a round clock with hands, it would look like ten to one, which gave me ten more minutes. But I was still roughly six or seven blocks from the hospital, and with everyone at a standstill like this, that could translate into twenty minutes…or more. I was used to heavy San Fernando Valley traffic, but at this hour things should at least be moving.

I'd never been called in by my boss for a meeting before. Trapped in my car, moving at two and a half miles an hour, I ironically had the luxury of time to again ask myself: *What did I do?* I racked my brain with a mental recap of all events that had transpired over the six months since Donarski had hired me at the Valley Hospital. I'd thought everything was fine. By now he'd accepted my rough edges. He'd even told me a couple of times that I was a good surgeon. (We never describe each other as "amazing" or "incredible" or even "great." From one surgeon to another, "good" is about the most you can hope for.) I hadn't had any more than the run-of-the-mill complications—an implant infection, a flap take-back. I hadn't stirred up politics with any of the other departments. *So, again…what could I have possibly done?*

You need to stop kidding yourself. It's not a what. It's a WHO.
Eddie.

Eddie, the sexy Latin scrub tech I'd been sleeping with on and off for the past few months. No, it wasn't the most politically correct maneuver of my career to date but…I'd practically been a prisoner of that hospital since I'd started working there. I no longer had any semblance of a social life out in the real world. I deserved *something* to keep me going, didn't I?

Besides, *he* started it. Not that I had exactly fought him off. But we'd been so careful about using the call rooms, always making sure the nursing stations on the other side of the wall were clear. Except, if someone *had* noticed the way we smirked at each other behind our O.R. masks…

But really, what more would Donarski do than give me a slap on the wrist? It wasn't like anyone had bled out or died or anything. So I'd apologize. We might even laugh about it. About how I could have done something so…cliché?

Besides, Eddie and I were done. I had finally ended it. Really, I had. I might not have officially let him know but in my head, it was over.

Because the *real* gut-wrenching problem was that, while I had started tasting the last name "Thomas-Fernandez" for our future children, he clearly had no interest in even being my boyfriend.

And I wasn't going to lie to myself that it was because I "intimidated" him. I learned it well from *Sex and the City*, and the book and the movie that followed. If a guy "ghosts" me, it's not because I intimidate him with the laundry list of degrees after my name. It wouldn't even matter if I was a pop icon or the descendant of a blue-blood family.

From what *I've* observed, there's only *one thing* that intimidates a guy. And you don't have to do individualized psychoanalysis of each one of them to figure it out. They're all the same. It's just *one* thing.

Beauty. The kind that's so exceptional it becomes painful to look at. I should know. I grew up in a house where beauty was the holy grail. The problem is, I'm just a "regular" girl.

Memorable snippets from my early childhood conversations with my judgmental mother? "Thank God you inherited my broad shoulders and not your father's awful narrow ones. All the models have broad shoulders." I was eight. The concept of "broad shoulders" went completely over my head. And I had no idea what a "model" was. Then, at fourteen: "Too bad you're kind of thick in the thighs." By then I knew what a model was. And that I wasn't even close.

With my mother's running commentary I perseverated on it. I measured and compared myself to all the women that she pointed out and worshipped. I evaluated the proportions of my body in department store dressing room three-way mirrors. I spent hours poring over Victoria's Secret and J. Crew catalogues, studying not the clothes but the models, the spaces between their legs, the shapes of their faces. I realized that I was missing the cheekbone "S curve." I became an expert on the perfection of the female human form.

I then started to wonder: what was *wrong* with me? Why wasn't *I* breathtaking? Over the years, I had gotten the message from my mother that somehow it was my own *fault* that I wasn't like her icons. Makes no scientific sense, I know.

Let's just say that when people ask me why I became a plastic surgeon, the whole thing is so fucked up I don't even know where to begin.

12:56. That was closer to five minutes left. I'd never make it. Shit. I was going to have to call. And it wasn't like I could lie and tell them I was stuck in the operating room or somewhere in the hospital—which was my excuse for everything I was late for *outside* of the hospital. Would she even be able to tell that I was calling from my cell phone instead of a hospital extension? Did her phone have caller ID? Probably not a lie I should risk with my chairman's secretary.

"Doctor Donarski's office, Brenda speaking."

Damn. I had hoped that she would be on the other line and it would go to voicemail. *"I called and called for like half an hour to tell you I was running late and nobody picked up,"* I would say when I got there.

"Hi Brenda, it's Dr. Thomas."

There were cops milling around the accident up ahead and I suddenly realized that I had a cell phone wedged between my shoulder and my ear while behind the wheel in broad daylight. It wasn't like I didn't know the law, but the Bluetooth was fairly useless with the background noise when my car top was down. I untied my ponytail and covered the phone with my hair.

"Hello, Doctor Thomas."

I could tell by the tone in her voice that she knew I was running late, and she was happy about it. She loved for me to screw up in front of Donarski.

"I'm…a few minutes late." I shifted from neutral into first and crawled the ten feet that had just opened up behind the minivan in front of me. Everyone makes fun of me for having a stick shift in this town, but in my opinion it's a crime to drive a sports car with an automatic transmission.

"What a surprise."

"Yeah, I was having…car trouble this morning." I knew better than to blame it on traffic. Traffic is a given in L.A. and unless there's a four-car pile-up that everybody knows about and the freeway is shut down you can't use "traffic" as an excuse. You're supposed to plan for it. And I wasn't about to tell her the truth.

12:59. Technically I wasn't late *yet*.

"But don't you have a new car?"

I raced through the light just as it turned red and made it past two more blocks by blowing by everybody from the turn lane. This was when that six-speed really came in handy.

"Oh, you know, these German cars, they have so many problems."

"No, I don't know. I don't have one."

Ouch. But I refused to feel guilty for my one self-indulgent splurge after suffering through over a decade of school and residency training. Besides, with zero down and a $50,000 loan, I wasn't even going to own one of the *doors* on this thing for another year.

"He has another meeting at 1:30. So I recommend you not waste any time."

Finally. The culprit. A totaled pick-up truck on the side of the road. Like everyone in front of me—as well as everyone in the unobstructed oncoming lanes—I slowed to gawk. The ambulances must have come and gone by now. There was just the truck attached to a tow by its mangled front end, and a layer of broken glass on the asphalt barricaded off by orange cones.

The truck's windshield had the characteristic star where the driver's head must have struck it. Hopefully he didn't mess his face up too much. Well if he had, I'd be meeting him soon enough—the Valley Hospital was the closest Level I Trauma Center within a twenty-five mile radius, and I was on call.

Hopefully it wasn't a woman. A *guy* could always handle scars on his face, but for *women*…just last month there was that girl I had with the gashes across her cheek…*so sad…she was so sweet, she'd just moved here with her life savings from the Midwest…she was so petite and perfect-looking that if the stars had aligned for her and the right sleazy casting director/producer/network exec had wandered into the place where she was "cocktail waitressing," she really could have wound up playing a teenage vampire or something for a few years…but now she couldn't even keep her day job because half her face was paralyzed from a nerve injury. She'd gone from being homecoming queen to "that poor girl who must have been really pretty before her accident."*

Wait, she didn't show up to her clinic appointment last week…I should call her…

"Dr. Thomas?"

"Be there soon." I hung up and raced through two more lights.

It really would have shut Brenda up if I could have just told her the truth about why I was late, but no way was I about to get into the whole saga with her. And I absolutely did not want it to filter up to Donarski. About how my morning had been sabotaged yet again by my brother, Jake. That because when I took him to the lab for his blood draw, the technician had to stick him so many times that he started to get belligerent and refused to let them try any longer and I had to plead and beg until he finally let me do it myself. That the whole sordid ordeal took more than the usual one hour I had allotted for it.

No, it was not time to pull out the Jake card. They didn't *really* know about him and it could put me in a worse light than I already was.

I made it to Donarski's office at one-thirteen.

"He's waiting," Brenda greeted me as I barreled through the door. I pretended that I couldn't tell how transparent her smile was, and I smiled right back. I always had to make a concerted effort to ignore how obvious it was that she hated me. It wasn't personal. She was just being territorial. She'd been Donarski's Right Hand Woman forever, and then he hired me and suddenly she wasn't the only girl. I got it.

I looked past her through the half-open door to Donarski's office. He was sitting at his desk arranging patient photographs into charts.

Brenda closed his office door behind me.

This was becoming uncomfortably ominous. *Was I really about to get fired for sleeping with a scrub tech?*

"Raquel, how are things?" Dr. Donarski greeted me in his thick Polish accent. He was middle-aged, slight in build and with sharp facial features that gave him a deceptively serious expression even when he was joking. Which wasn't now.

"Fine." I didn't bother to correct him on the pronunciation of my name. He had called me "Raquel" since my first day on the job and when I told him after a month had gone by, "You know, it's not Raquel, it's Rachel" he had said without missing a beat, "Too late. I already started calling you Raquel."

"So," he continued, holding up two of the photos from his desk. "What's this?"

It took me a minute to realize that they were before-and-after pictures of one of my breast cancer reconstruction patients. I recognized her pink leopard print underwear. *Okay, so I wasn't getting my wrist slapped for rendezvousing around the hospital with another employee after all.* Clearly, he was just congratulating me on one of my amazing results.

"Yeah, that's a really good one, right?" I said. "It's only been a few weeks though, there's still swelling…I might have to do another round of fat grafting on her."

"That's going to be difficult, considering you took all of her fat out the first time."

Funny, his tone did not sound congratulatory. I searched his face.

"No, I didn't. You can't tell from the picture but she's got a whole bunch of muffin top left there."

"Muffin top? And what anatomic part of the human body would that be?"

"You know, that fat that pokes out…" I grabbed at my lower back. "It was never an issue before low-waisted jeans but now, if you have any fat *at all* there it just spills over—"

"Raquel, why does this woman look two dress sizes smaller?"

"I know, isn't it great? I did her abdomen and thighs, but we're saving the back for next time—"

"Sit."

I did.

"Raquel, how much fat did you take out of this woman?"

"I don't know…two, maybe three liters…"

"And you put all of that in her breasts?"

I laughed at his obvious attempt at humor. "Of course not. Just about a hundred cc's on each side."

"And what did you do with the rest of it?"

I shifted a little in my seat, wondering where he was going with this. Was he about to make a *Fight Club* joke? "I don't know…they threw it out…you know, whatever they do with those hazardous waste containers…"

"So basically you're telling me that you gave this woman, in addition to her breast reconstruction, a total body makeover."

"It's not finished—"

"What I want to know is—*where* is the money?"

"What money?"

"The money that you charged her. Where is it? What—are you carrying around a credit card machine? Or now they've got that—that 'Square' thing, right? Let me see your phone."

He thought I was *charging* them and pocketing the cash. I actually laughed. I don't have enough business sense to even *think* of that.

"You are the last person I would ever have expected to do something so unethical. There are some that would not surprise me with such behavior but *you*—"

"Dr. Donarski, I didn't charge her. I just hooked her up with a little free lipo."

"And how much more time did that take you?"

"I don't know…maybe a couple of extra hours?"

Dr. Donarski frowned. "You really don't understand the problem here."

Problem? What problem? The patient was cancer-free—for now, anyway—and with her new body she had a whole new lease on life. Wouldn't that be considered a "win-win?" Unless… "What happened—did she come in with a wound infection or something last night? Is someone bitching about 'cleaning up my mess'?"

He sighed. "Raquel, she has an admirable result."

I felt the start of that uncomfortable internal glow that comes when someone's telling you how great ("good") you are.

But that's not where he was going with this. Instead he just clarified, "So you didn't charge her."

"No."

"Even if I choose to believe you, you are still committing a major insurance fraud. The hospital can get fined heavily for this kind of thing. And then you will lose your job."

"Oh." This was definitely news to me. "But, Dr. Donarski…I can't…I mean…I have to make her even. I can't just take it all from one thigh and leave the other one fat."

"Technically, you could. You might start a trend. Like asymmetric haircuts." He waited a comedic beat of silence but I was too confused to laugh. "All right, Raquel. I can see that you weren't intentionally being—what's the word—'shady' here."

Shady? I was getting in trouble for doing my best, going above and beyond, trying to *help* people and he was calling me *shady?* And if this really was a crime, then who had ratted me out? Who would even *bother* with this kind of intel? Everyone in the O.R. is always so bored with what's going on—I couldn't imagine that any of them were even paying close enough attention to notice. And what would even be the motive? The nurses all joked about getting up on the table after the case was over to have their *own* fat sucked out—if anything they wanted to stay in my good graces.

Would *Eddie* do this to me? To get back at me for breaking up with him? But I hadn't officially let him know about that yet. Besides, Eddie wasn't malicious. He was just…indifferent. He wasn't in love me. But he liked sleeping with me. He wouldn't try to get me fired.

None of this whole stupid non-issue made any sense.

"Doctor Donarski," I began, "How did you even—"

"How did I find out about this? That's irrelevant. But, if I may ask…how many of these have you done?"

I swallowed. "Four…five. Maybe six."

There was a pause, then he sighed, exhaling through his nose. "All right. You just need to stop."

Fuck. Just fuck fuck *fuck.*

"But you gotta let me do the lipo—" The words flew out of my mouth before I could stop myself. So then of course Donarski said to me with an appropriately perplexed look on his face, "But *why?*"

Exactly. *Why.* Why would *anyone* want to do all that extra work for free?

I couldn't answer him. If this really was insurance fraud, he wasn't going to care.

I took a deep breath and—uncharacteristically—thought out what I was going to say before opening my mouth: "Dr. Donarski, the extra lipo helps them get through the whole horrible disease process. Before the surgery they're all so depressed about losing their breasts and then afterwards, when they look skinnier, they get so happy. They come in smiling. They stop thinking about their breasts and get excited about how great their bodies look."

I thought about all of the other breast cancer patients I had lined up over the next few weeks, how excited they were about their lipo. "Can I at least just finish the ones I've started? They're going to be heartbroken when I tell them—"

"Raquel, we have a largely indigent patient population here."

"Just because they don't have money doesn't mean they don't care about looking good!" Jesus—now I was on a soapbox. "Maybe…if we can't do it this way, we could start a…a body contouring clinic, or something—"

"We don't have the demand for that kind of surgery."

"Yes we do. All my female patients talk about is how after having kids their bodies are never the same, and if they could just lift this or tuck that or suck this fat off here—"

"And how do you suggest that these women *pay* for their extreme makeovers?"

Whoever is still saying money can't buy happiness in this modern world is just an asshole.

"I could…put together a fundraiser to get the program going."

Dr. Donarski peered at me over his glasses. "Fundraisers are for disfigured war veterans. You are proposing one to raise money for women to have liposuction?"

Fundraisers for women to have liposuction. Okay, even I had to agree that this conversation had completely derailed. Still, I could give it one last try.

"But to so many of these women, it's as important as getting their breasts reconstructed. And, who knows…it could turn into something really big. There's nothing like it on this side of town."

"So what are you suggesting—that we try to really cash it in like one of these idiots?" He held up a *Star* magazine with a cover boasting a four-page spread of the life and times of the latest TV-Plastic-surgeon-*du-jour*. He must have found it out in the waiting room, since I doubt he had his own personal subscription to any tabloids. There was a fresh Brangelina story headline in the upper right corner. A new issue. I made a mental note to look for it next time I was in a checkout line. "Do you know that this clown never even got his Boards?" He leaned back in his chair. "Speaking of…how's the studying going?"

"Good," I said too quickly, and I could tell by the way he frowned and went, "Hmm," that he knew I was lying.

He was referring to my upcoming plastic surgery boards, the final rite of passage that loomed ahead in another few months. Analogous to the Bar Exam for lawyers, it was the last hoop they made all the new graduates jump through to get our certification. It was an oral question-and-answer session, a full day of torture held at the same resort in Phoenix every October, where they brought us all in for the massacre.

His phone buzzed and he pressed the speaker button.

"Yes, Brenda?"

"Your one-thirty is waiting."

He looked at me over his glasses. "So. Raquel. You have to stop with the free surgeries. This hospital is barely keeping its doors open as it is."

"Oh, I think they'll be open for a while," I joked. "There are too many human bodies in the way for them to physically close. Have you been to the E.R. lately?"

His upper lip quivered. I could tell he was fighting not to smile. He always did get my wit.

"Consider yourself on probation."

"Okay…" I waited for him to laugh. "And I would be breaking the probation…how? By doing a lipo?"

"Exactly." He kept his eyes averted from me. "An unnecessary one."

In any other context I would have said that there was no such thing as an unnecessary lipo, but I could tell he was over it and he was working hard to keep up a serious tone here.

"And you need to study. That test can be quite brutal."

"So I've heard."

"You know how important it is for you to get your certification."

Okay, so now we'd crossed over into serious *serious* territory.

"Yes, I know." I also knew the rest of what had been unsaid but was implied in that statement—that if I didn't pass, I really *would* lose my job. Regardless of whether or not the Valley Hospital doors remained open for eternity. And it wasn't like there was a plethora of jobs out there from which I could go choose another one. Not these days.

My generation was the last to enter med school with big ideas for the future. But by the time we'd finished our training, as in most other professions, the American-Dream-of-the-Successful Physician-Who-Comes-From-Nothing-and-Builds-a-Thriving Career-Based-on-Hard-Work-and-Compassion-Saving-the-World was dead. Insurance reimbursements had dwindled to near-nothingness. School loans followed you to the grave. Aside from the scarce few whose parents could bankroll them into their own private practices (and then if they had all that much money to begin with, why the hell were they working so hard anyway?) we all came out scrambling for whatever low-paying hospital and HMO jobs we could get. Not to mention the market crash.

In short, we had entered a post-apocalyptic era of medicine. I'm not expecting sympathy. It's just that I wish lay-people understood that not all plastic surgeons roll up to a mansion at the end of every day where their live-in housekeeper buzzes them in through a private gate and they are then greeted by their three children, still dressed in their adorable fancy private school uniforms.

Those were the "good old days" that the older surgeons reminisce about. "It's not how it used to be," you still hear them grumble as they fill out paperwork in the recovery room. In fact, in this second decade of the millennium, as crazy as it sounds—there really is such a thing as a financially struggling plastic surgeon. And I'm currently one of them.

Brenda smirked as I passed by her desk on my way out.

She shouldn't look so happy. She could've been first on the list for lower body lipo. I would've done it for free just to show Donarski what a life-changing operation it could be. Then maybe she'd actually meet a guy and stop drooling over him all the time.

I shouldn't be thinking such evil thoughts. The karma was going to get me.

But it was already done. All I wanted was to get out of the hospital—to go for a run (well, let's be real—a walk/jog), to get in my bed and finish my current Netflix binge…maybe even to stop by Jake's and see how he was doing. But I could just sense that I wasn't escaping any time soon. As I rounded the corner of the hallway, I got the call from the emergency room. The truck driver was waiting for me. And it was a twenty-three year-old girl.

2

I never made it home that night. The trauma patient had multiple injuries and I had to get in line behind the life-threatening ones. There were hours of scans to clear her brain and abdomen, and then I had to wait for Ortho to rod her femur. I didn't even get to start my part of the case until close to midnight.

I didn't walk out of the hospital until around 3:00 A.M. But there was my happy, shiny little car still waiting for me, all alone in the deserted physician's lot. My respite. Once I was in the driver's seat, I slid my shoes off and leaned my head back. It still smelled new inside. I breathed deeply in through my nose and closed my eyes. *I was just going to rest here for a second, just going to let my poor feet recover before I started driving.*

I woke up four hours later to the warm glare of the morning sun against my face through the open car window. I had a stiff neck and a sharp pain from where the seatbelt was digging into my side. When I went to open the door I realized it hadn't even been locked. *Great.* I could have been murdered.

I was almost done dragging myself around the fourth floor, making rounds on my patients with one more to go when Jake called, begging me to take him to the beach.

"Sorry, Jake. Not today." I signed the progress note I'd just scribbled and slid the chart back into the rack at the nursing station.

"Come on, Rachel it's the first real beach day of the season."

"Is it?" I peered through the open doorway of the patient room across the hall. Patches of sunlight streamed through the window and across the feet sticking off the end of the bed. "Well, I have to study."

"Can't you study at the beach? Please? It's a hundred degrees in the Valley. I'm going to die if I don't get out of here."

Crap. I looked up and down the hall and wondered if there was someone around who could prescribe me Xanax without a paper trail. Today was not supposed to be a "Jake day." It was the one day in weeks that I *completely* had to myself. But the image of my brother watching television, fanning himself on his futon couch next to the sweating AC box in the tiny window made me even more anxious than the thought of not studying. Even more anxious than the thought of wearing a bathing suit.

I reminded myself that I should just be thankful that he was okay enough to *want* to go to the beach again. And if I hung out with him today, I'd be off the hook until his doctor's appointment next week.

I exhaled. "I'll be there in an hour."

When I got home, I dug my bikini from the depths of my underwear drawer. It was my first encounter with it in almost a year, and I contemplated it for nearly five minutes before daring to put it on in front of my full-length three–way mirror. Can't undo the scars of childhood.

I'd had the same bathing suit for two years. Once I had discovered that the boy-short cut covered most of the cellulite from the fucked-up lipo one of my co-residents had done for me, I went and bought two more like it. I didn't care that boy shorts were no longer in style.

It was my own fault. I'd begged her to do it. I had started fixating on those saddlebags that were clearly there to stay (truthfully, without the three-way mirrors I would never have known about them,) and I'd wanted the coveted space between my thighs. Well, I got the space. Along with some divets from the amateur job. After that, I had ordained that my upper thighs required full coverage at all times.

So I learned the hard way. That all lipo is not created equal. If only I could have done it myself. But I did secretly love the thigh gap.

I know that my unhealthy body image issues came from my mother. To this day, she is still particularly obsessed with her "figure." Growing up, my brother and I were witnesses to the daily exercise regimen that she practiced with the discipline of a German soldier, not to mention her constant discussions of weight. Her weight, our weight, other people's weight. We thought nothing of it that, while standing in the middle of the kitchen serving us dinner she would suddenly lift up her shirt and examine her flat stomach to make sure it wasn't bulging that day. The two of us were raised on fat-free food before anyone else even *knew* about it, and I was programmed to think that anything anybody else was eating that hadn't been stripped of all flavor was "*poison*!" To this day, my sixty-seven year-old mother still discusses the fantastic shape she's in, as well as her yoga, Pilates and cardio schedules, with me and anyone else who will listen.

When I arrived at the trailer park, Jake was lounging in his favorite chair in the shade of the single tree on his site. Actually, technically it was *my* site since it was rented under *my* name. With Jake's multiple DSM IV diagnoses, and permanent unemployment, he couldn't even get a lease on a self-storage unit.

It hadn't started out like this—my being responsible for Jake's rent, as well as the majority of his other bills. At first I was just supposed to be coordinating his life. His doctor's appointments, his blood draws, making sure the invoices were paid. Which in itself was a pain in the ass, because obviously I didn't have tons of extra time for things like that, but there was nobody else to do it. My father had been out of the picture since we were kids. My mother couldn't make a decision about what to pick from a dinner menu, let alone focus long enough to do anything for Jake. And while she said that she "would do everything she could to help him," *her* psychiatrist felt that having Jake live at home with her "would not be a healthy environment." She'd even alluded several times to the fact that it might not be "safe."

She helped Jake out financially, but her shitty pension plan from the county school district wasn't enough to support him alone. So after I started working I began pitching in what I could, and between the two of us and Jake's disability benefits, the bills were—usually—covered.

But there was the other issue. Logistics. My mother's obsession with beauty didn't come from nowhere; she is a *true* artist, *the real deal*, completely orbiting her own little planet. Now that she was retired from teaching and didn't have to raise children, she didn't have to function in society either. She spent her days in a vacuum of yoga and painting. She had no concept of time, of deadlines. Finding her checkbook could alone be an all-day task. Then there was the moving money around so the check didn't bounce, her refusal to set up digital access to her bank account. What we really needed was a second mortgage on her house but her credit was wrecked. To have her participate in any business transactions was too emotionally exhausting.

Bottom line: When she sent the money we used it. But the trailer park lease was under my name. I couldn't let my credit to go to crap too. And I no longer had the energy to argue with her about how she needed to get her to get her shit together. Most of the time it was just easier to take care of things myself. Yes it was a financial hardship. But I had imagined that when I was done training I'd be a rich plastic surgeon and Jake's bills would be like pennies to me.

Well.

And yes, an apartment rental would have been a much more economical way to go than a single-wide in a trailer park. But my brother had a thing about having his own four walls.

"Hey, Rachel!" Jake waved over at me. As he lumbered up from the chair, his dog, Sam—a stray that had followed him home from 7-Eleven last month— jumped off his chest and ran up to greet me.

"I got us some snacks," Jake said as he rummaged around in his beach duffel at his feet. "Diet Dr Pepper okay? They didn't have diet cherry. Maybe we can stop somewhere."

"Jake, what happened to that shirt?" He was wearing the silk Hawaiian button-down Tommy Bahama I had given to him for his birthday. He had an unexplainable penchant for Hawaiian shirts and while I personally found them hideous, they made easy gifts to give him since they were such enormous, non-fitted things. However, this one looked about three sizes smaller than it originally had been—some of his stomach rolls were peeking out from underneath—and it was several shades lighter.

"What do you mean?"

"It looks a little…tight."

He glanced down and pulled at the edges. "Oh, yeah, maybe I accidentally put it in the dryer."

"Jake! That was an expensive shirt!"

"I'm sorry. It was a mistake. Look, it still fits okay." He pulled the edges down again.

I took a deep breath, reminding myself to put everything into perspective. *It's just a shirt.* "It's fine. Good to see you." I tried not to sound short. It usually took spending only about ten minutes with Jake until I wound up wanting to fucking kill myself. Before I'd left the hospital this morning I had pledged that today, it wasn't going to happen.

I gave him the quick obligatory hug and kiss on the cheek. If I didn't know Jake, and I saw him walking around by himself in public—down at the 7-Eleven on the corner where he was this morning, for instance—I would mistake him for a homeless person. And cross to the other side of the street. Not that he was dangerous, but the meds took all the life out of his eyes, giving them a scarily empty look. It didn't help that he was often muttering something unintelligible to himself, something that he claimed was in another language. Apparently, a dialect unknown to man.

But he was my brother, and we were only eighteen months apart, and I'd known him for as long as I could remember, and he hadn't always been this way. It was just that whenever I got close to him I was forced to see how physically grotesque he had become. How when he opened his mouth you could see that his teeth were stained from the combination of chain-smoking cigarettes and poor oral hygiene. As my face brushed up briefly against his, I struggled to ignore the stale odor of his breath, and the fact that there might be food particles stuck to his facial hair. That he had a beard growing down to his clavicle to cover the scars on his neck from before he went into the hospital the last time. And the tremor of his hand as he'd reached for the can of soda he wanted to show me.

"You look good," I said as encouragingly as possible, pulling away. "How are you feeling?"

"Okay. I feel okay. Hey…I forgot to give you this last time…" He put out his cigarette and pulled a crumpled piece of paper from his back pocket. It had that recognizably heart-sinking look of a bill. It also had the calmly typed threat across the bottom that the next one would be from a collection agency.

Jake saw the look on my face. "Rachel, I don't have to go there. I can go back to the clinic instead—"

"Yes, you *do* have to go there. He's the first guy who's been able to help you." It was true—this was the best Jake had been for a while now. "You're not going back to a clinic. Besides, how would that make *me* look?" I gently punched his arm, and tried to laugh. "Your sister's a plastic surgeon and you go to a Medi-Cal clinic? It's all about me, remember? Got to keep my image up." I didn't add that it was also because I couldn't handle waiting with him in some county clinic that smelled like piss for three hours.

He shrugged. "Mom came by yesterday." When they were working, those meds also instilled a creepy, dull monotone to his voice that I could never quite get used to. He laughed his throaty laugh. "She's pretty fucked up, isn't she?"

"What now?"

"She keeps coming by with vitamins and shit from the health food store. She's trying to cure me, I think. And she keeps giving me books about diets."

Jesus. You didn't have to be a doctor to know that it was the meds that made him sluggish and fat. Everybody knows that about crazy people.

He held up his boom box. I'd offered multiple times to buy him an IPod and speakers but he preferred his archaic technology. "What do you want to listen to?"

I followed him back into the trailer where I grabbed a few CD's from the stack on the floor. I didn't care what they were—I just wanted to get out of there as quickly as possible. I knew it would be like this today, since I could only afford to pay Maria once a month, and we were coming into the third week. The stifling, warm air inside the trailer felt contaminated, and the thought of breathing it in made me heave. I looked away from the half-open Tupperware containers on the counter, the mound of dirty clothes in the bathroom doorway, the stack of food-encrusted dishes piled in the mini-sink, with the fruit flies or whatever they were circling around over there. I tried not to imagine Jake sitting alone in this place.

"Wait, not that one!" Jake suddenly said, grabbing Steely Dan's *Pretzel Logic* from my hand and throwing it across the room.

"What? Why?"

"Have you listened to the lyrics? Really listened?"

"Not lately."

"'Rikki Don't Lose That Number.' It's about Devil worship."

Why was it that Schizophrenics always went back to that Devil and Hell theme? In Jake's case, it made no sense. We'd never even been a religious family. But I'd noticed the same thing during my psych rotation in med school. And I also knew there was never any talking them out of it.

"Huh." I nodded. "Interesting."

The summer season hadn't started yet and our favorite spot at the beach was nearly empty. As soon as we got there, Jake removed the too-tight shirt and then took off for the water with his snorkeling gear. He had never been coordinated enough to play a team sport, but our uncle gave him a snorkeling set for his sixth birthday and as a kid, Jake would use it in every body of water he encountered—the local neighborhood pool, the filthy Pacific Ocean at the Santa Monica pier, the bathtub. When we were younger, he would scour the lake at day camp for tadpoles. We would keep them in a jar at home, waiting for them to turn into frogs, but they never made it. They always died first.

Jake always offered to bring some extra gear for me, but there was no way I was putting a toe in that freezing Pacific Ocean. When I asked him how he could stand it so cold like that, he told me that when you were floating around looking down it was like flying. And it was so cold and silent that you couldn't even think. He said the underwater quiet was the only thing that completely drowned out the voices.

I needed to sleep or to study. *Hmmm.* Rather than pulling the pile of Board Exam questions out of my bag, I found my fingers—all of their own accord—reaching for and thumbing through an *Us Weekly* instead. Break-ups, make-ups, stars *without* make-up…

But I was too tired even for that. I'd barely made it through the introductory snapshots of celebrities doing errands "Just like us!" before I found myself lying on my back with the magazine rolled up next to me.

With my head tilted back like that I had a good upside-down view of the fabulous fantasy houses lining the bluff above me. Jake and I loved looking at those houses. We had this game that we'd play: "If you could live in any one of them, which one would you pick?" Jake liked the yellow colonial at the end because it had a tree house. I could never decide between the modern brown one with the wrap-around porch and the classic Cape Cod style with the Infinity pool. Sometimes I would get so caught up in my decision making— *well, this one has direct access to the beach, that one is farther from the parking lot*—that I'd forget for a moment that it was just a game. The sad thing was that those houses were probably all just second or third vacation homes. They always appeared empty. I don't think I ever saw a single person sitting on that wrap-around porch. Every time I came out here, I promised myself that one day, when I was a rich plastic surgeon, I would live in one of those houses and Jake could live in the guest house, and I wouldn't have to worry about him any more. And he could snorkel and bask in the sun all day long, every day.

We had instinctively picked our spot isolated far from the few beachgoers, but while Jake was in the water, two twenty-something co-eds getting a head start on their summer tans parked themselves nearby. They both lay on their abdomens, upper bodies supported by breast augs in the three to four-hundred range, bikini-tops undone in the back. Perfect asses. No cellulite. Shiny hair.

Okay, no need to start with the masochism. I closed my eyes and drifted off a bit to the hum of their hypnotic conversation. Until a sharp bark of "Rachel!" cut through my warm, dreamy state and jerked me upright.

Jake had emerged from the water and was heading toward us. The girls abruptly stopped talking and stared at him—and then at the two of us—as he dropped his mask and flippers next to me and toweled off.

"Get anything good?" I ignored the girls, but to expect Jake to ignore them would have been asking a lot. He didn't get out much. His high school friends had disappeared after his first psychotic break. Or it could have just been that he no longer had access to that good weed he used to get. Anyway, he probably hadn't seen girls that looked like that in real life since we were here last summer.

He showed me a handful of sea glass to add to his collection.

"What do you want to listen to?" I started sifting through the CD's, trying to distract him from the girls' open-mouthed gaze. I knew he wouldn't talk to them or even approach them but they didn't seem so sure. They continued to stare, unblinking, now even as they fastened the tops of their bathing suits. I'd become immune to caring about what other people thought when they saw Jake—but I couldn't help knowing.

I turned the volume up on the ridiculous 1993 boom box, as if that would drown out our awareness of what was going on. Wordlessly, the girls had gathered up their things and left, with the urgency as if they had just seen a storm rolling in. I wish I could say that they must have suddenly realized it was time to go home, but I saw them relocate about a quarter of a mile down the beach. I know Jake saw it too. Neither of us said anything. It wasn't like these things didn't happen all the time.

Jake sipped his soda and cleared his throat. I lay back down again and looked up at the houses.

"Jake—" I started to say, but he cut me off.

"Those girls had fake tits, didn't they?" he said.

3

My moonlighting job on Fridays was where I got the supplemental income to help Jake with the fancy shrinks and Maria.

Twice a month I honed my seemingly God-given body sculpting skills at a place where I actually got paid for them—at the office of Dr. Alberto Ferraro. Dr. Ferraro was one of a handful of famous plastic surgery old-timers whose combination of multiple marriages with alimony, child support and poor investments over the years had left him virtually unable to retire, and forced him to relocate his practice to a lower rent district in the Valley—far, far away from his old stomping ground of Beverly Hills.

And that's how I fit into the picture. There was another—more important—issue. When I first started working in his office, Dr. Ferraro told me that he was sixty, but I have a feeling he was closer to eighty. And no matter how technically talented he was, an old guy like Ferraro with back and neck problems was severely limited in the operating room. He was really only physically able to perform the delicate facial surgeries during which he could sit down while he was working. All of the heavy manual labor—breasts, lipo, tummy tucks—went to me.

Well, not exactly. When I met Dr. Ferraro in the cafeteria at the Valley Hospital last year and he said he had some "extra work" if I was interested, his plans for me were not exactly what I had anticipated.

I guess I was what one would consider a "ghost surgeon." The patient would sign up with the world famous Dr. Ferraro for her surgery, he would hold her hand as she went to sleep in the O.R., and then once she was "out"— she was all mine. He would go down the hall and get coffee and poke his head in about every half hour. When the patient woke up in recovery, he'd be standing over her, telling her what a great job he'd done. She'd never even known that I'd been there.

That last Friday in April had started out no different than any other. After I did a breast aug and lipo on a famous producer's second ex-wife, the office manager placed a light blue five-by-nine index card on the desk in front of me that read, "get Annette back in the room."

Dr. Ferraro was of the firm belief that verbal interaction in the workplace was inefficient and that conversations among staff should be kept to a minimum. Nearly all communication in the office was by written "memo" on light blue five-by-nine index cards, usually put in your inbox but placed right in front of your face if it was a more urgent matter.

Annette was one of my recent masterpieces, two weeks out from a breast lift and implants, and liposuction from waist to knees. Right now she was showcasing her new body, parading around the office in a string bikini and stiletto heels.

"Annette, you look in*credible*," I gushed, intercepting her before she made it out into the waiting room. Annette was of the attractive late-fifties divorcee race, hanging on to her astounding sex appeal with nips, tucks and augments. Since I'd started working at Ferraro's I had discovered that there was a whole population of these women who had already done their faces to the point of no return and had now moved on to their bodies. Inch by inch, they went after every bit of sagging skin and extra flesh, still trying to emulate whatever image of themselves they carried around from when they were twenty years old. The thing was, their success rate was pretty high. Especially with my help.

"Your breasts look insane," I continued. One of my best results to date.

"Didn't he do a wonderful job?" Annette beamed, squeezing her breasts together. Fortunately by then we were behind the closed exam room door. "They're so soft—I can't even feel the implants! Look at my legs. And my butt! I look like I'm twenty-five again. I just love that man. Here, I brought him a little present." She held up a shiny silver gift bag. "Is he here?"

"He'll be right in. Meanwhile, you have a couple of stitches that still need to come out..." ...*and I have to remove them since not only can he not see close up but he has no idea where they are.*

"Annette looks fucking amazing," I told my assistant, Jenny under my breath as I joined her back at the computer.

"You're so talented, Thom," she said. Out of respect, Jenny had never quite been able to call me by my first name. But after working together for a few months, she'd become like a little sister to me, and "Dr. Thomas" seemed too formal. So on her own she had just started calling me "Thomas" which had been eventually shortened to "Thom."

"You're just buttering me up so you can get up on the table yourself."

"And when *do* I get my turn?" She grabbed at her thighs. "But it's true. You're the best."

"Well, too bad nobody knows it but you." I glanced over her shoulder at the desktop monitor. In my absence, she'd predictably pulled up someone's profile from one of her hipster online dating sites. "He looks like he wears a lot of cologne."

"At least I'm trying. And frankly, your moping around about that asshole scrub tech is getting old."

"I'm not moping around."

"Holing up with Netflix counts as moping."

How ironic that I used to pride myself on *never* watching TV—hell, I didn't even *own* one in college or med school, and my current model was almost circa the same era as Jake's boom box. But once I started residency, I was left too exhausted in my few spare hours to do much else. *What do you like to do in your free time? Do you have any particular hobbies or interests?* Those admission interview questions…college, med school, residency… all the right answers: *read, hike, I'm learning to play piano…* Until the Valley Hospital interview. *What do I do for fun? Are you kidding? Sit on my couch and watch mind-numbing television.* I don't know why I'd felt compelled to tell Donarski the truth. But it was a good call. The corners of his mouth had curled up ever so slightly (which, I've now since learned is as close as he gets to busting out laughing) and he'd said, "Honesty is an important quality in a surgeon."

"And that shit that you watch…" Jenny was now on a rant. "That one about the vampire boarding school…I mean, come *on*…what is it—2008? If you're going to watch something stupid, at least watch something that's stupid and *real* -like the *Housewives* or something."

"I'm not watching it for the storylines."

"Right. I forgot." Jenny rolled her eyes. "The pretty-boy actors with the waxed chests. I get it. It's your porn." Jenny rolled her eyes. "But one day you're going to have to join the rest of us in the real world, where those boys don't *exist*."

I sighed. "Jenny how is it that I'm old enough to have been your babysitter, and yet, when it comes to relationships, you are more emotionally mature and grounded than I think I'll *ever* be?"

She shrugged. "I had a good father. However, the sad part is that *I'm* never going to meet anyone because no *guys* are mature enough to handle the fact that I have Zoey."

I couldn't think of anything encouraging to say. It was true—Jenny was a twenty-five year-old single mother from the wrong side of the freeway, and her six year-old child was not a key selling point.

She turned back to the computer. "I should probably just start a profile on that site where the rich old guys look. Age-wise, I'd be willing to go up to fifty-five. You?"

But I never did get to tell her that personally, forty was my absolute upper limit because that was when the commotion started. We heard Ferraro yelling and then he slammed out of one of the exam rooms, his nurse at his heels like one of those mini terrier dogs.

"Get rid of this delusional lunatic!" Dr. Ferraro bellowed and threw the chart at the nurse.

"But *all* of his facial implant patients are delusional lunatics," I whispered to Jenny, which was true. There's a big difference between wanting to look younger and better, and wanting to look like a completely different person.

"She's not Facial Implants," Jenny whispered back, showing me the day's printed schedule. "She's Lipo."

As Dr. Ferraro stood there fuming, he suddenly seemed to notice me. I'd been doing my best to blend in behind the 21-inch monitor. In the few months that I had been there I had never seen so much verbal communication.

"You." He grabbed the chart back from the nurse and threw it at me. "Maybe you can help this whack job."

"Of course, Dr. Ferraro." I flipped through the chart, glancing at the history. There must have been something really wrong with this woman if he was willing to give her away like that. Like as a real patient. When she was still awake so she'd know I was her doctor. *Forty-seven years old, divorced, living in the Palisades. Previous lipo here three months ago. No real medical history. No major red flags. Nothing treacherous. A couple of antidepressants, but in this town that was like taking vitamins.*

"Hello, Mrs. Green," I greeted her, closing the exam room door behind me. "I'm Dr. Thomas, Dr. Ferraro's associate."

A petite dark-haired woman wrapped in a blue paper gown was reclining in the exam chair. She was bent over her phone, but looked up and smiled when I entered the room.

"Call me Natasha," she said. I was surprised at how calm she was. After Dr. Ferraro's outburst I would have thought she would be a whimpering mess but no, she was relaxing with her feet up. Another woman, roughly the same age and similar in appearance occupied another chair in the corner. No doubt her friend, here for moral support. Neither of them wore wedding rings. Okay, *this* was the issue. I braced myself. A single, divorced woman with another single, divorced close friend in tow could potentially be…problematic. Any minute the friend was going to whip out her printed list of questions and interrogate me like she was a detective on the case.

"Natasha," I said. "What can I do for you?"

"Well, it's *this*." Her voice was filled with a loathing that is characteristic only of a woman at war with part of her body. She stood up in front of the full-length wall mirror and opened the gown so she could demonstrate by grabbing her inner thighs with both hands. "Dr. Ferraro did some lipo here a few months ago and he says there's no more fat to take off, but I just think he could…get a little more… you know?"

Overall, Natasha was a thin woman. Even *I* would have put her in my "thin woman" category, and—due to my own personal neuroses—my standards are fairly high.

I studied her legs, imagining that they were my own.

"You're in great shape," I began, and I was about to continue with the traditional mantra that you give a patient chasing perfection: "We women are much too hard on ourselves. You will never achieve happiness by trying to correct physical imperfections. You can only be as beautiful as you feel within."

But the truth was, she did have a little thigh action going on there. And the rubbing together drove her nuts. I understood.

So instead of comforting her with a line about how phenomenal she looked already, from somewhere inside me came the words: "You want to have a space between your legs."

"Yes!" She looked at me as if she and I were speaking a language that only the two of us could understand. She had one inner thigh grabbed in each hand and was pulling them apart. "It makes me not even want to work out at all, the way it feels. I can't stand it. I just want to wear my jeans and have that big space again! Like I did in my twenties. But Dr. Ferraro told me, 'You're a forty-seven year-old woman. Nobody is looking at your legs anymore.'"

"I don't know why she needs to do this again," said her friend from the chair. "She's a toothpick."

"But I'm not doing it for men to look at me," Natasha continued. "It's for *myself*. She let go of her thighs and turned to me. "I'm crazy, right?"

I bent down and palpated her inner thighs. There was just enough fat there to form a little triangle that touched the other side. She wanted her thigh gap back. I got it. The first secret thing I do when I get up every morning is check to make sure my thighs still don't touch.

"You're both nuts," said the friend.

"And your point is?" Natasha replied.

She was right. So what if she and I were the only two people in the world crazy enough to see what she was talking about? Did it matter? It was *her* body. And I had just become her surgeon. Besides, in this warped town, the only way you can be too skinny is if you're too skinny to be on television. And it doesn't help that these days, starving yourself with the goal of getting and staying as thin as a movie star is no longer a secret disease. At least in Los Angeles, it's a publicly accepted way of life.

I couldn't help myself.

"I can definitely get some fat out of there," I said. "But then, your body is going to look a little square if we don't—"

Natasha grabbed the small roll of fat above the elastic of her underwear. "Yes! Please! Get rid of this fucking muffin top!"

"Yes," I said. "Your muffin top."

4

Natasha Green's liposuction was a home run.

"I don't know where you're going to get it from," Dr. Ferraro said as I got to work once she was asleep. "She's a rail."

"Oh, Dr. Ferraro, it's just a woman thing," I said in my lightest, silliest voice possible while the nurse tied the back of my gown and the tech snapped on my gloves. It wasn't just a woman thing, though. It was a *neurotic-woman-obsessed-with-her-own-body-helping-out-another-neurotic-woman-obsessed-with-her-own-body* thing. But I didn't see any reason to piss him off by pointing out that although he had technically fired her as a patient, Natasha had chosen *me* as her surgeon because I could see something that he couldn't.

"You really are like a little superhero with that cannula," the nurse said after I'd finished, while we were putting the compression garment on. "I can't believe you got that much off her little body. She really had it packed in there."

Dr. Ferraro just grunted from the doorway. "We'll see," he said.

Since she was so thin to begin with, Natasha's swelling was quite minimal and the difference in her shape was obvious immediately at her first post-op visit. I had given her the perfect legs photo-shopped onto every actress in the tabloids.

"Miraculous," she said to her reflection in the mirror. "The space! And my back—"

"There's a lot of swelling right now," I started to tell her. "It's going to get better—"

"I *love* you!"

Even better than Natasha's new undying love for me was the check waiting at the office front desk. Ferraro must have been caught up that month because he gave me the whole surgeon's fee. Minus the taxes, the money I made doing Natasha's surgery was nearly an entire month's paycheck at the hospital. Almost enough to cover Jake's last round of bills.

I dialed Jake's number.

"Go take a shower," I said, knowing he probably hadn't for at least two days. "And please shave. What's that Italian place you like on Ventura with the really good calamari? We're celebrating."

5

When Natasha Green showed up for her second post-op visit in a pair of skinny jeans, she not only brought me a $500 Am Ex gift card (I briefly wondered if my landlord would take it as cash,) but her friend Sheila, also in need of emergency liposuction.

"Help me!" My soon-to-be-second patient grabbed at her abdomen with both hands. "Disgusting! We're in the fitting room, trying on dresses for this stupid charity luncheon and now I'm spiraling into a major depression."

"And you're already on three anti-depressants…" I murmured, glancing once again at her intake sheet.

"Exactly. I need a new approach. Let's just do this—I'll reassess my emotional well-being when I'm skinnier."

Sheila's surgery was also a great success. And then she sent Patrice. Who sent Diane. Who sent Gloria.

As soon as I met her, I knew Gloria Fitzgibbons was hands down going to be my biggest challenge. Before she'd even been invited to undress, she was sitting cross-legged in the exam chair, already stripped down stark naked except for the phone in her hands that she was madly texting away on. It had one of those extensions that made it still look like a Blackberry.

Ugghh. She was one of those hard-core entertainment manager/agent/producer types who still refused to give up their Blackberries. Those were the ones with the worst entitlement issues—like the whole world should revolve around their stupid shooting schedules. And the best part was that they were never doing anything you'd ever heard of—it was always some obscure show on deep cable, and the more obscure it was, the more entitled *they* were.

I reminded myself about the two unpaid invoices from Jake's psychiatrist that I'd shoved to the bottom of my purse and did an involuntary surreptitious survey of the room. You know, a wallet biopsy. There was the pink ostrich Birkin on the counter, a Dolce and Gabbana dress thrown carelessly over one of the chairs, and the red underside of a Louboutain platform visible at the foot of the exam chair. Her shoulder-length brunette hair was perfectly straight and shiny as if she had just left a blow-out bar, and she had what was at least a three-carat rock on her left ring finger.

"Gloria Fitzgibbons," the woman introduced herself without looking up, still texting.

"Hello, Gloria." I took a seat. "Did they not give you a gown?"

"That thing?" She nodded toward the paper gown still folded neatly on the counter. "What for? You were going to have me strip anyway. Save it for the next patient. Let's get to it. I'm here for body sculpting. And I hear you're the best."

"So you're here for liposuction," I said.

"No," she said. "I'm not here for liposuction. I'm here for lipo*sculpture.*" She finally stopped texting. "I'm getting thick around the middle. And I don't like it."

I glanced down at her chart, trying to review her demographics without appearing to be reading. Married. She had left her age blank, which meant she was at least mid-to-late forties. A house address in Beverly Hills, north of Wilshire. A laundry list of previous cosmetic procedures including a "mini neck lift" (translation: "facelift") and a breast augmentation in answer to the question: "Have you ever had surgery before?" I loved the way she'd left out the nose job, as if I couldn't tell. In fact, she was in desperate need of a revision. There was no way she could breathe through that thing.

Gloria stood up in front of the full-length mirror and without any prompting, proceeded to give me her wish list, starting with her upper arms and continuing on down her back, to her abdomen, buttocks, thighs and even her calves and ankles. She pulled and grabbed at the different small areas of excess flesh. She was a basically thin woman who no doubt looked great in her expensive clothes, but under the fluorescent lighting I could see the unwanted bulges, and the remnants of previous liposuctions, particularly the rippled effect on her abdomen.

She then went on with her other specifications. She didn't want any noticeable scars. She had to look good naked because that's the way her husband liked her to walk around the house. In short, it had to be a perfect job.

"So, can you help me? Or are you going to tell me I'm already too skinny like the last five doctors I've already seen?"

The stakes were high on this one. It was a real cleanup job. It would have been optimal if she'd been under forty, and didn't have so much extensive sun damage…but I couldn't help myself. It wasn't just the money. I was discovering that I had a problem. When I saw fat, I had to remove it.

I could make her better. If it came out right, I could make her perfect.

"I can get fat out of a rock," I said. "When would you like to schedule?"

6

Gloria's surgery was trickier than I had anticipated. Mainly because she was what you call "fat-skinny." That is, although she was a size zero she probably had a body fat percentage of about forty-five. As I always do, preoperatively I had estimated roughly how much I was going to get from each area. But in the O.R., I found that after I had reached the volume goal, the liquefied fat continued to flow freely out into the tubing. I was unable to see the shape of her body while she was lying down asleep because, well…it had no structure. The only thing supporting her shape was her skeleton. Underneath the hidden fat layer, her muscles were probably as atrophied as a quadriplegic's, as if they'd never been used. Instead of exercising, she must have just starved herself her whole life and decided on the liposuction when she got fed up and started to eat again and felt fat. What made my job even more difficult than usual were her specific regulations about where I could put the incisions, so I had to work from all kinds of crazy angles to get the fat out.

It was the first time that I had ever been unable to assess my end result on the table. I just had to go by my preoperative judgment and pray. I wished I had spent more time studying her body while she was awake standing up.

Even though Gloria was small, the surgery went a couple of hours longer than I'd planned. The nurse kept coming back into the O.R., asking for "updates" for her friend, who was out front in the waiting room, ready to take her home, wondering "what the fuck" was going on in there. As if I wasn't sweating it out enough.

Finally, I had to just call it quits. Well, that's sort of a lie. It was more like the scrub tech did an intervention and took the cannula away from me. I had started at 8:00 A.M. and it was almost one o'clock. I couldn't tell what the hell Gloria's body looked like. All I knew was that I had a liter and a half of fat in the canister and it sounded like her crazy friend was on the verge of calling the police. I had done the best I could but unfortunately nobody gets an "A for effort" in surgery.

After Gloria had been woken up and transported to recovery, and I had spoken to her friend, assuring her that "everything had gone perfectly" and she would be ready to leave in about an hour, I sat down and vented to Jenny.

"I don't know," I said. "I might have totally fucked her up. I mean, the fat just kept coming out, and I couldn't tell what anything looked like…"

This was her cue to champion me, and she acted appropriately.

"Now, Thom," she said. "Nobody's better at this than you. I'm sure she's going to look great."

Jenny then proceeded with her standard pep talk, reminding me how utterly fabulous I was, how talented, how I have changed so many lives, and if this one person wasn't happy, well, that was her problem.

In true frequent-flyer style, an hour later Gloria was already sitting upright in the recovery room with a ginger ale in her hand as if nothing had happened. I repeated to her how wonderfully everything went, how happy she was going to be with her results. I was glad that she was still too high to hear the doubt in my voice.

But even after she had been safely discharged home, I found myself not wanting to leave. I followed Jenny around while she shut down the front office, repeatedly describing how difficult Gloria's surgery had been. As if I talked about it enough, it would make the result better.

"What are you so worried about?" Jenny continued to file charts while she talked to me. "I mean, what's the big deal anyway, if it's not perfect?"

What's the big deal? The big deal was that my stretch of home runs may have just ended. If Gloria's body wound up looking worse than it had before she met me, my suddenly burgeoning career as a liposuction goddess would just as suddenly be over. And then what if Ferraro found out that I'd made a patient unhappy and he fired me altogether? That Valley Hospital paycheck would never be enough. I'd have to give up either Jake's doctor, or his trailer. And what if I had to let Jake move in with *me?* That certainly wasn't going to work, especially if I wound up having to move into my car. Come to think of it, what if I had to trade my car in for a *Toyota?*

"Why don't you come with us tonight?" Jenny said. "I'm taking Zoey and my sister to Cheesecake Factory. Come on, Thom, you know you love that Chinese chicken salad."

The Cheesecake Factory with someone else's family on a Friday night was an even more depressing idea than just going home alone to my cat. I politely declined. I didn't even call Jake to check on him. I even forgot to call Gloria Fitzgibbons to check on *her*. I just went straight home and got into bed, but I couldn't fall asleep. I toyed with the idea of taking a Benadryl, but that would leave me drugged for twelve hours and I had to get up early to take Jake to the podiatrist. I might be a surgeon, but his toenail fungus was one thing I refused to take on with my own two hands.

Then I remembered the two unused tablets of Valium that the vet had prescribed for Sushi to take for his teeth cleaning, which I'd had to cancel because I'd been called in to work that day.

"Sorry, Sush," I said to my cat, who was climbing all over me as I got back into bed. "Here, look, I'm saving one for you."

7

Normally I see all of my patients the first post-op day, but Gloria said she didn't have time to come in over the weekend, and since she'd had liposuction at least twice before, she knew how to take care of herself. The first time I saw her was Monday morning. She had a 9:00 A.M. appointment. I walked in at nine seventeen.

"She's in room two," Jenny said when I got there. I could tell she was about to give me shit for being late but then stopped herself when she got a good look at me. "Thom, are you okay?"

Jenny knew me better than anyone. I'd been sick to my stomach about Gloria all weekend, worrying about what she was going to look like when I took the garment off. Would there be big dents? Or still too much fat? I had spent the entire drive going over in my head the conversation she and I would most certainly be having in about two minutes. How she was going to complain. How she might demand her money back. How she was going to get on her Blackberry and Tweet and Facebook the whole world about how Dr. Rachel Thomas was a true *butcher*, that nobody should ever see me for liposuction again.

I found Gloria already in the exam chair, fixated on her Blackberry. This time she was wearing the gown. I braced myself for what was likely to ensue. *Is this fat here?* She was going to say. *And how come there's still some more over here? Am I swollen? Is this going to go down?*

"Incredible," she said into her phone. That is, I assumed she was talking into her phone, because she hadn't looked up at me.

"Call me when you're ready." At least I had a few more minutes before the barrage of scrutiny began. I turned back toward the door.

"Did you hear me? You're an artist. A genius." This time Gloria looked directly at me when she spoke. She removed the earpiece and stood in front of the mirror. "Unbelievable." She ran her hands up and down the sides of her body, admiring herself. "Sorry, I had to waste your gown, but I'm still dripping. Do you have a paper towel or something?"

She was indeed still leaking from the access sites but even with the cherry Kool-Aid-like liquid running down her legs, she didn't look bad. Actually, she looked surprisingly good. It might end up looking perfect after all. I guess I just needed to start trusting my instincts with this liposuction thing.

"And you're swollen," I said.

"Oh, I know. Dollface, this isn't my first rodeo. But I have to tell you, I've never seen anything like it. Such sculpting. I mean, look at my ass."

Well, my day certainly could've started out a whole lot worse. As the wave of relief washed over me, I started babbling: "I'm glad you're happy. Keep wearing the garment. You can shower tomorrow. I'll see you back in a week to take out the stitches—"

"This is the answer. *This* is the answer. *This* is the show." Gloria tore herself away from her reflection and whirled around to face me. "I've got it all worked out." She proceeded to get back into her clothes. "You're quirky. I like that."

I hate the way everyone calls me 'quirky' but I let it go. "A TV show?" I imagined myself sitting across from Matt Lauer, discussing the top five plastic surgery procedures of the year. I could be the national expert! Answer all the phoned-in live questions! *Yes breast reconstruction is a journey, but I'm with my patients all the way…* That could be some amazing media exposure. Usually you have to pay around six grand a month for a publicist to get you on those shows.

"I like you. You, Doll, are going to be the new *face* of liposuction." Gloria bounced up and down to pull up her jeans. "Look at this! I couldn't get into these last week, but thanks to you—they fit!"

Barely. "Liposuction is going to have a face?"

She looked me up and down. "Don't worry. After your makeover, you won't even recognize yourself. And we can always adjust the lighting. We just have to work out details. First off, we have to get you out of *here*. This *place*. We have to relocate. I need your info."

"My info?"

"Your info, your bio, your headshot, everything. I need it now. Where do you live? I need to come by your house, get some ideas. We have to set up a background. A story. The glamorous life of a fabulous female plastic surgeon. Your family. Are you married? Have a boyfriend? Hobbies? Interests? Email my assistant and set up a meeting. Preferably today. Damn. Can't do it today. Tonight. It has to be tonight."

"A meeting? For what?" She was talking too fast for me to follow her.

"For the show, of course! The show!" She hoisted her Birkin bag over her shoulder. Today's was orange.

"But what show?"

"I just *told* you." Now she actually seemed irritated, as if I was making her repeat obvious information. "*My* show. How on earth did I not think of this before? Of course! Liposuction! A show about liposuction. I mean, what woman would *not* stop the remote on something about liposuction? We really need to get going on this. We're almost in June. The first air date is in a month." At this point she was no longer talking to me at all, but having a conversation with herself.

It had to be the Percocet. I hoped she had someone to pick her up. She probably shouldn't be driving.

"But—"

"But what?"

Now, everyone in this town is forced to interface with unemployed actors on some level—these days, it's just as many unemployed potential Reality TV stars. Most of the time it's in a restaurant, where they rattle off the night's specials with such skill that it sounds like a Shakespearean soliloquy. *My* interaction with them usually took place in the Emergency Room, where I painstakingly sutured up their career-threatening facial lacerations. So even *I* knew from listening to all of their whining about this pilot and that pilot and how nothing ever actually got "picked up" that whatever Gloria was talking about sounded annoyingly far-fetched, if not ludicrous. And I didn't have time in my life for virtual reality.

"I don't know," I said. "Don't you have to do something else first, like, you know, pitch it to a network?"

"Dollface," she said, handing me her business card. "I *am* the network."

8

I opened my front door at seven-thirty that evening to find Jenny standing there.

"Surprise!" she greeted me, and waltzed into my living room with a couple of grocery bags.

"Surprise, all right," I said back. Jenny had never paid me an unsolicited visit. In fact, I couldn't remember her ever visiting me at all. I was shocked that she even knew where I lived. Not that there were any rules about it, but our BFF status was strictly limited to the office—I don't think we'd ever even spoken on the phone after work. "What's going on?"

She was dressed like she was about to go out clubbing in a crappy neighborhood: four-inch platform heels that just brought her up to five four and showed off bright blue toenails, a tight, almost see-through tank top and boot-cut black jeans that balanced out her pear-shaped body.

"Jenny, what kind of Victoria's Secret contraption is under there?"

"Actually, I borrowed a couple of implants from the office. Three-fifties." She turned sideways so I could admire her bust line, and as she tilted her head, one of her enormous gold door-knockers grazed her shoulder. "You think I can go bigger?"

"I think you're acting like you're high. Where's Zoey?"

"*Must* you remind me about my kid all the time? My sister volunteered to baby-sit, so I thought we could hang out. Can't a girl have a little fun?" She flipped her especially bouncy hair over her shoulder. "Thom, you really need to start doing some Botox on yourself. You look angry all the time."

"I'm not angry. Just confused. Why did you get dressed up to come visit me and my cat?"

"Must I have a reason to come hang out with you? And I brought some provisions. I know how you hate cooking." She headed for my walk-through kitchen.

"I don't *hate* cooking. I just consider it an occupational hazard." I do have an irrational fear of chopping off the tip of my finger with a kitchen knife. Can you really blame me though, after all those years of taking care of people who show up in the E.R. with their fingertips in freezer bags on ice?

"Where's your opener?" She held up a bottle of red wine. "You sit down and I'm going to put a plate together for you." She disappeared around the corner into my little walk-through kitchen and started bustling around, rattling plates and silverware. "Don't tell me you don't have wine glasses!"

"You're going to break your neck in those heels and just so you're aware, I don't have property insurance." When I got no response from her I added, "You stole implants from the office? Ferraro is going to kill you."

She carried two plates heaped with food and coffee mugs filled with wine back to the living room and sat down next to me. "They were expired. I'm doing him a favor."

Expired? Fuck. "How many are expired?" *Had I used any?*

She shrugged. "Oh, chill. They expire on the shelf, they expire in the patient. What's the difference, really? By the way, the Botox is no joke. You're getting to that age."

I took a plate from her. "Jenny. I know you didn't bribe your sister to watch your kid and steal a couple of implants from the office to come over here to tell me I need Botox."

"I just wanted to see you. *Swear!* Is that so wrong?"

"Thanks for the food. But I'm not hungry," I said with a grape leaf already stuffed in my mouth. "And actually, I've got someone coming by in a few minutes—"

"Really? Who? I'm sorry…am I interrupting?"

And as soon as I heard the stilted lilt in her voice, I immediately knew what was going on. As if on cue, that's when Gloria stepped into my apartment.

"Well, you're not easy to find," Gloria said, as if we were in the middle of the jungle and she'd just taken trains, planes and automobiles to get there.

"Gloria." My voice was muffled by the grape leaf. I quickly swallowed the entire bolus of it and balanced my plate of food on top of the pile of books and ancient mail on my coffee table. I muted the television.

"Sorry to barge in like this, but we don't have a lot of time." She didn't look sorry at all. "This is Blair, my line producer," she introduced someone else who had just slipped in through the front door and now silently stood next to her.

At first I wasn't sure if "Blair" was male or female. Everything about her was fascinatingly androgynous. She was probably about my age, with straight, limp brown hair cut in a bob that hung to her shoulders framing a face that I would not have been able to remember until I saw it again.

"Would you like something to eat?" Jenny held up the wine bottle. "Cabernet?"

I felt Gloria relax a millimeter. "I'll take a drink."

Blair shook her head. She hadn't yet smiled once.

"You look familiar. You're from the office, right?" Gloria said in Jenny's general direction, scanning the room as she talked. Without waiting for her to answer, she continued, "Tonight we work out the back story."

"Back story," I repeated, as if that would bring some sense to the situation.

"Yes, Dollface. My new reality show backstory. We are in a rush. A real rush." Gloria started pacing back and forth, but only a few steps in each direction so that she was almost walking in circles. "It *is* plan B. But we still have the time slot. We just have to do things a little differently."

"Can I ask what it's about? Or is it a *secret*?" Jenny winked.

Gloria ignored her and instead, started a self-tour through my living/dining/ common room area, curiously inspecting everything without touching, as though she were in a museum. I imagined I was seeing it for the first time through her eyes—the overflowing IKEA bookcases that had expired their life limit and could collapse at any moment, the funky throw rug from Target with the iron burn right in the middle, my cat approaching her and rubbing up against her leg. Not what she was expecting, I was sure. Especially when Jenny handed her red wine in a coffee mug. This was not the home of a "fabulous female plastic surgeon."

I cringed at the way her heels clicked loudly on the hardwood floor, praying that the tweaker below me wouldn't start screaming obscenities up the vent like he usually did whenever I accidently walked around with my shoes on.

"You knew she was coming," I hissed at Jenny while Gloria was checking out the bathroom.

"I might have overheard you guys talking this morning."

"Okay, I can see we're going to have to make a few adjustments," Gloria said when she emerged from the bathroom. She seemed to be speaking exclusively to Blair. "Nobody's going to tune in to *this* place for half hour. And that crack den below us could be a significant safety hazard."

"Oh, you should see my other place at the trailer park" I wanted to say.

"Call Gustavo and arrange for a condo in his new building on Sunset. Tenth floor or higher so we can get some good balcony footage." Gloria turned back to me. "What kind of car are you driving?"

"An Audi TT Roadster convertible. Dark blue." I felt my chest puff out a little. But I was met with silence, which made me feel like I needed to expound.

"It's brand new. A stick shift."

She still didn't say anything.

"You know, one of those round kind of bubbly cars with the roll bars—"

"Yes, yes, I know what it looks like," Gloria said. "What are you waiting for—a round of applause?"

"It's a luxury car."

"Too adolescent. You have to be taken at least somewhat seriously."

She had to be kidding. My beautiful brand new car, my fifty-thousand-dollar-including-the-five-percent-APR pride and joy that I was going to be paying off for the next five years was the *wrong car*?

"Blair, call Jim at Beverly Hills Porsche. Tell him I need a lease on a Carrera. 4S if he has it. White. No, no. Silver. No…black."

"Convertible?" Jenny suggested.

Gloria squinted her eyes. "Yes. Convertible. Good idea. Easier to see you coming and going on camera."

"By the way, I'm Dr. Thomas' assistant, so I would *have* to be in the show," Jenny continued, as if Gloria wasn't once again completely ignoring her. "I mean, I would think I would be a *major* character. Dr. Thomas and I are *extremely* close. Like sisters. I mean, I'm here practically *all* the time." She reached over and gave me a sisterly squeeze.

"Speaking of—any brothers or sisters?" Gloria asked. "Like, *real* ones?"

I wrestled with how to answer that. Jenny remained quiet. Gloria took the silence as a "no," and moved on to the next question.

"Boyfriend?" she said to me.

"What?"

"Do. You. Have. A. Boyfriend. It's not a trick question. If you do, we'll need to see him first. Bring him to the meeting. Wait, no…on second thought, don't bother. Show me a picture."

"She doesn't," Jenny assured us all. "She hasn't had one in years."

Gloria addressed Blair again, as she strolled into the kitchen: "Find one."

Then the near-tragedy ensued. Gloria reached for the wine bottle, but Jenny went to grab it—I guess hoping to pour Gloria's wine for her, since I heard her say, "Oh, here let me get that for you"—but instead she misfired and knocked the bottle off the counter. Some greater force intervened at that moment and she just missed splashing Gloria's outfit with the rich red hues of midlevel price-point Cabernet. Some of it did get on Gloria's left shoe, which—fortunately—was black.

"Oh, my God, I'm so sorry," Jenny moaned, staring down at the broken glass and wine all over the floor. While Gloria was distracted with her shoes, I scanned the photos and notes tacked to the refrigerator with the free magnets I got from the drug companies. *Was there anything there she would find fascinating?* Or, I wondered, as I spotted a photo of Jake and myself at the beach, *was there something she didn't need to know?* Without even stopping to think about it, I slid that single photo off the refrigerator—magnet and all—and into a drawer.

Then, when I looked over at Jenny again and saw what was going on, I yelled: "What are you doing?" and everybody jumped.

Since I didn't own a single dishtowel and the paper towel roll was bare, Jenny had grabbed the first thing she saw—a piece of laundry from the pile by the bedroom door—and was using it to wipe down Gloria's shoe.

"Jeez, Thom, chill out," Jenny said. "It's just a T-shirt. I'll get you another one." She held up what she'd been using to mop up the mess.

It wasn't *just* a T-shirt. It was *actually* a present from Jake. He'd had a recent T-shirt painting streak with that stuff that gets puffy when you bake it. I freaked out the first time I found him doing it—I rushed inside, thinking there was a fire, with that weird smell of burning plastic coming from the trailer. The art itself had been inspired by a TV game show that involved "rebuses." He'd had to explain to me—*"Rachel, how can you not know what a 'rebus' is? It's pictures that spell out a word. It's an ancient art that goes back to the Middle Ages."*

I don't know what the one he made for my mother said. Something about yoga. The shirt he'd given *me* was actually clever, though I couldn't bring myself to wear it outside the house. Still, it had sentimental value. And it *had* been white.

Blair and Jenny stared at me.

"Forget it," I said. "I…I thought it was something else."

Meanwhile, Gloria was trying to decode the rebus. It was like a game of charades. From left to right Jake had drawn—with puffed paint—a pair of red lips, the letter "O" in black, and a golden crown. "Lips O crown?" she said slowly. "Lips O—"

No worries. She'd never get it.

"Lip. Lipo."

No.

"L*ip O*—"

This could not really be happening.

"Lipo queen!" Blair said triumphantly. "It says 'Lipo Queen.'!" It was the first thing she'd said since stepping inside my apartment.

"Li-po queen," Gloria said slowly, as if tasting the words. "Li-po queen. Lipo *Queen.*"

"Where the hell—" Jenny started to ask me, but I shook my head and she knew.

I winced at how much cornier the words sounded when spoken out loud. Jake had meant well.

"*Lipo Queen,*" Gloria said, beaming. "Love it. It's the name of my new show. *Lipo Queen.*" She toasted us all with her still-empty glass. "Ladies, say hello to Dr. Rachel Thomas, the new *Lipo Queen.* She can get fat out of a rock."

9

"You really shouldn't be going to these things without your manager," Jenny said as I watched the valet at Gloria's building take my car to some underground abyss.

"Jenny, stop being an asshole. You know I don't have a manager."

"Well, you need one. Or at least an agent. This is a great building."

Gloria had scheduled—or as I soon learned to say, "called"—an emergency meeting smack in the middle of my Wednesday. When I had tried to explain to her that I couldn't make it until after I finished in the O.R., she explained to *me* that that was not an option.

"Dollface, this is prime time reality television on a major cable network," she had said on the phone to me the night before. "There's no room to fuck around. We're talking potential for multimillions in advertising and endorsements and international distribution."

It all just seemed too absurd to take it seriously. Except now I *had* to because she was asking me to cancel my whole day, which included someone who'd been waiting for their surgery forever, and we'd finally got it through insurance.

That's when I called Jenny for actual help. I figured that even though the whole Gloria thing had initially turned her into some kind of starfucker, she should be back down to earth by now. *She* understood what my life was really like. *She* would give me the sound advice I needed. Like: "You're right, Thom. I thought about it. Those people are all nuts. Don't waste your time."

I was a *surgeon*. I had an important job at a hospital and a cosmetic practice that was just starting to gain momentum. And I was studying for the most important exam of my life. All the while keeping an eye on my schizophrenic brother. I didn't have time for this Hollywood virtual reality bullshit.

"What?!?" Jenny had shrieked into the phone when I asked her if I should tell Gloria to forget it. It turned out that Jenny had already done her homework.

"I IMDB'd her," she'd said in between mouthfuls of whatever it was she was eating. Probably a medium Pinkberry since it was the week of her frozen yogurt and fruit cleanse. She insisted on doing it for three days every month even though I had tried to assure her multiple times that there was absolutely no scientific basis for cleansing one's intestines, that toxins do not "build up" in the body and that the bacterial flora repopulates the large bowel mucosa as soon as you flush it out. "Her *husband* is a network *president*. She's in *Variety*'s 'Top Twenty Most Powerful Women.' If she does something, it's *going to work*. And can you imagine—being on TV—you'll totally blow up. You're the one who's always complaining about your shithole apartment, and how you can't even pay off your student loans because of Jake. You're absolutely going to that meeting. And I'm coming with you."

Okay. So I was going to the meeting. But just to see. I wasn't getting caught up. Everyone knew entertainment people were crazy. Even crazier than plastic surgeons. And we're a pretty crazy bunch, considering that on a routine basis we make huge incisions on perfectly healthy people who think they're going to heal without any scars.

I waited until 4:30 A.M. that morning to call in sick for my case. Three hours before cut time was early enough for the O.R. to get a hold of the patient to cancel her, but not enough time for me to recover from my illness.

"You get yourself some rest, Dr. Thomas," the O.R. nurse said. "See, you work yourself into the ground and look what happens to you."

"I know," I said in what I hoped was a weak, raspy voice. "I just feel terrible about the patient…"

"Oh, she'll be fine. You're not doing her any favors if you're not feeling well." Her worried tone made me feel even worse. "We already got her back on the schedule first thing Monday morning."

"You know," Jenny whispered to me as the elevator ascended. "I read online that the *real* reason Gloria's production company nixed the other show was because the star was sleeping with her husband."

"Jenny, what's that in your purse?"

She pulled her arm down against her side to cover it.

I gasped. "*You* have a head shot!" I suddenly realized that this wasn't just Jenny trying to get in on the action. "Jenny, why didn't you tell me that you wanted to be an actress?"

She shrugged. "Doesn't everybody?"

She had a point. As an average-looking girl who accepted her aesthetic physical limitations, I was in the minority here in L.A. My mother had never marched me down to a talent agent's office when I was a kid. Though she did try it with Jake, and she made a little money off him with some local print ads in his pre-pubescent years. He was the beautiful child until he got sick.

When the elevator doors silently opened, we stepped out into the Fitzgibbons Entertainment loft-like waiting area, which had a stunning180-degree panoramic city view through the floor-to-ceiling glass walls. Against the only wall not made of glass sat an equally stunning redhead behind an aquamarine marble desk, flanked by lightly trickling fountains on either side.

The girl rose from behind the desk and approached us as the elevator door shut silently behind. She was that dimension of thin person who seems to float across the room without any center of gravity. "Doctor Thomas?"

"Jennifer Alexander," Jenny introduced herself. "Actress."

I have a secret trick that I use to keep from cracking up in front of a patient during a serious moment. I convince myself that I'm in a movie, and there's a camera, and I have to say my lines without laughing. For instance: "I'm sorry that your nipple sensation no longer connects to 'down there,' and sex with your eighty-five year-old boyfriend is not the same, but you *are* seventy-eight years old, and we discussed how it *was* a risk of the surgery."

So I managed to purse my lips together and say nothing.

The stunning redhead just nodded solemnly. "I do believe they're ready."

"Your last name isn't *Alexander*," I hissed at Jenny as we followed the red-head through the door to the back offices.

"I know, but don't you love the way it rolls off the tongue? It's my stage name."

"You've never been on a stage."

"Check this place out. Looks *exactly* like *Entourage*. Now *that* was a good show."

The redhead led us through a solid wood French double door engraved with Gloria's name. Just like in the lobby, the far wall of her office was a giant window through which the view stretched south forever. Or, at least to Orange County.

Gloria sat behind a large desk in the corner, plugged into her Blackberry-rigged smartphone, talking in a very fast, firm tone. In the center of the room was a rectangular glass conference table. The chairs were empty except at the near end, where two guys sat huddled in some private argument. Blair, dressed in another androgynous outfit, sat silently next to them, fixated on her laptop screen.

"Would you like a drink?" the redhead offered, pointing to the crystal bowl in the center of the table, stocked with an assortment of mini bottles of Evian, Perrier and Diet Coke on ice.

Gloria acknowledged our arrival with a general nod in our direction, but gave us no indication that she planned on getting off her phone or joining us at the conference table any time soon. Of the two guys at the table, the one facing us was the typical behind-the-scenes Hollywood wheeler and dealer you see in the movies. He had thick, slicked-back dark hair, his eyeglasses were riding that thin line between stylish and gay, and the front of his black silk shirt was unbuttoned just enough to show a little chest hair. The other guy, who was hunched over with his back to us, was nearly completely swallowed up in his charcoal hoodie sweatshirt.

"I've seen that guy on *E!*" Jenny pointed directly at Mr. Hollywood. "This is a sign." I'm sure she meant to be whispering to me, but I'm also sure everyone else in the room could hear her. She craned her neck to get a better view of the other guy, and then said, "Who's that?" Again, directed toward me but loud enough for everyone's listening pleasure.

"*Exactly!*" Mr. Hollywood looked at us, then back at the other guy and said to him, "That's exactly why you're doing this." He pointed at Jenny. "How old are you?"

"Twenty-one."

It took every single one of my muscles of facial expression not to laugh. *It's a movie, it's a movie, you cannot laugh…*I couldn't help starting to wonder how long this "meeting" was going to take, and if I could get back to the hospital in time to make a dent in my mountain of dictations before tomorrow.

"I'm Jennifer Alexander. I'm an actress—"

But the guy had dismissed her, and again addressed his full attention back to his friend, who now looked like he was *trying* to disappear inside his hoodie. "Devin, what did I tell you? You've got a twenty-five year-old mainstream pop culture junkie right here, and she has no fucking clue who you are. You need this show."

"Twenty-one," Jenny said. "And I'm not a pop culture junkie." She pointed an index finger at me. "But *she* is."

At this point, the mystery man in the hoodie turned around—as any guy would, to check out the twenty-one-*ish* year-old girl—and as soon as I saw his face, I knew exactly who he was.

I was staring straight at Devin Breeze, one of my favorite early millennium teenage heartthrobs. Well, I don't know if you could technically call him a *teenage* heartthrob. The TV show character he played was the hot, dangerous teenage bad boy but in real life he was probably closer to my age—already well into his twenties—at the time. He was the reason that most American high school girls—as well as plenty of closet watchers of my own generation—tuned in for our Wednesday night *Pacific Beach* fix. *He* was one of those "pretty-boy actors with the waxed chests that don't exist in real life" that Jenny had made fun of me for watching. My "porn."

Regardless, it was the usual nighttime drama guilty pleasure—gorgeous high school kids tackling all kinds of outrageously sophisticated storylines without any parenteral supervision. This one was about San Diego surfers and the complex struggles between their romantic relationships and their dreams of professional surfing careers. Escapism at its finest.

I was doing my residency during the years that *Pacific Beach* ran on prime time. I had discovered it while channel surfing in a half-conscious state after a thirty-six hour trauma on-call stint, and then once I started watching it, I couldn't stop. The mind-numbing, predictable plots were soothing to my burned-out, aching brain. Besides, I was training to become a plastic surgeon. So watching the absurdly beautiful actors was really just like research.

How random that *Devin Breeze* of all people would be here. Well, maybe he was a producer now—like Blair. I'd kind of wondered what had happened to him. After *Pacific Beach* ended he'd starred in a bad horror movie that tanked and then I never saw him in anything again. I thought I had read in some tabloid a few years ago that he'd spent the night in jail for a DUI. By then *Pacific Beach* and its inhabitants had long since evaporated into the second decade of the millennium, and nobody cared. I mean, it wasn't like a headline or anything, just in one of those columns in the back where there's a quick run-through of who's been Pregnant or Divorced or Dead or Arrested.

Who would've thought... He was smaller and skinnier than I had imagined— like a downsized version of himself, maybe five ten and 160 instead of six feet and 180 like he looked on TV. Some of his signature wavy, sun-streaked blonde locks had escaped out from the sides of his hoodie and framed his amazing face. Looking closer, I could see a short scar that barely violated the edge of his left upper lip. I wondered what lucky bastard got to sew that one up. It wasn't the greatest job—there was a definite mismatch at the vermilion border. Luckily for him there was no HD back then.

I'm not an amateur—I mean, I grew up in L.A.— running into someone famous doesn't really get me going. I've seen plenty of recognizable people over the years. Sure, you're caught off-guard, as your brain and eyes do the computation and then you're like: "Oh, yeah, there's that woman from that movie waiting for the ATM." However, someone like this—along the lines of Brad Pitt or Rob Lowe in their prime—now *that* could shake up your game a little.

He was the total opposite of Eddie, who you might not even look at until after you spent a few hours in the O.R. with him and those Latin pheromones got to you. No, this was completely different. Eye contact with Devin Breeze sent your hormones into instinctive turmoil and made you want to procreate. It was basic biology. Survival of the fittest. It was just science.

I sensed that I should act nonchalant. This was challenging, since having spent at least one hundred hours watching his image on television, I had the weird sensation that he must know me as well as I thought I knew him, and I was surprised when he looked straight at me with no recognition in his familiar denim blue eyes.

Devin did not look happy to be there. He didn't smile at us. Instead, he deliberately sucked the last of something from the end of a straw, creating loud slurping noises in the bottom of the huge take out beverage cup in his hand. Despite the scar—that probably nobody but me would even notice—he had those lips that were too good to be owned by a boy, centrally full like a child's, with a cupid's bow so defined it seemed to have been drawn on and shadowed in with a sharp pencil.

He looked right through us, then leaned across the table back to his friend and whispered, loud enough for *us* to hear, "I thought you said she was going to be hot."

Well, *that* was a punch in the gut. He wasn't talking about Jenny. Nobody was expecting *her*.

"Does it matter?" the other guy said to him.

"Who *is* that guy?" Jenny said to me.

Fortunately, Gloria suddenly sliced right through all of the awkwardness by finally ending her phone call.

"Rachel! Dollface!" She gave me a quick hug and then poured herself a Pellegrino while the rest of us assembled ourselves around the table. "Blair, you met Dr. Thomas the other night…this is Russell…" Mr. Hollywood nodded toward me and smiled, but he didn't bother to get up to shake my hand. "And I'm sure you know Devin."

Devin flashed an unenthusiastic smile in our direction.

"Or maybe not," Gloria added. "It *has* been a while."

"I don't know him," Jenny spat into my ear. "Who the hell *is* he?"

"So, we all know why we're here?" Gloria continued. It sounded like a rhetorical question to me but Devin responded with: "Not really," and slurped.

Russell shot him a look that even scared me a little.

"What, man?" Devin said. "I don't *do* reality television."

"Well, right now you don't do *any* television, so you might want to rethink that."

Gloria sipped her water and then cleared her throat. "There's a line around the block of all the *other* D-listers who would give a testicle for this job."

"Ignore him," Russell said. "We're in. It's either this or *Celebrity Rehab*."

"I don't have a drug problem," Devin said, then to me: "Can you believe this is my manager?"

"They can always say you're a recovering sex addict." Blair gave Devin a snarly smile.

"What would *you* know about sex?" Devin muttered. He then gazed at me through half-closed eyes, and leaned backward, balancing his chair on its back legs. "Fine. Then do I at least get a blowjob here and there? You know, to keep me from acting crazy?"

I was still reeling from his last comment, but I was so mesmerized by his mere presence that I had no emotional capacity left to even feel offended. Even in his nineties grunge outfit, with his faded T-shirt under a worn hoodie, ripped jeans and flip-flops, he was one of those helplessly handsome guys. Nothing could make him ugly. Not even the unkind words that flew from his mouth, directed straight at me.

"A true class act, Mr. Breeze," Blair said. "I can see it's going to be a great pleasure working with you. "

He sighed and smiled at me. "Sorry," he said. "You're going to have to get used to my sense of humor. Since she obviously has none."

"Great," Gloria said, as if nothing had just happened. "So, now that we've all become acquainted….*Lipo Queen*—by the way, the network just had an *orgasm* over the title—starts shooting in two weeks if we're going to make our deadlines. Blair, how are we doing on locations? All the permits in order?" Without waiting for an answer, Gloria waved her hand in the air and continued: "Rachel, as you've probably already guessed, Devin is your new boyfriend. We just need to flesh out the backstory a little. How the two of you met, et cetera—"

"My new…*boyfriend*?" I sputtered.

"I told you if you didn't have one we'd get one for you. You don't like him? We can get someone else. We've got a list—"

"No, no," I said. "Of course I like him—"

Devin looked up at the ceiling. "Oh, thank *God* she likes me."

"So, how did you two meet?" Gloria persisted.

"Starbucks?" Blair suggested.

"That's gay," Devin said.

"Any other suggestions?" Gloria glanced around the table at each of us. "Anyone?"

Nobody else opened their mouths and Blair smirked, satisfied. Inspired by Devin's upper lip scar I suggested, "Maybe he was a patient of mine...?" My weak voice trailed off into a scratchy whisper.

"Now that's *really* gay." Devin took a long last slurp on his straw, then tossed the Wendy's cup toward the wastebasket and missed. "I don't get plastic surgery."

"No." I was thankful that everyone at the table was too self-involved to notice the shaking in my voice. I addressed Gloria, because for some reason I felt like I couldn't talk to Devin himself. As if he existed in a whole other dimension where he might not hear me. "Like in the emergency room. Like he got a cut and I was called to sew him up."

"*Faaa*bulous!"

I loved the way Gloria lit a cigarette right there.

"Good," Blair said expressionlessly.

"I like it," Jenny said, as if anyone cared what she had to say.

"How romantic," Devin said.

Now that the crux of our whirlwind courtship had been solidified, Gloria moved on to more concrete logistics. She began describing to me the West Hollywood condo that was going to be my "home" on the show. The moving truck was scheduled to get me out of my current dump at 10:00 A.M. this Saturday.

"I can't," I started to say. I had promised Jake I would take him to the Memorial Day weekend parking lot carnival at the mall. It was one of the highlights of our childhood, and Jake still got excited about the "upside-down" ride and the food truck with the fried dough and playing those games you can never win. It was the one lucky thing for Jake—that with his life so limited, those simple things still made him so happy. "I can't do it Saturday morning—"

But Gloria just talked over me. "It's already furnished," she said. "So just bring what you *must*, and your clothes..." She looked closely at the suit I was wearing; the same one I'd worn to my med school interviews ten years ago. And maybe even the college ones before that. I prided myself on the fact that it still fit. "On second thought, don't bring your clothes. You're going to need a wardrobe. Blair?"

"She's not sample size," was Blair's response.

"So?" I said, instinctively defensive, even though I had no idea what "sample size" was.

"So it means we're going to have to *buy* everything."

"And hair and make-up," Gloria continued. "And the car?"

"It'll be in the garage when they move in," Blair said.

"Wait, wait a minute!" Devin stopped restlessly drumming his fingers on the table. "*I'm* not moving in."

"If you have to move in, you move in," Russell said.

"It's okay, Russ." Gloria put the end of her cigarette out in her half-empty Pellegrino bottle. "He doesn't have to *live* there. Just make it look like he does. What kind of drama and conflict can we have if they're not *living* together?"

It occurred to me to make a high and mighty comment about how it wouldn't be practical for *me* to move to West Hollywood, since it was so far from the hospital where I was a *surgeon*. But then it also occurred to me that here in this world, with these glossy people in this surreal mile-high-city-view office, places like the Valley Hospital didn't even exist. So I didn't try.

The middle part of the meeting was a general blur to me, mainly because Gloria's voice had faded into a background hum while I concentrated on trying to look at Devin Breeze without him noticing. It wasn't my fault. I was just so fucking fascinated. It was just—it was like the rest of the room was in black and white, and he was in Technicolor. It was impossible to take your eyes off him. Eventually I gave up trying to be discreet and just stared.

Gloria handed out thick bound booklets to each of us that contained a barrage of information written in lawyer-speak. Even though I didn't fully understand exactly what she was saying, I got the gist of it. The show's premise was the chronicling of the "real" life of a female plastic surgeon and the lives of the women on whom she performs life-changing body sculpting procedures.

Shooting would be twice a week, during which time there would be footage of myself in the office seeing patients, and performing liposuctions.

"Yeah, about that…" I started to say. "Does it have to be just about… *liposuction*?"

"What do you mean, *just* liposuction?"

I readjusted the weight on my ischial tuberosities. Sitting for so long on this hard wood chair was becoming mildly painful. "Like, maybe we could film some of the reconstruction stuff I do at the hospital…?"

Besides the fact that I was wondering when the hell I was even going to have time to do this—*if* I decided to do it—I was becoming concerned about being the front and center of a liposuction showcase. How could I explain to Gloria—clearly one of the millions of women who considered safe liposuction to be the greatest advance in modern medicine—that in the professional world of plastic surgeons, it was at the lowest rung of the totem pole, way below even breast augs and tummy tucks? Maybe even lower, like down in the dirt *underneath* the totem pole since the gynecologists and dermatologists had started taking "Weekend Lunchtime Lipo" courses and competing with us for patients.

Donarski would not like it.

Gloria exhaled smoke out of the side of her mouth and stretched her arm to ash perfectly in the narrow neck of the bottle. I marveled at how not a single ash dropped on the table, and she hadn't even been looking. "Dollface, this is not the *Discovery Channel*. The generic plastic surgery makeover show has been done to *death* already. We are in a world of niche markets. And this one is an unturned stone—pardon the pun." She turned and winked at me. "I just *love* that 'fat out of a rock' thing. The middle-aged women across America who fantasize about having liposuction are the same ones—" She paused and glanced at Devin. "—Who once fantasized about *you*. It's just the most brilliant non-celebrity pairing. So, what I need you both to do…" She pointed at my booklet. "Is sign that. And initial every page."

"I don't think they're middle-aged *yet*," Devin said. He had definitely looked at me when he said that. My stomach lurched.

"Whatever." Gloria waved her cigarette at him. "They're not teenagers and they're not senior citizens. Most of them have had a couple of kids by now and can't get the baby weight off…they're sure that if they could just be skinnier, their lives would be better…they *dream* about getting their fat sucked off. And most of them need someone to think about while they're fucking their husbands."

"Thom, this is going to be an insane practice builder!" Jenny chimed in. "You'll be like all those other guys on *Doctor 90210*. You'll never have to worry about money again! Just sign it!"

True, all "those guys" from *Doctor 90210* were cleaning up right now just from the exposure, and that show ended almost ten years ago. I would never get to where they were professionally, even with all of my business at Ferraro's. I wasn't in a financial crisis at the moment, but I was always teetering on one. Let alone ever owning one of those houses on the bluff.

Practice building software cost twenty grand. At least. This was free.

"Don't worry, Dollface. This will be a classy show. You won't be just another one of those social media whore plastic surgeons." Gloria turned to Devin. "This, Mr. Breeze, is going to put you back on the map. Women are going to want to suck your dick again."

Blair snorted.

"He still gets his dick sucked plenty," Russell assured us.

"Is this meeting over yet?" Devin said.

"Thom," Jenny murmured to me. "If you don't sign that thing right now I swear to fucking God I'm leaving you."

My phone buzzed on the table in front of me. I got that sinking feeling of recognizing the number, not being able to remember exactly who it was, but knowing it wasn't someone I wanted to talk to. Missed call. An 855. Oh, yeah. That would be about the copay on Jake's last hospital stay. My mother had promised to give me half of it, but in her loop-de-loop world she kept misplacing her checkbook or couldn't find a pen, and I kept forgetting about it until it got to a collection agency.

It was an opportunity that no other plastic surgeon would pass up in a million years.

What about my probation?

My phone did the short rumble to make sure I knew that the collection agency had left a voicemail message for me.

Jesus… I looked around the glossy room and at these glossy new people. At the glossy crystal bowl filled with glossy bottles of Perrier and Diet Coke on now-melting ice. At the glossy view to Orange County. And back at the motherfucking glossiest human being I'd ever seen in my life.

Eddie who?

I imagined paying off my glossy credit card. My student loans. And maybe paying someone *else* to be Jake's concierge.

Probation. As if I were some kind of criminal. Probation wasn't my problem. The fact that I had worked my ENTIRE life to get where I was—an underpaid employee of a hospital threatening closure at any moment, a place where I couldn't even give patients the care that I wanted to. The demise of the American healthcare system. THAT was the problem.

I was just saving myself. And Jake.

As if on cue, Jenny handed me a pen. It didn't even occur to me to have an attorney present while I scribbled my life away on every page of the document.

"One more thing, before everyone goes." Gloria retrieved a folder from her desk and splayed out its contents—an array of headshots of gorgeous barely-legal-looking girls—on the table like a hand of cards. "Rachel, you pick. Your new office assistant. If you want, you can take them home, give it some thought."

Devin leaned in to get a closer view and smiled. "Where do all these whores *come* from?"

"In case you haven't noticed, *you're* the whore here, asshole," Blair said.

"But I have an assistant," I said.

"Who?" Gloria's eyes widened as if she was noticing Jenny next to me for the first time. She stuffed her second cigarette into the Pellegrino bottle. "Okay, time out." She grabbed my arm and directed me to the other end of the room. "Not that chunky girl? *Rachel.* We're selling beauty. Fantasies. Dreams. She's fat in real life. Imagine what she's going to look like on television."

Gloria hadn't even attempted a stage whisper. I glanced back at Jenny. She was pretending to act like she didn't care, but I could tell she was devastated. It was only this past week that I'd started to understand that Simple Little Jenny wasn't as simple as I'd thought. And even though her recent behavior was more than annoying, she'd always been completely loyal to me. If I was really doing this, no way was I going to leave her behind.

"I'm not doing this without her," I told Gloria.

"You want me to pick one for you?"

"I mean it. If it wasn't for Jenny I wouldn't even be here."

"You say no to this and I'll have a line around the block of plastic surgeons ready to step in."

"Next to the line of D list actors?"

Gloria pursed her lips. "You already signed everything."

With Devin out of view, I could think clearly enough to be manipulative. "I'll get a lawyer."

A smirk flashed across her face. "You can't afford that kind of lawyer."

I shrugged. "There was a law school next to my med school, you know. I have a lot of smart friends."

It took about ten seconds, but the shift in Gloria's eyes told me that my bluff had worked.

"Just remember, she was never invited," she hissed, but led me back to the group. "Stand up!" she commanded Jenny, who obeyed. "Turn around." Gloria held one arm up by the elbow with her other hand, and tapped her free long finger against her cheekbone, as if she were deciding on a piece of art. "Okay, I'm willing to work with you on this one. Can you get her down to a size four by the end of next week? I especially need you to concentrate on the hip and thigh area."

It took me a minute to realize that she didn't mean for me to plug Jenny in to a Weight Watchers program. I just couldn't believe Gloria was asking me to lipo down my assistant to make her camera-ready.

Talk about turning a frown upside down. Jenny was even more ecstatic than the minute I'd finally said yes to Gloria. No big surprise there. She'd been trying to get herself on the table since I'd met her.

Blair nodded her head in agreement.

"Now that," Devin said, "is fucked up."

10

Having spent nearly my entire adult life in hospital settings where most of the patients can barely pay for the parking, it is still difficult for me to fathom how much time and money is used to get a reality TV show off the ground.

I had to completely tweak my hours at the hospital that next week. I switched my clinic to Tuesday afternoon by telling the nursing administrator that I had enrolled in an all-day-every-Monday Board Review course, my second lie in the history of my career.

Secondly, and not unhappily, Jenny and I said good-bye to Ferraro's—but not without getting in her three-liter hip and thigh liposuction before we left. With my oath to shrink her, Gloria had agreed to hire Jenny full-time as my patient coordinator in the new Beverly Hills office. It was a gamble for me to give up my steady moonlighting income, but Jenny had convinced me that the business I was going to get from the TV show would make it more than worth it. We left the night after her surgery. Right before we exited the office for the last time, I left a final memo on Dr. Ferraro's chair, saying "good-bye."

I still hadn't gotten around to explaining anything to Jake, though I planned to do so as soon as I saw him. When I told him that something had come up at work and we were going to have to go to the carnival later on, he was understanding, as always.

"I know how hard your job is, Rachel," he said. "Call me whenever you're done."

I'll make it up to him, I swore to myself. *But really, I shouldn't have to apologize. I mean, I was doing this just as much for him as for myself.*

As promised, the moving truck arrived at 10:00 AM on Saturday morning, and it was still half-empty when it left my place again for West Hollywood. Besides Sushi, his food and litter accessories, my books, computer and three-way mirror, and garbage bags filled with clothes that I couldn't live without (i.e., the three identical vintage boy short bathing suits) I didn't have much to bring.

My new "abode"—Penthouse 14A of the West Sunset Towers building—turned out to be just about as insane as it sounds. It was a 2000 square-foot loft, slick and modern, half of the entire fourteenth floor. Exactly the kind of place you would expect to find your young, hip, and single-but-living-with-her-ex-TV-star-boyfriend plastic surgeon.

"I cannot fucking believe you get to live here," Jenny said as soon as we opened the door.

It wasn't the moving in of my meager belongings that took the rest of that afternoon, but what happened when Jenny and I got in my new Porsche for a test drive. We found ourselves unable to get out of it.

Initially we had just meant to take it once around the block with the top down but, come on...would *anyone* just take a fully loaded brand-new convertible Porsche for a once-around if they could keep driving it? I couldn't be faulted for losing track of time. I felt like I was cheating on my poor little Audi, which we'd left sitting all alone back in the condo's underground parking lot. But the truth was, next to this sleek machine, my car did look adolescent and silly.

Jenny had insisted that we cruise down through the Beverly Hills shopping district, where the traffic is slow enough on a Saturday afternoon to leave you sitting in your car for hours at time, without even really going anywhere. For once, that was the objective. When one of those Hollywood tour buses pulled up next to us at a stoplight, some of the tourists up on the second level started taking pictures of us. It might have had something to do with our "Lipokwn" vanity plates that Blair had managed to swing at short notice.

Jake hadn't answered his phone when I tried to call him to let him know I was running late. By the time I showed up at his place it was close to eight, and he was sitting in front of the television with Sam.

"Jake, I'm so sorry," I said. "I left you a message."

"I know. It's okay." He was watching *Apocalypse Now* from a VCR tape that he must have had since he was ten. He yawned. His day was almost over and I had missed it entirely.

"I guess you ate already." I nodded toward the remains of a frozen dinner on the coffee table in front of him.

"Yeah. You want one?"

Jenny and I had stopped for a late lunch and I started to say, "No, I just ate not too long ago," but then realized that would conflict with the story that I had been working all day. And I could see from what he'd been eating that he had purposely gotten the Asian Chicken ones that I liked. "Sure," I said. "I'll get it."

As I prepared the frozen dinner in the kitchenette area, I tried to formulate the speech I was about to give Jake to let him know what was really going on. Then I spied the greasy waxed paper wrapping on the counter.

"You went to the carnival without me."

"Yeah."

"How did you get there?"

He made a face as he got up and handed me my own bag of fried dough. "Rachel, I'm not a cripple. I took the bus. Here, I wasn't sure if it was supposed to be in the refrigerator."

"Was it…fun?" *Why wasn't I glad he'd just gone without me? Why did I have to feel so guilty?* He was right. He was an able-bodied adult. *Good for him!*

"It would have been more fun if we went together, but I got a bunch of stuff." He ripped open a couple of garbage bags and dumped an assortment of stuffed animals on the floor. Sam sniffed at them.

"You won those?"

"The little ones. The big ones I bought." He held up a huge pink bear. "Here, this one's for you."

I tried to block out the image of Jake dragging those enormous trash bags full of stuffed animals onto the bus. But now I did feel that this was a perfect example of why Gloria and Blair didn't need to know about him. Not only was he not a piece of the world they were creating, but they might even turn him into a freak side show.

I wasn't leaving him behind. I was protecting him.

"We need to talk about something." I followed Jake back to the couch with my lukewarm dinner in my hand, a torn-off piece of fried dough in my mouth. "Jake, you know I do the best I can to take care of you."

He looked at me, suddenly stiffening. "Don't tell me you're sending me back to the hospital. I didn't bother anyone today, I swear. I take my meds. Every night. Check my blood tests. I bet they're perfect."

"No, Jake—"

"I won't go back there. I'll leave again." His voice would have scared me if I hadn't known him. Whenever we got on the topic of hospitals, Jake's voice took on the chilling, rough quality of someone who sounded like they needed to be exorcised.

"No, it's nothing like that," I repeated, but he took off into the bedroom, slamming the flimsy door behind him. It took half an hour before I was able to convince him that I wasn't talking about "locking him up" again. When I finally got him calmed down enough to coax him out of the bedroom and back to the couch, I told him about Gloria and *Lipo Queen*.

"It's going to help me make more money. So I can get you out of here. We're going to get one of those houses, remember? And just think, *you* actually named the show. How crazy is that?" I laughed.

"Pretty crazy." He was so relieved about not going to the hospital that he didn't seem to process much else of what I was saying. Except the Devin Breeze thing caught his attention.

"That's that guy from that TV show you used to make me watch," he said. "You were like in love with him." He started to laugh.

"Shut up. I was not." True, we might have watched a few *Pacific Beach* reruns together when there was nothing else on, but how the hell did he remember that shit?

"He's your boyfriend now? In real life?"

"Not exactly."

"But...you just said—"

"That's what I wanted to talk to you about. It's kind of...made up. It's not really my life...here. They got me this new place to live...it's over the hill in We Ho...it's unreal, I mean, I can't wait for you to see it...and the *car*..."

63

He turned to dump the remains of his frozen dinner tray into the garbage. He was silent for a moment, then said with his back to me, "It's okay, Rachel. I don't want to be in it, anyway."

"Jake, I'm still here for you."

"I know."

"Please don't be mad at me."

"I'm not mad." He turned to look at me. "I understand."

What made it worse was that I knew he really did understand. But the worst part of all was that not only did he understand why he had to be excluded, but I knew that he was genuinely happy for me.

11

Talk about not being a "sample size." Since we couldn't borrow from the downtown showrooms, shopping for the *Lipo Queen* wardrobe was—for the entire Memorial Day weekend—a full time job all on its own. Blair had me in and out of every outfit imaginable, from Conservative Professional Woman to Slutty Professional Woman, from Brooks Brothers to Frederick's of Hollywood. The show's stylist, Eva "yay" or "nay'd" everything in the dressing rooms, via Facetime. I liked Eva. She had the decision-making capacity of a surgeon. Her text responses to the photos were either "Fabulous!" or "Absolutely not!"

We finished off the third day at Marc Jacobs where Fitzgibbons Productions' final additions to the Lipo Queen's wardrobe included a $2500 pair of leather pants.

I'd gotten to wear some pretty swanky stuff during our shopping spree, but those leather pants were in a league all of their own. And it wasn't just the price. Maybe it was because they had actually been chained to the rack. Maybe it was because they sucked me in and smoothed me out in the places you just can't fight without a liposuction cannula.

Or maybe it was just because it had never crossed my mind to wear a pair of leather pants. I successfully squeezed myself into them without any significant compromise to my peripheral circulation, and then I was somebody else in the mirror. I wasn't sure who. But I couldn't possibly be someone who owed six figures in school loans, or who until a week ago lived in a crappy walk-up in Van Nuys, or whose main life priority was her morbidly obese mentally ill brother who lived in a trailer park.

Blair saw the look on my face. "Yeah," she grunted. "I guess we're gonna need those."

They had kept the store open for us long past closing time. It was eleven-thirty on that Monday night when Blair was finally satisfied that I had an adequate wardrobe to shoot the first six episodes, with an understanding that I was not to wear anything twice. "If you wear something more than once on a television show, people will think you wear it *all the time*," she'd said.

But when she started reciting off the condo address for the courier for the umpteenth time in the past seventy-two hours, I snatched the bag off the counter and said, "I'll take this one myself."

"Are you sure?" the salesman said to me, pen poised in the air, mid-transcription, shaking his head with a constipated look on his face. "It's going to be *heavy*."

Of course he was right, as it contained about ten other articles of clothing and two pairs of shoes. It was probably our heaviest bag of merchandise all day. Not the ideal time to start questioning the competency of the messenger. But I couldn't let those leather pants out of my sight. What if the messenger lost the bag or was held at gunpoint and my magic leather pants never made it home?

Blair didn't argue with me, just informed me that I needed to have everything unpacked in an orderly fashion by the time Eva arrived tomorrow to pick out the outfits for the first shoot. I pictured all of our purchases still stacked in boxes and bags in the entrance hallway, and decided to skip meeting Jenny for a drink—it was her night off from Zoey and she was out on the town somewhere with her sister.

When I got back to the condo, I was surprised that the front door wasn't locked. *Had I left it open? And with thousands of dollars worth of clothes sitting right inside the door…*

I exhaled in relief when I saw that, as far as I could tell, everything was still there. And when I entered the living room, I realized what was going on. *Fuck*. Devin was here.

12

At first he didn't see or hear me. He was stretched out on the couch with his bare feet propped up on the coffee table and his back to the front door, his famous sun-streaked wavy hair smashed against an oversized throw pillow. It was like the enormous flat screen television and the high-tech surround sound system had entirely cut him off from the rest of the world.

My palms instantly developed a layer of sweat and as I wriggled my fingers to uncramp my stiff hands, the Marc Jacobs bag hit the ground.

"Hey," he said, without even turning his head. It was like he knew it was me and he was so uninterested that he hadn't even considered that it might be an intruder instead.

My mouth had become dry and sticky so I was glad he didn't seem to expect a response.

Why was he here? He'd made it clear that he was only going to be around when he had to, and we weren't supposed to start shooting until next week. *Dammit.* It wasn't supposed to *go* like this. I had envisioned a whole Cinderella thing—that with Blair and Gloria's makeover, the next time Devin Breeze saw me, his heart would stop. Or he'd at least reevaluate my hotness.

But right now I was far from heart-stopping form. My scant morning makeup had long since faded, the jeans that I'd been throwing on all weekend were stretched-out and baggy, and I hadn't washed my hair in two days.

It doesn't matter. He's not here to see you. He probably has another girl here with him...somewhere. As I crossed the room toward the couch I did a quick survey of the kitchen and the upstairs bedroom through the door on the balcony. I didn't see any movement. I glanced in what I thought was a discreet manner toward the downstairs bedroom. The light was off.

He looked up at me and laughed, but not in a mean way. "There's nobody else here if that's what you're wondering. I'm not *that* much of an asshole."

I caught my breath. *So on top of his super-human physical attributes he was a mind reader as well?*

Okay, now I need to just stop acting like an idiot. This isn't a TV show where the cute boy turns out to be an alien. The only paranormal thing about him is how crazy good-looking he is. It's just pathetically obvious that you were craning your neck around, looking for someone.

And why did I even *care*? *He's a loser. He's just a prop.* For *me.* They didn't take *him* shopping. *He dresses like a homeless surfer.*

External beauty is temporary. I tried to picture him ten years from now, all weathered-looking: deep irreversible wrinkles from too much Southern California sun and trashed hair and loose abdominal wall skin hanging over a half-zipped-up wetsuit, like those old crusty surfers you see smoking pot around the pier. The ones that you look at and think: "Yeah, they were probably hot when they were young."

It didn't work.

The déjà vu was unnerving. I guess that's what Netflix binge-watching will do to you. Yes, I had recently recaptured the past by hunting down *Pacific Beach* and watching a few episodes. Purely for research purposes.

"So, what are you doing here?" Now that I was closer, I saw that he had Sushi sitting on the floor, looking up expectantly at him. He dumped a small pile of cat treats out onto the blanket next to him and Sushi climbed up and started devouring them like he hadn't eaten in weeks.

"The truth is…I have a curfew." Devin massaged the top of the cat's head with his thumb and forefinger while he spoke to me.

"A curfew? You mean, from your parents?"

"Yeah, from my parents. No, from Russell."

"Oh." The adolescent "fight or flight" response going on with me had finally started to wane. My voice no longer sounded smothered, drowned out by the hammering of my own heartbeat.

Thank God. I was a responsible, important adult. I should not be feeling like a swooning teenager.

Yet we all know that there are those things that never change. I took a few steps closer but his brief, direct gaze with those denim blue eyes totally knocked me off balance. I swiftly tried to disguise my stagger by flopping onto the end of the couch, and reaching out to pet Sushi, as if that's all I'd meant to do. This didn't work out very well at all, since Sushi was fixated on the bag of cat treats in Devin's hand, and completely ignored me.

Then I had my first logical thought.

"Why didn't you just go home?"

Devin dumped another pile of treats on top of the throw pillow and Sushi went for it. "I can't risk driving that far after I've been drinking. I've already had one DUI." He added as if to qualify, "It was a while ago. Like three years."

I had to stop myself from saying, "I know."

"I wasn't even drunk. I blew a .08 and I was sober, but they love to make examples of celebrities."

Was he watching my expression?

"That is, I was one back then," he added.

This time I figured it was appropriate to say, "I know."

"So, what's in the bag?"

I realized that I still had a death grip on that Marc Jacobs bag. I wanted to say something clever and flirty but of course nothing at all came to mind. "Just some clothes…"

He motioned for me to hand it over so he could take a look inside.

"*Niiiice.*" He whistled and held up the leather pants. He looked sideways at me and winked. "I wouldn't mind seeing you in these."

He sounded so sincere that I wasn't sure how to respond, and I felt that I had to switch the subject.

"You shouldn't give my cat all of those treats," I said.

He had just poured another pile of snack pellets for Sushi, who again consumed them like a wild animal attacks his prey.

"Why not? He really likes them."

"Of course he does. It's like crack for cats." I grabbed the bag. It was empty. "You gave him the whole thing!"

Devin laughed. It was a genuine, startled laugh.

I had made him laugh.

"That's funny," he said. "Crack for cats."

"It's true!" I wanted to keep making him laugh, so he could see how witty and charming I was. Maybe I wasn't a supermodel, but I did have a reputation for being somewhat entertaining. I blabbered on: "I swear, I think they put cat heroin in there. He gets like a drug addict. He loses interest in everything except sitting and waiting for them by the cabinet and starts losing weight because he won't eat anything else."

"I think he'll be okay." He smiled but didn't laugh hysterically.

He wasn't getting my brilliant parallel between the cat and the heroin addict doubled over, clutching a syringe, wasting away in a dark room. *Maybe he even found it offensive. Did he think I was making fun of heroin addicts? What if he used to be one himself?*

He rubbed the cat's ears. "What's his name again?"

"Sushi," I said, and then, as I always felt compelled to do, I added a disclaimer for being a single woman over thirty with a cat: "He wasn't really *my* cat, I mean, it's not like I'm one of those crazy cat ladies…he was my friend's cat…"

Gloria didn't think that a single woman with a cat was sexy either. She had wanted us to have a dog instead, "Because then it will seem like you're a real family." It wasn't like I was Angelina Jolie and I could just go get us a baby.

Devin continued to stroke his head. "He's a cool cat. He looks just like one I did a commercial with a few years ago."

He didn't say anything else. Now that I was over my initial episode of physiologic overdrive and could speak without my voice shaking, I couldn't think of any more conversation starters.

As if there had been an unspoken command, we both turned to watch the flat screen. Sushi realized he had been cut off and wandered away into the kitchen. Now we didn't even have the cat to talk about.

The awkward silence overpowered the noise from the television. Well, it was probably just awkward for *me*. I didn't get the sense that this situation was making Devin Breeze feel awkward at all. I stole a sideways glance at him. No, he actually looked quite comfortable, settled into the couch like that. He didn't seem the least bit nervous. Just no longer interested in talking to me.

He's a D-Lister…washed up…future crusty old surfer…

But that didn't necessarily mean I wanted him to leave.

"Is that new?" I blurted out, nodding toward the *Saturday Night Live* episode.

"It's Monday."

"Right."

He held the remote toward me. "Here, you want to watch something else?" His voice was neutral. At least he didn't sound like I was bothering him.

I hesitated. First of all, did this mean that he had given up on late night television and was going to leave me here alone? And if he was staying, was I up to this kind of responsibility? Selecting the television show to watch with a hot guy who isn't gay can be a very tricky matter. *And with a TV star?* Even with an *ex*-TV star—that certainly wasn't going to make it any easier. Besides *Saturday Night Live* reruns, what does someone who is *on* TV actually *watch* on TV?

I took the remote from him and started channel surfing as fast as I could.

"This high definition is really something," I said. I clicked rapidly past things that I really would have liked to watch—a *Friends* rerun, a chick flick edited for television, a *True Hollywood Story*…But any of that would likely make him flee…Where the hell were *South Park* and *Indiana Jones* when you needed them?

A cooking show. Definitely not. A wilderness show. That could be a possibility. I peeked over at him but he wasn't even looking at the screen—he was inspecting something on his finger. The delay between the picture changes was making me anxious. *How could this new technology be so slow?*

"Oh!"

I had involuntarily stopped clicking. But by the time I caught myself and was about to change the channel again, it was too late.

"Oh, come on," he said. "You're not going to make me watch *that*, are you?"

Busted. There wasn't even any point in quickly switching the channel because he'd already seen my now-burning face. I looked straight ahead and let my hair fall forward on the side to cover my cheek, which I'm sure was crimson.

It was an episode of *Pacific Beach* running on syndication on a basic cable network. But it wasn't even just any episode. The image of Devin in the familiar decorated high school gymnasium slow dancing with his co-star—and rumored-to-be-then-real-life-girlfriend—had sent me into a paralyzing tailspin of nostalgia.

"I remember this one," I said.

"So do I. That doesn't mean we have to watch it." He reached for the remote. "Sorry. I have to take over."

The on-screen Devin was gazing at the girl as if he was seeing a rainbow for the first time. "You're my soul mate, Kristy," he was saying. "You're the only person who makes me feel like myself." And then they were kissing and hugging each other so hard, turning together in a tight circle, clutching each other so that it looked like the room was spinning around and around them, and all the lights and decorations and other couples blurred together in the background until it looked like they were completely alone.

"Didn't you get dizzy doing that?" The words came out before I could stop them.

"Doing what? Come on, gimme the remote."

"Spinning around like that so…fast."

"*We* weren't spinning. The camera was spinning around *us*."

Then I just couldn't help myself.

"I loved your show," I blurted out. "I used to watch it all the time."

There, I'd said it. As if I was giving him novel information, not something that he'd heard from crazed groupies countless times before. Thankfully, I stopped myself before I went on to describe how I used to watch that scene repeatedly so many times that I had memorized the words to the saccharine high-pitched Wilson Phillips song playing in the background. But that wasn't *so* weird, right? I mean, who doesn't love a good hokey TV high school fantasy story? Kristy was the dorky one, the unpopular outsider who gets the hot guy because he likes her for who she really is. Of course in true television fashion she was the most beautiful girl on the show; they just frumped her up for the first season.

I wasn't sure how I had expected him to respond. He just kept staring at me with a half-smile. I tried to back pedal a bit. "I mean, I didn't really *watch it* watch it," I said.

"It's okay. It's people like you that paid my bills all those years. Just wish I'd saved more of the money."

People like me? I wasn't just his run-of-the-mill fan! That show had merely been an escape from my *own* very full life of literal blood, sweat and tears in the hospital.

"No, really, I was a surgery resident at the time—I even got myself in trouble for it once—" I said, as if that explained anything.

"Watching *PB*? You might be thinking of something else. It wasn't X-rated. At least, not that *I* remember."

He was actually starting to look more amused then bored, which prompted me to launch recklessly into a story that I had never told anyone before. "Here's what happened," I said, like I was about to tell a thriller.

There was one post-call Wednesday—my internship year of general surgery—that I was counting down the hours of my grueling day until I could get home for the *Pacific Beach* season finale that night. We had been left with a real cliffhanger the week before when Devin's character, Braden had cheated on his girlfriend with a professional female surfer he met at a competition, and this week the aftermath would start to unfold.

But just as I was about to walk out the door of the hospital at the end of the day, my chief resident gave me an assignment for the following morning's Morbidity and Mortality Conference. I was to present the succession of in-house events that had led up to the demise of our latest gunshot wound victim on the O.R. table. Of course, I was going to have to spin the tale and skirt around the key piece of information, which was that since the patient had arrived at two in the morning, unfortunately for her she got three unsupervised surgery residents mucking around in her abdomen instead of someone more senior who might actually know what he was doing. Had the attending surgeon gotten out of bed to help us that night, the bleeding from the back of the liver might have been stopped, and there probably wouldn't even have *been* a presentation to give.

Carrying out my chief's request would have meant spending half the night in Medical Records turning the patient's chart into a PowerPoint presentation, which would definitely make me miss my show. These were the days before "On Demand" TV and "streaming", and I hadn't bothered to set my TiVo because, being post-call, I was guaranteed to be home and in front of the television by 7:00 P.M. I hadn't slept at all the night before, and all day I had been anticipating curling up on my couch that evening with a Lean Cuisine and a glass of wine and losing myself in the fantasy world of gorgeous people and beautiful San Diego beaches.

I was beyond furious. I was panicking. I left the hospital with a half-hearted intent to return early in the morning to work on it, but with rounds starting at 6:00 A.M., that never happened. Confronted by my chief the next morning, pre-conference and empty-handed, I told him that my computer had crashed and I couldn't recover the file. The most fascinating part to me is that even though he made sure how "disappointed, shocked and disgusted," he was with me, I never felt bad about it. That's how much I loved *Pacific Beach*.

But while retelling the story to Devin I didn't get any further than the description of the operating room—which, in retrospect, was probably fortunate.

"So it was a girl that got shot?" he interrupted me.

"Yeah, a police officer. She stopped a guy on the freeway for speeding—"

"And you were looking inside her? Like at all her organs?"

"Well, yeah."

"Really." He sat upright and faced me, crossing his legs Indian style in front of him so that his bare toes brushed up against my thigh. "And it was bleeding? Like blood everywhere? Did you find the bullet?"

"We did, but it's not really about finding the bullet," I said. Lay-people always want to know about the bullet. You come out to the waiting room and the family is always like, *"Did you get the bullet?"* And you're like, *"We got the bullet but the bullet got the large intestine so he's going to have to shit in a bag on his stomach for the next three months."*

"It's about fixing the damage that the bullet causes," I said. "Sometimes you just leave it there."

"So there are people still walking around with bullets in them?"

And because when it came down to it, he was a guy and the story had something to do with gang warfare, the conversation veered off to one about guns and bullets, and people getting shot, and gang members walking into the emergency room dripping trails of blood. I told him all about the Crips and the Bloods, and how we had to put them in rooms at different ends of the ward. How there had to be two police officers guarding the door of every patient who turned out to be a prisoner, even if they were brain-dead in the unit on a ventilator, because there was some folklore that one such patient had woken up, and, unattended, assaulted the nurse and escaped from the hospital.

"That's some crazy shit." Devin yawned without covering his mouth and settled back into the corner of the couch again, spreading a throw blanket over his legs. "You don't mind if I crash here tonight, do you?"

I was still pretty revved up from captivating his attention with my stories, and I was trying to think up a few more that he might want to hear, but I took this as my cue to leave. The *Pacific Beach* episode had long since ended. Now there was just an infomercial about a combination Stairmaster-bicycle that toned your thighs in under thirty minutes a day. The digital clock on the cable box said 1:27.

"It's your place, too," I said as I stood up.

"I promise not to be too much of a burden." He closed his eyes and turned on his side. "Hey, can you turn the light off?"

Step away from the couch, Rachel. Thatta girl. Hit the light switch. Up the stairs. Don't go looking for the cat right now—he'll find you later. Don't look back. Not that it would matter, since the light is off and his eyes are closed but still...it had to be a nonchalant exit. Especially after how I'd bared my soul to him earlier. What was I thinking, anyway, telling him all of that?

I don't think I slept at all that night. I'm pretty sure I woke up at least once an hour, thinking: "Devin Breeze is downstairs in my living room right now. I can't just lie here. I can't stand it. That's it. I'm going down there."

It was such a dangerous and fantastic thought to entertain, and I loved scaring myself with the idea of going through with it. But the closest I got was sneaking out to the landing when the sun came up and watching him sleep under the daylight that filtered through the skylights. He lay in the fetal position on his left side and Sushi was curled up in the middle of the "C", right up against his abdomen. That lucky little son-of-a-bitch.

13

That first day of shooting *Lipo Queen* was like practicing medicine in an alternate universe.

Jenny and I pulled up to the legendary 436 North Bedford building at our anointed "call time" of 6:30 A.M. and became part of the succession of European cars creeping down the steep ramp to the underground lot. Six-thirty A.M. also happens to be the common "arrival time" for all other patients, staff and surgeons scheduled to participate in the practice of plastic surgery across town. And our new building—the one that Robert Rey, "Dr. 90210" himself, had made famous by dubbing it the "Holy Grail" in a *New York Times* article—was the mecca of it all. The rusted-red brick front with the circular courtyard surrounded by rosebushes and tulips had been featured on so many television shows and photographed for so many articles that it had a grand familiarity similar to that of the White House. The place where the most high profile clients underwent the most coveted procedures at the most outrageous prices—it was all going down right here.

I inched along behind a red Maserati, thinking I should have brought the Porsche. It was just that I'd been up the entire night before at the hospital fixing yet another mandible in a guy who got into a fistfight with his drug dealer, and I hadn't had time to make it to the condo to switch cars or even shower.

Jenny and I were late finding my new office. We were both so stoned—she on her post-lipo narcotics and me with my post-call fatigue—that we circled up and down the hallways for twenty minutes until we finally stumbled upon the door. *My* door, with the gold engraved glass placard "**Rachel M. Thomas, M.D., Plastic and Reconstructive Surgery.**"

"We've arrived," Jenny said. "But don't you think my name should be there too? My stage name. Smaller letters, of course." She tried the doorknob, which was locked. We started by knocking politely, but resorted to banging when we got no response. Eventually someone swung it open from the inside. Blair.

"You're late," she said. "Remind me to get you a key."

"Fuck *me*," Jenny said when we stepped through the doorway. At first I thought that was a response to Blair, but no—she was reacting to the room we had just entered. Presumably the waiting room. Someone had dropped some serious cash on this place. Just not with the interior decorator I would have chosen.

The office was a lavish explosion of gold lame and red velvet patterned wallpaper…mirrors everywhere…white leather couches…a marble floor partially covered with something that I'm pretty sure came in one piece off an animal. Since I know nothing about art, I gave the prints on the walls the benefit of the doubt.

The generous flat-screen television inset into the wall, and the large colorful orchids everywhere were good, though.

"I thought Gloria said it would be classy," Jenny giggled, then winced as a woman with spiky hair and a nose ring grabbed her by her recently liposuctioned arm and whisked her off to hair and makeup.

"Just so you know," Blair said. "The rent here in 90210 is twice as expensive per square foot as it is two blocks over in 90212. Now, I need you to come show us how close we can get the cameras to the O.R. table. And why do you look so pale? We need to get you into makeup."

"I'm fine," I said, though I wasn't entirely sure this was true. The only sleep I'd had since the mandible was the twenty minutes I'd accidently closed my eyes while I was dictating in the recovery room. While normally I can operate on no sleep for days, there was nothing normal about this specific situation. This wasn't the hospital where everyone was my friend, or even Ferraro's. When I caught sight of the cameras next to the sinks in the substerile area—with all of the lights and wires and umbrella things for the lights—I felt the nausea of a vasovagal coming on, and I had to lean up against the wall to keep from sinking to the ground. I swallowed the quarter-cup of saliva that had pooled in my mouth and closed my eyes.

When I opened them again, I looked past the expression of consternation on Blair's face—not, I knew, because she was actually concerned about me, but because she was worried I wasn't going to be able to do my job—and into the operating room itself. That, at least made me feel like I was somewhat at home. All operating rooms are pretty much the same. There's the table. An anesthesia machine. Oxygen connections dangling from the ceiling. A back table covered with blue sterile drapes.

The O.R. staff members had their backs to us. There were two of them. A large woman counted medication at the narcotics cabinet while a young guy with perfectly tousled and highlighted hair loaded a tray of instruments into the autoclave. The nurse and the scrub tech. *Okay, this was more like it.*

"Ladies, this is Dr. Rachel Thomas," Blair announced, and the two of them stopped what they were doing to acknowledge us. I wondered why Blair had addressed them as "Ladies" since the one working at the autoclave was clearly male, but when he spun around and opened his mouth I realized why.

"I'm *soooo* excited to meet you!" he crowed in the classic voice of a fun, flaming gay. "I'm your tech. What cannulas do you use?"

I was too dumbfounded to answer him. He was like his own reality show waiting to happen. He had an unnaturally tiny, upturned nose with complete loss of tip projection—a classic hack job and possibly the worst I'd ever seen. You'd need a rib graft to reconstruct that thing. And either cheek implants or at least four syringes of filler stuffed in there on top of his malar eminences. But the most fascinating thing about his oddly feminine face were his disproportionately large lips that had the rubbery appearance of silicone injections—which can only be done in a shady back room somewhere or south of the border.

From the neck down he looked like a Chippendale's dancer ready to strip down out of his scrub tech costume to his thong. The edges of his short sleeves skimmed across tanned arms, rippling with steroid and HGH-supplemented sinewy biceps and triceps, and just above the "V" of his collar you could see the glistening stubble of his shaved chest. His top was tucked in, exaggerating his perfectly proportioned wide shoulders and narrow hips.

"Well, we've got an entire selection here—flat, round, curved, straight. You just let us know what you need," said the woman, who was an entirely different story. She was a six-foot tall, two hundred-pound black woman who spoke with a heavy southern twang.

The pink scrubs they were wearing were also throwing me off.

"I'm Adeta. A D E T A," she spelled, leaning toward me as if to make sure I got it. "Adeeehhhtaaaah."

I nodded and looked at the boy.

"You can call me Mateus," he said.

"His name is Dan," Blair said.

"No!" he whined, hands on hips. "You promised! You promised I could be 'Mateus!' It's in the contract! I'm calling Gloria."

"We'll call you Mateus," Adeta said like he was her own bratty child. "Just get that stuff flashed so we can set up. We're already behind schedule, and I got my meeting tonight."

Mateus looked at me. "Oh, she's not a recovered alcoholic."

"It's my Bible study," Adeta said. "And I'm not going to miss it again because of you."

"Girl, if you miss it it's your own slow fat-ass fault." Mateus whirled around while waving his hand in the air and returned to the instrument pile on the counter. "Now don't bother me. I'm working."

"Just set up already," Blair said to them. "And save the fighting for the camera." She turned to me and added, "They're actually not just a sideshow. They happen to be the best staff in town. Gloria stole them from one of the big shots upstairs."

"How?" I said, wondering which "big shot" it was, and if they knew that their staff had been pilfered for a reality TV show.

"Oh, she's paying us a lot of money," Mateus said without turning around. "I don't come cheap."

"Who you kidding?" Adeta laughed. "You would have done it for nothing. All you want is to be on TV."

"Not true. I'm a professional. I have standards."

"Uh, Blair, Do I have to wear those, too?" I said.

"What?" Blair checked her phone.

I pointed in the general direction of Adeta and Mateus.

"Pink…ummm…scrubs?"

"It was Gloria's idea. We're working the female angle for you."

"As if he's not feminine enough already." That was Adeta.

"I can't help it if I have a pretty face."

"*Shut up* and work!" Blair bellowed.

"It's just that…" I started to say. *It's just that they look like Mary Kay uniforms.* Pink was for nurses. And gay scrub techs, if they so desired. Didn't Gloria know that no self-respecting surgeon would ever wear pink scrubs?

"We had them custom-ordered. And that pink looks great on camera."

But then my misgivings about being seen in pink scrubs were superseded by the incredible vision of what I thought at first might be a mirage from my own sleep-deprived delusional state. Through the window of the O.R. door—before Mateus even swung it open as he pushed through with the sterile tray to set up on the back table—

One glimpse of that shiny black chrome exterior with the red letters and it was like being handed the keys to a loaded Porsche all over again. Actually, forget Porsche—this was the *Rolls Royce* of all liposuction machines that I'd seen only in print ads in my plastic surgery journal. A brand-new double canister aspirator/infuser with a Microaire-powered component. I had never dreamed of getting my hands on anything like that before. Ferraro's liposuction machine was almost as old as he was, and every time I used it I prayed that the equipment would hold out till the end of the case. I could count on more than one hand how many God-awful times it actually gave out and we had to hook the tubing up to the wall suction to finish the last thigh.

"Where did that come from?" I asked Blair.

"What?"

"The lipo equipment. How did you know what to get? Who paid for that?"

"Like I said, she may have stuck you with that Devin Breeze loser," Blair said, "but when it comes to the important shit, Gloria doesn't fuck around."

Adeta caught my eye from across the room and smiled, nodding. "Nice, huh?" she said. And I could tell by the way she appreciated that Microaire machine with me, that she *was* the best in town.

By now the crew members—who, Jenny was pleasantly surprised to learn, turned out to be three cute college-age boys, clearly not in college—had trekked back to scout out the operating room for their cameras and lights. Jenny emerged from behind them, taking unnaturally short, slow steps. She was stuffed into a tight, black pantsuit, and her hair had been blown out and ironed flat to the same slippery, shiny tresses that every reality show and sitcom actress carelessly flips around on television. The make-up, while a bit exaggerated, was flattering.

"Thom, I can't breathe," she whispered to me. "But look how skinny I am!"

"Hey Doc," one of the crew called out to me. "Is it okay if I put these lights over here?"

"Look at the guy in blue," Jenny murmured with a big hair flip. The nose-ringed woman, whose name turned out to be Betty, led me to the room that Jenny had emerged from, plunked me down on the exam chair, and started applying layer upon layer of makeup to my face. The one without the nose ring—Leticia—proceeded to wet down my hair and furiously blow it out.

It took them well over an hour to shadow my facial features to what they considered camera-ready. When they were done, I saw a version of myself in the mirror that I hadn't known was possible.

Where was Devin Breeze *now*? Or at least *Eddie*? This way beyond what I'd ever imagined could be done to my face without surgery. I know I'm not hideous, I'm just plain. I'd always been just an eyeliner, blush and lip gloss kind of girl, and usually my make-up lasted in the bottles for years at a time. I had never taken a great interest in my face because I just never saw much potential there.

Betty saw my expression. "It's the fake eyelashes," she said. "The extensions are miraculous. Especially for girls like you who have so little to work with around the eyes."

"*Betty*!" Leticia hissed at her.

"What?" Betty glanced apologetically at me. "Oh, I'm sorry, I didn't mean you're not—you're *very* cute, you know, and you look *just* beautiful!"

"It's okay," I said. "I'm not offended." I really wasn't. It was actually a relief to hear someone around here speak the truth for once, so I could drop this charade of pretending to everyone that I didn't know about the huge elephant in the room. That their "star" was not beautiful. "Looking beautiful" means having the right lighting, perfect makeup, a flattering dress. A good night's sleep and a good hair day. All women have the capacity to "look beautiful." But *being* beautiful—that indisputable physical beauty of heartbreaking facial harmony; the S-curve of a cheekbone, full lips and almond-shaped eyes with long lashes that only gets more intense with animation—that's a completely separate ball game.

Eva herself made a brief appearance—long enough to have me in and out of six designer business dresses before she selected an emerald Donna Karan—and then she was off to style another reality show down the street.

"Let me know what you think of the lab coat," she called as she flew out the door.

At least it was a less offensive shade of pink than the scrubs. Tailored at the waist and flared out just below the knee, with my name embroidered in darker pink along the left lapel, it was a flattering, feminine twist on the usual baggy doctor's ensemble.

When we joined the rest of the crew out in the waiting room, they were already shooting a scene with Jenny answering the phone. She looked so small sitting all by herself behind the long reception desk. When she saw me, Blair lifted her finger to her lips and nodded her head toward the monitor.

"Pull back a little," Blair instructed the camera guy. "More of the stack of charts behind her. It has to look like something's going on in here. Once more. Stop looking at the camera, Jenny."

She'd already shushed me so I didn't bother to inform Blair that Jenny wasn't looking at the camera, but at the guy holding it.

"Good. Now look like you're doing something at the computer. And pick up the phone. And please try not to look so miserable."

"But I'm suffocating," Jenny said.

Blair handed me a manila folder. "You might as well go meet your patient. Looks like we're going to be here for a while. She's in room two. Jenny, enough with the expressions. This isn't theater."

I opened the folder and started thumbing through the documents, impressed at their thoroughness. There was a demographic sheet, signed consents, and a full medical history and clearance from some primary care doctor whose foreign last name had no vowels in it. There were even pre-op photographs—all of the anterior, posterior and lateral views—

"Wait a minute," I said to Blair.

"What?"

"What am I supposed to be doing on her?"

"Umm, *lipo*suction, he*llo*."

"But—which part—"

Blair sighed and glanced down at the picture. "I don't know. Everything. Make her skinny."

Everything? Her abdomen and thighs alone was going to be pushing close to five liters, the outpatient legal limit in the state of California.

"It might be…too much," I said.

"What do you mean, too much? This is TV. There's no such thing as 'too much.'"

"But I can't do all of it at once. I could do her legs this time, her back next time—"

"Dr. Thomas. We need you to do the whole thing. Today."

Shit. It wasn't that it wasn't doable, it was just that—I don't know, I guess I'd assumed all of my patients would be Natashas and Glorias. Neurotic skinny women who wanted to be skinnier. Donarski would kill me if he knew about this.

"But it could be a seven liter lipo—"

"She's got a medical clearance." Blair tapped the chart. "You want to review your contract? Her name is Sheryl."

I could tell the minute I met Sheryl that she wasn't completely on board with this whole thing, either.

"Do you think I could have a Valium or something?" was the first thing that came out of her mouth when she saw me. She stood up in the paper gown with her arms folded in front of her.

"I'm Doctor Thomas."

"I'm Sheryl," she said, ignoring my attempt to shake her hand. "Can I have a Valium?"

"Why don't we relax for a minute and talk about the surgery and then I'll see what we can do." I sat down.

"That's what the Valium's for, you idiot. To relax. You know what—I know I promised, and you can't beat a free lipo, that's for sure—" She reached for a pair of jeans in a pile of clothes on the floor. "But I just can't. I can't do this. Forget it."

Fantastic. I watched Sheryl struggle, one leg at a time, to get back into her too-tight jeans. Finally, when she failed on the third attempt to button the front, she fell backward into the exam chair, fly still undone, her face in her hands, and cried.

"These used to be my *fat* jeans! And I'm going to my best friend's daughter's wedding in a couple of months," Sheryl stuttered in between sobs. "And the bride's dress cost $50,000!"

She looked up at me as if she had just explained everything. In a way, she had. What she was telling me was that this was a typical L.A. society wedding (if there even is such a thing as "L.A. Society.") And she, a close friend of the bride's mother, as a member of the exclusive inner circle of partygoers, was expected to look the part.

"And you can't get anything you want to fit you—" I started to say.

"It's worse than that! Marla, my friend, she's been sending me all these dresses—these designer gowns to choose from, and nothing fits because of this!" She pulled her jeans back down to her ankles and pulled sequentially at her thighs, her back, her arms and her abdomen. "I look disgusting! I look like my mother! I'm going to have to wear a mumu!"

"Let's look at your pictures."

"Oh, no, don't show me those!" She burst into tears again and covered her eyes as I held up one of the photos. "Don't make me look at that!"

"Okay, well, then…" I turned the photo face down back in the folder.

She opened her fingers slightly and peered through, like a five-year-old playing hide-and-seek. "Did you put it away?"

"Yes, Sheryl, I put it away."

"Okay." She took her hands away from her face.

"Sheryl," I said. "Do you not want to do this surgery?"

Her fearful expression changed to one of horror. "Of course I want to do the surgery! I've wanted to do it since I was fifteen. I've never had good legs. Or arms…or waist…or…*anything*. I work in an office and I can't even wear straight skirts. I want to wear sexy clothes and start dating again. But I'm a single mom. What if I die on the table? Who's going to take care of Charlie? How will someone explain to him that I died getting a *liposuction*?"

Perfect. Everybody in plastic surgery knows that one thing you *never* do is try to talk a patient into a procedure they don't want. It's a surgery recipe for disaster. That and operating on another physician's wife. Murphy's Law. Surgeons are a superstitious bunch. Something bad will happen. If we were at Ferraro's I would have just told her to have a great day, and gone home and crawled back into bed.

But we weren't at Ferraro's. And after the way I left, I certainly wasn't going to be invited back. I didn't care so much about the contract, or the fact that there was already a crew out there filming a pretend scene with my starfucker assistant. It was more about the fact that Sheryl was my new Ferraro. Without her I'd never be able to keep up the private shrink for Jake. And what about the caretaker, so that I wouldn't feel so guilty whenever I freed up the portion of my brain that constantly worried about him? And the house on the bluff in Malibu—that was stretching it, but at least somewhere we could live together so he wouldn't ever have to go back to a halfway house if the market crashed again and the money got too tight for the trailer park.

Sheryl was my house. My freedom. My sanity.

I had to make this work.

I'd done some pretty big lipos in the past at the hospital and never had a complication. And this place was clearly legit. We were in a fancy accredited facility. We were going to have a board-certified anesthesiologist here. I'd take good care of her. Everything was going to be fine.

I just needed to convince Sheryl of that. I started by quoting her the statistics of safety. That the risk of anesthesia in a young healthy person like herself, especially one with a medical clearance, was less than the risk she would take getting back on the freeway and driving home right now. I finally got her to look at her pictures and I used a Sharpie to shade out all of the bulges that would be gone when I was done. And over the next hour, while Blair directed take after take of Jenny answering the phone, I was able to show Sheryl that not only was this not a mistake, but the best decision of her life. By the time Blair and the crew were ready for us, I had Sheryl raring to go.

"Thank you," she said to me. "I'm sorry I called you an idiot. Now just put me to sleep."

I would have loved to do just that, but there was more preliminary footage to go. Now Sheryl and I had to *act out* meeting for the first time. Blair loved the story about fitting into the dress for the wedding. She had the girls bring one of my dresses in from Wardrobe, pretending it was something Sheryl's friend had sent to her, and tortured her with making her try to get her size twelve body into it.

It was already 2:00 P.M. when Blair finally had a take of me marking Sheryl in the pre-op area that she was happy with, and then we broke for lunch before surgery, something that never happens out in any *real* O.R.'s. Surgery is, by tradition, an early morning sport. Especially for the anesthesiologists, most who get grumpy and lose interest if anything goes past noon. I could only imagine the mood the anesthesiologist was going to be in when he showed up to start a late afternoon case.

I wasn't wrong. And it only got worse. The anesthesiologist turned out to be one of those doctors who introduce themselves as "doctor" to other doctors.

"I'm Doctor Jones," she said, in a British accent that to this day I still debate whether or not is real. "I can't believe you left her NPO all day without an IV. She's so dehydrated, I may not even be able to get a line in her. I can't believe I agreed to do this."

"Well, you did," Adeta said. "So stop complaining and put the patient to sleep already."

"This could be a huge liability for both of us." Dr. Jones glared at me and went to set up her drugs.

Once I was scrubbed in, I examined the liposuction cannulas that Mateus had laid out for me on the Mayo stand, each one at a time, as if I were inspecting them.

"What are you doing?" Mateus asked me.

"Stop dawdling and get on with the show," Adeta said.

"Let's start with this." I handed Mateus the five millimeter. "She's kind of big."

"*Kind* of." He loaded it into the hand piece.

"Do we have the infusion?" I said.

"It's right here," Adeta said.

"Twenty lidocaine, one amp of epi?"

"Just like you told us to make it, Dr. Thomas."

"How many bags do we have?"

"Five, Dr. Thomas. Just like you asked for."

"Can you make another bag please?"

Adeta dropped her chin. "Stop stalling. We'll make it when we get there."

"I'm not stalling," I said as I frantically tried to think of something else that had to be done before I could start.

What was my problem? I'd been doing surgery nearly my entire adult life. Why should it matter if a few laymen with cameras were watching me? It would be way more stressful to have some surgeons in here who could actually criticize what I was doing wrong, like in all those years of residency.

I palpated the rolls of fat on Sheryl's lower back and outer thighs.

"Eleven blade," I said to Mateus.

This must be what it feels like to go to the Olympics. You do something every day of your life and then one day you have to do it and it's like it's the only time that it really matters.

"I'm going to make the first incision," I announced when Mateus handed me the knife.

"Thank the Lord," Mateus said.

"Okay, Dr. Thomas," Blair said. "Now, just talk as you're working, tell us what you're doing at each step. Like you're teaching someone how to do a liposuction."

Was my hand *shaking*? This was crazy. I needed to get a grip. My hands never shook. I prided myself on having the steadiest hands in my whole residency class. Donarski loved for me to assist him with the micro cases because my hands were even steadier than his were.

I made the first two incisions in the lower back. Mateus handed me a sponge and I reflexively started wiping away the small amount of blood that trickled from the holes.

"So tell us what you're doing," Blair demanded.

"I'm…I'm making access incisions," I said, as I made two more in the infragluteal crease. "These incisions here are hidden in the fold, and they give me the best access to the fat on the outer thigh." The camera guy moved in to get a close-up of my hand, which was still noticeably shaking.

"You don't have to yell," the sound guy said. "You got a mic on you."

"Oh. Sorry." I had forgotten about the microphone taped to the inside of my bra with the wire running down to the box in the back pocket of my pink scrub pants.

Mateus handed me the infusion cannula and I started tumescing Sheryl's lower back, then her thighs, my main areas of attack.

"What's that?" Blair said.

"This is wetting solution. For numbing. And epinephrine, which prevents bleeding." I heard the monitor start to sound like a piano metronome set on a fast staccato as Sheryl's heart rate sped up from the epi and the alarm went off and instinctively I called up over the drapes to Dr. Jones, "Maybe we should wait?"

"No, we absolutely *should not*. She's fine."

"Dr. Thomas, we should be ready." Adeta motioned toward Sheryl's now bulging lower back and thighs, tumesced and blanched from the epi.

"This is called pre-tunneling," I told them as I manually ran one of the bigger cannulas through the incisions. "It breaks up the fat so you get a more even contour." It was getting easier to talk, and after a few passes with the five millimeter I started to relax a little more. After all, it was just another surgery day, only with television cameras in the operating room. And I could tell Sheryl was going to be a slam dunk. She was one of those pale white women whose fat just spills out like cotton candy. Like Gloria, except with a bigger skeleton and more muscles so I could see what was going on. Even without the suction on, the disrupted fat was already starting to ooze through the cannula sites of its own accord, begging to be released.

And as soon as I turned on the magnificent new suction machine, and I felt the comforting vibration of the heavy hand piece in my palm, I was home. Sheryl's fat was coming out like gangbusters and I had a captive audience. Liposuction always evokes such an enthusiastic response from everyone watching, including the scrub tech who has seen it hundreds of times. It's the *one* surgery nobody gets tired of. At least for the first half hour when all the good yellow fat comes out. And this one was going to be a great show.

"You can see how much better she looks already," I said to my millions of viewers, running my hand over the area that I had sculpted. "See how her back no longer looks square, but curvy, and her butt appears lifted." By the time we turned Sheryl over so I could sculpt her from the front, I was actually enjoying myself.

Thrilled with all the reels of graphic footage, Blair told the crew that they'd gotten enough for the first episode and to just get some "B-roll."

"B-roll", as I learned, was footage without sound. It's the stuff that you see while someone is narrating the story, fractions of scenes to give you the overall flavor of what's going on.

So the hard part was over.

I, on the other hand, was just warming up. I was coming into my own, now sculpting away Sheryl's abdomen and sides. Today I had discovered a latent talent of mine. I liked operating on stage. It's a hell of a lot more fun with people "oohing" and "aahhing" in the background rather than asking you when you thought the case would be over, because it was time for shift change and they were going to have to call in more staff.

"You know, you two are done for the day," Blair said to Betty and Letitia, who hadn't left the doorway since the case had started. "You're free to go."

Neither of them budged.

The camera guy moved closer to the suction machine and zoomed his lens in on the foaming fat that dripped from the tubing into the two liter plastic canister. "That shit's nasty," he said.

By now the fat had settled out nicely. Pristine yellow slurry floated on top of pink, blood-tinged fluid in the three full canisters that Adeta had lined up in a neat row on the windowsill, with the sunny background of the Beverly Hills shopping district beyond the glass.

"Classic!" Blair shrieked when she saw it. "We'll close with that shot."

"You really are quite something with that cannula," Adeta said as I finished off the right knee to match the inner thigh in a perfectly angled line. "I been in this town for thirty years, and I've worked with the best."

"There's really not that much to it," I said. "But most plastic surgeons are men, and men don't get it. They think we just put clothes on and look okay and that's the end of it." I had been thinking a lot about this issue lately—why should *men* be sculpting women's bodies?—but had never actually verbalized it.

"That is so true!" Betty or Letitia said.

I had clearly hit a chord. "Usually male plastic surgeons think it's just sucking fat," I continued. "They don't focus on the things that we see. They don't see saddlebags and muffin tops. They only see breasts." I knew I was walking a fine line with the "girls against boys" blanket statement, but I couldn't help myself. I'd always felt this way. Besides, all the women in the room—Dr. Jones included—were nodding in vigorous agreement.

"That's not true!" the camera guy said. "We see other things besides breasts."

Another one of the crew guys whistled, and thank God the sound was off because I could sense that, as it usually does when the case has gone on for more than a few hours, this operating room conversation was about to rapidly degenerate into the final common denominator—a raunchy discussion about sex. But that's what happens. It's like with alcohol—after a couple of hours in here, your inhibitions diminish. You're completely covered from head to toe with gowns and masks and hats and gloves and you feel protected, like you're at a masquerade ball. Incognito. As if nothing you say counts. What happens in the O.R. stays in the O.R.

So what if it was a poor man's Vegas? For the first time in my life, I was feeling like a star.

14

"Thom, I can't believe you're going out with him tonight when he was such an asshole to you." Jenny's voice cut in and out over the Bluetooth. I strained to listen as I wove through the freeway traffic, once again racing the digital clock on the dashboard from the Valley Hospital back to West Hollywood.

"It's not my choice. Besides, I think he meant to apologize," I said. I hadn't told Jenny about the "moment" Devin, Sushi and I had had together on the couch. She would only trivialize it so I could focus on the bigger picture of my career. *Our* careers.

"I can't imagine what would make you think *that*. And don't even talk to me about that stupid show he was on."

"*You* would have taken a role on that 'stupid show.' Besides, I haven't even seen it in years," I lied.

"Where are your scrubs?" Blair demanded as soon as I walked in the front door. "You're supposed to be coming home from work."

"But I don't wear them home."

"Well, you do on television. Everyone else does." She sent one of her lackeys to get a pair from the van.

Really? I was going to have to have my first "date" with Devin Breeze wearing scrubs? There is nothing sexy about scrubs. Not only are they shapeless, but they're made out of some scratchy, stiff synthetic material that is capable of washing completely free of all blood and body fluids. How was I going to shock Devin Breeze with my new upgraded, improved self in a pair of baggy pink scrubs? "Then why did you guys buy me a whole new wardrobe if you just want me to walk around in scrubs all the time?"

"America wants to see you in scrubs. We have to set in motion one of our major conflicts—is your relationship going to withstand the pressure of your demanding careers? Although he doesn't really have one, but that's Russell's problem. So…we show *that* by having you storm in here—" Blair pointed at the front door. "—late and disheveled. In scrubs. And he's furious. Like he's been waiting all night and the food is cold."

It seemed like a pretty tame conflict to me, especially since there were shows out there with names like *I Didn't Know I Was Pregnant*.

"And hey," she called to Russell, who was out on the patio with his back to us. "Where the fuck is your boy, anyway?"

After multiple phone calls and arguments between Blair and Russell, Devin finally showed up an hour later. Well at least with him around, I wouldn't be the "late" one all the time.

I was busy attempting to strike casually seductive poses at the living room wet bar, a virtually impossible task in my pink scrubs, when he strolled in.

"Hey," he said when he saw me. "What's up?"

He could not have been more nonchalant, and yet I literally felt my breath catch somewhere in my proximal bronchi. Now that he was all cleaned up, you could really see how undeniably striking he was. And he had that skin— that skin that tans so easily, smooth as a rubber bath toy. He had that freshly-washed look of a guy in jeans and a T-shirt, as if I got close enough to him he would smell good.

"You want a drink?" he said. Without waiting for me to answer, he ducked behind the bar and started examining the multiple bottles of liquor.

"I thought you were sober," I blurted out, realizing too late that I was letting him know that, like the crazy, obsessed fan that he already thought I was, I had retained every piece of information from the tabloids that I had ever read about him. *And besides, how had I already forgotten that the only reason he'd been here last time was to sober up after a night of drinking?*

"Really? Who told you that?"

"Nobody, I mean, I read you went to rehab…I thought…it must have been someone else."

He half-smiled and leaned toward me on his elbows across the bar. "Yeah, well, luckily, it wasn't for alcohol."

"Luckily?"

"If you're going to rehab, you want it to be for something hard core—you know…like crack, heroin. If you have to give up alcohol, where do you go from there? At least a recovered crack addict can have a drink every once in a while." He spoke solemnly, without a trace of a smile left on his face.

I must have looked as if I'd just witnessed a murder. He touched my hand, and my arm immediately bristled with goose bumps.

"That was a joke. Like what you said about your cat. No, I've never been to rehab. So, enough about me. What did *you* do today?"

Was he making conversation with me? I was so taken off guard that I found myself babbling away in response, and realized too far into it that the detailed description of my paraplegic patient's pressure sores must be completely grossing him out. And yet, his eyes emanated a warmth that made me want to keep talking…a warmth I had never felt from another person before, something I hadn't even picked up from watching him on television all those years.

Charisma, I reminded myself. *It's called charisma. And it has nothing to do with you.*

It was an intimate dinner on our fourteenth-floor balcony where we could enjoy the early summer evening. Just the two of us…the two of us, two camera operators and the sound guy, and Blair and Russell, all of who stood immediately outside the breathtaking shot of Devin and me and the backdrop of the Los Angeles city lights. Sidetracked by her own argument with Russell, Blair had forgotten to stage our "fight," and we went right into the storyline of how Devin had surprised me after my long day of surgeries with a three-course dinner he'd prepared himself.

The first shot was a close-up of him standing over the barbecue pit. "I *love* to cook," he said. "*Mmmm*….smell that." He grinned like a goon, moving the tongs around. What the viewer wouldn't see was that the gas was actually off and there was nothing cooking. The steaks that Devin had supposedly so lovingly grilled were already waiting for us on the table, prepared by someone from one of Wolfgang Puck's restaurants who was now whipping up a chocolate soufflé back in the kitchen.

"Tell him you didn't know he was such a great cook," Blair said to me once we sat down.

"I didn't know you were such a great cook." *Why did my words sound so stiff?* Devin's voice sounded so natural when he spoke, even with Blair telling him what to say.

"There are a lot of things you don't know about me yet." The way he lifted his fork and knife without averting his eyes from me…there was that impossible warmth again…now spreading from the back of my neck up to my scalp and cheeks and down to my toes.

"Say something!" Blair's voice broke through my haze and I realized that they had moved the camera on to me while I had zoned out. "Drama, drama, give me drama! Be mean, be sexy, be dirty—I don't care—just be *something*! Wait—I got it—talk about how much your sex life is suffering because you're too tired all the time. Is your relationship doomed?"

"Ohhh, there you go," Devin said. Then to me: "Honey, it's been *weeks*. The online porn is getting lonely,"

I think after the way he looked at me that it was normal to feel a pulse somewhere down in my groin. But I *shouldn't* have had this feeling like someone had paralyzed my vocal chords. I cut people *open* for a *living*—how could something like *this* be even the slightest bit challenging?

I pretended to be chewing to buy myself some time—which wasn't going so well since I didn't have any food in my mouth—and I cursed myself for not having watched more reality shows so I'd at least have something to imitate. Everybody—Blair, the crew, Russell, and Devin—waited. I swallowed saliva.

"Come on, do I need to feed you every line?" Blair said. She turned to Devin. "And stop fucking hypnotizing her! We'll be here all night on the same shot."

"I'm not doing anything." Devin was wide-eyed.

"Unbelievable. Now I need a fucking script. We didn't budget for a *writer*. I *told* Gloria to get someone with media training."

Then I felt something press up against my ankle. *Devin's foot.*

"Find your voice," he whispered.

"What?"

"Find your voice. If you have to, rip off somebody else's."

Find your voice? Did actors really say that kind of stupid shit to each other?

The only voice I kept hearing was Blair's ordering me around, then—in my head—Jenny's making fun of me for liking *Pacific Beach* on the car ride over here—-

Wait, now there was an idea.

"Brad—I mean—" I began.

"Speak up!" Blair yelled.

I took a meditative breath, then started again: "Devin, you're the only person in the world who gets me—"

"Louder please!"

I raised my voice—aiming at decibels but I think what I got was octaves because it just started sounding squeaky: "…and I know I'm the only one who gets you. So we'll have to make time for me to learn *everything* about you. And for *you* to learn everything about *me*. No matter what they think." It was a line from the episode of *Pacific Beach* I'd watched the night before. And the voice was that of Devin's TV girlfriend. The two of them were a pair of star-crossed lovers, hiding under the pier from her parents. I closed my eyes for a split-second to imagine the smell of the damp wood, the waves lapping at our bare toes, the setting sun.

"Who's 'they'?" Blair said.

"Oh, sorry." Thank God I had all that makeup on to cover my face, which was probably a deep shade of magenta by now. "I guess I got a little…carried away."

I wasn't sure if I was relieved or disappointed when Devin didn't even blink at my plagiarism. There was zero recognition in his face. I guess he hadn't been paying as close attention to that episode as I had.

"Okay, well…corny but America loves corny. Elaborate. Breeze, tell her that's the problem—there *is* no time. She works too much."

Devin folded his arms across his chest.

"Well, how do we make 'us' time?" he said. "You work too damn much. I don't exactly appreciate being sloppy seconds. Or is it not some*thing* but some*one* who's keeping you there?"

"Okay, I won't…I won't work as much." My voice echoed like it came from somebody somewhere else, far away in an amphitheater.

"Are you fucking kidding me?" Blair barked. "Respond! Get angry! Your fucking loser boyfriend just accused you of cheating on him! You're a career woman! Tell him he doesn't understand, maybe because *he* hasn't worked in so long—"

"Uhhh, uhhhh." Russell said. "We're not going there. And I'm the only one who gets to call him a loser."

Devin rolled his eyes and then, leaning on the table with his elbows, covered his face with his hands.

"You want us to break up with him and get someone else?"

While Blair and Russell began bickering again in the background, Devin peeked at me through his fingers and said, "Speaking of drinking…" I liked the way he opened the bottle of wine and filled both of our glasses without asking me. He started to say something I couldn't hear but Blair interrupted with, "Moving on. Let's talk about how lucky you two were to meet."

This time I was sure I heard him mutter to himself, "I cannot fucking believe this shit." But then he turned to Blair with a big smile. "And how did that go again?"

Blair sighed. "We went over this, Breeze. She sewed you up in the emergency room a few months ago—that scar on your face. Remember?"

"But I've had this scar since I was seven." He rubbed his upper lip with his finger.

"So? Close-up on the scar."

"We can't see it on the monitor," the camera guy called.

This time I actually had something to say.

"It's a mature scar," I said.

"What?"

"That scar is too old," I said.

"See?" Devin said.

Blair stared blankly at me so I elaborated, "If it was something recent it would be more red, a little swollen…" With the bronzer they'd put on his face, the scar was almost imperceptible—except for the vermilion mismatch, you couldn't even see it under the bright lights of the set. Any plastic surgeon would know that a thin white line like that without any inflammation was at least a year old.

"Then someone go get a lip liner. Make it red," Blair barked at the Betty, who swooped in with her makeup.

"We could make it…a year ago." I suggested. "That might be believable."

"I think you should listen to the doctor," Devin said.

"Jesus! This isn't the *Discovery Channel*. It's not a fucking science show! He was surfing and cut his face. She got called to come fix him. And the two of them fell in love, Goddammit!"

"Only problem with that," Devin said. "Is that I don't really surf."

"Breeze, stop being difficult."

"What? What do you mean, you don't surf?" I said. "On *Pacific Beach* you—I mean, Braden—and there were all those surf contests—"

"That was my stunt guy."

How was that possible? In all the pin-up posters of him that they used to sell at CVS he was always standing next to a surfboard.

"I'm sorry you're so disappointed," he laughed. "I'm an actor, not a surfer. Besides, they didn't have enough insurance for me to wipe out and fuck up my face."

I was silent. Come to think of it, he was never standing *on* the surfboard in those posters.

I wasn't *disappointed*—that was silly. I didn't really *care*. It's just that…I guess I still hadn't yet shaken Eddie from my brain. Eddie, for whom surfing was like a dick size competition. *Hanalei Bay was just five feet? Can't compare to Frigates. Have you ever towed? Paddle only? So you're just a pussy with a long board?* Eddie had constantly reminded me how all the locals gave him his space because he was the best surfer at the pier. Always first in the pecking order. Whenever I stayed over at his place, the first thing he did every morning was walk down to the end of the street to "look at the water." Was it "big" enough for him to call in sick and surf all day instead? Even better was when one of his neighborhood pals would just slide open the bedroom window and poke his head in to give us a full surf report, completely unconcerned that we were half-naked, twisted around each other under the blanket, about to get busy. And then Eddie would stop and *listen to him*.

In Eddie's world, that surfing shit was serious. And I'd been drinking the Kool-Aid. Even *I* knew when the "south swell" was coming. For a guy to admit that he sucked at it and didn't even care was unfathomable to me.

"Fine," Blair said. "Nobody cares about your dated beach show. So you fell off a bike. I'm assuming you know how to ride one of *those*. You know what? On second thought, let's take a break from this amateur hour. I can't get what I want here. In the living room in ten." The crew moved off inside.

"So does this mean I can finish eating?" Devin called after them. Then he looked up at me and said, "What—is there something stuck in my teeth?"

"No!" I *was* staring at him. I do admit, I have a problem with that—as if my job description gives me the license to openly stare at people and imagine the physical changes that might transform them. In this case I was just admiring his impeccable bone structure. Very few people look that good from a straight-on view.

"Oh, I get it. It's cause you're a plastic surgeon. You're looking at my nose, aren't you?" He had been rhythmically cutting up the rest of his steak into tiny pieces and sliding them off the edge of his knife into his mouth, but stopped.

"No!" I said again, too quickly. *But now I was.*

"It's big, right? That faggot Russell thinks I should get it fixed."

I did a quick analysis. "Your septum deviates off to the right and there's some collapse of the internal valve—"

"What's that? And why would I have it?"

"Usually just genetics. Trauma. Heavy cocaine use—"

"What?"

"Or not! But if you don't have trouble breathing…well, it's a little prominent, but it's in complete harmony with the strong features of the rest of your face."

"What's that supposed to mean?"

"It takes up the precise aesthetic ideal of the distance from your hairline to your chin."

He remained silent, fork poised in the air, as if waiting for more of an explanation.

"Your nose is fine," I said. Oddly, something in his voice had given me the need to reassure him.

"Hey." He reached over and squeezed my hand. "You okay? Don't look so worried. You're doing great."

"How do you know I'm worried?" I said.

"Because you've had this 'V' in the middle of your forehead the entire time." He pointed to my frown lines, then reached up and pushed gently on my contracted corrugator muscles.

So Jenny was right. I needed to start doing some Botox. I rubbed the spot between my brows when he took his finger away, as if it would feel different after he had touched it.

He gently squeezed my hand again and a thrill starting from my fingertips rushed throughout my entire body. *Dangerous.* Especially in this absurd, contrived situation. I refused to enjoy this feeling. I needed to will it away.

"Dr. Thomas, go upstairs for a touch-up," I heard Blair yell from inside. "And yes, now you can change."

I nodded to Devin as casually as if I hung out with guys that looked like him all the time—and walked away from them just as easily—and turned toward the staircase, surprised to find myself a little wobbly at first. *Damn, I already had a buzz going after that one glass of wine. Must be because I'm so tired.* With my head still tingling from the alcohol, I played that game with myself that he was watching me walk up the stairs and that I would ruin everything if I turned around. *Now I was grateful that those baggy scrub pants were hiding my leftover saddlebags and an ass that I was convinced was too big for my body.* I swayed my hips ever so slightly with each deliberate step. *He's watching, he's watching*, I told myself. By the time I reached the bedroom door, I couldn't bear to turn around to find out if he really wasn't.

15

When I came back downstairs, a limo was waiting out front in my building's half-circular driveway.

"Now *that's* what I'm talking about." Devin smiled and ran his hand down the side of my right leather pant leg as I slid onto the seat next to him. "They look even better than I could have imagined."

I knew that argument I'd just had upstairs with Blair about letting me wear them was going to be totally worth it. He handed me a glass of champagne, and toasted me with his own. "To us. We really need this night out." He slipped his arm around my waist, letting his hand rest on my thigh. Even through the leather, the touch of his fingertips sent an unwelcome rush of prickling up my spine. "You know, you've *got* to relax more," he whispered in my ear.

"My…my job is very stressful," I said, and gulped. *Keep the buzz going. Keep the buzz going and I'll be fine.*

"I'm here for you." He lightly kissed the side of my head through my hair, and the prickling made its way up the back of my neck to my posterior scalp. I shivered.

It was then that a light came on somewhere and I realized we weren't alone. Once my eyes had adjusted to the sudden brightness, I saw that Blair and the crew were sitting across from us with a camera rolling just a couple of feet from my face.

"Lift your chin up a little. Turn to the side. Dr. Thomas, tilt your head, please. Dammit, does she not have *one* good angle?" That was Blair.

"What's wrong?" Devin said to me, and without waiting for an answer he leaned in close and brushed the hair back from my ear. "Don't let them bother you," he whispered. "Pretend they're not here."

His face was only inches from mine. He had the smallest hint of blond razor stubble and the way his hair curled at his ears and the nape of his neck was just unruly enough to be sexy. He smelled faintly like a combination of soap and fabric softener. I wondered if he did his own laundry. The tinted window rolled up behind him, immediately silencing the noise from outside and enclosing us in our own little black leather cocoon. That heart-wrenchingly wistful theme from *Titanic* piped from the speakers above our heads.

I don't know when we started kissing. Only that our faces were close and the champagne had taken over and then it seemed to make perfect sense that he was kissing me…my lips, my face, my neck. His mouth was parted slightly open. My first thought was, *how bizarre that he could so naturally be intimate in front of a camera*, until I reminded myself that this is what a nighttime soap actor does for a living. This is his *job*.

"Stop," I murmured because I felt it was the appropriate thing to do. "Shouldn't we…you know…?"

"Are you kidding?" he whispered. "This is what they want."

Got it. So this part was still pretend. It absolutely was *not* that those leather pants made me so fascinating and irresistible that Devin Breeze couldn't keep his hands off me.

I found myself responding to him, kissing him back, running my hands through his hair—a little stiff from hair product, I was surprised to discover—feeling the taut, lean muscles of his chest and shoulders up against me. He was as beautiful as he had ever been five years ago on prime-time television. I prayed that we would be stuck in traffic all night, but all too soon we stopped moving and someone swung open the door from the outside.

Blair ushered us onto the curb and the camera guy got some shots of our arrival at the front entrance. Wordlessly, Devin led me by the hand, weaving our way through the small crowd of club-goers up to the door. I tried to appear blasé, which was really unnecessary since nobody paid any attention to me. I could tell a few people recognized Devin but it wasn't like a Hemsworth had showed up. There wasn't any stampede or anything. A few lackluster paparazzi took his picture. I wasn't close enough to be in the frame, but I don't think they were even trying to get me in it.

"Hey, man, what's going on," the bouncer said to Devin and unclipped the red velvet rope for only us and the crew.

"Welcome to 'Villa'." A pretty young cocktail waitress in four-inch heels and a skirt that barely covered her crotch greeted us inside. Her eyes skipped over me and she smiled at Devin. "Nice to see you, Mr. Breeze." Well, they might not sell CVS posters of him holding surfboards anymore, but obviously Devin Breeze had not dropped off the radar of the Hollywood club scene.

The waitress invited us to a back table where Blair and the rest of the crew were congregating. Devin fell into one of the huge plush armchairs, pulling me down next to him.

The room was small and dark and crowded, with a hip-hop rhythm that vibrated off the walls and the ceiling. I had never been inside of a Hollywood club before, but it was pretty much what I had expected from the movies. The women were all tall and skinny, scantily-clad twenty-somethings who towered over their much shorter, older, and less attractive male counterparts, magnetized I'm sure, only by their Black Am Exes and bank accounts. I had never seen so many pairs of breast implants *in vivo* in a single room.

Behind the bar, there was a cage built into the wall, and inside a girl writhed against a stripper pole, wearing only a G-string and a bra. It was impossible not to stare at her.

"Are you checking her out?" Devin said to me.

"No!" We had to yell directly in each other's ears over the music. "I was just…wondering how she got up there."

"Liar," he laughed. "Don't stop on my account. It's okay to like looking at women's bodies. I do."

"Look, I'm not a lesbian." I don't know why I felt so strongly that I had to defend myself, since it has been so well established that all men are either turned on by Lipstick Lesbians or they pretend to be. "It's my job."

"Whatever you say." He tightened his arm around my shoulder. "Personally, she's not my type."

"Why not?" If we were on a real date, this would be the perfect segue for him to then tell me how *I*—so different from the nearly naked girl in the wall—*was* his type.

But it's not a real date.

"Not a big fan of breast implants."

"How do you know she has implants?"

"Come on." He made an exaggerated serious face. "Oh, that's right. You're the expert."

I studied the dancer more closely as she twirled around her pole. "She's so skinny—I doubt she's a C-cup on her own."

He watched her. "She's not *that* skinny."

"It's a tough angle. Her body's pretty much perfect." I suddenly felt embarrassed for being an expert on such a weird topic, especially since he was no longer listening. Which was actually fine, because my throat was starting to kill me from all of the yelling.

Blair handed each of us a fluorescent green martini.

Devin made a face and yelled at her, "So you want me to vomit?"

"Then just *hold* it," Blair yelled back, then added, "How is it possible that you're even more of a dick than I thought you'd be?"

Devin put his mouth next to my ear again. "So, how does it feel, being a sell-out?"

Not only did his words come out of nowhere, but also—out of nowhere—I sensed that tinge of that anger I'd seen when we'd met the first time, back at Gloria's office.

Blair was a lip reader. "Shut the fuck up, Asshole. You're drinking for free. Besides, you're lucky anyone even considers you positive promotional material anymore *at all*."

You didn't need to read lips to see the "Fuck you" come out of his mouth. He tightened his arm around me. "Who's complaining? Certainly not me." When he turned back to me, his face nearly up against mine, he stared for about ten seconds, then frowned. "Did you know that your left pupil is bigger than the right?" he shouted at me. The anger in his voice had vanished.

I swallowed and shouted back, "I know. It's actually pretty common. It's called 'anisocoria.'"

"You make it sound so sexy."

The alcohol was doing its thing, and now he was being so charming again, that I almost wasn't even nervous anymore. I started to cozy up to him the slightest bit, then at the last second chickened out and pretended that I was just getting more comfortable in the chair.

"She wants us to dance." Devin crossed his eyes and pointed at Blair, who was signaling for us to get up.

We made our way to the dance floor, the camera guy in our wake. Out of curiosity, the other couples cleared a space for us. Nobody took a second glance at me, although quite a few of them stared openly at Devin.

"I'm warning you, I'm a shitty dancer," I said.

He shook his head and entwined his fingers through mine. I did my best to imitate his moves and even though I'm sure I looked like a complete idiot, he leaned in and yelled, "See, you're *excellent!*"

Devin Breeze said I was an "excellent dancer." Actually, he hadn't specified that he was describing my dancing skills…maybe, even better, he was telling me I was just overall "excellent." That was pretty spectacular. In fact—despite myself—this whole *night* was inarguably turning out to be rather spectacular. No matter how it had come about, whether it was real or not, I was on a date with Devin Breeze. We were physically together. Dancing in a club. Did it matter whether something was "real" or not, as long as it was happening? And I was having fun. And as long as Blair wasn't within close proximity, *he* seemed to be having fun. *I was on a date with Devin Breeze and we were having fun. Fuck stupid Surfer Eddie and his not-being-that-into-me bullshit. He'd be so jealous if he saw this.*

I was so caught up with congratulating myself about burning Eddie, that when Devin abruptly pulled away from me and dropped his hands in the middle of the song, I assumed he was going to get us a couple more drinks.

"I would *love* another apple martini," I said, speaking with what I hoped was a flirty lilt, even though I was shouting. "What are *you* having?"

But he never answered me because that's when someone's arm reached in front of me and I heard a male voice from behind: "Hey, man, what's going on?"

I turned to see a tatted-up hipster flanked by two younger blondes. Each girl looked like she could have had a month on the calendar that I knew Jake kept hidden behind his CD collection.

The music stopped. We didn't have to shout anymore. There was an announcement about switching DJ's.

"Ted, man, what's up," Devin said. The two of them did their cool-guy handshake. I tried not to be jealous as I saw him size up the girls.

"This is Chrissy." Ted spoke specifically to Devin. "And you know Kona." I could tell by the way Devin's eyes lingered on her, that Kona was more than just an acquaintance.

"Devin, I haven't seen you in *forever*," she purred, her tongue flicking in and out between her youthful, naturally plump lips.

"Hi," Ted said to me, as if he felt like he had to.

"Oh, yeah, this is Rachel," Devin said, seeming to suddenly remember that I was there. He was no longer holding my hand. In fact, he was no longer touching any part of my body.

I forced a smile and the three of them gave me an unenthusiastic "Hi." Ted asked Devin if he wanted to get a drink.

"We got a table over there." Devin pointed to where we had been sitting earlier. "We'll get the waitress."

"Niiiice. A table. You baller." Ted jokingly punched him in the shoulder. When Devin only half smiled, Ted looked at me again and then carefully back at Devin. "Hey, man, I'm sorry, are you guys, you know…are we interrupting..?"

"No, no," Devin said, too quickly. "It's that…I'll tell you about it later."

That was when I realized that the crew was packing up all their equipment. *So that's why he let me go.* We were done.

Blair stopped to say good-bye on her way out. She leaned in toward Devin and said, "You're just lucky Russell's gone already."

"They're old friends," Devin said.

She shrugged. "Get yourself in trouble. Anything stupid you do is only going to help the ratings." She smirked at him, then turned to me. "Dr. Thomas, we'll see you Tuesday."

"Oh, this is that job you were telling me about," Ted said after Blair was gone.

"Yeah…you know…" Devin's hands were in his pockets, and he didn't look Ted in the eye as he spoke. As if he had just been busted for something shameful.

"Hey man, you don't have to explain to me. At least you're working."

I watched Kona settle herself into the armchair where Devin and I had sat together earlier. Her presence somehow diminished all of the previous events of the evening. Or maybe it was just clarifying reality for me once again.

Still. We'd been having so much fun. I decided to give it one last shot.

"You know, Blair gave us the limo for the rest of the night," I said to Devin.

"Oh, go ahead. You take it."

I could tell that he was genuinely trying to be generous. He watched my face. "I mean, unless…you're welcome to come have a drink with us…"

I shook my head, silently praying that he hadn't heard me ask him about the apple martini.

"Well, that was kind of fun, wasn't it?" His eyes were as wide and open and blue as ever, but there was no more abyss. No more forceful pull into his stratosphere. He was just a polite, incredibly out-of-my-league guy standing there talking to me. "Guess I'll see you next time." When I didn't move or say anything, he added, "Oh, don't worry—I don't need to crash at your place tonight. It's all yours."

"Van Nuys," I said to the limo driver as I tumbled into the back. I still had the key to my old apartment and a few more weeks on the lease. I couldn't bear the thought of going back to the condo tonight. I needed to be in a place where I could pretend that this excruciatingly embarrassing moment had not just happened.

I leaned my head back on the seat, uncapped a bottle of water from the bar, and started swigging. My cell phone said 1:30 A.M. A little late to start hydrating, but I had accidently left part of my stash of I.V. supplies and a bag of fluid back in my apartment if it came to that.

Kona? She didn't even look Hawaiian.

A pack of cigarettes called to me from the shelf under the bar and I went through three of them before we hit the freeway. Since my internship year I'd been one of those people who never really "smoked" but never really quit, either.

Even though my reflection was distorted by the curve of the window, I could see how disheveled my hair was and how the dark eye makeup had smudged into circles around my eyes, giving me the likeness of a Goth rocker.

So I wasn't going to ride off into the sunrise with my golden hero after all. Well, really, what *had* I expected? Somehow, I wasn't even that upset. I was exhausted. Disappointed. Sexually frustrated. Furious at myself for thinking for even a minute that Devin Breeze might actually *like* me. But above all, I was enlightened. Because tonight I had discovered something. Something that probably very few people knew. Tonight I had learned that Devin Breeze of has-been-early-millennium-teen-drama fame, was actually an unbelievably good actor.

16

The *Lipo Queen* premiere aired the next Sunday night. He didn't outright ask me, but I knew Jake wanted us to watch it together.

"Don't you have that great big TV?" he said when I mentioned it.

"I'll just come to your place," I told him. "You want Kentucky Fried?"

Somehow I still hadn't gotten around to inviting Jake over. I wish I could say that it was because I was afraid that Blair would walk in and have a melt-down when she saw him, but it wasn't even that. I couldn't articulate why I felt weird about having him there. He'd asked about it a couple of times and then stopped asking.

"I'm just waiting," Jake greeted me at the door, then summoned his dog back to the couch with him and resumed waiting, even though there was still a good half hour until show time. Apparently, he'd been sitting there waiting all day. With the DVR set, just in case. I unwrapped the take-out and arranged it on the coffee table.

"Why did you even get that?" Jake said, watching me squirt salad dressing from a plastic pouch onto an indecipherable mound of vegetables and what was supposed to be chicken. "You know you're just going to want these." He held up a handful of ketchup-smeared French Fries and stuffed them in his mouth. "So, are you nervous? To be a TV doctor?"

Nervous? *Nervous. Hmmm…* If I allowed myself to even go there, "nervous" wasn't really the word. To be honest, I wasn't sure *what* I was feeling. Severe anxiety? Panic, perhaps?

I wasn't worried about the surgery. Sheryl had been a true home run. While she still wasn't done "cooking," the dramatic transformation in the before-and-after photos was sufficiently impressive. *That* wasn't the problem. *There* I was the big hero. It was the *other* stuff that knotted up my stomach.

*Devin and our date and...*We hadn't spoken since, and I dreaded seeing it all played out in front of me. How out of my league was I going to look standing next to him? Was the bullshit love story going to be painfully obvious? That the production company had to hire an actor to be the loser doctor's boyfriend because even the lowly scrub tech she'd been sleeping with wouldn't have shown up?

"That actor guy. That's the part I want to see," Jake said, as if on cue. I always figured that it was because we were siblings so close in age that we were often on the same wavelength. Any other explanation was a little too frightening.

"Remember, when you used to visit me in the hospital you made me watch that show he was on?" he continued. "I didn't mind. They had some hot girls on that show."

"Jake, you have a cigarette?"

I sat out on the front stoop by myself, slowly smoking one of Jake's Marlboro Reds, savoring the burn against my trachea. No light cigarettes for me. When I smoke, I really smoke.

"Rachel, it's on!" Jake yelled from inside.

I missed the first four seconds of the intro. I walked in to a panoramic view of Beverly Hills on the TV.

"Don't worry, I'm taping it," Jake said. "Not sure I like the music."

I stared hard at the screen, waiting. I hadn't seen anything except the bits and pieces they had played back on the monitors while we were shooting, and I had no idea what to expect.

"Do you think I'll look fat?" I wondered out loud. I had been so busy worrying about my patient looking skinny enough post-op to impress everyone else that I'd forgotten that the camera was going to add ten pounds to me as well.

"I think *I* would've looked fat," Jake said.

The camera panned up the classic palm tree-lined Beverly Hills residential streets and then zoomed in to the commercial district, and then to the 436 building. And then there I was. Driving the Porsche into the underground lot with the top down.

"That's *your* car?" Jake said.

Now I was sitting and talking to the camera in an "interview"—or what I referred to as the "blue background Hamlet monologues." You know, those parts of a reality show where one of the main characters sits there all decked out and made up in front of a marbled blue backdrop and makes a bunch of philosophical statements about whatever is going on in the show.

"My name is Rachel Thomas. I'm a Beverly Hills Plastic Surgeon. My goal is to become the 'Lipo Queen of the World'," were my first words.

I cringed. *Did I really say that?*

"They made me say that," I said. "It wasn't supposed to sound like that. I was kidding—"

Now I was in the exam room with Sheryl. "This woman is *plagued* by her saddlebags," I heard myself say.

Jesus. It sounded like I was making fun of her, the way I was so life-and-death serious about it.

They cut back and forth between me marking Sheryl to different scenes in my office. Then there was me and Jenny hanging out at my new place, talking about how we're all each other has, how neither of us have families. Gloria hadn't been interested in adding Zoey to any storylines ("This show is supposed to be an escape from reality. Our demographic has to look at their *own* ugly kids all day. Why would they want to look at yours, too?") and she never even asked about my own parents. I didn't offer up any information, since getting my mother involved would have been a nightmare, and tracking down my father would have been pointless. But I still couldn't bear to look at Jake during this scene.

Then they cut to the "date night" which, I was relieved to see, had been slashed down to almost nothing. Maybe Blair herself had realized it wasn't working and they were better off just getting rid of it? In fact, they'd cut almost all of the dialogue and just used voice-over for most of it. The part out on the patio was shortened to about ten seconds, and it was just a voiceover of Devin saying, "Rachel and I have so little free time to spend together…when we do, we really like to make it count." And while we were walking into the club, my voice: "After a hard day's work, I really like to unwind."

Well, *that* was slightly out of context. When they'd asked me that question I'd meant watch TV. Not go clubbing in the middle of the week.

"You look beautiful, Rachel," Jake said.

Jake was right. While Devin was still outrageously handsome, with the miraculous TV makeup I *looked* beautiful. And not fat. I started to breathe a little easier at the second commercial break. Ten more minutes to go.

The last segment began with me scrubbing at the O.R. sink, then cut to the middle of the surgery. The whole thing was totally out of order, but Blair had explained that this would happen, that the actual liposuction was what everyone wanted to see, so they left it till the end.

"Fucking awesome," Jake said when they panned to close-up shots of the fat-filled canisters.

And then it started.

"As a woman, what's better than sucking fat out of another woman?" I heard myself say. "It's a fantasy!"

Wait a minute. This was from the "B-roll." The microphones had been *off.*

"I think 'Body Dysmorphic Disorder' is B.S.," were my next words.

"That's not what I said," I said to Jake. "They asked me if I thought I was playing on Body Dysmorphic Disorder in women and I just meant—if someone has something on their body that I think I can fix, I'll do it."

This was the only part where it seemed like they'd kept every word that came out of my mouth:

"It started with Kate Moss and really never went back. Aren't you sick of all these actresses who talk about embracing their curves, saying that they refuse to succumb to the Hollywood ideal, and then the next time you see them on TV at an awards show or in some magazine, they're stick-thin? Well, let me tell you—this is the big secret. One of four things: weight loss surgery, lipo, coke, or Photoshop. Oh, and Adderall. Sorry. Five."

"They weren't supposed to put that part in," I said quietly. "I was just talking."

It actually got worse. They had a close-up of me in my scrub cap and mask, still going full-force, spouting off my personal theories about women's bodies and external beauty.

"When women act like they're 'above' being thin, they're so full of—" Of course, "shit" was wiped out with a disturbing bleep sound, more offensive than the actual word, drawing even more attention to what I'd just said. "Like my chairman's secretary."

Oh, no. Please God, stop this from happening. Give me a little earthquake. Just a "four." Just something that can knock out the power across the city.

"She moons over him day and night but someone really needs to take a liposuction cannula to those hips before he'd ever consider having an affair with her." My words were synchronized with camera angles of Sheryl's lower body bulges and the cannula moving in and out.

But the on-screen me was not to be stopped, with nearly six full minutes left. "There was this one time in med school when I was at the beach with a couple of girlfriends…"

Why oh why had I launched into that stupid story? "We were watching a bikini model get photographed down at the edge of the water." *Because what happens in the O.R.*—"And my friend said, 'There are a lot more important things in life than looking good in a bathing suit, you know.' So I said, 'Really? Name one.'"

It was just a joke. And everyone in the O.R. had laughed.

Because they knew it was true.

It's the kind of true thing that *you never say.* Because even though it's true, it makes you look mean and shallow.

Makes *me* look mean and shallow. In front of the entire world. Or, at least, whoever was watching this piece of shit show.

Jake was silent. I couldn't look at him. I glanced at the clock. Four more minutes. There couldn't possibly be time for it to get any worse. It wasn't a Laker's game.

But of course there was. Plenty of time. That last four minutes is an eternity filled with possibilities. That's where the sit-com predicament gets resolved, the drama sets up the dilemmas for next week, someone wins a million dollars on a game show...

"Oh, I've had a younger boyfriend," I heard myself say. Next a two-and-a-half-minute description of how Eddie and I used to romp around the hospital together. How we "hit" every call room, the stairwell, the roof. "They don't just do it on TV!" I had assured everyone. And then the whole stupid story, play by play, about how I had been *madly* in love with him. And then how he'd stood me up. How I'd splurged on those stupid $500 tickets for that big charity gala and I'd just wound up sitting at home drinking alone on my couch all night. I wondered how I'd managed to turn something that had been so painful into a stand-up routine? Did it have something to do with the fact that I was annihilating a woman's thunder thighs with a four millimeter liposuction cannula while I was telling it?

"But Rachel, isn't that the night you came *here*?" Jake said, not accusingly, just curious. Of course it was. But I couldn't exactly tell everyone how, all dressed up and nowhere to go, I'd wound up at my secret mentally ill brother's trailer park.

I wasn't even watching anymore when they got to the triumphant finale of Sheryl, successfully wearing a pair of expensive tight skinny jeans and thanking me profusely for my miraculous work.

They closed with cliff-hanging scenes from next week's episode, specifically a close-up of me consulting with my next patient about her "bra fat," assuring her that, "I can get fat out of a rock."

"I need to smoke," I said, and returned to the stoop with Jake's cigarettes. This time I took the entire pack. Jake, Sam and I sat together and they watched silently as I burned through the first one.

How could Gloria have aired something so offensive and tasteless? What happened to not making me look like a "media whore?" This was supposed to be a show about a glamorous, fabulous young female plastic surgeon in Beverly Hills. Why would they bother doing that makeover on me if they were just going to make me a laughingstock? *She must not have even known.* It was the only explanation. She was too busy with all of her other, more important shows to deal with this last minute time-filler; she'd trusted Blair implicitly to make it work. She was probably reaming her a new one right about now. Then she'd get to me.

And what was this going to do to me professionally?

"You looked great, Rachel," Jake said.

"I don't think that's the issue here."

He was silent for a moment, then: "I didn't know what a dick that scrub tech was." He shook a cigarette out of the pack and lit it for himself. "I'm sorry."

They'd cancel it for sure. Well, easy come, easy go, right? And it's not like I was getting paid for it, anyway. The only real benefit for me would have been the free marketing. So I wasn't going to be a big, famous Beverly Hills Plastic Surgeon. At least I still had a day job.

"I bet the network's server's crashed from hate comments," I said after a few minutes, and tried to laugh. "Gloria's going to kill Blair. It was supposed to be classy." I looked up at Jake and moaned, "She promised that it was going to be classy."

"I think that's what they call a 'bait and switch,' right?" Jake laughed. "Come on, it's reality television. What did you *think* they were going to do? And really, it wasn't that bad."

"Which part?" I said. "The part where I champion anorexics, or the part where I make an ass of myself talking about how I got dumped and my heart broken by a scrub tech?"

"I have to go to bed." I could hear the yawn in Jake's voice. His meds were starting to kick in. He sighed and stood up.

"Jake, please tell me I'm not a terrible person," I said.

"You're not a terrible person, Rachel."

I buried my face into my knees. "Then why am I this way? Why do I say such fucked-up things? What is *wrong* with me?"

I felt Jake's hand on my shoulder. "Do you *really* have to ask that?"

"I can't blame mom for the rest of my life. I'm an adult."

"I'm not saying *blame* her. It's just…it's not your fault. I mean, maybe do you think…it's just like…each one of those surgeries you do is like a 'fuck you' to her? Like a…a reckoning with mom or something?"

Okay, if Jake was truly going to be the voice of reason here amidst this whole mess, I knew I was in trouble.

I heard him ground out his cigarette with his foot. And again, as if he could read my mind, he added, "That's pretty deep, huh?" and then he started howling with laughter.

17

By the time I was on my way to work the next morning, I still hadn't heard from anyone yet—not Gloria, not Blair, not even Jenny. Which gave me a moment to start focusing on a whole new crowd of people to worry about—*what was everyone at the hospital going to say?*

I was uncharacteristically on time for the O.R. Rather than blowing into the pre-op holding area at my usual 7:10—when really the patient was supposed to be on the table at 7 A.M. sharp—I was there by 6:50, ready to mark her.

The pre-op nurse greeted me with the purple marking pen. "Did you have a pleasant weekend, Dr. Thomas?"

I searched her face, and saw nothing except the surprise that I was actually on time.

"Do you need my signature on anything?" I felt like I was in slow motion as I started thumbing through the pages in the chart, trying to engage her in small talk. "Everything should be faxed over but just to make sure…the labs are here…"

"Everything's fine, Dr. Thomas," she said. "They're ready to go in the room."

I took a deep breath and stared long and hard at her face. It was blank. *She really doesn't know anything.*

I surveyed the pre-op area—ten beds partially curtained off, physicians and nurses milling around the patients waiting to go to surgery. There was the occasional "Hello, Dr. Thomas," from someone familiar passing by, but nobody treated me any differently.

I should probably just stop flattering myself. These days, there were a million TV channels and about two million reality shows. And this wasn't my demographic. There was no reason for any of these self-important medical professionals to be tuning in to a silly reality show on a basic cable network.

I kept a low profile at the sinks. The other surgeons and I acknowledged each other with the customary gruff "How's it going?" from behind our masks while scrubbing in to our respective rooms. Nothing unusual here, as far as I could tell.

Not only had I been uncharacteristically early, but I kept my mouth uncharacteristically shut throughout the entire case. None of my usual rambunctious stories or sassy jokes. Topics were limited to things like the weather, the insane real-estate prices and how amazing this patient's reconstructed breasts were going to look when I was done. By the time we were struggling with the hook-and-eye closure of the post-surgical bra, I had almost forgotten about *Lipo Queen*.

Until, on our way to recovery, the scrub tech leaned across the gurney and whispered in my ear, "Dr. Thomas, I had no idea what an asshole Eddie is!"

I stopped walking and the gurney rolled over my foot. "Excuse me?"

"You know, what you said on your show. I saw it. Last night."

She was a heavy-set Mexican girl who wore too much eye makeup and probably commuted from an hour east of here so her mother could take care of her four kids while she was at work. I didn't even want to *think* about what the Lipo Queen could have said to offend *her*.

I abruptly snatched the chart and marched off to a desk but once I was sitting, I was too stunned to work. I looked around the recovery room at the other surgeons sitting in front of computers, filling out charts, fiddling with their phones. At the nurses giving patients sips of water and charting vitals from the monitors. Nobody was staring at me. Things were still the same.

"Dr. Thomas!"

I jumped at the sound of the nurse's voice.

"The family's waiting to talk to you. Are you done with the chart?" She frowned at the blank order page. "Well, please give it to me when you're finished. The patient's almost ready to go."

As I made my way to the door, I smiled at everyone, regardless of whether or not I even knew them. I even smiled at bleary-eyed patients waking up from their surgeries on gurneys behind half-drawn curtains. Not one person yelled out after me, "Hey you, you crazy bitch! I saw you on TV last night and you really made an ass of yourself! And you are a despicable human being!"

By the time I got to the waiting room, I had convinced myself that I really, truly had nothing to worry about. That scrub tech was just one person. And she was just a scrub tech, anyway.

Until I felt my phone buzzing in the back pocket of my scrub pants. It was Donarski's office.

18

It would have been too tricky for me to work my quirky charm with Donarski over the phone. But certainly I'd be able to smooth everything over if we could just talk in person. And after all, it *was* possible that this call had nothing to do with *Lipo Queen*. Maybe he just had some paperwork for me to sign. Maybe he had some information about another study course for the boards.

I had my apology for Brenda all worked out in my head but when I got to the office, her chair was empty and her computer was off. Dr. Donarski sat at his desk with his arms folded, framed by his wide-open doorway. I guess he knew me well enough to figure that I was going to just show up.

"Hello, Rachel," he said.

This was definitely not good. He rarely called me by my real name.

"Dr. Donarski."

"You might want to close the door."

I was about to start my usual endearing chatter, but the no-bullshit tone of his voice stopped me, so I just sat.

"I let Brenda go home early today," he said. "To say she was upset would be a grotesque understatement."

How had I not at least *anticipated* this conversation and *attempted* to plan for it? I hadn't the faintest idea of my next move. Would it be possible to make him believe I'd been *tricked* into being on television?

"Rachel, I am extremely disappointed."

"I know, Doctor Donarski, and I can explain. It wasn't supposed to be like that—"

"Was it supposed to be like *this*?" He didn't raise his voice, just held up a glossy tabloid magazine to show me a right-hand side full-page ad for *Lipo Queen*. There was an illustrated outline of a skinny person inside of a fat person, a photograph of me, gowned and gloved in the upper right hand corner,

121

and in the bottom left, a picture of Devin looking like a dork with his arms crossed, wearing a pair of sunglasses pushed down to the end of his nose. In bold print across the middle of the page it said "Sundays at eight!"

"She can get fat out of a rock," he read.

"It's a figure of speech," I said. "It means—"

"I understand what it means."

"Doctor Donarski—"

"Gallivanting around at clubs, having sex with actors in limousines—is this how you want to be portrayed? Reinforcing the stereotype of the Hollywood plastic surgeon? How can you expect to be taken seriously?"

"I did not have sex in the limo."

"How could you do something like this without asking me?"

"I guess I didn't realize it was such a…big deal. Did you…see it?"

"I didn't have to," he said. "My kids saw it. You can imagine the family discussion that ensued."

"Doctor Donarski, I'm so sorry. I really didn't think—"

He sighed and leaned back in his chair. "No, you didn't think. That's the problem. How could you do a large volume patient like that? *On television?* You know the Task Force guidelines. What if something happened? Your malpractice would never cover you. And the hospital would have been liable."

I tried to laugh. "Actually she wasn't that big. It came in under five liters—you know how TV adds ten pounds—"

"You made the operating room look like a carnival."

"That wasn't my fault—"

"I received a call from Mr. Hopper this morning."

Fuck. I was pretty sure that was the hospital CEO.

"He understands what a valuable asset you have been to this department since you started here," he continued. "And everyone agrees that you're the hardest-working surgeon I've ever hired."

I felt myself relax a little.

"And technically you're quite superb."

Superb. That was a first. It was going to be okay.

"But I'm afraid that the Valley Hospital can not endorse the *Lipo Queen*." I forced another laugh that came out more like a squeak. "Doctor Donarski, you don't have to endorse me. Believe me, I'm sure by now it's been cancelled anyway, and even if it's not, I'll never do it again—"

He cut me off, monotone and unwavering. "By keeping you on staff here we are silently endorsing your behavior. And that television show. I'm afraid that under Mr. Hopper's recommendation, I'm going to have to terminate you."

He couldn't have said what I just thought he did. *Terminate* me? I had been prepared to be embarrassed, to be hated by everyone who knew me, to have to apologize to Brenda at a formal assembly, to promise to never step in front of a camera again, but—*I was going to lose my job over this? A stupid reality TV show?*

"Doctor Donarski, please," I began. "I promise, nothing like this will ever happen again—"

"It already has," he said.

"But I need this job!"

And then he said the words that ripped through me like a fresh stainless steel number ten blade cuts through flesh: "Then you probably should have thought of that before."

The worst part was that he had not even raised his voice once. I was sitting across the desk from the very same Dr. Donarski who had hired me, who had a soft spot for me despite my roughness around the edges, who appreciated what a good surgeon and ethical, caring physician I was.

"Can't you talk to Mr. Hopper?" I pleaded.

"I'm not going to be able to change his mind. And Rachel, I tend to agree with him on this. I'm sorry."

"But…but what about all of my patients? Who's going to take care of them? The breast recon I just did—"

"I will," he said. "Until I get someone to replace you. The chief residents graduate in a month. Everyone's looking for jobs."

This couldn't be happening. I searched his face, but it was closed.

"Dr. Donarski—" I stood up on my rubber legs.

"I really am sorry, Rachel," he said. "I wish I didn't have to do this. You're a fine surgeon. I wish you luck." He bent his head, redirecting his attention to a pile of papers in the middle of his desk.

Just as I put my hand on the doorknob to leave, I couldn't help myself. "It was what I said about Eddie, wasn't it?" I blurted out.

"Excuse me?"

"Eddie. The scrub tech. But I swear, it's completely over, we don't even speak anymore—"

Without looking up he said, "We all knew you were sleeping with the scrub tech, Rachel."

This just could not be happening. Not that I'd never been fired before, but those had all been waitressing jobs back in high school and college. This was my *real* job—the career I'd been working toward my entire life. I slipped out a side entrance of the hospital so I wouldn't have to look anyone in the face, retreated to my car, and proceeded to chain smoke.

I was in the middle of my second stale cigarette when I felt my phone buzzing in the pocket of my white coat. Unknown caller. My heart jumped. Donarski's cell was a private number. It had to be him, calling me back, telling me to forget everything he had just said, that he had reconsidered and called Mr. Hopper and convinced him to let me stay.

It wasn't Donarski. It was Jenny.

"Jenny, where are you?"

"At the office."

What was she talking about? Ferraro's? "What office?"

"*Your* office, dummy. Your Beverly Hills office, remember?"

"Oh, yeah." I'd forgotten that even though we had only used it for filming, there was an empty office with my name on the door in the most coveted real estate in Beverly Hills.

"Thom, you're smoking, aren't you? I can hear it. What's going on?"

"Jenny, are you kidding me? You saw that thing last night. I'll tell you what's going on. I just got fired."

"That's interesting."

"Interesting? What do you mean—interesting? How am I going to pay my bills? Or go out in public—I'll never be able to drive around with the top down again! Someone might shoot me."

"Well, I don't know about all that," she said. "But I wouldn't worry about the getting fired part. You don't have time to work at that hospital any more."

"What does that even mean?"

"Your phones have been ringing off the hook all day here. I've got you booked out for consults for the next two weeks, and two people have already scheduled surgeries sight unseen! I took deposits with credit cards! You made five thousand dollars today!"

I called Blair.

She picked up right away and greeted me with a dry, "I wondered when I'd be hearing from you."

"Blair, what's going on?"

"Well, let's see. The ratings were stellar. We have a hit TV show. So that makes me a genius, I think. Dr. Thomas, are you near a computer?"

My phone had one bar. The browser would never work. Fucking Sprint. I glanced across the parking lot at the Emergency Room side entrance. I still had my badge.

"I could be."

"Go Google yourself and call me back."

I may have been fired, but the electronic passkey at the "Staff only" entrance didn't know it yet, and so I ducked back inside to the end of the E.R. Nobody noticed me sneak past. The break room was empty. I locked the door behind me before I sat down in front of one of the desktops.

First I typed in my name on the home page browser. A few links came up, most of them having to do with my previous residencies, the Valley Hospital staff. Physician databases offering to give the searcher a background check on me for only $9.99.

Then I replaced the entry with "Lipo Queen." Immediately an entire page of links came up. I clicked on the first one and started reading. It was an online *Entertainment Tonight* review. "*Lipo Queen* Tells It Like It Is!" was the headline, and it proceeded to describe the guilty pleasure of the uncensored "behind the scenes" approach of the show. "This is like no other plastic surgery show, real or scripted," it read. "No holds barred, this is racy and cuts to the heart of the matter, no pun intended. Dr. Rachel Thomas is endearingly candid and fresh."

I read the next one. "*Lipo Queen* gives us an authentic taste of the world of plastic surgery. This is the real deal."

And the next one: "*Lipo Queen* goes where no plastic surgery show has gone before. Rather than capitalizing on a makeover freak show with 'total overhauls' *Lipo Queen* taps into what we can really relate to—the psyche of the everyday American woman."

And *People* online: "With the combination of the 'ultimate fantasy' of body sculpting and Thomas' boyfriend, our favorite *Pacific Beach* heartthrob, what woman will *not* be glued to her television for this on Sunday nights?"

Down at the bottom of the page were some comments. "Dr. Thomas is so down to earth. I just love her! She really understands women. As soon as I have the money I'm going to have her sculpt my body!"

"Finally, a TV doctor I can relate to, instead of some chauvinistic guy who doesn't know the first thing about how a woman wants her body to look and just wants to give us all humungous breast implants!"

"I like the way they let us see all sides of her, like a real person. I just went through a terrible break-up. It makes me feel better knowing that someone as pretty and successful as she is goes through the same thing."

Pretty. Someone out there said I was *pretty*.

"I'm so glad she and Devin Breeze got together. I know he had some problems in the past but now he seems like a great guy and like they are really in love. She deserves someone like that after what she went through."

There were pages and pages more, but I needed to get out of the break room before someone caught me red-handed, Googling myself. My phone buzzed again. This time it was a hospital extension.

"Dr. Thomas, this is Connie calling from human resources. We have some paperwork that we need you to come finalize. No rush, of course. At your convenience. But, uh, today if possible." The woman's voice sounded very uncomfortable and sympathetic.

I smiled into my phone. "Hi, Connie," I said. "I'll be right down."

19

believe that there are two kinds of people in this world. Those who are interested in plastic surgery, and those who are interested in plastic surgery and won't admit it. So basically, everyone. Now, imagine the cross section in a Venn diagram of "everyone" with "people who are addicted to reality television." With the help of this cult following, *Lipo Queen* became somewhat of an overnight sensation. The network re-aired the pilot every night until we had another half-hour episode ready to go.

The sting of getting fired didn't last long. Jenny had certainly been spot-on about that free marketing—without even trying, we were booked out with office visits and surgeries until Labor Day. Not only had I become the star of the most-watched show on our network, but I had instantly become one of the most sought-after plastic surgeons in town. We got phone calls from all over the country. All women, ranging in age anywhere from eighteen to seventy. There were the twenty-somethings cursed with unfortunate congenital fat deposits and then there were the ones in their fifties and sixties with menopause-induced weight gain that wouldn't disappear, no matter how many hours they spent on the elliptical. And even though their husbands and boyfriends said "don't be crazy," and "do it if you want but you're fine the way you are," I knew I was helping them. I *got* it. I got *them*. With my neurotic passion, I had tapped into a population of motivated women whose general conviction was that if they could just be skinnier, their lives would be better. Who was *I* to tell them otherwise? What they thought was true. After I made them skinnier, they *were* happier. At least temporarily.

And while I was helping women from all walks of life rebuild their self-esteem from the outside-in, the money was flowing into my bank account so easily that I felt like I was doing something illegal. For the first time since I could remember I was handling my bills—and Jake's—without the unpleasant sensation that I was being choked to death during the process.

"Pull, Mateus, pull like you fucking mean it!" I yelled. When Blair first told me she wanted me to yell at people on camera in the O.R., I hadn't been able to do it—you learn early in residency that mistreating the staff is *the* biggest misstep a surgeon can make. But after a few times with her coaching me, I got used to it pretty quickly. I had to admit, being given free license to yell at people at work was a great stress reliever. Besides, when you're secretly freaking out in the O.R., the last thing you care about is hurting someone's feelings. In fact, at this exact moment, the *only* thing I cared about was stuffing that too-big silicone implant in through that too-small peri-areolar incision. Right then, it was the only thing in the entire world that mattered. I could apologize to Mateus later.

We were struggling through an aug redo. The patient had assumed that I would be just as artistic and intuitive with her breasts as with her body. And despite Gloria's initial desire to keep an "exclusively liposuction feel" to the show, once Blair saw a breast case, she insisted on staying and filming. No comment.

I felt Adeta peering over my shoulder. "I'd make that incision about twice as big," she said.

There's nothing more annoying than an O.R. nurse who thinks they're a surgeon. Except maybe a scrub tech who thinks they're a surgeon. I glared at Mateus, daring him to open his mouth.

Yes, I could have made the incision bigger but honestly, I was afraid. It was a revision surgery and the patient had some old scars and I wasn't one hundred percent certain where the blood supply to the nipple was coming from anymore. In an ideal world I would have gotten the patient's old op report from the previous surgeon, but the constraints of the shooting schedule hadn't left time for that.

"If we can't get it through that hole, then we really suck," I said. I'd gotten much bigger implants through much smaller holes. These were only three hundreds. "Jesus, Mateus, show me those muscles you spend your entire life on at the gym." I could hear him grunting from the strain of retracting against me, as I continued to unsuccessfully try to stuff the implant through the tiny incision.

"Nice! Barbaric!" Blair said from behind me. "Make it look really hard to get it in there!"

It *was* really hard to get it in there. I gave Mateus a quick rest, then signaled to try again. He repositioned the retractors to spread open the wound. I started to stuff an edge of the implant back through the hole with my forefingers. It was going, going…then the whole thing slipped back out and across the drape and I caught it before it landed on the floor.

Finally, with a healthy shriek of: "*Motherfucker!*" I got it in on the third try.

Mateus and I switched sides. I started dissecting the left breast pocket and things got routine and boring again. As usual, the second side went faster and I was able to finish by early afternoon.

Another success story. The patient's body was now streamlined to perfection, and the breasts were round and full, natural in appearance, yet not so natural that she would want her money back.

They shot me talking to her as she woke up in recovery.

"Everything went perfectly," I told her. "You look uh-*maaazing*." I snuck a peek under her bra one more time, just to make sure. The nipples looked right back at me, pink and warm and happy.

"Ouch," the patient said.

"And she still has nipple sensation," I said to the camera.

"Make sure you get that," Blair instructed the sound guy. "Dr. Thomas, once more, with a little more vigor."

"How'd the case go?" Jenny always waited for me after surgeries with lunch and a list.

I sat at the break room table opposite her and poured dressing over my Chinese chicken salad from across the street. You can rarely go wrong with a Chinese chicken salad.

"I don't know why you ask for it on the side," Jenny said. "You always put the whole thing on anyway." She turned to the camera guy, who had followed me into the room. "Leave her alone when she's eating."

She then proceeded to rattle off to me the numerous messages. Except for the ones from the patients, I had no idea what to do with them and they all got handed off to Blair, anyway. But it was still fun to go through the long list of phone calls and emails and feel popular.

"You want some?" I had noticed that Jenny had nothing in front of her so I raised up a forkful of salad in her direction.

Jenny shook her head and put her hands on her stomach. "I'm not eating this week. Being around all these skinny women down here is killing me."

"Now *that* is an insult to *me.*"

"It's not your fault, Thom. It's my body. You did an amazing job. But all the other office assistants in this building look like lollipops. Boobs on a stick."

She was right. Everyone down here was trying to out-skinny each other. Still, it didn't make me want to leave Beverly Hills. Less than a month ago my lunch had been someone's leftover M&M's in the chart room of a dingy county hospital clinic and no time to eat them. It was surreal, the way things could change so fast.

But nothing was more surreal than Jenny's next words:

"Now please don't go getting all crazy on me, Thom. We still have a lot of work to do this afternoon. Stay focused when I tell you this." She handed me a Post-It with a phone number scrawled across it that I recognized with a pang in my gut. "Eddie called. He said to tell you there's a party out at his place this weekend, if you want to stop by."

20

Eddie's party was Saturday night. When I woke up Sunday morning to my cat chewing my hair, my first thought was: Good. I'm still home. I didn't somehow wind up at Eddie's Malibu shack in an Ambien-induced coma. And the second was: "Fuck, I gave Jenny my car last night."

We'd had a long shoot on Saturday down at the beach and when we were finished, Jenny had driven me home and taken my keys. She swore it wasn't just because she wanted to borrow my car.

"This is the only intervention I can think of," she said. "I know you, Thom. You won't show up at Eddie's without the Porsche."

She was probably right.

"And how could you even *consider* going?" she continued. "How can you give him the *satisfaction*? I can't believe he had the nerve to even *call* you!"

About that…I can't say I was completely shocked. Because I knew Eddie. I'd figured I'd hear from him eventually, I just wasn't sure when.

After Jenny had left, I'd toyed with the idea of somehow getting out to Jake's, where I kept my Audi because I didn't have space for it down at my fancy condo. But I didn't have a number for a cab company, and my Uber app wasn't working, and I was so sleepy from having been out in the sun all day, that I dozed off trying to remember whether or not I'd thrown out the phone book.

I checked my phone. Not a message from either of them. Which just proved I'd made the right decision about going to Eddie's. And the *wrong* decision about letting Jenny have my car.

I should have been extremely specific with her about exactly when I needed it back. I was supposed to be doing one of those interview shoots here at the condo in an hour…and I still had my Friday patient coming into the office for a post-op check beforehand. *Shit.* I considered calling the patient and switching her to tomorrow instead, but it had already been almost forty-eight hours since the surgery and I really needed to see her before another day went by.

I waited until my hair was dry and I was dressed in the outfit in the Polaroid picture taped to the closet to start getting pissed. I sensed a time crunch that *for once was no fault of my own*, and Jenny wasn't answering her phone. Not only was I going to have to endure Blair's bitching, but the office door was locked and now my patient was going to be stuck out in the hallway, waiting.

I finally got Jenny on the sixth try.

"Get up," I said. "I have someone waiting for me at the office. I need my car back. I'll drop you off after."

"Hmmm…" I could tell she was still waking up. "Thom, I would but I'm a little…far."

"Far? How far can you be?"

"Dr. Thomas, makeup!" someone called from the living room.

Shit. What were they doing here already? I hadn't heard anyone come in.

"Well, I'm kind of in…Vegas."

"*Vegas*? How could you be in Vegas?"

"I drove. Your car's pretty fast, you know. And Bentley has this app on his phone that can track highway patrol."

"What are you doing in Vegas?" *And where was her kid these days?*

"Well, we were already halfway there—"

"Halfway there from *where*? A gas station in the desert?"

"We were at a party in Pasadena—"

"Jenny, Pasadena is nowhere near the Nevada border. How could you just take my car like that?"

"Helloooo up there!"

Great, Blair was already downstairs yelling for me.

"It was the launch party for that new flavored vodka, at the Palazzo. Bentley got invited and you know how important it is for me to make appearances at these things. Thom, you wouldn't believe it—all the 'Housewives' were there—"

"Who's Bentley?"

"You know Bentley. The actor I'm seeing."

"The one on unemployment?"

"He's not unemployed. He's on hiatus."

It wasn't worth even asking if Bentley had a car they could have taken instead. Or to point out how ironic it was that his name was "Bentley" if he didn't. It didn't matter. I was about to have to be in the city of Los Angeles in two places at once and for the first time in my life I actually had *two* cars—and access to neither of them.

Bracing myself, I shut my phone off and headed downstairs, where I found my entourage already hard at work.

"Doc, gotta move." Lately Blair had taken to calling me "Doc." She stood in the middle of the living room, pointing to Betty and her make-up bag. "Let's go."

Devin and Russell strolled in from the patio.

"Hey, Rachel," Devin said when he saw me. Just hearing him say my name—and the way he looked like he'd just rolled out of bed himself—made my stomach squirm.

"Hi," I said. "I didn't know you were here."

"Just having a little *kibbutz*," Russell said.

"Are you ready?" Blair said to me.

"But, you said noon," I said.

"It's eleven thirty-five."

"I know," I stammered. "I just…I have to see a patient in the office really quick."

"*Now*? You couldn't plan that on your own time?"

"I'm outta here," Devin said to Russell. "Later, man."

"Doc, we don't have all day to wait while you take care of your personal affairs."

"It's okay, let her go," one of the crew members called over from where they were assembling the lights and the blue screen. "We could use more time, anyway. We're having a problem with the sound."

"So, go!" Blair said to me. "Go now!" When I didn't move, she said, "*Now* what?"

"I kind of need to…get a cab," I squeaked. When I saw the expression on her face, I assured her, "The car's fine."

"You're fucking kidding me, right?"

"It's not a big deal. It's just—Jenny took the car and the patient from Friday—I have to check her really quick—it'll take like five minutes—"

"Doc, how the hell you made it through all that school being such a dumbass—"

Russell sighed. "Jesus. Dev, you wanna just take her?"

Without saying anything, Devin pulled his hand from his jacket pocket and dangled his small ring of keys in the air, letting them jingle back and forth. Then he looked at something on his phone. My heart skipped a beat. *Was he going to refuse? Was he about to give me the number for a good cab company? Or tell me to Uber it like everyone else?*

He didn't. Instead, he stuffed his hands back in his pockets and nodded at me. "Sure," he said. "Let's go."

21

I had never before really paid attention to what Devin Breeze drove around town himself. I was surprised when he led me to a forest green vintage BMW parked at a meter across the street. He must have noticed my expression when he manually unlocked the passenger side door for me from the inside.

"Everything okay?" he asked as I slid onto the seat. *Was I imagining it or did he seem amused?*

"Yeah, I was just…" I fumbled for the words. "I mean, is this like an antique or something?"

"Kind of. Bought it when I moved out here."

"Well, it's a real…classic."

He started the engine—which, fortunately, ran like new—and we pulled out onto the street toward Beverly Hills.

"Yeah, I know you're supposed to trade them in every few years but…I'm kind of attached to this one," he said.

"I have a car like that," I said.

"What, that loaded Porsche they've got you tooling around in?"

"No," I started to say. "I have another one…" I was about to tell him about my beautiful TT that I had been so proud to be able to purchase and finance all on my own, sitting all by its lonesome in Jake's driveway, but then I realized he wasn't listening anymore. In fact, he was making a phone call.

At least the door to the office was unlocked, so there was no angry patient waiting for me in the hall when we got there.

"Your patient's in the first room," Mateus greeted us from the reception area behind Jenny's computer. "Well, hell*ooo there*," he whistled when he saw Devin, who visibly cringed. I didn't bother to introduce them.

135

"What are you doing here?" I smelled nail polish. When we got closer I saw that Mateus had his bare feet resting on the desk with toilet paper wedged in between all of his toes. His toenails were hot pink.

"I had to autoclave some stuff for Monday, so I figured I'd get a pedicure in while I waited for the instruments. And a 'thank you' would be nice, by the way." He wiggled his toes. He still hadn't taken his eyes off Devin, who by this time was probably wishing he'd waited for me in the car.

"Mateus, get your feet off the desk," I hissed. Then I said to Devin, "Just wait here for a sec. I'll be right back." I waved in the general direction of the waiting room and as I did, I noticed a girl who looked to be in her early twenties—as blonde and tan and half-dressed as they come—sitting by herself on the couch in the corner. I assumed she was my patient's ride, since there was no other reason for her to be there. I caught Devin checking her out and sensed their gaze catching for a split second and I hated myself for hoping Mateus *did* pester him after all.

"Hey, how's it going?" When I entered the exam room my patient was already in the chair, dressed in a blue paper gown. "Nancy," I added. I almost hadn't been able to remember her name. A sign that I was successful, I suppose. I now had too many patients to remember all of their names off the top of my head, or even sometimes exactly what part of their body I'd operated on.

I didn't even wait for her to answer me and I tried not to seem like I was rushing as I helped Nancy off with her gown so I could see how everything was healing. She didn't look bad for two days post-op. Her swelling was minimal and her color was pretty good. I helped her stand in front of the three-way mirror so she could see her fabulous new figure from all angles while I changed the lipo incision dressings on her back.

"Wow," she said. "I'm a new woman. You really are as amazing as they say."

She was an easy one. No whining, no pain. This would be quick. Now just a peek at the breast incisions and I'd be out of there.

I unhooked the surgical bra and removed the gauze.

"Oh my God! They're perfect! I love them!" Nancy moved closer to the mirror to get a better look.

Crap. This could not be happening. Surely I was just imagining it. I looked back and forth between Nancy and her reflection in the mirror.

"You're an artist! Unbelievable! *Sooo* much better than before. Will they stay this big?" Nancy put her hands on her hips and posed, admiring herself. "When can I start having sex again?"

"Here, can you just…sit back here in the chair…let me take another look at that," I said, trying to keep my voice in a monotone. Maybe it was just the lighting. It *had* to be the lighting. It was dark over there by the mirror.

"Sure." Nancy hopped up onto the exam chair, beaming at me. She must have been high as a kite to move around like that without feeling anything. "Everything's okay, right?"

"Of course, it's just…" *It's just that your fucking nipples aren't getting any blood supply.* Well, maybe that was my hysteria blowing things out of proportion. There were patchy areas of pink color that blanched and refilled when I pressed on them, but the majority of the areolar skin was blotchy blue and purple. Venous congestion. The dreaded congested nipple. I'd been preemptively concerned in this case, and—it appeared—rightly so. *But how could this have happened?* I had been so meticulous, so careful in the O.R. When she'd gone home two days ago, everything had been fine.

Two days ago. I pushed gently on some of the purple areas. *It had been two days. Why hadn't I come in to see her yesterday morning instead of going to get that stupid spray tan for the shoot?*

"Doctor Thomas, is something wrong?"

"No," I said. "They're just a little…bruised."

"Yeah, but that's normal, right?"

"Well, they're a little more bruised than I would like." I took a 27-gauge needle from the cabinet and swabbed each areola with alcohol. *Dammit, had I pigeonholed myself into such a "niche" area that I couldn't even do a stupid breast case anymore? Did this mean I shouldn't be doing anything anymore except sucking fat?*

"Dr. Thomas, what are you doing with that needle?"

"Just checking something. This might sting a little bit."

It is a true art for a plastic surgeon to deal with disaster in a cosmetic patient. When a general surgeon has a complication like a leaking bowel anastomosis, or postoperative internal hemorrhaging, the patient is usually too sick to understand what's going on. But it takes real skill to successfully sugarcoat some downright scary shit to a healthy, very-much-awake patient, in the middle of a posh Beverly Hills office where bad things aren't supposed to happen, and then to successfully treat the problem without the patient ever really understanding the gravity of the situation. All the while keeping a poker face.

"What are you checking?" Nancy still didn't sound worried, just curious.

"Just the blood supply." That was an understatement, considering that in plastic surgery blood supply is pretty much everything. Then I went through the routine bag of tricks that I'd read you're supposed to use in this type of situation. I loosened a few of the stitches to take tension off the incision. I covered the whole dusky area of skin with nitro paste from the crash cart. I stuck the needle in a couple of places on the areola where I had swabbed with alcohol and prayed for blood. At first nothing, then slowly dark red spots appeared. Not good. There was definitely an outflow problem.

Now what do I do? I couldn't afford to lose a cell of that skin.

I knew that Donarski would have picked up the phone if I called him for help. I just couldn't bear the satisfaction he'd get out of knowing I'd had a major fuck-up on my own out in the big world. The first thing he'd say was, "Raquel, why didn't you have her old op report so you could see what was done before?" and I'd have to say, "Because I couldn't get it in time for her surgery, which was—more importantly—part of a shoot schedule set in stone."

I tried to picture the textbook algorithm of "congested nipple after mastopexy/augmentation." It was a board question. I should know this. What was the next step—take her back to the O.R. and do free nipple grafts? No, it was too early for that. There had to be something in between. Something else less drastic.

And then I remembered. I knew what I had to do. We'd done it plenty of times in residency for big reconstructive muscle flaps on open ankle fractures, and for the replanted fingers that struggled along with their blood supply. I had never had to do it before in my private practice, but there's always a first time for everything.

"I'll be right back," I told Nancy. I took a deep breath and went out to the front of the office again, where Mateus was marveling at his toes.

"You know, it's hard to get them this good," he said.

Devin waved at me with his phone through the reception window. "Hey, Russell keeps texting me. You ready?"

How pathetic was I that even in this desperate moment I couldn't help feeling satisfied that he was completely ignoring Nancy's gorgeous friend?

I held up a finger and slid the frosted glass window closed, separating the reception area from the waiting room. Then I minimized Mateus' Facebook window.

"What now?" he whined. "Don't start bitching at me about doing my toes in here. It's a week*end*."

The autoclave buzzer went off and drowned out my next words. Mateus ignored me and after slipping on a pair of throwaway salon sandals, hobbled back to the substerile room on his heels with his toes splayed out.

"What do you want?" he whined as I followed him.

He unlocked the autoclave and it hissed steam out in our faces as the door swung open.

"Leeches," I said. "I need to get some leeches."

Mateus opened his eyes wide and his mouth turned into a huge "O" that he then covered with his hand. "OMG! What happened? It's not the nipple, is it?"

I nodded. "Both."

"OMG, OMG, OMG!" He sucked in his breath and started jumping up and down. "I saw that once at Smith's place and oh my God we had to put them on her nipples and—"

"Shhh…" I jerked my head toward the exam room.

"Where do we get them?"

"We have to order them."

"Order them? Where do we order them from?" He seemed to have forgotten about his toes, because he ran after me down the hall like a puppy and

139

watched while I furiously swept the computer mouse across the desktop and brought the screen back to life.

"You really need new batteries," he said.

Through the frosted glass window I could make out Devin's silhouette as he paced back and forth in the waiting room with his phone to his ear. "She's doing something," I heard him say. "*I'm* not going in there. I don't know, tell them to get some B-roll or something."

"Come on, come on," I begged the computer. Sunday afternoon. The worst possible time to try to get online.

The thing is, medicinal leeches don't come from a local swamp. The hospital keeps them in the pharmacy refrigerator. But since I was no longer part of a hospital, I was going to have to deal directly with the source. The leech farm.

The only reason I could Google it by name was because the company—which basically had a monopoly on the medicinal leech market in North America—took out a full-page right-side ad in the plastic surgery journal every month.

"Leeches, America."

"Yes," I said. "I'm a plastic surgeon here in…Los Angeles…and I need some leeches stat. It's an emergency."

"Well, it's always an emergency, now, isn't it?" The "Leeches, America" operator went on to inform me that I was going to have to do an emergency custom order, and that the leeches were shipped by Fed-Ex Air and took twelve hours to arrive when traveling cross-country.

"Twelve hours!" I zoomed in on the website address. I hadn't realized they were coming from the East Coast. "I can't wait twelve hours! I need them now!" *Great.* I was going to have a couple of sloughed nipples on national television. As quickly as it had started, my career was going to be over. I could just see the tabloid headlines coupled with pictures taken with telephoto lenses of me back in my Van Nuys apartment, smoking cigarettes with no make-up on. "*Lipo Queen* spirals downward to disaster." No, I wasn't going to let this happen. I refused to go back to Van Nuys.

"Please," I said. "I need them now."

"I'm sorry. It's the best I can do. If you have a more urgent situation, I suggest you borrow from a local hospital in the meantime. Would you like to place an order? They start at $15.50 each, but our minimum stat cross-country order is forty leeches for five ninety-nine plus shipping. Can you hold please? I have another call coming in."

Forty leeches? What the hell was I going to do with forty leeches?

"Would you like to place your order now?" the operator said when she came back.

I heard the door to the exam room open and Nancy step out into the hall-way. "Dr. Thomas, are we done because we parked illegally and we're gonna get towed if we don't get out of here."

"Do I really have to buy all forty?" I said into the phone.

"It's the minimum stat order."

"What if I don't use them all?"

"No returns. But they're good for a month, if you keep them refrigerated."

I imagined hiding the canister of leftover leeches behind the case of Diet Coke on the second shelf of the office refrigerator. "And then what?"

"Then you sacrifice them with formaldehyde and dispose of them accordingly with the other hazardous waste. Would you like to give me your credit card? We take Visa and MasterCard only."

I guess I wasn't as famous as I thought, because the operator had zero reaction to the name "Rachel M. Thomas, M.D." that I read off with the card number. I didn't even get a word when I gave her the Beverly Hills address and the 90210 zip code. That leech farm really must have been in the middle of nowhere.

"What's wrong?" Mateus said when I hung up the phone. "Are they coming?"

"They won't get here till tonight."

"Tonight? Those nipples are gonna be dead by tonight!"

"Shhh…She said to borrow them from the hospital."

Mateus nodded. "That's probably a good idea. I mean, you might want local ones anyway. Those ones from back east—they're going to be all jet-lagged the first day."

"This is not a joke!"

My phone buzzed. A text from Letitia. "Where are you? Blair's getting super pissed."

Come on, I told myself. *I've been through worse before. Hadn't I?* Well, not really, but…there had to be a way to get my hands on some leeches and get them on Nancy's nipples before the tissue damage became irreversible. Just like on all those television shows, everything would be wrapped up and fine by tomorrow. It had to be.

My survival instinct kicked in and I completely tossed the remains of my pride out the door. Why did I care if any of my colleagues found out? My patient was more important than stupid politics. I dialed one of the phone numbers that had been burned into my memory, and prayed.

"Valley Hospital inpatient pharmacy."

Miraculously, my old buddy, Hector, was working today. Even more miraculously, Dr. Donarski had used some leeches on a flap last week and there were still ten left in the refrigerator. But the biggest miracle of all was that—despite the fact that I no longer had any affiliation whatsoever with the hospital—Hector was going to give me the leftover leeches as long as I promised to replace them tomorrow with the new ones before his boss found out.

The catch was that Hector was only going to be there for another hour and it was unlikely that the next guy coming on shift would cooperate. Not only did I have no way to get there, but at this very minute I was supposed to be sitting in front of a muted blue canvas screen, spouting off my insightful theories about women and their bodies with a camera rolling.

The glass window slid open and Devin poked his head through. "Blair's blowing up my phone."

"Hey, is she okay?" Nancy's ride called from across the waiting room without looking up from her magazine.

"She's fine," Mateus answered her.

"Sorry," I said to Devin. "I'm just trying to figure out how to…well, I kind of…have to get something from the hospital."

"I'll go," Mateus said. "I can get them."

"It," I corrected him, widening my eyes at Mateus to tell him to keep his mouth shut about what "It" exactly was in front of Devin. "And no, you can't. You drive a scooter." I could just imagine Mateus hitting a pothole, sending the last of the medicinal leeches on the west coast flying off the side of Mulholland Drive to the bottom of the canyon.

I turned to Devin. "Just give us a moment," I said and I slid the window shut again. "He can't know about this!" I hissed at Mateus.

"Why not?"

"Because I don't want Blair to find out. She'll be over here in a second with five cameras, and no way am I going to let her film me leeching somebody. This *cannot* get on the show. It'll ruin me."

"He wouldn't tell Blair." Mateus shook his head. "I'm sure he hates her. She's such an *angry* girl…and by the way, did I mention how *yummy* he is—"

"Mateus, stop! He can't find out about this!" The truth was, I didn't want Devin to know and it had nothing to do with Blair finding out. I didn't want him to know because of what he might think. *Of me.* Not that I should really care what a D-list-yet-absurdly-hot-actor thought of me but still…he'd never understand this sort of thing. He'd think that I was more pathetic than he'd even imagined when he found out that I used to watch his show. That I was just like all of the other fame-hungry doctors around here—lucky because Gloria picked me—and not even good at my own job.

"Where's your car, anyway?"

"Jenny took it to a vodka launch party. In Vegas."

"Oh my God!" Mateus started bouncing up and down on the balls of his feet, with his hands clasped to the sides of his head. "That looked so fun! I saw it on '*E!*' last night! That's not fair! Tell her to take me next time!"

"Mateus, *focus*! I have to figure this out!" I opened the window again.

Devin hadn't moved from the other side. "Do you need me to pick something up for you?" he said. "Because I really have to get you home."

"Now, that's an idea," Mateus said. "Let him go."

I heard Devin sigh. He couldn't have looked any more bored.

"Or maybe Eddie can go."

"Eddie? What Eddie?" I spun around to see Mateus slowly scrolling down through the screen of my phone with his forefinger.

"The Eddie that's been texting you. 'Wish you'd been able to make it last night. How are you?'" he read before I was able to grab the phone away from him. "There's a missed call from him too. But he didn't leave a voicemail." He turned to Devin, "You should see this guy. Pretty hot. At least in the picture she's got." He winked. "You might have some competition. Look at the effect he gets with a measly text. Can't even *imagine* what the sex is like. OMG."

Mateus was right. Just seeing Eddie's name pop up on my phone made it feel like I was suddenly going fast in a down elevator.

"See, look how red she is?" Mateus laughed. "Now Dr. Thomas, why haven't you told us about Eddie before?" And then I saw it on his face the second he put it all together. "Oh you *did* tell us about him! You told us *all* about him! Hot Eddie! The hot scrub tech with the big dick—"

"Mateus, please shut up—"

"Call Eddie to get the stuff! I want to meet Hot Eddie—"

"Jesus Christ," Devin interrupted him. "I said I'd get it already. Rachel, can we please get out of here?"

22

"Just promise me I'm not your drug mule," Devin said as we pulled up in front of the condo. "Because that could be a problem for me. If I got caught, I mean." When I didn't laugh, he said, "You really never know when I'm kidding, do you? Man, you're so serious all the time."

I watched him drive off down the street, now in the direction of the Valley. In the direction of the Valley Hospital, to be specific. It would be nice to imagine that he was doing it because he wanted to help me, but I knew his generosity had more to do with getting Blair and Russell off his back, and getting on with his day.

The best part was that he didn't know exactly what it was that he was picking up, so he was probably only half-kidding when he made that comment about being a drug mule. Somehow, I had managed to keep him completely out of the loop. And as long as he didn't open the cooler Hector was going to give him, it would stay that way.

Now that I was alone, I couldn't stop myself from reading Eddie's text once more. And even though it was only two lines, less than twenty words, sent over an hour ago, I let that warm churning start up in my gut again.

Mateus had been wrong. There *was* a voicemail.

I was afraid to listen to it. Afraid to hear his voice. Afraid that—as always—his words would be a letdown. The chances were pretty low that the message would be: "Rachel, I'm so sorry for all of the pain I've caused you. I had no idea how much I've hurt you. It's just that I've never loved anyone as much as I love you and it scares me."

Girl. Pull it together already. You haven't heard from the guy in months. He sent that same text to five girls. He probably doesn't even know who he sent it to. That's what a scumbag he is.

But he did call.

Remember sitting on Jake's couch in that ruined Calvin Klein dress you couldn't return?

But maybe he was just—

Don't say it!!!!

—intimidated.

Don't start with that shit.

I wound up not opening the voicemail. Truthfully, because the unknown leaves room for possibilities. For pleasant surprises and fantasies. For me, the unknown is better than a sickening halt. I'm a weak, blithering coward.

Anyway, as soon as I entered the condo, Blair abruptly ended my routine tortured internal Eddie struggle. *Who did I think I was, some A-list actress that could just saunter onto the set whenever I felt like it? And I better not be getting any bad habits from my loser co-star, or I would wind up just like him.* I wasn't sure what that was supposed to mean, since he was an actor and I was a plastic surgeon, but I just listened silently, waited for her to finish. And then we got back to work like nothing had happened.

"So, what makes you the 'Lipo Queen?'" was the question from Blair that I was supposed to be answering. She was like a professional heckler. "What makes you so unique? What makes you better at your job than everyone else?"

I was uncomfortably perched on a wooden barstool in front of the blue canvas backdrop and all I could think about was my phone, tucked in the inside front pocket of my jacket. I folded my arms, pressing it tighter against my chest. What if Devin got lost? Or what if there was an accident and he needed to take the back roads to get around the traffic? He didn't have a navigation system in that old car of his.

"I'm good at liposuction?" I shifted my weight around on the stool. Those lights seemed especially hot today. The back of my neck felt sunburned.

"Can you be just a *little* bit more convincing?"

What if the cooler fell onto the floor while he was turning a corner and the container spilled all over the back of the car?

"Dr. Thomas?"

"Maybe because I…" The truth was, I didn't have a good answer. At least not a tangible one that I could put into words. I'd never really thought about it. As far as I knew, I wasn't doing anything new or different. From a technical standpoint, I was just sucking fat off like everybody else.

"Don't use weak words like 'maybe.'" Blair said. "No 'maybes'. Why are you better? Why are you better than the other two hundred plastic surgeons down the hall from you?"

"Because I—"

"Come on, Doc, you know how to do this. Start with 'What makes me the Lipo Queen.'"

"What makes me the 'Lipo Queen…'" It was impossible to concentrate on anything besides an image of the leeches writhing around on the floor mats and under the front seats of Devin's car.

"Doctor Thomas!"

Oh, fuck. No matter what was happening, I wasn't going to be able to do anything until this stupid interview was over. The faster I came up with some dramatic statement for Blair, the faster I'd be out of there.

"What makes me the 'Lipo Queen,'" I began again, still not sure where I was going with this. Was it time for me reveal to the world my crazy neuroses about my own body? Was I going to have to air out my own personal skeletons to keep people watching? Should I talk about how—as Jake put it—each liposuction case was like a 'reckoning' with my warped childhood?

No way. No way was Blair going to get that from me.

Besides, wasn't it more than just that? And as I thought about it—*really* thought about it for the first time—I found some words that actually made sense, without sounding like I was undergoing psychoanalysis: "What makes me better at my job than anyone else…is that I see things that other people don't see. I see the potential in everyone."

"What do you mean?" Blair said, doing impatient circular motions with her hand to speed things up.

What *did* I mean? Let's see…maybe if I just kept talking the words would make themselves up. That approach seemed to be working for me so far.

"Everyone walks around with an ideal in their head of what they would like to look like."

"So what are you saying? That you're just helping people strive for some unobtainable level of perfection?"

"No." I paused. "I'm not talking about that perfect photo-shopped image of a supermodel. Of course, everyone wants to be beautiful. It's human nature. It's not even just human nature—it's in our genetic imprint, and to deny it is just going against our DNA. Did you know that we're the only animals who use intellectual reasoning to alter our choices for our mates? We're constantly fighting our inclination for natural selection—"

"Okay, please don't go all scientific here, Doc. Remember, the IQ of our average viewer is—"

"But this is important." I took a deep breath, reaching for the perfect words, because I felt like I was finally on to something, and I wanted to say it right. "We cannot deny that natural selection exists. And as humans we think about everything—and as women, we *talk* about everything—and natural selection affects not just how we pick our mate, or get picked, but how we feel about ourselves. What I do helps women feel better about themselves, not necessarily because they're looking for mates, but because we all want to feel attractive. And as women, how we feel about our bodies affects us more than how we feel about our faces."

Not only was this making sense, but I was actually no longer bullshitting.

"You don't *feel* your face," I continued. "You get up in the morning and you look in the mirror and you put some makeup on and that's it. You forget about it. But you *feel* your body. You *feel* your thighs rub together when you walk, and you *feel* the flesh hanging over the back of your jeans when you're sitting in traffic. Not everyone worships the unobtainable. Most of us have realistic ideas about improving our bodies in the areas that bother us."

I held my breath, waiting for Blair to tell me to stop trying to sound so intellectual but instead she said, "Keep going."

"For instance, *my* ideal for *my*self is different than a swimsuit model's, and hers is different from someone who's lost a hundred pounds with a gastric bypass and just wants to get rid of all the extra skin. It's just that some of these things we can't change on our own. And that's where I come in. I help people get closer to their personal ideal."

"Okay."

An "Okay" from Blair was like an A+. On par with being a "good" surgeon. I silently congratulated myself.

"Now tell us about your personal liposuction experience."

"*My* experience?"

"Yes. I heard you wish you could've done it yourself."

When I didn't say anything, she continued, "Come on, Doc. We all know about your fucked-up little liposuction."

This was nuts. How could they know? The only person who'd seen my bare thighs since 2013 was Eddie and straight guys don't usually notice those things. Especially once your clothes are off and they have full access. Not even Jenny knew about it. And I certainly hadn't mentioned it to anyone since my reign as "Lipo Queen" began. I mean, what was I going to do with a new patient—tell them how I was going to change their life and then pull down my pants and say, *"But I promise, yours won't look like this. If only I could have done it myself"*?

"Doc, what do you think happens when you go on TV? You don't think your friends and colleagues are gonna start coming out of the woodwork with all kinds of good dirt on you? So they can become famous too? Or at least make a little money? Besides, do you want to be a hypocrite?"

I hadn't spoken to any of my colleagues since I'd left the hospital. And aside from Jenny, with everything that had been going on, I didn't really have any other friends left. "But Blair, don't you think it's counterproductive to scare people about it? I mean, don't you think that it would hurt my practice?"

"Your practice isn't my responsibility. The 'Lipo Queen' Neilson ratings are. This is a great storyline."

And then, only because my phone started buzzing—and it could have just been a junk email because it was a little early for Devin to have made it back from the Valley but I couldn't take any chances—and I had nipple viability on my hands, I fabricated a detailed story for Blair about my humiliating truth, and that it was my lifelong goal to abolish the stigma of liposuction.

"Now *that's* good TV," Blair said when she finally let me go.

I didn't even check my phone—just ran downstairs and found Devin waiting for me at the curb. I was relieved to see the intact cooler on the floor of his car and no sign on his face that he'd figured out what was in it.

"I guess you found it okay," I said as I got in.

He didn't say anything to me until we were back out into the nearly standstill traffic on Sunset. "That place is something else. You *worked* there?"

I nodded.

"Pretty sketchy area."

"Tell me about it." I almost launched into a description of the grueling experience of working in a trauma center in such a high crime district, but then remembered who I was talking to. *He doesn't care about the ins and outs of your fascinating career. He's an actor. He's acting now. Practicing being interested in me. This is probably like a workshop for him.* I cut myself short and just said, "Thanks so much. For going."

"No problem." He smiled. "I felt bad for you. Blair's such a bitch."

"I've dealt with worse." I stared out the window, willing the barely moving cars in front of us to make it through the light.

"Yeah, I guess residency training and all, it's pretty rough, huh?" he said.

Maybe I was wrong. Maybe he was interested? No, I didn't have time to get all caught up in a roller coaster ride of emotions while Devin Breeze charmed me into thinking he was interested in anything about me. He was just being polite, making conversation while we sat in this ungodly traffic. Besides, what if he was the one who ratted me out on my shitty lipo? Had he felt the waviness under the leather pants?

"It's tough. Just like the military." There. That was a flip, cool answer. I remained detached and uninterested, concentrating on what was important— the task that lay ahead.

I had figured the best way to do this would be to break the whole leech thing to Nancy at the last possible moment. Like the moment I scooped a couple of leeches from the container and placed them on her nipples. All she knew was that she and I were going to meet back in the office for a couple of hours this afternoon so I could give her some extra "treatment" to help the bruising go away faster. Right now, she and her friend were killing time with some lunch and shopping. Lunch, shopping and leech therapy. Just a typical Sunday afternoon in Beverly Hills.

We'd moved two blocks in ten minutes and I could tell Devin was getting extremely bored the way he kept sighing and checking his phone.

"So." He took me off guard by suddenly turning toward me and grinning. "Are you going to tell me what's in the cooler?"

It was impossible to ignore the unmistakable sloshing sounds coming from the back of the car.

I shook my head. "Trust me. You don't want to know."

He laughed. "Now I *really* want to know." Maybe he wasn't interested in *me*, but he did sound as though I'd genuinely piqued his curiosity. It really was the first time he was even *pretending* to pay attention to me outside of filming anything. Still, my lips were absolutely sealed on this one. We began a very cute chitchat back and forth of, "Come on, just tell me," and, "No, really I can't" and at one point he even playfully squeezed my leg with his free hand to try to get me to talk.

Then it was back to reality once we were in the office again and I had to prepare the newsbreak to Nancy about how live leeches were going to be attached to her nipples. There's nothing couture about leeches, even the ones that have flown first class across the country and cost almost six hundred dollars. And *these* were just the bargain basement leftovers.

At least this time Mateus was wearing shoes.

"Quiet," he whispered, holding his finger to his lips. "She's in the room."

Oh, God. Now he was acting like he was in some kind of detective show.

"Mateus, go wait in there and tell her I'll be right in," I said.

Devin had insisted on carrying the cooler inside for me, so I directed him back to the substerile area where he placed it on the counter. I expected him to take off then as fast as he usually did when the work was done. But this time he just continued to stand there, arms crossed, blocking the cooler.

"Thanks," I said.

"Sure."

Why wasn't he leaving? I needed to take the leeches out. *In private.*

When he still didn't budge I added, "You can go, you know."

"I know." He smiled.

This was an ironic turn of events. Now all I wanted was to get rid of him and he didn't seem to want to leave. "Don't worry about me. I can get a cab later." I forced a laugh. "If Jenny's not back with my car by then—"

"You're really not going to show me what the big secret is in there?"

I shook my head. "Please, don't ask me to do that."

"So, I just risked my life in the worst neighborhood in town and I don't even get to find out why?"

"Even if I told you, you wouldn't understand—" When I tried to reach around him to get to the cooler, he stopped me by grabbing my shoulders.

"You're killing me." He pressed his fingertips just underneath the end of each side of my collarbone and when he released them it left the tingling sensation of a massage.

Killing *him*? *He* was killing *me* with that TV star grin of his while I had a real-life crisis to tend to.

I closed my eyes so I wouldn't have to look into his beautiful face and I could remind myself what I was doing here on a Sunday afternoon in my office in the first place. I had a potentially serious complication on my hands. I didn't have time for this playful banter. I'd already lost my job at the hospital. Patients like Nancy were all I really had left of my professional life and I'd already fucked up enough by not seeing her yesterday. Fine. If it was the only way I was going to expeditiously get on with this business, I'd let him see the damn leeches. And why did I care so much what he thought, anyway? *Again. D-lister. Prop. Loser.*

I opened my eyes. "You have to promise not to tell Blair. Or anyone else. Ever."

In retrospect, he never actually promised. He just took hold of my shoulders again, and I tried to will away the warm feeling that started spreading over my entire body.

"Jeez, why would I do that, anyway? You should have figured out by now that I can't stand her."

"Fine."

He leaned over my shoulder and watched as I unlatched the cooler lid and pulled out the clear plastic Tupperware container. There was a clump of leeches attached to the inside of the walls. With gloved hands I uncapped the top and plucked one of the little guys out for examination. He was slippery and writhed a bit between my two fingers. I lost my grip and he flipped out onto the counter.

"What…is that?" Devin said as I went after the leech before it slithered off between the cabinet and the wall. That was when I heard a thump behind me and I spun around to see Devin collapsed in a chair that was—fortunately—right behind him.

"Rachel, I'm not…feeling so hot…" His eyes fluttered. The sun-kissed color had drained from his face.

Crap. I'd seen that look before. I suddenly realized I had a second patient on my hands.

"Devin!" I yelled at him but he didn't respond. Instead, he promptly slumped over, his head hanging to the side.

I shook his arm but it remained limp. His eyelids were still half open and I could see that his eyes had rolled up and back into his head. I was up to speed with my CPR and ACLS, but Devin had a strong radial pulse and he was breathing fine. I wasn't good with this simple stuff like dizziness and passing out.

Crap. I'd expected him to be grossed out by the leeches, disgusted, or even let down by the anticlimactic element of the "reveal"—I mean, the way I was carrying on about it you'd have thought I had some green glowing kryptonite rock in that cooler. But I hadn't expected him to lose consciousness.

What did the nurses do when this happened? I propped his feet up on a nearby trash can and tried to drag his body down in the chair to lower his head as much as I could. I lay some cool, damp paper towels across his forehead. I'd seen someone do that before. I wasn't sure if it was on TV or in my office but it seemed like a good idea. He still didn't wake up. I glanced around the room. *Aha!* There was a package of smelling salts that Adeta kept taped to the cabinet door. I activated it and waved it under his nose. He immediately grimaced and shook his head to get away from the ammonia stink.

Devin opened his eyes. "What happened?"

"You had a vasovagal," I said.

"What?"

"You fainted."

"Oh." He looked like he didn't believe me.

"It's a physiologic mechanism triggered by pain, or fear, or—anything, really," I prattled on. "Normally when your blood pressure drops, your heart speeds up to compensate and keep it up, but in this case the vagus nerve stimulates both to drop."

"I fainted? That's never happened to me before."

"Oh, don't worry, it happens all the time," I lied. It seemed that I had successfully revived him. Was I done? Was it safe to just leave him here and take care of my real patient with the dying nipples now? What else would Adeta do?

There was a portable monitor in the corner of the room. Oh, right. I could take his vitals. I really was a terrible nurse.

"Doctor Thomas?" Mateus yelled from down the hall.

"Give me a minute!" I wheeled the monitor over to Devin and stuck the pulse ox on his finger. As I had anticipated, he was fine. One hundred percent and his heart rate was hanging out around seventy-eight.

"Hey, can you get that thing away from me, please?" Devin shrunk back in the chair.

"Oh, sorry." I'd forgotten I still had the leech clutched in my left hand.

"Hey, you'd better—I think they're getting away." He pointed to where a few of the leeches had navigated over the rim of their mobile home and started dropping to the floor. I scooped them all back inside and closed the lid.

"Rachel, what are you doing with those…things?"

After I had secured the cap back onto the jar I wrapped the blood pressure cuff around his arm and pushed the button. I lowered my voice. "Leech therapy."

"What's that?"

"They help the blood supply."

"But…how? What are you going to do with them?"

This is exactly what I had been trying to avoid—explaining the nitty gritty, and somewhat nasty, details. I avoided eye contact with my next words. "Put them on her nipples."

"You're kidding, right?"

"I wish I was." I spoke as fast as I could, hoping that if I could wow him with the science of it all he wouldn't concentrate on the graphic image he was probably conjuring up in his head. "It's a mainstay of treatment. They relieve venous congestion by sucking out the blood, and they have this chemical they inject from their saliva—it's called 'hirudin'. It thins the blood so it flows better."

"Does *she* know about it?" He motioned toward the hallway and the closed exam room door.

"Not yet," I admitted.

"Yeah, well…good luck with that."

"She'll be okay. Usually the patients are surprisingly open-minded about it. The last one I had to do this for actually gave them names." Yeah, but that guy had been sitting in the ICU for two days with a thumb replant after a work accident. This was an attractive party girl who'd just had elective surgery, and we were in an office where the parking was twenty dollars.

One-fifteen over seventy. The automatic blood pressure cuff deflated itself.

"Am I gonna live?" Devin said.

"I should get you some water."

"Hey." He grabbed my arm as I started to walk away. "Sorry about that. I guess I kind of have a problem with slimy little creatures like that."

"It's not your fault." I tried to smile. "But don't say I didn't tell you so."

When he was done drinking, he made a weak effort to get up but I pushed him back down. He didn't fight me. He still didn't look like himself. The honey glow of his tan hadn't completely returned to his face.

"Just wait here," I ordered. "I need to check you again before you leave."

It was true. I *should* check him again. In fact, I really should keep him here for observation for at least an hour. Maybe longer. *What if he stumbled around and hit his head?* It could become a major medico-legal issue. I was just being a cautious physician.

"Sure," he said.

Fortunately, even with Mateus squealing uncontrollably to the point where I had to step on his foot to shut him up, neither Nancy nor her friend reacted to the leeches the way Devin had. In fact, they seemed to find the whole activity rather intriguing.

"Whatever you think, Dr. Thomas," Nancy said. "You're the doctor."

"I've heard of that," her friend said, without looking up from her stack of tabloids. "The leech thing. I saw it on the Discovery Channel."

But this is not the Discovery Channel, I could hear Gloria's voice.

And then, as I got close to Nancy, preparing to unveil her breasts once again, I got an unmistakable whiff of a scent that was normally very comforting and familiar. Though, this time, it was just the opposite.

"Nancy, were you smoking?"

She hesitated, then said, "Just one."

"I thought you told me before the surgery that you didn't smoke."

"I don't. I mean, not really. I don't buy my own cigarettes."

I don't buy my own therefore I am not really a smoker. Sadly, I did understand the logic. That bumming cigarettes off your friends when you're out drinking doesn't count. But operative sites don't know a bought cigarette from a borrowed one. Nicotine is nicotine, and it doesn't matter what shape or form it comes in. Even just the tiniest bit can squeeze down on all those microscopic blood vessels and cause bad things like this to happen, and make your surgeon tear their hair out and want to jump off a bridge. Especially if they're trying to sneak it by a power-hungry producer who would showcase anything for ratings.

"Nancy, I told you I wouldn't do this operation if you smoked," I said. "I told you what it could do to the blood supply. Especially since this was a re-do."

Although I was furious about the deception, I would be lying if I said I didn't feel a twinge of relief knowing whatever happened wasn't going to be my fault. I *knew* I'd been careful and done everything right.

I was also relieved to discover that when I removed the dressings and washed off the nitropaste, the color of the areolas had somewhat improved.

At least now some of the dusky areas weren't as dark, and the borderline areas looked pinker. I had prayed to the nipple God and he had answered me. Still, I wasn't taking any chances. I started with two leeches on each side.

"They're so skinny," Nancy said. "I thought they'd be fatter."

"Oh, they will be," Mateus said. "They start out skinny and then after they get full from sucking all the blood they get fat and fall off."

"Thank you," I said to Mateus. "For giving us that visual."

It was also a good sign that the leeches attached themselves right away to the skin. If you try to put them on dead tissue that's already beyond hope they'll start shifting around, looking for greener pastures.

I left Mateus in charge of leech duty and slipped out of the room to check on Devin. I had to make sure he was okay, didn't I? It was just the responsible thing to do.

I caught a glimpse of myself in the hallway mirror and smoothed down my hair before I swung open the door to the substerile room.

"Devin, how are you feeling—"

The room was empty. I did a quick search of the rest of the office but he was gone.

Fine. So he got better and left. What had I expected him to do, anyway, sit around and wait for me? I'd already told him I didn't need a ride.

I should have known. Sure, today I'd gotten to be his doctor. But who was I kidding? I wasn't his girlfriend.

23

I leeched Nancy the rest of that afternoon. Fortunately, she was distracted enough with Mateus' little sideshow that she didn't seem to mind what was going on. We went through two rounds of leeches and by that evening I was satisfied with her improvement. When I saw her the next morning, her nipples had totally turned the corner. And at her first "official" post-op visit, with Blair and all of the cameras there, it was like nothing had happened. And just like I'd hoped, I didn't lose a cell of skin.

"Okay, I have a few *questions* from the network. Starting with—what is *this?*" Blair shoved a photograph across my kitchen table at me.

It was the next Saturday morning. We were preparing to shoot a scene of Devin and myself, sharing precious moments together over a leisurely weekend breakfast. It was the first time I'd seen or even spoken to him since—as Mateus liked to refer to it—"the leech fiasco." Today he'd shown up without even a subtle wink of subterfuge in my direction. As if our prior escapades had never happened.

Which was for the best, really. That's the way I'd wanted it to go. *Then why was his pointedly neutral facial expression bothering me?* I wondered, when Blair snapped me back to the present with her grinding voice.

"Excuse me?" I said.

"I said, 'What's this?' One of Gloria's interns found it on TMZ."

"It looks like a picture." It was a close-up of me walking by a Forever 21 store. Whoever took it had caught Jake in the shot. It must have been taken with a zoom lens because I don't remember anyone getting any pictures of me. Not that I often worried about that sort of thing. I wasn't really recognizable and alone, I wasn't worth much to the paparazzi. I wasn't a famous pop singer or a socialite heiress. I was still just a doctor.

"I think that was supposed to be a rhetorical question," Devin said, without looking away from the back of the cereal box.

"Where was this?" Blair demanded.

"At a mall in the Valley, I think," I said. It must have been shot a while ago, because I hadn't had time to get Jake out to any of our usual haunts for almost a month. Which made seeing that picture all the more painful.

"And what were you doing there, at this mall in the Valley?" Blair said to me.

"Ummm—shopping?"

"Doc." Blair rolled her eyes. "The Lipo Queen *does not shop* at malls in the Valley. What could you possibly need from a mall in the Valley? At Forever 21?"

"I wasn't *at* Forever 21—"

"If you want to shop, go to Robertson," she continued. "Go to Melrose. If you feel the need to hit a mall, go to the Beverly Center. But please, don't be seen walking around ghetto malls in the Valley. It's bad publicity."

"I thought there was no such thing as bad publicity."

"Okay, then we won't call it 'bad.' We'll call it *'harmful.'*" She rolled her eyes. "Now. Someone's bound to ask about the creepy guy with you. So who should we say it is?"

I had anticipated that that would be Blair's next question, and fortunately she had given me enough time with her ranting about where I should be shopping to formulate a well-constructed answer. It was just that I could taste the awfulness of the words I had to say: "I don't know. I've never seen him before. I guess they just caught him in the shot."

"He's walking *extremely* close for a stranger. You better make sure nothing's missing from your purse."

Devin leaned in to study the picture over my shoulder. "She's lying," he said, and my heart stopped for a second until he added, "It's her other boyfriend."

He glanced at me. "I'm kidding, dummy. That. Was. A. Joke."

"How nice for you. There's one more thing." Blair returned to her phone and started scrolling. "Shit, I keep forgetting about this email. Doc, we need a copy of your certification thing. Yeah, I think that's…" She was silent for a second as she squinted at the screen and made the image larger. "Yeah. That's what they want. 'Proof of board certification.' The network keeps asking. Legal needs it for something. I promised Gloria I'd have it to her by Monday."

When I didn't answer her immediately, Blair said, "What?"

"Duh," Devin said. "She doesn't have it. What do you think she's been studying for?" He pointed at the prop newspaper that neither of us was reading. Partially hidden under it was my stack of study material. Photocopies of the old board questions circulating around on the black market. Now that the exam was creeping up closer on the tangible horizon, I had started to seriously buckle down. I was no longer just studying lazily on the weekends, or falling asleep at night with the book on my face in bed with the lights on. I had kicked it into high gear, carrying books and flashcards around with me during the day, using every small window of studying opportunity. Sometimes there would be time in the office or between cases, or—in this case, this morning—while we waited for the crew to finish setting up for the shoot. Basically, I was in cram mode.

"Isn't that the big test coming up?" Devin spoke while he crunched through spoonfuls of cereal. "Your boards, right?"

There was a reason I had never brought this subject up with Blair. I instinctively did not think she should know about the boards, the way I didn't think she should know about the leeches. It was too serious of a situation to let her turn into a circus.

"How do you know about the boards?" I demanded.

"Oh, I pay more attention to detail than you think."

No time or space to spend interpreting the possible flirtatious innuendos there. Blair was back in my face. "What do you mean, you don't *have* it? How do you not *have* it? How did we manage to hire the only fucking plastic surgeon in Beverly Hills without any media experience *or* board certification?"

I tried to start explaining that I actually *wasn't* the only one, how the process takes a couple of years to finish even *after* we're done with all the training, that it's not automatically handed to us like a high school diploma, but she ignored me and instead got on her phone.

Devin and I listened to her pace back and forth in the next room, alternately blurting expletives and apologies to who must have been Gloria.

Devin raised his eyebrows at me. "Straight down the pipeline on a Saturday afternoon."

When she returned to the kitchen, Blair was an even paler shade of her usual chalk.

"Doc, we've got a problem. This show was contingent on us having a board-certified surgeon."

I saw no reason to ignite her fire any further with the most obvious question: *Then how come nobody asked me?*

So I just said, "It's not my fault."

"It may not be your fault, but it's your problem." Blair ran both of her hands through her greasy hair. "Fuck, it's *all* our problem. It's *my* problem. They could pull the show."

Pull the show? Really? All the crap on the air these days and the way they made me act and the network was going to cancel a show because the surgeon wasn't board-certified?

"That's stupid," I said. "Nobody even knows what it means."

"Legal knows. And Legal needs it."

"But I can't—the test isn't for another month." *Lipo Queen* had become my livelihood. *What would happen without it? Would patients still come to see me? Would my unpaid bills start piling up again?* "But how—what about Gloria's husband?"

"Legal trumps everything." Blair glared at me. "For now she said just go ahead today as planned while she figures something out."

"Shit," Devin said. "And here I thought I was about to get the day off."

24

"Thom, how long have you been up here? Your coping mechanisms suck, by the way." Jenny faked a cough. My half-hearted attempts to get the cigarette smoke to blow out the bedroom window had not been successful, and the room air was getting hazy.

"You found me."

"When did you guys finish shooting?"

"About an hour ago." I exhaled smoke toward the window, but it blew right back in my face. "Jenny, if they cancel the show and we're on our own again, are we fucked?"

"You want to look at the bank account?"

I looked back out the window. "Of course not."

Yes, this was how I ran my small business. At least it was consistent with the way I ran my life right now—avoiding true reality.

But it was Jenny's ensuing silence that tipped me off. Normally in a situation like this she would be running her mouth at high speed in an attempt to make me feel better.

I turned so I could see her face. "What."

"What?" Her voice was a little too high pitched.

"Jenny, you're a fucking terrible actress. Tell me what you know."

"I don't know what you're talking about."

"You know something."

She sighed. "I don't think we should do this right now."

"Stop with the cryptic bullshit and give me the intel."

"I think you should get some rest—"

"What. Do. You. Know."

She crossed her arms and looked away from me. "Put that out first."

"*What do you know?*"

"Put out the cigarette."

"Don't be judging me—you were the one doing crack cocaine until six weeks into your pregnancy."

"Fuck you! How do you know that?"

"You were bragging about it."

"Oh." Her tone went down a notch. I think she realized she had just said "Fuck you" to her boss. "I stopped as soon as I found out. And Zoey's fine. She's really advanced for her age, you know."

I pulled my knees up to my chest and shifted my weight around to get more comfortable on the windowsill. "Everyone's kids in L.A. are advanced for their age."

We both smiled weakly. It was one of our running jokes. "Jenny. Please. What's going on?"

"Fine, but maybe you really should get away from that window." She remained in the doorway. "I heard the crew guys talking about it when I came in."

"How do *they* know before *me*?"

"Blair was on the phone with Gloria again while they were packing up."

"And?"

"She's going to keep the show going. Thom, this chain-smoking thing is fucking disgusting."

"Shut up." I waited. Then: "So she's keeping the show."

"As long as you pass the test."

"Okay." I exhaled. I hadn't realized I'd been holding my breath. So…*okay*. Not such a big deal. I'd never failed a test before in my life. I was *planning* to pass. Before this show became my whole life, even my job at the *hospital* had been riding on it. So now *this* "job" was riding on it. So what was the difference? "That was easy, right?"

Again, Jenny's uncharacteristic silence and see-through face confirmed my gut.

"There *is* a but."

I exhaled smoke directly at her. "Cut the bullshit."

"It's not bullshit. There is a but."

"Well, here's a butt for you, bitch." I stubbed out the rest of the cigarette and threw it at her. She jumped away but she really hadn't needed to. It only made it a few feet across the room and landed in a pile of Sushi's toys.

"Thom! What is wrong with you?"

"Nothing." I put a new cigarette in my mouth and unsuccessfully struck a match. "Just that my entire life rides on this stupid TV show that even *I* wouldn't watch."

"Stop smoking."

"Not until you tell me."

"Fine." She looked away again. "They want to shoot it."

"Shoot what?"

"The test, the resort, the whole thing…They're going to follow you to Phoenix."

"Don't you dare fuck with me like that."

Jenny shrugged her shoulders. "I told you you wouldn't like it."

"But why would they want to bother with that? How is that even interesting?"

"From what I understand…They're going to make a big point that the survival of your show—and, I guess, you—hinges on whether or not you pass. Like a real-life thriller." She contemplated. "No, more like an elimination show with one contestant. It's kind of brilliant, actually."

I was starting to feel so dizzy that I actually did slide off the windowsill and into a nearby chair. *Wasn't it enough that I had to endure what was historically the most grueling ritual in a plastic surgeon's professional career? Now I was going to have to do it with the rest of the world watching?*

"Oh, come on Thom, chill out and think about it for a minute. What's the problem? You're going to pass. And to be honest, they need to liven things up around here. The storyline with you and that dude is boring."

"I am *not* boring!"

"You know what I meant. There's no real angst in your life. They need a good struggle for you."

I successfully lit the cigarette on my third try. "Ha. Now *that's* funny." I thought about the picture of Jake and myself and Forever 21 and how it was like re-opening a scab.

No angst.

It's good to keep a scab on a wound because then you can't see the ugliness festering underneath.

25

I'm still trying to understand exactly what's going on in the Middle East. And no matter how many times someone explains it to me, I don't get what happened in 2008 to make the market crash. But I am always shamelessly up to date on pertinent celebrity gossip. I will say that I know that I'm not alone in my thirst for pop culture knowledge; you could do a Candid Camera in my office, the way the patients beeline over to the magazine rack and fish out the latest rags the minute they walk through the door.

But now that *I* was the occasional subject of the photographs inside these magazines, it was fascinating to learn how the pop culture machine really worked.

I *know* that most of what we read is sensationalized, or hearsay, and shouldn't be taken as gospel. But the *real* news to me was discovering that a lot of what I *saw*—the internet celebrity home pages, the magazines, the spots on *E!*—was just part of a virtual reality that *really* only existed in the reader's mind.

For instance, with a once-a-week half-hour TV show and just a few images of Devin and me placed strategically in trash publications and on the internet, Gloria's production company was able to paint the deceptive picture of a loving—but tempestuous, with great sex implied—relationship.

It's not like we were *everywhere*. We wouldn't even have been considered "B list." Devin was getting recognized more frequently, but we never had photographers pressing up against store windows like flies and we weren't even close to cover material. But if you were living in Ohio, and you were thumbing through the back pages of *Us Weekly* or *In Touch* on the check-out line at Wal Mart, and you happened to come across one of those pictures of us shopping...eating...walking arm in arm down the street...in our own private little world of bliss...you would think, "How annoyingly cute are they?" and maybe even, "What does he see in *her*?" when the reality was that, aside from those few digitally captured moments, we rarely saw each other.

And even though I knew the truth, there was still a part of me that was that girl living in Ohio, who wanted to believe. I would secretly scour the magazines out in my office waiting room to see what I could find. And in case I missed one, I had Jake to help keep track for me. He had made it his job to park himself at 7-Eleven every Tuesday morning, as soon as the new ones hit the stands. He would comb through every single one of them, cover-to-cover, and he purchased everything that had even the slightest mention of *Lipo Queen*, all for an ongoing poster board collage that he was constructing at home.

One classic example of our fake relationship was a recurring staged "lunch" shoot at the same outdoor café. We made a big show of having it look like we were rushing during a small break in our busy work day, but we always did it on the weekend. Devin and I would meet in the front, both of us in a big hurry, Devin talking about some "promising meetings" he had on the horizon, and me showing up in scrubs like I'd just come out of surgery. At least I was able to convince Blair not to make me hang a stethoscope around my neck so I wouldn't look like a true asshole.

In Reality Show Land we were near my office, but the restaurant we shot at was actually a new bistro located across town in Santa Monica where the owners fed our entire crew for free. I hated going there. The thing about Santa Monica is that—from a distance—it's a beautiful city, with its famous palm tree-lined walkway along the ocean and the exhilarating Ferris-wheel-and-roller-coaster skyline at the pier. But when you look around closely—when you *really* look—what comes into focus are the scattered human figures wrapped up in blankets, slumped over and sleeping on the ground under the palm trees. Up close, in front of the sunshine and the blue sky and the brilliant aqua water, are the spaced-out loners wandering around, pushing shopping carts, talking to themselves. This end of the city housed many of the local soup kitchens, and notoriously had one of the highest homeless populations in all of Los Angeles.

It wasn't that I was disgusted because all of the filthy loiterers ruined the scenery. It was just that I couldn't look at them without knowing the real reason they were homeless; pretty much all of them were mentally ill. A bunch of schizophrenic and bipolar souls, psychotic and delusional, segregated from society. I couldn't look at them without seeing Jake.

This particular day I had actually miscalculated and arrived early. While I waited on the bistro's outdoor patio for everyone else to show up, I couldn't stop staring at a little gnome of a woman taking down her cardboard house in the doorway of a cupcake shop across the street. She couldn't have been more than four feet tall and she wore a baggy sundress and flip-flops that exposed her permanently dirty feet. She spoke to the air as she dismantled the structure, neatly folding it up and leaning it against the wall of the building. When she was done, she settled herself down on the ground with a cigarette.

My study materials sat in an untouched pile on the table in front of me as I sipped an iced tea, unable to tear my eyes from her, yet desperately wishing I hadn't seen her. Then I couldn't stop myself. I felt around in my pocket as I crossed the street and when I reached her, I held out my hand with what I had been able to find. A five and two singles.

She took the money without saying a word. I was unable to tell from her empty expression if she could even see me. In her defense it was an unusually hot day, but she reeked of pungent body odor as if she hadn't had a shower in a month. I felt my eyes grow moist and I had to collect myself before I ruined my makeup. As I crossed the street again, I thought about how a cupcake from the store she lived in front of sold for almost as much money as I'd just given her. Money that would last her all week.

As painful as it was to come over to this part of town, I needed the reality check. It was like getting an ice bucket dumped over my head, waking me up from the hazy daydream of my new life…my fancy new practice…my pictures in tabloids…wasting my time with a guy who was completely indifferent to my existence…

I had to remind myself why I was doing this stupid TV show in the first place. As I poured another packet of Splenda into my iced tea, I took a silent oath to start saving my money for that house on the bluff again. That Jake would never wind up like these drifters, that he was never going to be an unkempt, overweight man pushing a shopping cart around and talking to the air.

I was just about to call and check in with him when everyone else started showing up. *So I'll surprise him later on with a visit. Instead of working out at the downstairs gym I'll take him to the movies or something. I'll call him as soon as I'm back in the car on my way home.*

Turned out I didn't have to. Just as we were served our food I got three calls in a row from him. I hit "ignore" the first two times, figuring I'd call him back when I was done, and as always, he would understand. But the microphone had picked up the vibration from my phone.

"Whose phone?" Blair said.

"Not mine," Devin said, his mouth full of french fries. It was annoying how magically fit he was, even though he ate like a teenager. Someone his age should at least have love handles.

"Who is it?" Blair said to me.

The phone was buzzing for the fourth time, and I looked at the number, praying it would be someone else. It wasn't.

"Uhh…Jenny …" I said because at that moment I couldn't think of a single other name. "It's Jenny."

"Why don't you answer it?"

"Ummm…because I don't feel like talking to her right now," I said. "We're in a big fight."

I should have known better.

"Perfect. Answer it and have a fight with her on the phone. Liven this episode up. You guys are getting so boring. And it's fucking hot out here today."

The phone continued to buzz.

"Doc, answer it!" Blair yelled at me. The usual handful of oglers shrank back a few steps behind the roped-off restaurant terrace.

Could I have a phone conversation with Jake on camera without Blair catching on? And why wouldn't he stop calling me? If there were a problem, wouldn't Maria have called? It was a Saturday afternoon. *One of the days she cleaned and stocked his refrigerator. What could possibly be wrong?*

Really? This was *Jake.* I tapped "call receive."

"Yeah, what is it?" I said, hating that I had to talk to him like that. But supposedly it was Jenny on the other end, and *supposedly* we were fighting. "What's going on?"

"What is it, *Jenny*," Blair commanded. "Say her name so we know who you're talking to. And sound bitchier."

But Blair's words were drowned out by Jake's voice into my right ear: "Rachel, your car has been in an accident."

It took me a few seconds to orient myself to the conversation. My *car…?* *The Porsche…?* What now? Had Jenny taken it again? Hadn't I just parked in the lot down the street? And why would *Jake* be calling me about it?

"I'm really sorry, Rachel. There was a deer. It was an accident. The roll bars work pretty well, though. I guess they're not just for decoration."

He was talking about my TT. *My brand-new little blue TT.* My zero-down-900-dollar-a-month present to myself for finishing residency, that I never missed a payment on and would be paying off for the next five years. My poor little car that wasn't sophisticated enough for the Lipo Queen and had been parked at Jake's trailer site so that Maria could do all the other concierge things I now paid her for.

"Are you and—okay?" I stopped myself just in time from yelling Maria's name. "What happened?" I lowered my voice to a hiss and put my hand over my mic. "Did Maria fuck up my car?"

"It wasn't Maria."

"Someone broke in and stole the keys?"

"Doctor Thomas! He*lloo*! We need to hear you! It's not a silent movie! You *know* how to do this. Put her on speaker, please."

"It wasn't Maria, Rachel. It was me."

Apparently what happened was that Jake had decided it was too hot to wait outside while Maria cleaned. So he would just drive himself to the beach, where the wind brought the temperature down at least ten degrees. Perfectly logical. I'd never told him he couldn't use my car, but I thought we had an understanding since he hadn't driven since his diagnosis and *he'd never learned to drive a stick.*

"What's going on?" Blair demanded. "*Tell us!*"

"I swerved so I wouldn't hit the deer," he said. "But I hit one of those big rocks and went off the road. The car flipped on its side."

"Oh my God!"

"Doc!" Blair barked at me. "Would you mind sharing?"

"I'm sorry," I said, pushing back my chair and stepping away from the table. "I have to take this privately." I made sure I was out of earshot at the other end of the patio, then I reached under my shirt and yanked the microphone off my bra, keeping it covered in a tight fist so it wouldn't catch any sound. "Jesus Christ, Jake! Are you okay?"

"I'm okay. The police are here. Can you please come?"

Fuck. This could not be happening.

"I can't come now, Jake. I'm in the middle of something important."

"They ran me on their system and they found my record. They think I stole the car and they're going to arrest me if you don't come."

"What record?"

"From that time I got arrested selling nitrous hits."

"What?"

"You know. At those concerts."

I'd forgotten about that. It had been the summer before his diagnosis. He had ingeniously gotten his hands on some nitrous tanks and sold hits at about ten concerts at arenas across the country before someone turned him in. But not before he'd made a good chunk of money.

"Jake, where are you?"

"On Kanan. Halfway to Malibu. After the first bridge."

Fuck. Fuck fuck *fuck.*

"Jake, let me talk to the police."

"He said if you don't come now they're going to arrest me."

I was tempted to let them do it, but the image of Jake in handcuffs stopped me. How could I let him go to jail when I couldn't even bear the thought of him aimlessly wandering the streets in dirty clothes as a free man?

Jake put the officer on the phone and I assured him that I was the owner of the car, and to please wait, I'd be there as soon as I could—which, based on my current location, was going to be at least an hour.

"Dr. Thomas, would you care to join us?" Blair had her hands on her hips, and was rocking back and forth on the balls of her feet when I returned to the table.

"What's going on?" Devin said. "Babe."

"Blair," I said, "I have to go."

"Now?"

"Yes. It wasn't Jenny. It's a…patient." That wasn't a complete lie. After all, Jake *was* a patient. Just not mine.

"Is everything okay?"

"I think so," I said. "But she might have to go to the hospital."

I had long since discovered Blair's Achilles heel. She aimed for drama, and she would have *loved* the leeches, but her one big fear was that if a patient really *did* go south it would be blasted all over the news and she'd lose the show. If I was going to pull out the patient-in-trouble card, now was the time. When she didn't bite immediately, I threw in some medical jargon: "I mean, if she has a seroma I'll need to drain it percutaneously, maybe put a drain in…" I could sense her getting anxious, but not quite ready to let me walk, so I tossed in the kicker: "You know, that actress we did last week…I'm sure she's fine but she's concerned about some swelling and she has a red carpet thing tonight…"

That should do it. *Actress on her way to a red carpet but might wind up in the hospital instead…talk about 'harmful' publicity.* I was getting to be a very convincing storyteller.

"Then at least let's shoot this," Blair said. "Doc, go back to the table, pretend you're getting the call, you have to leave—"

"No." I unclipped my mic and handed it to the sound guy. "I'm sorry. I really have to go. Now."

"Fine," Blair said. Even if she suspected I was lying, she'd never risk it. Motioning toward the crew and all of their equipment, she muttered, "That's certainly a waste of a day."

"Why don't we just shoot it like she never showed up because she got stuck in the O.R.?" suggested the sound guy.

"Shoot *him* by himself?" Blair said. "How boring would *that* be?"

"So you mean I got stood up? I don't know how realistic that is." Devin cocked his head to one side and said to me, "Would you ever really stand me up?" Then he signaled to the waiter, pointing at my uneaten Asian chicken salad. Actually, at this place it was an "Oriental" chicken salad. Someone needed to tell whoever was writing the menu that you can't call it that anymore. "Hey, can she take this to go?"

Blare scowled at him, then said, "Fine. Breeze, take out your phone and act like you're texting her and she's not answering you."

"I'm sorry," I said to her as I gathered up my purse and my now brown-bagged salad. "I'm not trying to be difficult. Really, if it wasn't an emergency—"

"Just go," she said. "We'll manage. I'm used to dealing with divas."

"Blair—" I started to say. I wished I could tell her what was really going on, that I wasn't just whimsically ruining the shoot and wasting everyone's time and money. If there was one thing I'd learned during all of my years in surgery, it was how to be a team player. I've never been the weak link.

Devin grabbed my waist as I passed by. He leaned up and whispered, "Hey. Be careful driving, you diva."

It took me over an hour to get to the accident scene, which had turned the canyon road into a parking lot. The beach traffic was bottlenecked in both directions, with people slowing their cars to stare at the destroyed luxury sports car and the creepy-looking obese guy standing next to it. From an onlooker's perspective it *did* look like a case of a stolen vehicle.

At least I'd had the foresight to pull my own highly identifiable flashy car with the vanity plates out of sight and into a private driveway a few houses up the road. Aside from when I was surrounded by a camera crew, I'd never had anyone recognize me in public, but I could just see the *Star Magazine* headline: "Lipo Queen's Secret Brother Almost Dies in Car Wreck—Is She as Crazy as He Is?"

I needed a better camouflage than the stupid pink scrubs. I took them off and wriggled into my emergency dinner outfit—not the easiest thing to do while hunched down in my front seat. Once I was out of the car, I made sure my face was covered with my floppy driving hat and huge sunglasses.

I avoided eye contact as I hobbled along in my Louboutins up the dirt shoulder of the road. By now most of the drivers were done staring at the sideshow up ahead and were just looking pissed-off about getting stuck and were either talking or texting on their phones. Nobody even gave me a second glance. Only in L.A. could you trek along the side of a mountain road in high heels and a designer mini-dress and blend in with the scenery.

When I saw the car up close, I couldn't believe I wasn't in a dream. That what I was seeing had really happened. My poor little TT, once a symbol of my hopes and dreams, my pride and joy since the day I drove it off the lot less than a year ago, was now tilted on its side, smashed up against the embankment and crushed in on its front end like a tin can.

I spoke as little as possible to the officer and signed everything he handed me. By showing them my I.D. and the car registration—which, fortunately, I still carried around in my wallet—I was able to assure them that this guy shuffling back and forth in the middle of the road was my brother, and that the car was not stolen.

As the officer glanced back between me and my license, I couldn't help thinking, *is he staring intensely at me, trying to see me through my huge sunglasses, trying to figure out where he knows me from?* I had to get out of there before someone from TMZ showed up. The leeches paled in comparison to this. *Did TMZ have helicopters?*

"These little cars are made to take all the impact in the front," the officer was telling me. "Bad part is that all the important stuff is right there behind the bumper. Most likely totaled." He handed my driver's license back to me. "Glad your brother's okay, Miss Thomas. Good thing the car didn't roll the other way."

I'm sure he was waiting for me to chime in wholeheartedly about how thankful I was that Jake hadn't flown over the guardrail down the side of the canyon, but all I could manage was an: "Mmmhmmm." Of course I was glad that Jake was okay. In fact, I was glad enough now, and recovered enough from the initial fear and worry, that I was stark-raving furious at him.

I had to wait for the towing company. It took them forever to get there around the backed-up traffic. By far the best part was that I hadn't bothered to renew my AAA membership and it was going to cost me $250 to drag my totaled car back to Jake's place.

"Can we put the top down, Rachel?" Jake said as soon as we started driving back.

"No."

"But it's hot."

I turned on the air conditioning.

A cigarette would have helped, but I had never really mastered the art of smoking while driving, even with an automatic transmission.

Then Jake rolled his window down and lit one.

"You can't smoke in here," I said.

He tossed it out the window.

"Jake, are you insane? You're gonna start a *fire* now?"

"It's just in the road. There's nothing there but dirt."

"Well, put the window back up. The air conditioner's on."

"Rachel, it was an accident. There was a deer."

"Right." I stared straight ahead at the road. I had to stay angry so that I couldn't feel anything else. It was the middle of August and I hadn't taken Jake to the beach once this summer. I had barely spent any time with him at all, and I couldn't decide which reasoning was worse. Was it because I had so many new, more exciting time commitments? Or was it because after Blair's reaction to the photo of the two of us at the mall, I knew that I couldn't take him anywhere public anymore?

"I just really wanted to go to the beach."

Of course he would eventually try to leave by himself. And he would have actually gotten there and back if he'd been able to drive a stick.

"Why didn't you wait for Maria to take you?"

"She said she couldn't."

"What about Mom?"

"You know she'd never come."

"Why didn't you just wait for me?"

"I couldn't wait."

"Why not?"

He just stared out the window.

"I could have taken you later."

"No, you couldn't. You don't even live here anymore. Besides, they were coming. I had to leave."

I looked sideways at him. There was that familiar inflection in his speech that gave me a bad feeling. And I didn't like the way he was staring out the window.

"Jake, what did you say?"

"Nothing." And then he mumbled something under his breath that I couldn't completely hear.

"*Who* was coming?"

"Nobody."

"Jake," I said. "You weren't going to the beach just to snorkel, were you?"

He remained silent and staring.

"Jake, are you taking your medication?"

He didn't answer me so I asked him again.

"Yes," he said, still staring out the window. "What kind of a question is that?"

"An important one."

"I'm taking it," he muttered, refusing to look at me. "I'm fine. There really was a deer, and then the fucking rock on the side of the road. I'm sorry, okay? I'm sorry about the fucking car."

Every time Jake and I had fought in our adult lives, it was for the same reason.

"Jake, I need to know."

"Need to know what?"

"If you're taking your meds. You have to tell me the truth."

"I said yes! Stop fucking asking me."

"Then who were you talking about—someone coming to get you?"

"Nobody. I was kidding."

I looked over at him again. It was unbelievable that the car could look like that and he didn't even have a scratch except a small cut above his left eyebrow.

He refused to talk to me again in the car, although I could have sworn that under the hum of the turbo-charged engine I heard him making little whispering noises to himself.

Back at his trailer I supervised the tow company's placement of the wreckage. After I finished signing everything and the tow guys had cleared out, I discovered that Jake had gone inside and locked me out.

"Jake!" I pounded on the door and then started ringing the doorbell repeatedly like little kids do. "This is really important. I don't have time to be worrying about you every minute."

He opened the door. "I'm not asking you to worry about me."

"You know what happens when you stop taking it."

"What—you're gonna put me back in the hospital? You know you can't do it against my will. I'm an adult."

"Jake, if you need help—"

"What would you know? You're never even here."

"Jesus Christ, one of the reasons I'm gone all the time is to pay your fucking bills. Who knows where the hell you'd even be living if it weren't for me? And the least you could do is not be such an asshole, since you just totaled my car."

"Yeah, well, it's not like you don't have another one. Stop fucking nagging me." And he slammed the door in my face.

I was just about to try banging again when I heard a voice behind me: "You know you can't keep that there."

I spun around to see the trailer park manager standing at the end of Jake's driveway. She was walking her dog but I think that was just an excuse to see what was going on.

"What?" I said.

"This isn't a junk yard. You need to have that thing towed by the end of the week."

I returned to the Porsche but I didn't start the ignition. I fished under the seat for my pack of stale cigarettes and smoked through the open door. I turned my head so I wouldn't have to stare directly at the remains of my car.

How could I have let this happen? Why had I left the keys with him instead of just giving them to Maria? Jake had never exactly been an angel. I thought about all of the times that he'd taken my mother's car without asking while we were growing up. Before he even had a driver's license.

My phone vibrated and Devin's number glowed on the screen. I tried to kid myself that I was so upset that I wasn't going to answer it, but of course I did.

"Hey, how's your patient?" he said.

His question threw me for a minute until I remembered the story I had told everyone.

"My patient. She's…fine."

"So…no leeches this time?"

"No. No leeches." I tried to guess why he would be calling me so I wouldn't be let down when I found out it was about work. "Does Blair want me to come back?"

"What? Oh, no, we've been done for a while. I'm home." I took that to mean his place in Silver Lake, not "our" home. "Listen, what are you doing tonight?"

"Why?"

"Well, there's this party I need to go to…"

"Blair wants to shoot it?" I had been in this long enough to be suspicious. Devin had never asked me out on a bona fide date before and there was no reason to expect that he would start now.

"Not exactly…but Russell thinks I should make an appearance."

"And he wants you to take me."

"Some rich kid's twenty-first birthday party. There's going to be a red carpet. I know, it sounds really lame. But, hey, if you're not doing anything—"

"I was just about to go running." This wasn't entirely a lie. I was still toying with the idea of working out.

"I'll get you at seven."

"I don't know."

"Come on, you're killing me here! You'd rather go running than go out with me?"

I sighed and put out my cigarette in the dirt driveway with my heel. *Oh, who was I kidding? Of course I was going to go.* "Okay, see you at my place at seven," I said and hung up without saying good-bye. Like they do on TV.

26

Since I didn't have a stylist for this one, I had to make do with an impromptu phone consultation. Jenny's opinion was to wear the leather pants again since I'd had so much success with them the last time.

"That's a joke, right? Because he went home with someone else," I said as I continued to rifle past the leather pants and everything else that hung in the walk-in closet that still didn't feel like mine. "Besides, leather pants are a bit obvious, don't you think?"

"So? Who cares if it's obvious? It's obvious that you like him."

"It is not. And no, I don't." *Red strapless BCBG minidress...too cold for nighttime, I'd have to wear a jacket with it and then I'd look like a flasher. White jeans...maybe, but then what top would I wear? And what was that blue mark on the back pocket? Did I get ink on them?*

"Oh, come on, Thom. Of course you like him. He knows it. And he must like you at least a little. That's why he asked you to go."

"It's not a real date. It's our job." *Should I wear a long silk skirt? That would be something different, and it could be super sexy the way it shimmers around down at the ankles.*

"Don't bullshit me, Thom. Blair didn't say you had to go."

"If she knew about it she would." What about the leather *skirt?*

"Well, whatever you do, you need to be fully recovered by Monday. You've got Whitney Whatsername in the morning and then about ten new consults to see."

"Remind me who Whitney is." I stopped concentrating on the clothes long enough to picture the patient.

"That girl from Arizona. So save your energy. You've got a lot of work to do on her. And now that I'm thinking about it...jeans. Absolutely. Tight dark jeans and one of those James Perse t-shirts. And the highest heels you've got. Where's the party? Can you get me on the list?"

I took Jenny's last bit of advice, and slipped on some four-inch Jimmy Choos that I could barely walk in. But I was right. About it not being a date, I mean. Devin called me from his car and by the time I met him out on the sidewalk, he was already on his phone talking to someone else. He barely looked up to greet me when I slid into the passenger seat. And between his multiple phone calls and the fact that it was getting dusky out, even by the time we arrived at our destination, I doubt he noticed what I was wearing.

It was an intimate Hollywood affair. Just the birthday girl and her five hundred closest friends. Devin gave me the back story while we waited in line for the valet to take the car.

"I think her name is Lilah. This thing is a launch party for her new clothing line."

"She's twenty-one and she has a clothing line?"

"It's a birthday gift from her father. He's some kind of foreign mogul."

"Interesting place for a party." Aside from the line of cars in front, we were in an area of downtown that was otherwise completely deserted by this time of day.

"It's a warehouse party. A pop-up."

I had never seen such a good-looking crowd. *Here I am. At some kind of underground invite-only thing, where they don't let the regular people in. Was it wrong to feel like I had accomplished something by being here?*

A girl who looked like a sit-com star—but clearly wasn't, because she was the gatekeeper with the clipboard—blocked the front entrance. Her permanent smile got even bigger when she saw us.

"Come on in. I *love* your show, by the way," she said to me.

Okay, she wasn't talking to *me*, she was talking to *us*.

Devin took my hand and we stepped through the entrance and found ourselves standing next to not a red, but a *pink* carpet. The whole place was decorated with white twinkle lights and sparkling streamers. Pink and white helium balloons floated. everywhere above our heads. Pink looks good on camera. I was so "in the know."

There was a lineup of photographers, their cameras labeled with their different domains—*E!, Extra, Entertainment Tonight*. Another could-be-TV-star guarded the carpet entrance. When she saw Devin, her face lit up and she beckoned us through.

"They are seriously desperate for talent if they're this happy to see us," Devin said. He squeezed my hand and nodded at the empty space on the carpet between us and a couple of the girls I recognized from the TV shows I never had time to watch anymore. He took a deep breath and mumbled something like, "Let's get this over with," and before I knew what was happening, we were standing out in that space on the carpet, with the photographers all pointing their cameras at us. The lights from the flashes made it impossible to see even a foot in front of me. I hadn't been prepared for this, and all I could think was that I was glad I had chosen the black jeans instead of the white ones and I hoped I didn't look fat standing next to those girls from TV.

A television journalist leaned in toward Devin with a microphone.

"Hey, Devin Breeze! What brings you out here tonight? The birthday party or the fashion line debut?"

Devin gave him that exaggerated toothy grin that I now know he uses when he's basically making fun of you. "Well, they're *both* such monumental occasions."

His sarcasm was completely lost on the reporter, who continued: "So how's it going? I hear things are really picking up for you! Tell us what's happening!"

"Hey…I'm on a hit show, I've got a plastic surgeon by my side to fix my ugly face…what could be better?"

To everyone else I bet he couldn't have sounded any happier; I knew I was the only one who could hear the undercurrent of annoyance in his voice. I knew how he hated having to be constantly reminded that he was coming back from the dead, and how he was doing it.

"So…" Now the reporter was talking to both of us. "Your demanding schedules…both professionally and personally…how have you managed to balance everything?"

"My friends say I'm finally growing up." Devin now spoke in his mesmerizing between-you-and-me voice—the one with which he made the rest of the world disappear —while he pulled me in closer. "It's my first time with someone who's not in the business—"

"*First time?*" the reporter cut in. He turned to me. "It's not *really* his first time, is it?"

"Very funny, man." Devin said. "Rachel here—" He gave me a squeeze around my shoulders. "Her whole job is taking care of *other* people. And I just find it so refreshing."

Okay, that *had* to have been scripted by Russell.

"So she takes good care of you, is what you're saying?"

"That's none of your business," Devin replied, winking at me.

Again, Russell.

"So, Lipo Queen." The reporter thrust the microphone in my face. "They say you're the best. Any comment?"

I was so busy concentrating on not laughing at what had just come out of Devin's mouth, that at first it didn't register, but then I saw Devin nod slightly and suddenly I realized, *he's interviewing me!*

At least he was *trying* to interview me. The sudden jolt of adrenaline that came with having all of this attention—with cameras rolling and light bulbs flashing and everybody looking—had immobilized my mouth. I wanted to talk but my tongue was stuck and I couldn't find my voice. Just like in one of those dreams.

"I'm sorry, what was that?" The reporter leaned in closer.

I took a deep breath and in true Red Carpet Smile fashion—perfected from watching too many segments of *Entertainment Tonight*—I tucked my chin back into my neck, tilted my head to one side and—baring all of my upper and lower incisors back to the canines—I said, loudly and clearly into the microphone: "I can get fat out of a rock." There. Nailed it. Blair would be ecstatic.

"That's what they say! And your show has really taken off! Why do you suppose it's so popular?"

The blinding flashes left spots of bright light, so I couldn't see the reporter's face. This was tough, trying to come up with something profound, yet pithy, while I basically felt like I was talking to air.

"So…Lipo Queen…any comment?" the reporter persisted, his voice now sounding a bit weary, like he was bored with me and ready to move on to someone else who was not only more famous, but who knew how to talk.

"Because…" I wracked my brain, trying to remember some of the heartfelt things I'd said in that last brilliant Blue Background Interview with Blair. *How did Devin and all these people here do this and make it look so easy?* "Because I can make people skinny! And there's nothing better than being skinnier."

I still couldn't see his face, but I sensed a resurgence of interest. "That's a pretty strong statement. On that note, would you mind telling me—and this is probably a question you get asked all the time—how many pounds of fat can you *really* take off?"

Okay, a technical question. *Easy. This* I had an answer for. I was gearing up to give an expert, scientific response about the fat and the fluid, and how thirty percent of the fluid you put in comes out again and how seventy percent gets absorbed, so there's really a period where the patient *gains* weight, when Devin grabbed the microphone.

"She can't talk about that stuff," he said, putting his other arm around me, while pushing me toward the door. "Top secret. You have to tune in to find out." He put his head next to mine and hugged me close for a few pictures, then waved at everyone.

"Thanks, guys," he said to the crowd. "Don't want to miss the festivities!" He then led me a little too briskly down the rest of the carpet into the party. I tried to walk slowly so that the photographers could get all of their pictures but he kept pushing me along until we were inside.

"What was that about?" I demanded. "I was getting better at it."

"You really think you should be talking about your job that way in a place like this? I mean, what you do is some serious shit. You're talking about cutting people open."

"It's just *liposuction*."

"Still. Should you be talking about pounds of people's…fat…like that?"

"Liters," I corrected. "It comes off in liters."

I thought he was going to do that thing he always did, laughing and telling me I was too serious. He didn't. He sighed and shook his head. "I shouldn't have brought you here."

"No, no, it's okay!" I said. "Really!"

He narrowed his eyes for a second and then the corners of his mouth turned up in an amused smile. "Don't tell me you're turning into a little paparazzi whore?" He squeezed my hand and laughed. "You know what? For some fucked-up reason, with you…it's actually an endearing quality."

The party was young Hollywood decadence at its finest. The inside of the warehouse had been converted into a pink explosion and it was already packed. Club music blared. The decorations—mostly flowers and a banner that said "Happy Birthday Lilah!"—encircled a runway centered in the middle of the room. The fashion show had not yet begun. Strobe lights cast sparkling reflections across the partygoers, and cocktail waitresses in pink mini-dresses carried Cosmopolitans on pink trays.

"C'mere." Devin led me through a passageway in the crowd to a roped-off area, where I found myself surrounded by a bunch of indifferent-appearing hipsters, sitting on plush pink velour couches and sipping drinks, staring off into space. All of the guests *outside* the rope were packed together like they were at a fraternity party, standing in clusters and trying to shout at each other over the music. But curiously here, in this roped-off area with these comfortable couches and all of this luxurious space, everyone was ignoring each other.

And then it dawned on me. I suddenly realized that I was now in a world that I had never been before. *A galaxy far, far away. The VIP section.*

Devin led me to a vacant end of one of the couches where it was a relief to sit. I slipped my feet out of my shoes to give them a breather, then remembered my pedicure was three weeks old and shoved my toes back in. A server handed each of us a very watered-down Cosmopolitan.

I tried to get a bearing on my surroundings without seeming too obvious. There was the smattering of recognizable faces/sometime celebrities. I figured that the others must be the industry people who had wrangled their way in. Regardless, there seemed to be some unspoken code that everyone here in this VIP area understood. It was okay for the common folk to gawk from the other side of the velvet ropes, but none of us in here were supposed to acknowledge the celebrities, let alone talk to them.

It was like a human safari, the way the partygoers stared as they walked past. And was it my imagination or was Devin striking a pose?

"What are you smiling about?" he said to me, and I abruptly stopped. I wasn't going to be the only smiling goof in the VIP lounge. I had to seem as detached as the others sitting around me. But the more I recognized their famous faces, the more I couldn't stop staring at them.

That's when I turned my head and caught a girl quickly averting her eyes from me. Huh. *She* was trying to pretend not to look at *me*. It hadn't occurred to me—if it was a safari, then I was one of the animals. *I* was one of the people being secretly stared at.

I turned my head slightly and arched my neck. Like a giraffe.

Devin, on the other hand, was the caged lion. After only about ten minutes, he started tapping his foot on the floor, and his eyes flicked back and forth like they did when a shoot was running too long and he was getting restless.

Finally, he leaned in toward me and said into my ear: "Okay, we can go now."

"What?" I was busy not looking at an impossibly beautiful girl who sat across from me. She caught me staring at her and shot me a look, as if I was being rude. *Oh, please*, I wanted to tell her. You were fucking *born* to be stared at. *Just deal with it.*

"Let's go."

"Why?" I said.

"We can go. I only had to stay for an hour."

"What do you mean—had to? And it hasn't even been an hour."

"By the time we get the car it will be."

"What are you talking about?"

"I'll explain later."

I would have been content to sit there all night exactly as we were, doing and saying absolutely nothing. But I wasn't about to argue with him and cause a scene while a bunch of strangers were pretending not to watch us.

"Man, I hate all that crap," Devin said. We had waved our good-byes to whoever was interested and were back in his old BMW, headed toward the freeway.

"So, then why did you go?"

He didn't answer me.

"Devin, why'd you let Russell make you go if you hate parties so much?"

He kept staring straight ahead as he spoke. "It's good money."

"You got *paid* to go to that?"

"Not as much as that guy sitting next to us, I'll bet."

"You mean...*everyone* else—"

"Not *everyone*." He seemed to think about it. "Oh, wow, I'm sorry. You want a cut of mine?"

I couldn't help laughing.

He scowled at me. "It's not funny. You think I'm happy about it? I never used to have to do shit like this."

"I'm not laughing at you. I just...can't believe it, that's all. That people get...*paid*...to go to...*parties*."

"Well, what did you *think* was going on there?"

"I don't know...that Lilah was really...*popular*?"

"Yeah, right," he said as he made a sharp U-turn to get us back to the freeway. "I bet nobody there could even pick her out of a crowd."

Crazy. But then as much as I wanted to just sit and mull over and digest this astounding new spin on things, I couldn't. With the visual and auditory overload of the party now gone, the earlier events of my day had started to bubble up and resurface and my brain did an involuntary recap of the whole afternoon. I dug my phone out of my purse, unsure if I was hoping that Jake had called or that he hadn't. He hadn't.

Fine. I was not going to call him tonight. Why was the burden always on me, anyway? Just because my mother was in denial and my father lived hundreds of miles away? I know they all just assumed that I was the best man for the job because I was a doctor, but Jesus Christ, I was a plastic surgeon, not a psychiatrist. And he *was* an adult.

"So you're not angry?" Devin said.

"Angry? About what?"

"That I dragged you to that lame-ass thing. I really am sorry…it's just… you know…"

"It's fine," I said. "You don't have to explain. I actually had a good time."

"Okay, then. Well, that's cool." He saw me fiddling with my phone. "Everything okay?"

"Oh, yeah, it's just…Jenny," I lied. "She left me a message about coming to the party."

"That Jenny…she's a handful, huh?"

"Yup." I looked out the window into the dark, and watched the glowing white words of the freeway signs flash by overhead. Which was when I realized where we were. "You passed our exit."

"I know."

We passed another exit. Shit, I hoped he wasn't somehow drunk off that weak Cosmo.

"So…are you going to turn around?"

He continued to stare straight ahead.

"Devin, where are you taking me?" I was actually on the verge of being nervous. After all, how well did I *really* know him? And supposedly he *did* have some kind of torrid past. I could see the byline in the center column of the MSN home page: "Lipo Queen's body found in abandoned 1996 BMW—TV Boyfriend is Prime Suspect."

He turned his head slightly to look at me. "You want to go to another party with me? A real one?"

My stomach did a somersault. *Was he asking me out?*

"Now?"

"Unless you're too tired…"

"No, no—."

"Good." He smiled. "And don't worry—I'm not getting paid for this one. Russell doesn't even know about it."

27

He took the Sunset exit and headed east.

"Are we going back to Hollywood?" I asked.

"Bel Air."

"Oh. Whose party?" I said as casually as I could.

Once, about ten years ago I had tried to take a sightseeing detour through Bel Air, but soon learned that unless you had your own helicopter, there really wasn't much to see. The over-the-top houses of the Hollywood greats that were so plainly depicted from the birds-eye view in all of the magazines were frustratingly hidden behind elaborate landscaping with twenty-foot high shrubbery.

"A friend."

I settled back into my seat and returned to silently staring out the window in what I hoped was a bored fashion. At least with this turn of events I could forget about Jake again for a while.

There were no streetlights on the narrow, winding road beyond the faux Bel Air gates. The road curved sharply, and forked suddenly multiple times as we climbed the hill, but Devin drove through the darkness without hesitation, as if he had been here many times before and knew exactly where he was going. We ended up at a driveway blocked with a closed iron gate. Devin punched in a code as confidently as if he had just arrived home.

Until the gate opened, I was sure that we had finally hit the apex of this mountain, that we couldn't possibly travel uphill anymore. But, there in front of us was a driveway that snaked on up an incline for about another quarter-mile, ending at a Victorian-style home that in size, resembled a federal building. The driveway was lit up with a row of columns on each side, and in the dark, the expanse of land seemed to go endlessly in every direction.

Two Hollywood parties in the same night, and they couldn't have been more different. We'd just left a place where the guest of honor was drinking legally for the first time—to club music in the middle of an explosive pink fashion show. Here in this mansion, the members of the crowd were, on average, at least one decade older than me, dressed in elegant yet casual evening attire. This was a true grown-up, no nonsense party.

A waiter in formal tuxedo attire stopped us in the front entrance hall to offer us glasses of wine from his tray. I chose my standard white—not because I like it better but I can't drink while standing in crazy shoes without spilling and white doesn't stain.

"I think I need a little something more than that," Devin said, nodding toward the full bar at the far end of the room. Just beyond it, through a wall made of double glass doors and windows, there was a stunning view of the city lit up for the night. We were about to head in that direction when an older gentleman emerged from the crowd and approached us.

"Ha! I was wondering if you found something better to do." The man, whose Dodgers cap was on backwards, leaned forward and gave Devin a big bear hug without spilling a single drop of the drink in his hand. Judging from the texture of the skin on his face, I pegged him at about seventy. But a *good* seventy—not the seventy year-old with a forty pack-year smoking history and five coronary artery stents.

"What could be better than this?" Devin said.

"Don't bullshit me." The man gave me a wink that I think was supposed to be conspiratorial. "He's always got 'things to do.'"

"This is Rachel," Devin introduced me.

"Nice to finally meet you." The guy shook my left hand since we both had drinks in our right. *Finally?* Who was this—his father? "Guy Tanaday."

It took me a second to register what he had just said and then my next thought was: "*Holy Shit.*" No wonder we were in the middle of Bel Air, at a private estate that looked like a great Georgian plantation home. And why Devin had just sauntered in here in front of me like he owned the place. It suddenly became so crystal clear that in my excitement I *did* spill some of my drink. This was the house that *Pacific Beach* had built.

The man shaking my hand was Guy Tanaday, the creator of *Pacific Beach* and about half a dozen other nighttime dramas of the guilty pleasure genre.

"Guy Tanaday!" I squealed before I had time to stop myself. "I mean, Mr. Tanaday, I'm honored, I mean—"

"She's a big fan," Devin said.

I felt Devin's arm tighten around my side. Definitely a cue to shut up. But he had nothing to worry about—there was no opportunity for me to gear up for a conversation about plans to bring back any of his old shows. As soon as he let go of my hand, Guy gave me what was clearly a dismissive nod and smile and a "Very nice to meet you, Rachel," and turned back to Devin.

"So, you got a minute? Or do you want to go mingle for a bit with your girlfriend and get back to me?"

I felt Devin's eyes on me. "Go," I said to him. I wasn't thrilled about being abandoned into this roomful of strangers, but I wasn't going to stand in his way if Guy Tanaday needed to talk to him privately.

"Thanks," Devin mouthed, then said, "Have fun. I'll come find you."

Guy draped his free left arm over Devin's shoulder and the two of them strolled away, through an open door into another room where their conversation was swallowed up into the overall buzz of the party. They had turned their backs to me so I couldn't even read their facial expressions to guess what they were talking about. What I *could* see was Guy summon over a cute blonde twentysomething in hot pants and a tube top and introduce her to Devin.

Another Kona.

Oh, well. I knew going into it that this night wasn't a real date. I finished off the rest of my drink and as I started to feel it, I reminded myself that tonight I was at a fabulous Hollywood party, and that *I* was just as fabulous as anyone else here. If Devin wound up leaving with someone else again, I could still have a great time without him.

But even with the open bar, mingling was strangely difficult. You would think that at such an exclusive party people would be friendly. Like, the cut had already been made at the door, and even if nobody knew who you were, you were grandfathered in once you stepped inside. But it soon became apparent to me, as I cozied up to the bar by myself—I'd made the switch to hard alcohol—that all the little groups and clusters of people already knew each other. The only person who spoke to me was the bartender when he handed me my second martini. And, it wasn't just me. There were a couple of women sitting on a nearby couch next to each other but they must have come separately because they both sat in solitude, staring straight ahead at the wall.

How strange, I thought, that people should come to such a swanky gathering, just to ignore each other like they were sitting at a bus station. Maybe it wasn't so different from the other bash after all? But this wasn't like back at Lilah's, where it was a matter of people pretending to be cool in the face of celebrity. Aside from Devin, nobody here was blatantly recognizable. This was just a matter of good old-fashioned snobbery.

I listened to the snatches of conversation whirling around me. It was all disappointingly dull. The couples beside me at the bar were bemoaning their trip to Europe and how the accommodations had been so "unbearable" they'd had to fly back early. To my left two men talked about golf.

There was a buffet table that extended the length of the room, but it was late, and all that was left were the empty warming vats. However, the dessert table was still going strong. In fact, it looked nearly untouched. It was like something out of *Willy Wonka*; an ornate display of fruit and cookies arranged artistically around a five-foot tall actively flowing chocolate fondue fountain. Jake would have gone crazy over it.

Jake. I felt for my phone in my purse and then stopped. He wouldn't be up this late anyway. I'd call him tomorrow. Give him a little time to atone for what he'd done.

*For now…I was starving. Fondue choices. Strawberries, pineapple, marshmallows, coconut…*sounding so good with all that alcohol on board. I reached for one of the wooden sticks and accidently knocked my hand against someone else's.

"Sorry," I said automatically.

"Oh, no, go ahead," the owner of the hand said. She was smiling until she saw my face. In fact, she froze at the same moment that I recognized her.

It was one of my lipo patients who always insisted on going in and out the back entrance even though nobody knew who she was. Merle Something.

When she first came to me she was already in amazing shape for her sixty years, but her husband had just left her for a younger woman, so I slimmed her down so she could "get back out there."

"Hello," I said.

"Well, hello." She looked much better than when she'd shown up in my office a few months ago, in and out of crying spells about her divorce. She seemed to have gotten herself back on track. She had that not stunning—but perfectly polished and preserved—look of the over-fifty west side woman. Tasteful barely-there makeup that probably came from the Chanel counter at Barneys and took an hour to apply. Subtle paralysis of her corrugators and central frontalis muscle and arching of her lateral brows with an estimated fifty units of Botox. Not a stray strand of gray in her sleek shoulder-length hair. But the best part was how she was rocking a pair of skin-tight jeans that she never could have worn without me.

"Don't you think so?" a woman standing next to her said.

"What's that?" Merle spoke to the woman without turning away from me. I recognized the petrified look in her eyes. It was the "don't you dare let anyone here know how you know me," look.

"Merle, I thought you were going to take some fondue," the other woman said.

"I've changed my mind." Merle placed her fondue stick back in the tray.

By now the two other women seemed to realize that she knew me.

"Hello," one of them said. She seemed to be waiting for Merle to introduce us. When she didn't, she said as if I weren't there, "Who's this, Merle?"

I watched the color drain from Merle's perfectly made-up face, leaving just blue eye shadow and patches of blush and bronzer on her cheeks. She took a deep breath and said, "This is—"

"Rachel," I said, shaking each woman's hand. "Rachel Thomas."

"Oh, I know who you are!" The second woman squealed. "You're that fabulous new plastic surgeon on TV. We were just talking about you! Diane, Diane—over here!" The second woman beckoned over another one of them. "Look! Look who's here!"

Diane's eyes grew wide. "The Lipo Queen!" she exclaimed. "We need to talk!"

Then, a group of five or six women clamored around me, becoming a chorus of voices, questions about lipo. Where? When? How? How soon? What was the recovery? How big are the incisions? Is there a way they can do it so their husbands don't find out?

"I've been meaning to call you. Your work is magnificent! And I just love the fact that you're a woman—and so in touch with what women want!"

"I can't tell you how many times I've been to a male plastic surgeon and they just don't get it. I mean, if I want small hips, I want small hips. It means yes, I want to look like a twelve-year-old boy. Take it off!"

"Goldstein did my breasts three times. *Three times* and he never got it right. They're still too big. 'Full and perky,' I told him. What part of that did he not understand?"

"They like saggy breasts. Men like saggy breasts."

"Men just like all breasts. That's why you should never have one do yours. They don't care what they look like."

"You're so cute! You look like a baby! How can you be old enough to be a doctor?"

"Are you married? I should set you up with my son."

"She has a boyfriend," one of them said. "She goes with Guy's kid. That little hottie. Don't you watch the show?" She raised an eyebrow and did a cougar scan of the room. "In fact, I just saw him a minute ago." She then summoned Merle out from behind the fondue fountain. "So how *do* you two know each other?"

Merle's face changed different shades of crimson.

I decided to save her.

"I think we met at the gym," I said.

"You joined a gym?" one of them said to her.

"Of course she did! She's been working out like crazy. How do you think she got that body?" another one said.

"Equinox. In West Hollywood," I said. "They have really great classes."

"You know, they do," said the one who offered to set me up with her son.

This might not have been a congregation of rocket scientists, but it was still unbelievable to me that none of them had put two-and-two together. I nodded and sipped my drink.

Then, just as suddenly as I had become the star-studded attraction, suddenly everything felt awkward. It wasn't just because Merle looked like she wished she could make me disappear. The subject of liposuction had been exhausted. The buzzing banter centered around me had stopped. My moment was over and the conversation had moved on to a debate about who had the best private trainer, and who looked better and skinnier than who these days. I don't have a whole lot of party savvy, but my instincts told me it was time to move on.

I pretended to see a message on my phone.

"Excuse me," I said to the women collectively. "I have to take this call."

"Oh, yes of course. You're a doctor!" one of them said.

I glanced around half-heartedly, already sure that Devin wasn't anywhere in the vicinity. I was drunk enough to convince myself that if he *was* nearby, I wouldn't have to look. My body would just *know*. Again, *oh, well*. I slipped out through the back doors onto the patio, grabbing a vodka soda on the way.

28

"There you are." I felt Devin's hands on my back before I heard his voice from behind me. "Where've you been?"

Hmmm…let's see…right here at this party where you left me. Well, not exactly. In order to avoid another run-in like the one I'd had with Merle, I'd slunk off to a corner of the patio by myself, and started downing mixed drinks in solitude.

He picked up my still-full glass from the railing. "Hey, what's this? You're not drinking?"

"I'm good." I'd already had more than enough and decided with this last one that dirty martinis sounded better than they tasted.

"You're not bailing on me, are you? We're just getting started!" The way he looked when he cocked his head to the side like that—he could have convinced me to jump off the patio into the swimming pool in front of the entire party. Naked, even. I forced myself to take a huge gulp.

"Thatta girl!" His mood had improved so drastically from earlier in the evening, that I wondered if he'd just finished off a couple lines of coke in one of the upstairs bedrooms. Or, at the very least, if he'd gotten lucky with the Tube Top Girl. I was actually feeling drunk and brave enough to make a joke about it, and I was just opening my mouth when he wrapped his arms around me from behind and leaned both of us up against the railing. "Rach, we're celebrating."

Okay, something had definitely happened. He'd never once before called me "Rach." Or voluntarily wrapped his arms around me without a camera present.

"Celebrating?" I turned to look up into his face, something I knew I shouldn't do with that much alcohol on board. "What's the occasion?" I was right. I started getting a little dizzy.

He seemed to pause for dramatic effect, then said, "Guy wants me to do his new show."

"That's…wonderful." I wasn't sure what else I was supposed to say. I was used to talking to anesthesiologists about surgical start times and device reps about different styles of breast implants, not actors about their new gigs. "What's it about?"

He sipped his cocktail before responding.

"Two young professional guys starting out their careers in Beverly Hills."

I must not have given him the reaction he was looking for because he added hastily, "I know, I know, not very original—"

"No, really, it sounds…*amazing…*"

"Hey, Rach, it's okay," he laughed. *There was that "Rach" thing again.* "It sounds stupid as fuck. But it's got a green light. Based solely on interest from the Middle East."

"The Middle East?" Political unrest in the Middle East seemed like the last thing that would affect the kind of shows that Guy Tanaday made.

"The whole 'Beverly Hills thing' is huge out there. That *90210* show is still cleaning up based on foreign syndication alone. I'm sure Gloria's planning the same thing with *Lipo Queen*."

Funny. I had never thought about people across the world, sitting and watching American television with Arabic subtitles.

"And get this…" Devin leaned in closer, past that understood boundary of personal space that is reserved only for those people that you would be willing to have sex with. "I'm going to be playing a *doctor*." When I didn't say anything—mainly because having him so close made just breathing *alone* a struggle—he continued, "Guy said he thought of me because my real-life girlfriend's a doctor…And you know, he's right. It really is genius P.R." He gave me a big wink and hugged his arms even tighter around my waist. "So you can't break up with me, yet, okay? At least wait until pilot season's over."

Still unsure how to react, I went with the next logical question in *my* mind: "What…kind of doctor will you…*be?*"

"Does it matter?"

"Well…*yeah.*"

"I don't remember what he said…that stuff's not totally worked out yet. I think maybe a pediatrician?"

"A *pediatrician*? You can't be a *pediatrician!*" *I* have more testosterone than any of the male pediatricians I know. "Listen, just tell them you have to be a surgeon."

He laughed. "Look at you…all fired up. Makes sense, though..." He raised his eyebrows. "Seeing as now I have all this experience…with the leeches and all…"

"You have to bring that up right now?"

He laughed again, raising his finger to his lips. "Although wouldn't it make a great headline in one of those magazines you love to read…?"

I scowled but I knew that it was impossible for me to look angry at him.

"Anyway, why would I do anything like that to you when you've done so much for me?"

I waited for the punch line. When he didn't give me one, I said, "What do you mean?"

"Come on, Rach. You know." He voice had shifted from playful to serious.

"I know what?"

"Please don't make me say it out loud."

"Say what?"

He sighed. "You know…you…and…are you really going to make me say this?"

"Now I am." I genuinely had no idea where he was going with this, but it was fun to watch him squirm.

"…Fine. Jesus." He exhaled. "You and…this stupid show…I know it was asking a lot…I get what an inconvenience it's been for you…I heard you even lost your job…"

I waited for him to finish, secretly dying, standing so close to him, having to pretend that I could take him or leave him, enveloped by that wonderful boyish aroma of detergent mixed with Speed Stick Sport Scent.

"Look, what I'm trying to say is…I've been such a fuck-up the past few years…I cost some people a lot of money and…it was hard getting someone to take me…you know…seriously…"

Wait a minute. Was he going where I thought he was going with this? "You *really* think you're being taken seriously by association with *me* and our stupid show?" The look on Donarski's face when he fired me flashed through my head and I started to giggle. "Taken seriously by *who*?"

"It's not funny." He rested his glass down on the railing and the ice made a clinking sound as it shook back and forth. Weird, but the almost forlorn quality to his voice made me want to reassure him.

"Guy Tanaday wants you because you're a good actor," I said.

"No, I'm not. I'm a good-looking guy who can act."

"That's not true."

"What, you don't think I'm good-looking?"

"You know what I meant."

"It's okay." He smiled. "Do you think I really care?"

"Yes, I think you do care. And you *are* a good actor." *Was I, really and truly, at this moment giving Devin Breeze a pep talk?*

"And you would know that from what, watching all of my Emmy-worthy performances carrying a surfboard around when I can't even surf?"

I should never have finished that martini—the words escaped before I could stop them: "From that night in the limo."

He frowned, like he was trying to remember.

"That first night we went out," I said. "Before we went in the club." Now *this* was embarrassing. He didn't even remember what had been to date the most exciting night of my life.

"Oh." He looked directly into my eyes and I felt everything start to get cloudy. "What makes you think I was acting?" His hands skimmed up and down the sides of my body and then, lingering around my hips, he hooked his fingers into the empty belt loops of my jeans.

He had turned me around so we were facing each other, *Dirty Dancing* style. Being this close to him, knowing that I could never enter his "beautiful people" plane of existence, was just fucking painful. No other way to describe it. I squeezed my eyes shut so I wouldn't have to see the way the moonlight bounced off the perfect S-curve of his cheekbone, how small shallow dimples formed at the corners of his mouth when his full lips turned up into a smile…

the mild ptosis of his upper eyelids that gave him such a mysteriously sexy gaze *all the time, no matter what he was looking at.*

"This is the first time Guy's offered me anything since *Pacific Beach* ended," he said.

"I'm happy for you."

I felt his hands slip into my back pockets, palms forward.

"I'm glad you're here, Rachel."

I felt my heart hammering away against my sternum. *Don't do this to me,* I should have said. *You can't do this to me again...please, not now...*But instead I joked, "Why, so you can grab my ass?" And I didn't force his hands away. I liked the way they felt, although I knew they were just on loan. You could tell they were experienced hands, even when they weren't doing anything.

And I made the mistake of opening my eyes.

"No," he whispered in my ear. "But now that you mention it...it *is* pretty great."

I was about to fire back that I took that as the ultimate compliment, since he had undoubtedly had his hands on many great asses, but I was immobilized, once again trapped in the black hole of charisma that surrounds someone like Devin Breeze. I couldn't see or hear anything past his face.

"If you're trying to show everyone in there what a great couple we are then we should really move over to the left a little," I said. "I don't think they can see us through the door."

I felt his fingers moving around gently in my back pockets.

"Rachel, if this were a performance I would have brought you back inside."

"So...why don't you?"

The way he had me pressed up against him, I was sure he could feel my heart banging away as well as I could. And for a second, I thought I could feel his.

"I don't know...I kind of like the privacy. Don't you?"

"I guess." I wasn't going to be fooled into thinking he actually liked me. Not again. But it *was* possible he had decided that, in light of his limitations of the evening, to close the deal with me after all. And that in itself was flattering. That Devin Breeze found me attractive enough to want to fuck. I'd take that.

When he saw that my glass was empty, he handed me his and I took a fast swig so I could immediately feel the burn of the vodka in my chest and even more lightness in my head. Alcohol is such a fantastic crutch. Honestly, I don't know what sober people do in these situations.

I was feeling bold again.

"Tell me the truth," I said. "I'm here with you because of Russell."

He took his hands out of my pockets and delicately ran his fingers through my hair as he spoke. "Yes, Russell asked me to take you to that PR disaster. But I brought you here because I wanted to."

"Why did you want to?"

He looked up at the sky, which was appropriately illuminated with the requisite millions of stars. Or isn't it that they're actually burned out and not really there any more by the time you can see them? So the technical description would be "millions of already-burned-out stars." *A coincidentally symbolic metaphor for the moment.*

Then he laughed. "Why did I want to? I don't know. Because you liked my show. Because I figured nobody else would appreciate meeting Guy Tanaday more than you would."

"Well then, maybe we should go talk to him—"

He cut me off by nuzzling the back of my neck and then kissing my forehead. Dammit, how could a boy's lips be so soft?

"Come on," He whispered. "Isn't this more fun than talking to Guy Tanaday?"

"Like I said, you're a good actor." I tried to sound coy, but I'd given up resisting him, and he knew it. I was going down. But I was only game as long as he understood that *this* time, I knew what was happening. That I was just an afterthought, the girl of the moment. That he was drunk and horny and there was nobody else out here on the patio to choose from.

He had gone back to gently brushing his lips up against the back of my neck but pulled away for a moment.

"Do you think I'm acting now?"

I didn't answer him right away. Even if it was method acting that had made his breath quicken and his heart pound so hard that now I could definitely hear it with my ear pressed up against his shirt, it didn't matter. It wasn't going to matter next week, or even tomorrow. All that mattered was that I was here with Devin Breeze, the hottest boy I'd ever met in person. And fuck it, I was going to sleep with him. I deserved it. Everyone thought I was doing it anyway.

Maybe it came from watching too much crappy television, or maybe it was just all the alcohol I had on board that enabled me to say the smoothest words that have passed through my lips to date: "If you are, then I expect a fantastic performance."

29

We took a cab back to the condo. It was a Yellow Cab with the pungent stench of body odor and stale cigarettes and duct tape across a tear in the back seat but somehow, all of that just made it better. All I remember is feeling Devin's mouth and tongue and hands everywhere, and the two of us sliding back and forth on the slippery vinyl seat as the driver made our way back down the hill.

I don't remember walking to my bedroom. I do remember pushing the door open and turning on the light to find Sushi sitting in the middle of the bed. And I remember running quickly into the bathroom and having one of those "Wow I'm really drunk," and "What's about to happen out there is blowing my mind," bathroom moments while relieving my bladder in solitude with Devin on the other side of the closed door.

"Hey, this is nice," he said when I came back out. *That's right, he'd never actually been in the master bedroom before.* He grabbed my hands and pulled me in close.

"Welcome to my lair," I said as he cupped my face in his hands and started to kiss me again. *Damn, I was coming up with some really good lines tonight.*

We continued the whole making out thing without missing a beat, even when he pushed me backwards onto the unmade bed, forcing Sushi to evacuate in disgust. I kept my eyes open the whole time. I was afraid that if I closed them my alarm would wake me up and I would discover that this had just been a dream. The bed was strewn with the rejected outfit choices of the evening, and I vaguely felt the zipper of the leather pants digging into the back of my neck.

"You're really cute," Devin said with genuine surprise in his voice, as he started to undress me. "How come I never knew how cute you were?"

I'm not twenty-one. I knew that this was the alcohol and his lower half (which I could now clearly feel against my thigh since the only thing covering it was the worn cloth of his boxers) talking. If I recounted this scene at a round-table discussion with a group of women the next day, they would all immediately roll their eyes and think, "Player!" Yet women are just so hopelessly programmed to believe every cheesy thing that comes out of a guy's mouth in the heat of the moment. Like *this* time *this* guy really means it.

"You feel good," he continued. "You must work out all the time."

I felt his light breath on my neck as he whispered into my ear.

"Not really," I said. I wasn't being coy. The truth was that I hadn't had any time to work out since *Lipo Queen* started, and I was feeling uncomfortably soft in this situation.

"I don't believe that. And your arms are incredible."

"It's just from sucking out other people's fat." It was true. It was the only upper body exercise I'd gotten in the past few months.

He had managed to get my bra down to my waist without undoing it.

"Damn. Your boobs are perfect," he said. This I believed. Whenever people ask me why I have never gotten a breast aug myself, I always tell them it's because I really don't need one, that from my neck to my navel I could pass for eighteen.

He was paying way too much attention to my nipples, but I didn't want to insult him so I just let him continue. Male plastic surgeons write articles and hold intense hour-long discussions about how important it is to preserve nipple sensation during breast augmentation. I can tell you that after years of consenting women for breast procedures, when I warn them about the risk of loss of nipple sensation, there are definitely those that care, but I'm one of the nine out of ten who shrugs and says, "*What* nipple sensation?"

He grabbed my anterior superior iliac crests like they were handles and slid down my body, then ran his tongue along my inguinal ligament, sending electric shocks up my spinal cord. My peripheral nervous system was on fire.

I have often tried to analyze exactly what it is that makes intimacy with a hot guy so incredibly exciting. It wasn't that fleeting ten seconds of pure physical bliss that used to make me ache for Eddie. And I certainly never lay awake at night dreaming about watching his dick slide in and out. Like most women, I'm not even anatomically wired internally and after about five minutes of the sole act of penetration I'm usually left staring up at the ceiling, wondering how much longer he's going to take and when it's going to be my turn. So if it's not the technical "sex" act, what is it that makes us unable to stop thinking about it afterwards, and to repeatedly describe the whole thing over and over to anyone who will listen?

It was this. This part where Devin was undoing my jeans, the part where his eyes lit up upon seeing my bare abdomen and appreciating it with a wondrous smile like he has just discovered something new, even though you know he's seen plenty of bare abdomens before. There is just something so simple and pure about raw physical attraction, where the complications of real life don't exist. Where it's all about lips and eyes and soft skin and his hands running up and down your freshly shaved and moisturized legs and knowing that he just can't get enough of you. Almost like he can't control himself.

I propped myself back up against some pillows and as I did so I caught a glimpse of us in the full-length closet door mirror. My ripply upper thighs had not slowed him down. And dammit, he didn't even have the *hint* of any love handles. But most of what I saw in the reflection was Devin's back, straining and arching toward me just enough to define the edges of his latissimus muscles, which tapered down nicely from his broad shoulders to his narrow pelvis…that rubber-bath-toy skin luminous under the dim recessed lighting. We could have been in one of those romantic scenes from *Pacific Beach*

Except this was real life.

"Do you…have anything?" I whispered.

He said, without looking up, "Don't worry. I'm clean, Honey. Russell makes me get tested every three months now." He continued to kiss me, working his way up from my knee to the inside of my thigh.

I had meant a form of protection, not an actual disease, but since he was mentioning it…

"You know, there's a window period where it still doesn't show. And have you ever been tested for Hep C—"

He moaned and pressed his body up against mine with a force like he was trying to get through me to the other side.

"Rachel, I know you're a brilliant doctor, but can we just stop all this medical talk and have some fun? I swear, I'm clean. I haven't had sex in like… forever…"

"Really? What about Kona?"

He sighed. "That was forever ago." He tilted his chin up to look directly into my eyes. "Relax. I'm the one who should be worried. What if you get pregnant?"

"I won't." After all of the unprotected sex with Eddie I had come to the conclusion that my risk of getting pregnant from a pull-out was slim to none. Unless the issue was that Eddie's sperm were just too stoned to swim.

But the STD risk was a real one. Not to sound like an infomercial, but I had managed to make it through nearly a decade of surgical training, where I'd been splashed and stuck so many times with contaminated body fluids that it was a wonder I hadn't sero-converted by now.

Finally, after ten minutes of him saying, *Well, what can we possibly do, he didn't have one*, and me saying *Absolutely we need to use one*, and him saying, *Well then you should keep a stock in your linen closet*, and my empty threats of putting my clothes back on and kicking him out, Devin magically produced a condom from his wallet.

It wasn't a Magnum. I hated myself for even noticing. Early on in our "courtship" Eddie and I used condoms a few times and that's the only reason I even knew what a Magnum was.

He was working with it in that rushed way that guys do like they're on a meter, and I wished he would hurry even more. I was still so afraid that I was going to wake up from a dream. I heard the crumpling of the package and watched the movement of his hands under the sheet. He didn't lose eye contact with me the entire time until after what seemed like hours I heard him say, "Dammit," and he looked down at what he was doing.

"What's wrong?"

He fumbled around with it a little more but I couldn't see what was going on.

"Shit!" He threw the condom across the room without aiming anywhere near the wastebasket.

Oh. I saw the problem. I had not offered to help him put the condom on but maybe I should have.

Yikes. I had no idea what to say. This had never happened with Eddie. Or anybody else that I could remember. I thought this sort of thing was only supposed to happen with older men…much older. Like men Guy Tanaday's age.

"Here…" I moved closer to him and started kissing his stomach. He lay there quietly, not saying anything, just staring up at the ceiling sulking while I made a futile effort to bring things back to life. Then after a few minutes he reached down and pushed me away.

"Forget it," he said. "It's not going to work."

"Is it me?" I felt a wave of nausea course through me. *I knew it. No matter how drunk he is, I can never be pretty enough for someone like him.* I needed to stop fooling myself. To get back to reality. *My* reality. Not this fake one. *How stupid I am to have thought, even for a minute…*

"It's not you." He sighed and looked up at the ceiling.

Well, of course unless he was truly evil he was going to say that.

I wished I believed him. "I can do something else," I offered. "Like give you a blow job." I thought he might at least laugh but he didn't say anything. "I give really good ones. So I hear." I lay down next to him.

"I'm sure you do."

I couldn't tell at first, because he remained quiet for a while, but it felt like he was stroking the top of my head, ever so slightly with the tips of his fingers. Even though I was extremely uncomfortable and barely able to breathe with my face smashed awkwardly into his chest like that, I didn't want to move. The bare skin of his arm felt warm against my shoulder. It was completely quiet and still except for our breathing. I felt Sushi jump back onto the bed and walk right over us like we were just part of the clothing pile to get to his favorite spot by the pillows.

"It was probably just all that alcohol," Devin said after a few minutes.

"Of course."

"I must have had like seven or eight drinks tonight."

"Me too."

"We should get some water."

"We should," I said, but I didn't want to get up. For now, at least, I didn't even care about what had just happened. So he drank too much. That was all. It wasn't me. He was still touching me, wasn't he?

It felt so good to be lying so close to him that the next thought in my head just slipped out of my mouth. "I still had fun," I said, and immediately wished I could retract the words.

"Me too," he said. Even if he was lying, at least he had the decency to say it. It was just basic manners. Like when a guy says he's going to call you, even if he's not. *Maybe he'll call me, maybe he won't...* I felt myself going in and out, and realized that I was falling asleep.

"We can try again in the morning," I said. But Devin's regular, heavy breathing pattern told me he probably hadn't heard me.

30

O f course he automatically tried again the next morning.
"Forget it." Devin sighed and rolled off me underneath the twelve hun-dred count Egyptian cotton sheets.

"You're sure it's not me?" I said.

"I told you already—it's not you. How many times do I have to say it?" He lay on his side, facing the mirrored closet. So he had his back to me, but not really.

"I'm sorry," I said. It was true—I'd lost count of how many times he had sworn that it wasn't me but I needed to keep hearing it. Especially after this morning's unsuccessful effort. We had even foregone the condom and it hadn't worked. I could rationalize away a one-time occurrence at 2:00 A.M. after a night of indulgence…he was drunk, he was tired…it was the first time… maybe he was even nervous. But morning sex for a guy is a given. He should wake up ready to go. And if it wasn't my fault, fine. But I needed to hear him say it. I needed to know for sure that it had nothing to do with my lack of resemblance to one of his gorgeous TV show girlfriends.

"I don't know," I said. "It's just that…" *Shit.* What I had thought at first were hunger pangs were waves of nausea. *Dammit, I should have at least tried to drink some water last night.* I tried to visualize which box in the bathroom closet had all of my hangover supplies.

"What?"

"I don't know…I feel kind of…"

"Kind of what?"

I stopped myself. It was impossible to finish what I really wanted to say. How could I possibly tell him how ugly I felt when I was around him?

I couldn't.

"…hung over," I finished. "I'm really hung over." I took a deep breath. My chest stung and I imagined how raw and inflamed my trachea must look from the inside. All those cigarettes I'd smoked when I found myself alone out on Guy Tanaday's terrace last night. Without anyone to talk to, I had had time to start grieving again for my car, and wondering if I should call Jake back, and whether or not Devin was ever going to rematerialize.

"Me too. I feel like shit right now. I'm getting too old to drink that much."

He rolled onto his stomach, keeping his head turned away from me

I stayed very still and quiet, mainly because I suddenly felt that any movement at all was going to result in severe projectile vomiting. But now I was plagued with the next obvious question in the algorithm: *So if it wasn't the fact that I just wasn't up to par, what the hell was wrong with him?* Purely from a medical standpoint...Impotence at his age was a major issue. What if he had a life-threatening disease that he didn't know about—like some kind of cancer that was growing into his perineal nerves? I managed to force out the words: "I'm worried that you might have a problem."

"I'm not gay so don't even go there."

Whoa. I hadn't even considered that, which was probably the most obvious answer. I didn't remember any rumors of Devin Breeze being gay ever floating around in the tabloids. Certainly I would have remembered that one.

"I don't have a problem," he snapped at me. "It's normal. It just happens sometimes, that's all."

"It's not normal."

"Just because you're a doctor doesn't mean you know everything."

"It's not normal in a thirty-one year-old guy."

"How do *you* know how old I am? Do you know my sign too? My favorite color?"

"Devin, this is important." I ignored his cheap insults. His *life* could be at stake. "Has it ever happened to you before?"

He didn't answer me right away. Then: "I don't know. Maybe. Once."

"Do you have any medical problems? High blood pressure...diabetes...?"

"No. I said no. You got any Advil here?" He avoided my eyes in the mirror.

"But do you know for sure? Have you ever had a fasting glucose?"

"Enough, Rach, okay? Drop it. There's nothing wrong with me." He moaned. "Except that I feel like I'm going to die."

How could he not take this seriously? "Are you on any medications? This is important. I'm not kidding around."

"Neither am I."

"Do you take any meds?"

He sighed. "You're not going to give me that fucking Advil, are you?"

"It's not a trick question."

"I don't know...allergy stuff, sometimes..."

"Nothing else?"

Silence.

"Well, maybe one other thing," he finally said.

"What?"

He was silent again for a minute. *Jesus, had he lied to me last night? Was my life now in danger too?* If it was possible to feel even more nauseous at that moment, then I did.

"Please don't tell me you're on antiretrovirals," I said.

"What the fuck are those?"

"Nothing. Forget it." I didn't see the need to tell him they were HIV meds. "So what is it? Your other... 'thing'?"

He mumbled something that I couldn't understand.

"What?"

"Stuff for my hair."

"Like what?" I was thinking along the lines of essential oils or something to keep it shiny.

"You know, stuff." Then he added almost under his breath, as if he hoped I couldn't hear: "To keep it from falling out."

"*What?* Why?"

He turned to face me for the first time that morning since he'd lost his erection. "Why do you *think*?".

"I don't know," I said. Devin Breeze's thick, sun-kissed wavy locks were part of his brand. "Your hair looks great to me—"

"Well, it's not!" He pulled apart the roots up at the crown of his head. "Look at this!" he said, as if it were *my* fault. It did look a little thinner and darker there when he was shoving it in my face like that, but it still didn't keep him from being the best-looking male specimen I'd ever seen in real life.

"It's fine," I said.

"Fine! Fine is fine if you're an I.T. guy. I'm an actor, Rachel! I'm *supposed* to be a sex symbol. I can't have a bald spot in the middle of my head."

Well, taking something to keep his hair on his head could certainly explain why he'd been unable to perform. I tried to be delicate about it. "You know that stuff can have side effects, right? I mean, I'm not saying for sure, but it could be the reason—"

"Yes, I know. You don't think I know? Why the fuck else would I tell you?" He started massaging his temples. "My head. I'm going to die. Just start putting the nails in the coffin."

Even on his self-proclaimed deathbed he resembled a Greek God. Certainly not someone who needed to risk his potency to keep his hair on his head. What a shock, when all this time it had seemed that being gorgeous was so effortless for him.

"So why don't you stop taking it then? And see what happens. Maybe it'll start—working—again."

"I'm not stopping it." He had his hand over both eyes. "Can you close those shades or something?"

"So you'd rather keep every single hair on your head than be able to have sex?"

"Basically, yes."

"But that's…" *Unheard of* is what I wanted to say.

"I told you, it's not all the time. It's just when I drink a lot. If you don't like it, you can leave. Are you going to get me the Advil or what?"

"I'm not leaving. It's my condo."

"No, it's not. Nothing here is yours."

Nice. Just like a slap on bare skin. For a moment, I felt my throat start to ache and the corners of my eyes sting, and I prepared to fight back tears. Then I realized that I was too dehydrated to cry. Besides, I could feel the dry heaves coming on. My physical illness had taken over, squashing any "hurt feelings" I might have. My survival instinct had kicked in.

I managed to drag myself and a chair into the bathroom.

"Easy," I cautioned myself out loud like I was talking to an animal. I stepped up onto the chair so I could swing open the door to the top of the linen closet.

After a few moments of silence I heard: "Did you find it?"

I ignored him, and continued to rummage around in the back of the cabinet, where I was sure I had packed my stash.

It was no longer about our unsuccessful attempts at sex or his persistence in taking hair preservation products that caused impotence. It was now all about taking care of the nausea centers in my brain.

Things were not staying still. I had to hang onto the shelf edge to keep my balance while I pushed a few of the boxes out of the way. It had to be here. Somewhere behind all of this other inane shit that I somehow couldn't seem to let go of because it had been given to me by grateful patients…gift packages of decorative soaps, bath salts and lotions that I'd had for years and would never use, jewelry that just wasn't "me"…the T-shirt and other weird presents from Jake.…*Where the hell was that box? Oh, God please don't tell me I left it in the kitchen somewhere. I'll never make it down the stairs.*

"What are you doing?"

I glanced down to see Devin standing in the bathroom doorway in his boxer shorts. "Getting something." *Wait, was this it?* I pulled a box toward me and tilted it, pushing the broken cardboard leaflets out of the way to verify what was inside. *Thank you God, thank you. I'll call Jake as soon as I'm better and forgive him for wrecking my car.*

It was the stash. Five bags of Ringers, a pile of I.V. tubing. A string of angiocatheters in beautiful pink packages. Eighteen gauges. Those were the big ones. You could get a liter of fluid into your vein with one of those and a pressure bag in under twenty minutes. And there in a flat sheet of foil… *come to Mama.* The sublingual Zofran. The most powerful anti-emetic drug in existence. The ones I had confiscated when we packed up at the end of that last Mexico mission trip we did in residency. They were expired but they'd still work.

I popped one of the pills into my mouth.

"What's that?"

Okay. The magic potion was in. Ten minutes and the feeling that I was in perpetual motion was going to stop.

"Here." I held out a second pill for him in my palm. "Take this."

"Advil?"

"No, just take it."

"I don't do drugs anymore. And after today I may never drink again, either."

"Just take it. You'll feel better. I promise."

He closed his eyes and grabbed his head in both hands.

"Devin, stop being so dramatic. Trust me. You need this."

He sighed and I could smell the alcohol in his system from two feet away.

"Okay, Alice. Bring it on." With his eyes still closed, he opened his mouth and stuck out a parched tongue.

I dropped the pill into his mouth to an immediate "Eeeewwww!"

"Just let it dissolve!" No time for his wimpiness. I grabbed the precious box, wobbling around for a minute under the uneven weight of it. I had to hold onto the shelf for balance to step off the chair without killing myself.

"Rachel, what the fuck are you doing?"

I had made it back down to ground level, clutching my box of supplies. I had to move. There was only a short window of time that the Zofran would work well enough for me to do what I had to do. I had to get things going before the dehydration took my body beyond return.

"Putting in an I.V.," I said. "You want one?"

31

"Pepperoni or cheese?" Devin opened the pizza box again. "There's still three of each."

He pulled at the strings of cheese forming between his mouth and the piece he was inhaling. "You're an incredible doctor. I have to say...what you've done here is miraculous."

Two hours ago we had been about to take turns praying to the porcelain god and now we sat comfortably side by side, polishing off a pizza that could not have smelled or tasted any better. It's incredible what eight milligrams of expired sublingual Zofran and a couple of liters of crystalloid will do.

"It's just Surgery 101," I said. "Fluid fixes everything."

"So how come *I* didn't know this trick?"

"I don't know...maybe because you didn't go to medical school?" I bit off the corner of the crust and looked sideways at him. "But my hunch is that you wouldn't have been able to do anything about it even if you had."

He chewed slowly, as if considering. "No, you're right. That took some talent, the way you put your own in like that. Listen, Rach—"

We were propped up next to each other in the bed on a mountain of pillows, with our bags of Lactated Ringers hanging from jerry-rigged IV poles made of wire hangers hooked to the top of the bedposts. The shades were drawn and the television was on, though neither of us was really watching it.

A commercial came on and Devin started flipping through channels with the remote. I noticed he was keeping it up in the five-hundreds, staying safely away from all of the basic cable networks where we might run into one of us on screen.

"I'm sorry about what I said before," he said. "You know I didn't really mean it."

"I know," I said. "And I'm sorry about your hair."

We both kind of laughed.

"It's not a common side effect. Apparently, I'm part of the lucky two percent." He paused, then added, "But they say that once you start taking it, you can't stop—that you could lose even *more* hair. Like it might *all* fall out."

"I understand," I said, even though I really didn't. I guess I had just never met a guy who wouldn't sacrifice anything for sex. I almost felt sorry for him.

"Besides, you don't want a bald boyfriend, do you?"

I shrugged. Devin Breeze bald. I could think of a lot of worse things. "But why did you even bother to tell me? If you're not going to stop taking it, I mean."

He landed the remote on the Animal Planet. Couldn't get any safer than that. No way was *Pacific Beach* or *Lipo Queen* going to show up on Animal Planet.

"I don't know." He sighed. "I guess I didn't want you to think…I mean, you know how everyone always thinks actors are gay…And last night I really *did* want to…you know…."

I was uncomfortable with where this was going. I didn't want to hear next that he wanted me last night and maybe even a little this morning but now that the alcohol had worn off and he was all rehydrated, he didn't want me any more, so I steered us into a more objective, scientific conversation.

"So, does it happen all the time?" I said. "Like, does it *ever*…work?"

"Oh, yeah, yeah, of course it does."

"Like how often?"

"What do you mean? You want a *percentage?*"

"That would be helpful." I tried to sound as clinical as I could. "I'm worried about you."

"Well, trust me, you don't need to worry…" I was glad he just let his voice trail off—I didn't need to hear the unspoken "…because I get laid all the time" part of it. He looked up at the ceiling and narrowed his eyes, as if calculating. It was taking him a long time to tally up the numbers and I was starting to feel sorry that I'd asked. At least he hadn't started listing *names*.

"Okay, probably this happens like thirty percent of the time."

"Hmmm. Those are not great odds. Can you…umm…take something to…uhh…counteract it?"

"What, you mean like Viagra? I usually do. If I have fair warning."

I wasn't sure how to take that. Should I be flattered that he respected me too much to anticipate trying to get into my pants when he asked me out? Or should I be insulted that it hadn't crossed his mind to try?

It was like he was reading my mind because then he quickly added, "But it's probably better that we didn't. I don't want you to hate me or anything."

"Why would I hate you?" I said, even though I knew exactly why.

"Oh, you know how girls are…" I could tell he wished he could give me a telepathic message so he wouldn't have to explain it. "It just always makes everything so complicated. And we don't want to start *really* fighting on camera."

"Why not?" I said. "Blair's always asking for drama."

He propped himself up on an elbow. "Because if two women fight on a reality show it becomes a hilarious screaming match. That's drama. If a couple fights on a reality show the guy always looks like a douchebag."

"I see."

The tone of his voice changed. "Hey, that right pupil of yours is like twice the size of the left. It's kind of cool, the way it does that."

I didn't think it was necessary to point out that pupil dilatation was commonly stimulated by pheromones and physical attraction.

When I didn't say anything he became serious again. "You better take this to your grave. I mean it, Rach. The last thing I need is for this to be front page of *Star* or something."

"Don't flatter yourself," I said. Although he probably wasn't wrong. Something this good on a *dead* Has-been could probably make the cover of a tabloid. I could see it now: "*The truth revealed: Why he never had children. Teen idol unable to deliver in the bedroom!*"

"Well, I'd appreciate it if you could just forget it happened."

"As long as you forget the leeches happened."

"What leeches?" He sat up and put his I.V.-free arm around my shoulder. "Don't worry, Rach. I got your back."

Without him saying it, I knew he meant: "Because nobody else does." Gloria, Blair and even Russell would prostitute anything at our expense for ratings. I was loving this "us against the world" feeling. It would have been so nice to be able to lean in and kiss him right then, but it was clear that that chapter was way over for him, and I was better off pretending the same.

"Rach, you're a pretty cool girl." Devin stretched and while doing so, caught a glimpse of himself. "Holy shit! What happened to my stomach? Where's my belly button?"

I looked down at his abdominal wall, which like mine, was swollen with all the extra fluid third-spaced into the tissues. His six-pack was gone.

"Relax," I said. "It's just the fluid. You'll be back to normal by tomorrow. But it looks like we've had enough."

"So," he said at the door, where he gave me a quick good-bye hug. "What are you going to do today?"

It was already four.

"Study," I said.

"That's right. You've got that big test coming up."

"What about you?"

"I don't know. Stuff. I got a lot of stuff to do." He had his hand on the doorknob. "But hey, Rach, listen. Thanks for everything. I owe you. Really."

"Thanks for bringing me to the party," I said. "I had a…lot of fun."

"Yeah, it *was* fun, wasn't it?" There was an element of surprise in his voice as he seemed to be reviewing the events in his head. "But…maybe it's better if we kind of…keep all this on the down-low, you know? Like, don't tell them? I mean, yeah, I know, we're supposed to be together and all, but the crew, and Blair, Jenny…"

Oh, sure, of course. I get it. We were going to play "See you in Biology class tomorrow and it will be like nothing ever happened." I knew that game well. And I knew he wasn't just talking about his lack of performance.

"Tell them about what?" I said.

He seemed startled, maybe surprised that I accepted so easily. I guess he usually had to physically peel off most of his one-night-stands.

I offered to drive him to pick up his car at Guy's house but he declined twice, insisting on getting a cab. He didn't have to tell me. I knew that his refusal was more his desire to put an end to this "date" than a true effort to be courteous and not waste my precious time. The worst part was that I could feel his sympathy in the way he waved good-bye, like he knew I understood.

At least Jake and I called a truce. Sort of. He wouldn't answer his phone so I tried texting him and after half an hour he finally responded. Though he still didn't apologize. In fact, *I* apologized for accusing him of not taking his medication. He accepted my apology.

And in the *would-you-rather* game of being good with Jake versus having Devin Breeze fall in love with me...well, I needed to keep my priorities straight. To drive it home, I pictured the sad gnome living in front of the cupcake store. Yes, if I could only have one of the two things, I had the one that mattered.

32

The national Aesthetic Meeting was held annually exactly two weeks before the oral board exam, and although I had absolutely no time, I was anxious to go. For the past few months my whole world had consisted of *Lipo Queen* and my solo private practice. I had become my own little oasis in my office, and as insulting as Donarski had been to me, *he* wasn't *everyone*. I had other colleagues, and I wanted to be amongst them again, even if it was only for a day. Any kind of gathering this close to the boards was bound to be a mass group bonding on the upcoming legendary terror we were about to endure, like it had been for all the other exams we'd taken together over the years. It would be our form of a pep rally, and I needed to be there.

Of course, Blair turned the meeting into a filming field trip. Except the day started with some minion at Fitzgibbons Entertainment getting fired when we arrived in San Diego and learned that the permits had not gone through. The hotel refused to let the crew follow me inside. The closest they could get was the valet station in the front entrance courtyard. I tried not to look happy about it.

After I was able to get rid of Blair—who made the most of her restrictions by filming my entrance into the hotel six times—my first stop was the registration booth to collect my nametag. Normally I hated wearing the nametags at these things because they always got so tangled up in my hair, but today I proudly displayed mine clipped to the front of my blazer: "Rachel Thomas, M.D., Beverly Hills, CA."

The presentations had already started and clusters of attendees loitered outside the closed conference room door in the hotel entrance hall. It's no secret that out here was where the *real* meeting was happening. Out here in the hallway, between the restrooms, where all the political stuff between the Powers-That-Be went down.

It was a typical crowd. Eighty percent men—half older and paunchy, the other half, the new generation of Plastic Surgeon Pretty Boys hailing from places like Los Angeles and Miami—and twenty percent women.

I approached a group of what I would call my "meeting buddies"—familiar-looking surgeons in my age bracket whose names I could never remember. I'm sure they didn't know mine either, and it didn't matter; after over a decade of medical school, interviews, residency, exams and meetings like this one, even if you didn't really *know* each other, there was an unspoken code of solidarity. A "we're all being tortured in this shit show rat race together."

The four of them were discussing labiaplasty, now one of the most in-vogue plastic surgery procedures around. It's kind of crazy, really. I mean, who could have predicted that women would become fixated with the aesthetics of their vaginas?

"It's like the new breast aug," said a skinny guy with a bowtie and a painfully long comb-over. I recognized him from a residency interview back when his comb-over wasn't quite so long. "All of my patients ask about it. They get obsessed."

A few of them chuckled and I saw this as an opportunity for a smooth entry into the conversation.

"Oh, I know!" I said. "These women are always showing me what they don't like—'this skin hangs too low here, I don't like this over there.' How do they even *know* it so well? I mean, I couldn't pick *mine* out of a lineup!" That was one of my favorite original jokes. Whoever I told it to would always start cracking up. Just the visual of a lineup of vaginas made it funny every time.

But nobody even smiled. They all just stared at me blankly as if they'd never seen me before, even though we'd all crossed paths multiple times and I'm sure they knew who I was. I figured it wasn't the time or place to continue with my follow-up line, but I just blurted it out to fill the unbearable silence: "And you don't have to worry about a guy seeing the scar, because they won't see it unless they have their head down there and if somebody's got their head down there then, well you're having a really good day!"

"Hmmm." The guy with the bow tie/comb-over combo looked down and started thumbing through his program. I was close enough to get a whiff of his coffee breath but he acted like I wasn't there. The other guy looked past me through thin-rimmed glasses, and pulled on his tie a bit. And then the girls on either side of me sort of quarter-turned their bodies away.

"Great meeting, isn't it?" the one on my right said to the others. Clearly none of them planned on acknowledging me again. When I stepped back to walk away, I heard one of the girls whisper, "She's got some nerve, showing up here."

"That's the one on that crazy show, right?" one of the guys said.

"I can't believe people actually watch that crap."

"What she's doing is disgusting," one of the girls said. "So degrading to the rest of us. It makes us look like we're not even real surgeons, like we just do liposuction all day long."

"Seriously. It's so 'trailer park.'"

A verbal sucker punch. Maybe they weren't my "friends," but these were the same people that I used to get drunk with at drug rep dinners. And now they were my haters.

I did a quick survey of the rest of the hallway minglers as covertly as I could, but nobody—not even those whose names I knew—gave me so much as a non-verbal nod to invite me to join their group. I could see my *Lipo Queen* posse through the revolving glass doors, and I was surprised to feel a comfortable pang of familiarity at the scene of them in the hotel front courtyard. The crew guys were sprawled out lazily on a strip of grass, looking perfectly content to get paid for sitting on their asses, doing nothing. Blair was pacing back and forth with her Bluetooth, waving her hands wildly and speaking to the air. Earlier, she'd mentioned having me bring one of my colleagues outside for an on-camera discussion to give our viewers the inside dish about the "latest and greatest" plastic surgery advances. Well, that didn't look like it was happening, since nobody would even talk to me.

Nobody except—

"Dr. Thomas! There you are!" someone shouted into my ear. Ah, yes…the one person here who *did* want to talk to me. Tiffi—that was her real name, short for nothing—the sales rep for "Softsilk" post-liposuction garments She beckoned me toward another group of "meeting buddies," all with vaguely recognizable yet clearly unfriendly faces.

Out of the corner of my eye, I spotted one of my colleagues, Jessica Bernholtz across the room deep in conversation with a couple of the more senior, much more powerful players. Jessica and I had trained together and we'd lost touch after we'd graduated, which was a miracle considering our offices were now in the same building. Well, not exactly a miracle. I can't say that I'd been trying to run into her. But unfortunately today our eyes caught and I involuntarily waved. She nodded and waved back in a dismissive manner. Then she said something to the guy she was talking to, while frowning as if she smelled something bad. She pursed her lips and nodded. The senior guy glanced momentarily in my direction, then said something back to her.

Had she just said something about *me?*

Tiffi continued to jammer away in my ear about a new, even more breathable fabric line, but I was too busy wondering what Jessica was talking about with those two big shots. *Why did they keep looking over here?*

Then, there Jessica was—standing next to me.

"Rachel!" she squealed, hugging me too tightly and then air-kissing my cheek. "So good to see you! I wish I'd known you were coming! We could have carpooled! It's been absolutely *forever*, hasn't it?" she continued. "And you look just *fabulous!*"

Tiffi leaned in toward Jessica. "Doctor….?"

"Bernholtz." Jessica pumped her hand and held up her nametag at the same time. "Jessica Bernholtz. Beverly Hills." She turned to me with a conspiratorial smile. "How's it going, Rachel? So much buzz about you lately!"

"Really." I glanced around the nearby group of angry faces and I quickly tried to steer the conversation as far away from *Lipo Queen* as I could. I figured it wouldn't be too hard, since Jessica was so good at talking about herself. "What have you been up to?"

"Oh, studying wildly, of course!" she chirped. "I'm just trying to pack it all in these last few weeks. You know, cram, cram, cram. Between my *frantic* work schedule and redecorating our new house—did I tell you we moved?— I just have teeny, tiny bits of time here and there for all of that last minute studying." Jessica pinched her fingertips together as if explaining to me what "teeny tiny" meant. She had this irritating habit of curling her fingers up as if she were holding whatever she was talking about, even if it wasn't an inanimate object. "Speaking of," she added. "I don't know how *you're* getting any studying done, with all that you've got going on. I'm just a busy plastic surgeon, not a *TV star*. *However* do you find the time? *You* are just a *Phenom*! So, anyway… isn't it *exciting*? I mean, it's less than three weeks away! Three weeks and we're going to be *board-certified*! In fact—" She had her left hand on her hip again and she waved the right one in the general direction she'd just come from. "I was just talking to John and Phil about it."

"John and Phil?"

"You know, John is head of the boards committee. Phil is a senior examiner."

The way she had the balls to call legends by their first names—it made you wonder if she *herself* had a couple of undescended testicles hidden up in her abdominal wall. She raised her thinly plucked eyebrows and fake-laughed. "In fact, just now we were talking about *you*…"

I knew it. "What *about* me?"

"Actually…they were asking me about your little television show."

"Really? Why?"

"They're curious. I was just filling them in."

"And what did they say?"

She looked me squarely in the face and suddenly her voice completely changed from a grating sing-songy pitch to a concerned, motherly tone. "I'll be honest with you, Rachel. You need to be careful."

"Careful of what?"

She stared into my eyes and spoke with the intensity of a female character on a daytime soap. "You know what happened to those guys who did reality shows in the past, don't you?"

"What happened to them?"

Jessica's eyes darted both ways before she spoke, as if we were now discussing a tragic secret. "They *failed* them." She exaggerated the enunciation of the words as she lowered her head toward me with a hushed voice.

Except for that day back in my old lifetime, when Donarski had accused me of insurance fraud and called the plastic surgeon on the magazine cover a "clown who never even took his boards," I hadn't thought about it. I'd just assumed that all of those pioneer reality-show plastic surgeons passed the test. Especially after the way Gloria's network had made such a huge deal about it.

She took my silence as a sign of needing more information.

"It's the *politics*," she continued. "I'm surprised they're even letting you take it. Some of those guys got *totally* blackballed *forever*. I know one who did a few laser lipo segments on *Extra* five years ago and they *still* haven't passed him. They just let him keep taking the test to torture him. Isn't it just awful?" Jessica pursed her lips and shook her head. "I mean, I just wouldn't want that to happen to *you*."

Well, I would have had to be an idiot not to know that of course she really *did* want that to happen to me. I was, after all, the competition right down the hall.

"Especially after the way you got caught up in that insurance fraud scandal at the Valley Hospital," she added. "You know how they are about insurance fraud."

Wait, *what?*

"There was no scandal," I said. "And how do you know about that, anyway?" Jessica had never stepped foot into the *neighborhood* of the Valley Hospital. How could *she* know about the internal politics going on there?

I could tell I'd caught her off guard, but she still answered smoothly, "Oh, just a patient who came to see me for a lipo consult—when I examined her, I realized that half the case was already done by another plastic surgeon!" She gave out an obviously forced laugh that sounded more like a cough. "One of your breast cancer patients. Great job, by the way."

She still hadn't answered my question. "But how did you know I'd gotten in trouble for it?"

"Oh, you know how everyone talks. My tech told me. He must have heard it from a friend of his who worked with you. You know how it is—Los Angeles plastic surgery gossip is better than celebrity gossip any day of the week!"

Uggh. That high-pitched condescending voice of hers. I averted my eyes so she couldn't see how successfully she'd upset me, and as I did, I saw Dr. Donarski across the room. He was engrossed in a conversation with a woman about my age that I didn't recognize.

"I wonder who that is," I mused, not really expecting Jessica to know.

"Who?" When Jessica saw where I was pointing she said in her know-it-all manner—which is especially annoying because she really *does* know it all—"Oh, you mean Paula. You haven't met her? She's your replacement."

"My replacement?"

"Well, I don't know if she's your replacement *per se*, but she's Donarski's new girl."

I looked back at the two of them. Paula was unusually tall for a woman—she actually towered over Donarski—and her straight brown hair trimmed in a sensible shoulder-length bob made her look even taller. She stood poised on the soles of her feet, like a tennis player waiting for her shot.

"I've never seen her before." I said. "When did she graduate?"

"With us. But she spent the last year on missions around the world."

"Missions?"

"You know, those cleft lip and palate ones where they don't have any toilets. I can't believe she did that for an entire *year*. She risked her own life under the worst conditions to help kids all over the world. For *free*. She's truly a *saint*." Jessica shook her head in what I guess was supposed to be reverence. "I hear she's a *gifted* surgeon," she continued. "She does replants in one and a half hours skin-to-skin. Artery, vein, nerve, everything. Isn't that incredible?"

"That is," I said. Good for her. Good for fucking her if she was better at my old job than I was. She could have the Valley Hospital. And who the hell wanted to do replants, anyway? Even if you could get it to stay on, the finger never worked right again.

"She's taking the boards with us this year," Jessica said, then added sweetly, "I can introduce you if you'd like."

I didn't get a chance to respond, because at that moment, Tiffi sidled up to the two of us.

"Are you ladies going to be in town tonight?" she said. "I'm taking a group to a fantastic steak house and I'd love for you to join." She addressed both of us but she looked directly at me as she spoke. I was her cash cow, after all. Who was going to use more "Softsilk" postoperative liposuction garments than me?

"Love to," Jessica purred. "Is my husband invited?"

"Absolutely!" Tiffi chirped, still looking at me. "Dr. Thomas?"

"Of course she's coming." Jessica flashed her motherly smile at me. "Don't you *dare* say 'no', Rachel."

One look at the hostile expressions from the group milling around Tiffi assured me that I was not welcome at her little dinner party.

"I can't," I said. And then I just couldn't stop the next words that flew out of my mouth, sounding even more obnoxious than they had in my head. "We're shooting tonight. At a big Hollywood party. In fact, I have to leave now. See you guys at the boards."

The break was over and people had started to re-congregate back into the auditorium. I was fighting upstream and had almost made it to the front doors of the hotel lobby when I felt a hand on my arm. I whirled around. It was Dr. Donarski.

"Rachel," he said.

I stopped, and felt my chest tighten. "Congratulations. You got my name right."

"Rachel, don't do this to yourself."

"Do what?"

He waved his arm at Blair and the crew, who stood waiting for me on the other side of the revolving glass door. "Come on. What are you—a surgeon, or a TV star?"

I took a deep breath. "I'm a surgeon *and* a TV star."

"What about Phoenix?"

"What about it?" I said.

He sighed. "They will never pass you, Rachel."

I kept my voice as monotone and steady as possible. "Of course they will. I'm totally ready. I've been through the syllabus twice."

"It doesn't matter." Dr. Donarski lowered his voice. "They will never pass you behaving like this. But there's still time. If you quit now, I can talk to them—"

"About what?"

He sighed again and tilted his head. "How much longer do you think this idiot show of yours is going to last? A few more months? And then what will you have when they fail you? After all those years of hard work. You're a good surgeon, Rachel. But what you're doing right now—it's not even…surgery. It's not even *real!*"

"It's real to me."

"It's difficult for me to watch you ruin your life over this stupidity."

"Then don't watch," I said. "Besides, I don't really have any other options. Somebody fired me, remember?"

"If you'd like I can get you some work at the hospital."

I saw Paula The Superhuman Surgeon watching us. She hovered uncomfortably around the conference room entrance, as if waiting for Donarski, but unsure if she should.

"I don't need work at the hospital. You think I want to spend the rest of my life in that ghetto place fixing mandibles and debriding dead butt sores?"

I felt so sick after saying that that I couldn't bear to look him in the face. Instead I checked my buzzing phone from the bag pressed tightly against my shoulder. It was Blair, calling me from the other side of the door. She must have seen me.

"My crew is waiting. I have to go," I said. "You don't need to worry about me. I'm better than ever." And I pushed through the door, leaving him standing alone on the inside.

"I thought you were going to get one of your friends to come out here and shoot with us," Blair said. She peered through the window. "Anybody attractive in there?"

"Let's just go," I said. Then loudly, almost hoping someone important would hear, I added: "This meeting sucks. And no, they're all ugly."

I didn't get any arguments about leaving. Blair wasn't excited about paying the crew overtime if she wasn't getting anything good, and I'd heard one of the camera guys talking about a Dodgers game that he was missing.

I spent most of the drive with my face pressed up against the cold tinted glass window of the town car, replaying the day's events in my head. Had I *really* not seen this coming? How many times in the past had I heard the snide comments among my peers about the flashy plastic surgeons on reality TV? Calling them "idiots," "a disgrace to our profession"? And I used to laugh right along, even though I knew deep down that the nasty things that were being said were really fueled by envy.

I didn't blame those older guys for hating us. They might be the top guns in our little political plastic surgery world, but those of us on TV were the most *famous* plastic surgeons out in the *real* world.

Besides, this whole *Lipo Queen* thing wasn't my *fault.* Didn't they understand that it wasn't my *choice* to become a famous fat sucker? That I was just doing what anyone else would have done in my situation? That maybe I didn't have three ex-wives and four kids to put through private school in Los Angeles, but I had bills to pay too?

Really? Was I being *completely* honest with myself? Was it *really* all about my struggling financial situation? About helping Jake with his bills so he could live the way he wanted to? It wasn't that I really *liked* being the *Lipo Queen?* That I actually *enjoyed* all of my cool patients and the fabulous parties and clothes and hanging out with Devin Breeze? And so if I did…why wasn't that *okay?* Why wasn't it okay for me to finally be happy? Why wasn't it okay for me to have fun?

Up until I'd met Gloria, my life had been an exercise in delayed gratification. For the first time I was starting to actually feel like I was living in the present, like I could enjoy the day and appreciate my accomplishments instead of just constantly reaching for something more, the next thing, so that things would one day be better. For me *and* Jake.

It wasn't my fault if my colleagues were haters.

But no matter how I tried to spin it, I couldn't. Being snubbed like that back there really hurt. They weren't just anybody. They were members of an elite club that I had worked my whole life to join. I didn't just need to be a member for professional reasons. I *wanted* to be one.

And what if it was true—what Jessica had said? That the old guys were just bringing me out there to Phoenix to fail me?

"You can't come with me when I take the boards," I said to Blair as we turned onto the toll road, halfway home.

"Of course we can," Blair said. "*Those* permits have been taken care of already, thank God."

"No, I mean—I won't *let* you."

Blair snorted. "Maybe you'd like to speak to Gloria about that. Or review your contract one more time."

Of course she was right. That head-spinning first day in Gloria's office, I'd signed off on the rights for them to follow me anywhere, including the one place I was going to have to make everyone else forget that *Lipo Queen* existed. Surely any lawyer I called *now* would just laugh at me for not having had one there in the first place. And then if I failed the boards…I wouldn't just be failing them, I'd be failing them in front of an entire audience. Not only would they cancel the show but what patient in their right mind would ever walk into my office again? Forget about being on TV. My career as a *surgeon* would be over. As usual, Dr. Donarski was right. I *was* ruining my life.

33

"Hey, what happened in here? An earthquake?"

"I didn't hear you come in."

It was the night before I was to leave for Phoenix and *Surprise!* Devin standing in my kitchen doorway. I hadn't seen him since our shared morning of I.V. hydration. He'd completely disappeared—again.

Well, to be fair, maybe *I* was the one who had disappeared. I'd been staying late at the office every night so I wouldn't have to shoot any scenes with him, and it wasn't because I was so swamped with paperwork. I knew that I was avoiding him. It was just that I knew the next time I saw him and he smiled at me, all open-faced and friendly, everything we'd had together would once again be erased. And I needed something to help me get through these last grueling days of studying for hours on end. Whenever I felt like I couldn't bear to go through the differential diagnosis of limited thumb flexion, or the risks of a pedicled TRAM flap one more time, I would think about tossing around in bed with him, the feel of his lips and his skin and his muscles…it was like having a shiny new toy just to pull out and look at. I had to be able to preserve it so I could put it back and take it out again.

I was sitting in the kitchen with books and papers spread out in front of me across the counter, on the barstools next to me, and on the floor. What might have resembled the incomprehensible aftermath of an earthquake to someone else made perfect sense to me. "Scalp Reconstruction" was in front of me. "Lower Extremity" on the chair to my left, "Abdominal Wall" to the right and "Head and Neck Tumors" were on the floor. "Breast Reconstruction" was also somewhere in that pile.

"Studying hard?" Devin said. He reached up and grabbed the doorframe above his head. As he stretched forward, his shirt lifted up slightly and his jeans slid down just enough to reveal his anterior superior iliac spines and the waistband of his boxers crossing a touch of the inguinal ligament.

"So how's it going?"

"Fine." I had thought a clinical description in my head instead of *"there he is showing me those sexy hipbones with the diagonal dents below them"* would keep my hormones and emotions in check. It did not. He was the ultimate sun-kissed man-boy. *How could he even stand himself?* "What's up?"

"Can I just print this out really quick?" He held up a thumb drive. "I need to get it over to Russell tonight."

"Sure. Over there." I waved in the general direction of my makeshift "corner office," where my laptop and printer were set up on a side table. I expected him to beeline over there but he just stood there, surveying me in all of my misery.

"So, are you ready?" he said.

I shrugged. "You're never ready for these things."

"You're not *cooking*, are you?" he joked, motioning toward the humming microwave in the background.

"Reheating Chinese."

"What time do you leave tomorrow?"

"Eight."

"We must be on the same flight."

"What? *You're* coming to Phoenix?" It was one thing to have the crew following me around, but how was I supposed to concentrate with *that* kind of a distraction?

"Whooaa…don't sound so happy about it. Talk to your buddy, Blair. She's the one who's making me go."

"It's not that…it's just…I mean, I need to be able to study and sleep and—"

"I promise not to interfere." Again he grabbed onto the doorframe above his head and stretched out his torso. "I'm kind of looking forward to it. I could use a break from this place. And I hear it's a killer resort." This time his shirt rode up a little more, exposing a few inches of his taut lower abdomen. *Fine. His "six pack."*

Asshole. He did that on purpose. Now he was just fucking with me.

I looked away from him and back down at my mess of study materials.

"I might have come along anyway." He bent down to pet Sushi, who rose from somewhere in the middle of the pile of papers on the floor to greet him. "You know, to cheer you on."

"It's not a sporting event." I stared hard at the posterior scalp algorithm I had drawn out for the fiftieth time on the card in front of me and sighed.

"Are those flash cards?"

As was the standard practice, I had transcribed every one of the sacred questions from the past five or six years onto a five-by-seven index card with the answer on the back. The idea was to study with a colleague, but for obvious reasons, I'd just been quizzing myself.

"What's this?" Devin said, grabbing Posterior Scalp from me.

"It's a picture of a head."

"And what's that?"

"That's a hole in the head."

"So what's the question?"

"Are you trying to help me study?"

"Maybe."

Dammit, why did he have to be so disarming? The microwave shut off with a "ping" but food was now the farthest thing from my mind.

"Okay." I took a deep breath. "So ask me how I'm going to cover it."

"Cover what?"

"The hole. It's on the posterior occiput. Ask me how I'm going to cover it."

"Dr. Thomas," he said with a stern voice. "How are you going to cover the hole on the posterior occiput?"

"Well, first I need to know is it full thickness or partial thickness? Is the bone involved? How did it happen? How old is it? Has there been any radiation to the area? Is the patient otherwise healthy and how much surgery can they withstand? If it's partial thickness I could use a skin graft and even turn over the periosteum and lay it on that if necessary or if it's less than two centimeters I may be able to do a direct closure or rotate in a local skin flap. Bigger than that I would consider a tissue expander or a fasciocutaneous or muscle flap." I stopped for a breath.

Devin blinked hard and shook his head.

"Turn the card over and see if I missed anything. The answers are all on the back."

He flipped the card. "I really can't tell."

"Well, if the defect is on the posterior occiput and they've had radiation treatment then I have to bring in healthy tissue with a flap. I could use the Trapezius muscle based on the Supraclavicular artery. If I need it to reach farther then I could use the Latissumus based on the Thoracodorsal. If neither of these will reach then I have to think about a free tissue transfer like a Rectus based on the Inferior Epigastric or a Free Lat. And I'll have to doppler out recipient vessels like the superficial temporal. Now ask me what I do if it dies."

"If the person dies?"

"No, the flap. Ask me what I do next if the flap dies."

"What do you do if the flap dies?"

"If the flap dies then I would do local wound care first to see if I could salvage enough of it to advance it into the wound later. Or I'd have to try another flap. Now ask me what happens if brain becomes exposed."

"Can we not do that part?" He put the index card back down on the table. "But see? You really know your shit."

"I kind of do," I said. I had even surprised myself with all that knowledge.

"You should practice saying it. You know, record yourself talking and listen."

"Is that what *you* used to do for work?"

"For *PB*? *No*. Shows like that—those scenes are all like one minute each. You never have to memorize anything. You just show up at the crack of dawn and they hand you like two pages…" He started laughing.

"What's so funny?".

"Nothing…it's just…I mean, most of the time I was still going from the night before. Straight from the club."

"Still fucked up?"

He dug his hands into his front pockets and suddenly became very interested with something on the floor. "I wouldn't necessarily say '*fucked up*.'"

When I just stared blankly at him, clearly unable to connect with what he was saying, he explained further, "You know, just stuff to keep me going. How the hell else do you get through a twenty-two hour day that starts at four in the fucking morning?"

"With respect to my medical license, drug enhancement is really not going to be an option for me."

"No, I didn't mean—"

I nodded my head to let him know that I got it. He wasn't giving me pharmaceutical advice. Just simply reminiscing about the good old days, when his life was one big happy moneymaking party.

"But it wasn't like *this*," he added hurriedly, as if he were apologizing. "If you remember, most of the lines in *PB* were super complex like, 'Dude,' and 'Check out those girls.' What *you* do is serious. And you're a genius. You're gonna nail it."

I didn't know where he got "genius" from. Just that he meant in no way was he comparing long days on a set with strict unions and doughnuts and macaroni and cheese continuously ladled out by Craft services to my endless work stretches in a hell hole, putting people back together.

Still, the moment was awkward enough that he abruptly ended it by turning his attention to the computer and fiddling around with the keyboard to make the screen come on. "Hey, can you help me with this? I don't want to mess anything up here."

"It doesn't matter if I'm the best one there," I muttered as I sat down next to him. "They're still going to fail me."

"Who's 'they'?"

I was wary about answering him because his voice was starting to get that far- away sound, like he was rapidly losing interest. "The old guys who give the test."

"What would they want to do that for?"

"Oh…all this *Lipo Queen* stuff."

"What does that have to do with anything?"

Well, I'd managed to sound ominous enough to spark his curiosity. But now I had that problem again where if he really *did* start paying attention to me, I was going to completely lose my focus for the rest of the night, even long after he left. I looked down and I started making small tears in the corner of the index card I was holding while I spoke. "Politics. Historically, they don't look fondly on those of us who go on these reality shows."

I was surprised by what he did next. He leaned back in the chair, balancing it on its two back legs and played with the sides of his hoodie, pulling it back and forth over his ears, much like he had done the day that I met him in Gloria's office.

"But everyone says what a great surgeon you are. How can they fail you?"

I sighed. "This test has nothing to do with what kind of an actual surgeon you are. Besides, most plastic surgeons don't consider liposuction to be 'surgery,' really."

"Why? Because you're not fixing a hole in someone's head?"

"It's complicated." I took the thumb drive from him and popped it into the USB port.

"Oh, well look at that," he said when the monitor came back on.

I immediately minimized the image, but he'd already gotten a good look at it.

The last thing I had left open on the screen was a patient before-and-after photo. It was actually a dangerous distraction to have these pictures on hand in my laptop because before I knew it, what would start out as a little "look-see" to break up the drudgery of endless studying would turn into an hour and a half of poring through photos, admiring some of my work and crucifying myself for the rest of it, making lists of who needed to come back, who might need touch-ups, and who looked good enough to put on the website.

"Huh," Devin said. "You did that to her?"

"Well, yeah. I mean, what do you think I do all day?"

"You really helped her. Did you do her boobs, too? They look good."

What the hell. I brought the image back up on the screen. "Knock yourself out." *Her face wasn't in it and she'd signed a photograph waiver, anyway.* "But I thought you weren't a fan of boob jobs."

"Did I say that?"

I clicked on a few more views. "It changed her life."

The twenty-six year-old girl in the picture was one of my favorites. She was "cute," but unfortunately cherubic and pale in comparison to her three older half-sisters, all of whom had inherited the stunning dark, lanky looks of their mother's first husband. Her procedure—a full-body lipo and breast augmentation—had transformed her from a cute girl hiding in baggy clothes to a shapely young woman who was no longer afraid to draw attention to her curves in flattering, form-fitting outfits. I remember her ex-supermodel mother telling me that I was an artist, that she had never seen her daughter so happy. I'm not saying the surgery solved all of her life problems, but that's still something.

Now looking at me instead of the picture, Devin said, "You really love what you do."

"I guess." His intensity made me uncomfortable. I reminded myself that he was an actor, and that he could turn the intensity on and off as if he had his hand on a wall switch.

"Do you mind if I ask you…" He paused and tugged on the strings of his hoodie. "How did you get into this, *ummm*—line—of work? I'm just wondering, I mean…how does someone—"

"Wind up sucking fat off other people all day for a living?" I shrugged. "It's not exactly like I grew up *dreaming* about becoming this *Lipo Queen*, or anything." I tried to laugh.

He was either seriously pondering what I had just said, or thinking about something else entirely. Finally, he said, "I know how that goes."

When I clicked on the icon to pull up his document, the title, "Tanaday Productions contract for pilot, working title *Professional Men*" slid up to the top of the screen. I remained silent while the printer started cranking through the pages.

As he collated the two copies, he waved a few pages at me and muttered, "This is kind of the same thing, you know."

"Your pilot is like liposuction?"

"No, I'm just saying. Guy Tanaday makes stupid shows. That's not a secret. But they're stupid shows that people like to watch."

"You want this back?" I disconnected the thumb drive.

He was so into whatever he was talking about that he ignored me and continued, "Why do we have to be judged all the time? Why do we all have to be world conquerors? So what if you're just doing liposuction? So what if I'm just a dumb TV actor? *Someone's* gotta do it."

Was he trying to draw a parallel in our lives? And using metaphors, no less.

But I had no time to even think about it because that was when the shit really hit the fan.

"Rachel." A joltingly familiar voice from across the room. And then—as if this night couldn't get any weirder—

There *he* was, standing in the doorway where Devin had just been. The *other* him. It was so out of context that at first the only thing I recognized was his voice. Then, as the synapses between my eyes and brain reconciled…There he was, in all of his self-righteous sexy Latino glory. Like he should have been wearing a crown. And a royal robe. With a couple of minions holding up the tail.

He must have just gotten out of the water. He was wearing soaking wet board shorts and flip flops and you could see the sand stuck between his toes. His preternatural burnt-sienna skin had a reddish hue to it, like it got when he spent a lot of time in the sun. His hair was much longer than I remembered, almost shoulder length, and it dripped from the ends, leaving dark spots on the hardwood floor. Pissing on his territory.

A cross-breeze filtered through the room and I was hit with a waft of skunky pot odor.

"Eddie," I greeted him, too dumbfounded to even get up.

"You're Eddie." Devin didn't get up either.

Eddie nodded. "Hey, Dude. And you are…?"

Really? He was going to be *that* much of an asshole—after all this time, after I had finally been able to cut myself loose from him—that he was going to stalk me, sneak into my building, show up in my home and then pretend to be oblivious as to what was going on in my life?

"I think you know who he is," I said. "Eddie, what are you doing here?"

He batted his puppy eyes at me. "I heard you were leaving for the big test tomorrow. Thought maybe you might want some help packing. I know you've got all those heavy books." He turned to Devin as if he were an afterthought.

"Right. You're that guy from that show my little sister used to watch." He strolled across the room toward us and the skunk smell got stronger. He must have had a bag of it in the pocket of his board shorts. "What was it again? Your TV show. That *girls* liked to watch...'*Beach*' something?"

"Pacific Beach." Devin spat out the words in a monotone.

Clearly there was room for only one man-boy in here.

"Right. That's right. About the surfers." Eddie pushed his hair out of his eyes with one hand. "You guys must have been so bored, sitting around with nothing to do all day."

Devin glanced at me like, "What is this weirdo talking about?" but I just shrugged. And there was silence as I started to see where Eddie was going with this.

"I'm sorry...?" Devin said.

"No, Dude, *I'm* sorry. You must have been freezing your ass off, just hanging out in the water like that."

"I'm not sure what you mean."

Eddie helped himself to a bottle of water from the counter. "Oh...you know...I did a lot of the surf stunts for that show. I know they kept you guys around for the close-ups."

"Funny." Devin rolled his eyes at me. "I don't remember you. I mean, while I was hanging around, *freezing my ass off*."

"Wow. Look at this thing." Eddie leaned up against the refrigerator. "Stainless steel. Must've cost a lot, huh, Rach?" Then to Devin: "I only did it a few times. They loved me and they kept begging me to come back but the pay was really low and you know, my sponsor wasn't happy."

"Well, I can't imagine whose stunts you did," Devin said evenly. "You don't resemble any of the main characters."

I sucked in cold air. I know he hadn't meant it that way, but Devin had unknowingly hit Eddie where he really lived.

The thing about Eddie was that although his charm and sex appeal and natural talent—in bed, on a surfboard, in the operating room (yes, in that particular order)—seemed to make his life so easy for him, it couldn't *ever* get him the one thing I knew he wanted the most. It wasn't something that he'd ever put into words. He didn't have to. It was this unspoken thing about him that I just *knew*. Ironically, I think I had picked it up from listening to him brag about himself. And it was so much more crystal clear *now*, after spending time away from him.

It made no sense, but in this modern world where it seemed like everyone else aspired to be an urban gangster—more specifically, a hip-hop star from Compton—Eddie wanted to be white. A *white* surfer boy. Not on *Pacific Beach*, but in real life. It didn't matter that he was the best surfer at the pier and he got the most girls. He was the only Mexican on his street in Malibu who wasn't "the help." He laughed along with his friends when they jokingly called him "Pedro the Gardener." Or about how when he walked around his neighborhood, rich white women would pull over and ask how much he charged for a car wash. He would laugh when he told the stories, but I never believed that deep down he really thought any of it was funny.

And right now he was lying. His transparency was so pathetically, painfully obvious. Yes, Eddie had a "sponsor"—some local surf shop that gave him free boards and wetsuits—but he had *never* done professional surf stunts on a popular TV show. I would have heard about it a million times already. Besides, any time Eddie started using the vague pronoun "they" and got all grandiose, he was bullshitting. Like how he used to tell me that "*they*" wanted him to scrub on certain cases, or "*they*" begged him to work for another hospital, or "*they*" were going to pay for him to go to medical school. When I was sleeping with him and I thought I was in love with him, I excused it as his "big personality." *This* was my Latin Lover? This dick size-measuring idiot? Incidentally, a contest he would have won, but that wasn't the point. I used to be impressed. Back then I wanted to believe that he was great. Now I was just embarrassed for him.

"Eddie, what do you *want*?" I pretended to start organizing some of my papers so I wouldn't have to look at him.

"Well, you never got back to me after I left that message on your cell, so I thought maybe I had the wrong one. Really just wanted to come by and see if you needed help. How you're doing. And wondering if you've heard from Jake."

"What?"

Outside of my family, Eddie was the only person besides Jenny who knew about Jake. We'd actually taken him to the beach a few times together. Confiding in Eddie about Jake was one of the things that had made me feel close to him. Like our relationship meant something, that it was more than just a booty call.

Now I was forced to look at him. To look at Eddie with his stupid big brown saucer eyes to see if he was still lying. "What about Jake?"

"You know, just wanted to make sure he was okay. I've seen him around down at the beach once or twice. He doesn't look that good."

Dammit! That manipulative bastard. "Don't talk to me about Jake, like you even give a fuck about him."

"Whoa, Rachel. You really need to learn to control your emotions better." The corners of his mouths curled up and he shook his head a little. "It's not good for you to get yourself all worked up."

"Jake?" Devin said.

Eddie looked at him. "Oh, you don't know about Jake?" He glanced around the room. "Nice place you got here. Too bad you don't have room for him."

"Eddie, you need to leave!"

"Rachel, you should really calm down. You're going to make yourself sick."

"I said, get out!"

Devin stood up. "Maybe you should hit the road, *Dude.*" He wasn't bigger than Eddie but he was about half an inch taller.

"Eddie. Get. The fuck. Out of here."

Eddie threw his hands up in the air like he was some kind of peacemaker. "God, all this violence. I was just coming to wish you luck. To be a friend. To help you out. You want me to leave, fine. I'm going. Just don't say I didn't tell you so." Then, just before he slammed the front door behind him, he called over his shoulder, "It really is too bad you don't have room for him here. It's such a nice place."

I turned away from Devin so he couldn't see my face. He waited for Eddie's footsteps to fade down the hallway before he said anything. "So. That's Eddie."

"That's Eddie."

He touched my shoulder lightly with his hand. Not the time for the pulse in the groin. "Ummm…You want to talk about it?"

How I wished I could. How I wished I had someone to talk to right now, to wrap their arms around me and tell me that Eddie was full of crap. That Jake was fine. *Fine.* And that keeping him separate from this life was also fine because it was how I paid for *his* life. His health was what was important. His doctors. The *right* doctors. And the right medication. And they were expensive. Who would pay for it if I didn't? My mother couldn't do it herself. That was more important than my spending time with him. And if I didn't do all of that for him, where would he wind up—eating pudding packs in a state institution for the rest of his life?

So maybe I didn't see him every day. So what? I saw him a week ago. He even apologized about my car. We were working things out. He was his usual removed self in our conversations. Maybe a little more distant. But that was okay.

If he wasn't taking his meds, one of his doctors would have certainly called me. Besides, it took a while for him to really go off the wall and wind up in jail or something. And even if there was the slightest bit of truth to what Eddie had said, and he was a little nuttier than usual and people at the beach were scared of him, he'd never hurt anyone. Regardless of what my mother said, he wasn't dangerous. After I got through this last professional hurdle, I'd fix it all. Family therapy. That was the answer. I could afford it. We could even invite my mother.

If only I could tell all of this to Devin. Hearing the words out loud would make it okay. And then Devin could hold me and tell me I was doing my best, that Jake couldn't hope for a better sister…the way Eddie used to when we lay in bed, before or after he fucked me.

But Devin wasn't Eddie. He wasn't especially interested in fucking me. He didn't need to pretend to care about my schizophrenic brother. He was definitely turning out to be a lot more *human* than I'd originally thought, but that didn't mean he'd understand about Jake. He'd see me completely differently. Like I might be crazy too. Most people don't know much about mental illness, but the one thing everyone seems to know is that it's hereditary.

Anyway, how would I even *begin* to tell him, to untangle myself from this embroidery of lies about who I really was?

"Rachel, you want to talk about it?" he repeated.

"No," I said. "And thanks for not asking me who Jake is."

34

"Non-smoking, please," I said to the girl at the hotel lobby registration desk.

"Of course," she chirped back. Her gold-plate nametag said "Marcie."

"Why are you getting a non-smoking room?" Devin dug his elbow into my side. "We all know that you smoke."

"Please shut up."

"Great," Blair said to the camera guy, then back to us. "Keep that. Conflict. Tension. Love that. Argue about something else, like how he wouldn't help you carry in your luggage. Let the audience in on your anxiety."

My initial plan—before Blair had turned this serious milestone into a dramatic escapade—had been to drive to Phoenix alone. I had actually been looking forward to it. I imagined six hours of nothing but flat desert landscape and familiar soft pop music on the radio. Maybe even with the top down, flying along on some of that straightaway road where the speed limit is seventy but you can go ninety, with the wind and sun in my face. It would be a time to relax and decompress so that I could make a smooth transition into what was surely about to be the most terrifying experience of my life.

But instead I got this. The on-camera tracking of my whole sordid travel itinerary from the Southwest Airlines terminal in Burbank to the resort check-in. Blair's primary mission was to capture my anxiety, heightened by airport security and a packed plane that felt like a bus. The best part was having to check my bags, and trying not to visibly panic while waiting for the two tons of books that I'd packed for last minute studying to show up on the carousel in Phoenix.

I turned back to Marcie. "Non-smoking," I repeated, imagining the pack of Marlboros at the bottom of my carry-on.

"Yes, ma'am."

"It's 'doctor,'" I said. The only time I ever insist on being called "doctor" is when someone calls me "ma'am." Besides, didn't she have some kind of advance warning that a horde of doctors was going to take over the place for the weekend, and that she should be addressing them appropriately?

I couldn't have conjured up a worse nightmare in my own head. I was surrounded by a hotel lobby packed with a herd of agitated young plastic surgeons, each fighting their way to check in. I, in my usual short skirt and sexy top ensemble and my entourage—all in matching pink and white *Lipo Queen* T-shirts and baseball caps and beige Bermuda shorts—contrasted painfully against the roomful of men and women in business appropriate attire.

The plastic surgery oral boards was an exercise in tradition and suffering. The first tradition was that the venue for this rite of passage was the same luxury resort where the old guys *giving* the test could enjoy themselves socializing and playing golf on their downtime while the examinees like myself sat caged in our rooms with the shades drawn against the bright sunlight, doing our last-minute cramming, chewing our fingernails until they bled, and—in my case—illegally smoking cigarettes until we asphyxiated. As far as I knew, nobody had ever hanged themself from a shower rod.

"Would you like some information on our spa services?" Marcie said.

Was she *joking*? Was she *that* oblivious to the terror in the air? Could she not sense the sadistic massacre that was about to ensue?

"*I* would," Devin said, taking the glossy pamphlet from her hand. He winked at her. "I could really use a massage."

The girl's eyes widened. "You're that *guy*—"

"Yes, he is," Blair said. "Can you please do that one more time?"

"Do what? Oh, my God, am I on television?"

"If you sign a release," Blair said. "Now, Breeze say that one more time and Doc, give me a look like you're irritated. Like you're angry because he's flirting with her."

Really? I had just come from a town where I had to compete with Playmates and actresses and every other girl who looked like a bathing suit model and I was supposed to be jealous of *Marcie*?

It only got better when Marcie actually read Blair's *Lipo Queen* baseball cap. This time she looked at me. "You're the *doctor*! I *looove* your show! I watch it all the time. What happened to that one pregnant woman who wanted—"

"Excuse me," I heard one of my perturbed colleagues call out from behind me on the line. "But I would really like to check in."

I didn't recognize the voice and I didn't turn around. Knowing who it was would only make it worse. Especially if it was someone who didn't already hate me and was just about to start now. If only I could escape through a secret portal into another dimension like they did in those sci-fi thrillers Jake used to watch when we were kids.

Somehow we made it through check-in and to my room without running into anyone I knew, which had been my first clear-cut goal. I had figured if I could hole up inside my room and just concentrate on the test and have minimal negative interaction with all the haters around I might be able to mentally prepare myself to have a fighting chance at this thing.

"Two beds?" Devin said to me when the door swung open. Blair and the crew had left us to get some general footage of the resort, and I was to meet up with them at the exam sign-in, for the unfolding of more drama.

"I told you. I have to concentrate." I hoisted one of my suitcases up onto the dresser.

"Damn." He lifted the other one next to it. "You brought a whole fucking library. You won't even have time to look at all of this shit."

"It makes me feel better knowing they're here."

"I could help you unpack. If you want."

"I'm fine. Why don't you go check out the pool or something?" I marveled at how effortlessly I was able to resist him. My survival mode had taken over. The same survival mode that had gotten me through relentless years of rigorous training and the countless standardized tests that went along with them. I had suddenly become a horse with blinders on. No, better—a dog with one of those cones around his neck after he's been castrated. Basically an animal with the ability to keep my eyes only on what I needed. To pass the boards. Devin had become peripheral vision material.

Which I think was becoming confusing to him.

"Okay. It does look pretty awesome," he said. "See ya." He dropped the two bags of books he was carrying and they hit the ground with a perfunctory suit-yourself thump. And he left.

Blair ignored my desire to isolate myself in my room. *Her* goal for the day was to capture my intense suffering on camera as completely as possible. She got footage of me strolling, solitary around the golf course, deep in thought about my future, running off steam on the treadmill in the workout center, "talking to Jenny" on the phone about how hard the test was going to be. When I finally convinced her that I had to get back to my room to study, she followed me for one last interview.

"Fine," I said. "But at six I have to start waiting for the phone to ring."

Perhaps this was the most sadistic ritual of all. One third of the test was based on our notorious "blue books." Basically, it was an audit of your practice. Each year, the Board would pick five operative cases from the year-long log you had to hand in with the exam application. Then they sent you five blue binders, one for each case. If any information from a single case was missing—no matter what the reason—you had to inform the Board immediately. They didn't care if the hospital burned down with your X-rays in the basement, or a mass murderer broke into your house and killed your whole family and then took your camera with all the pictures inside. As punishment for missing the information, the examinee was assigned *three more* cases to prepare in place of the one that was incomplete. I'd noticed several unfortunate candidates carrying more than five blue books, and one girl who wheeled them in on a dolly.

The case books were handed over at registration for review by our examiners prior to the test. One of the three forty-minute test sessions consisted of in-depth grilling about these cases. Now that I knew the political "rules," I realized that this was one place where I had them beat. The whole case collection and selection process went down long before I had become the *Lipo Queen,* so I had a plethora of mandible fractures, pressure sore flaps and breast reconstructions for the examiners to choose from. There wasn't a single lipo for them to crucify me on.

The night before the test, all of the examiners gathered in one room and reviewed the case books. If a case book was found to have any misinformation—anything from incorrect billing codes to missing photos to improper notary signatures—the owner of the book was excused and sent home before the exam had even begun. According to plastic surgery lore, at least one or two people were "sent home" each year. As painful as it was to have to take the test, getting sent home was worse. That just meant prolonging the torture for another year until you could take it again.

The method of contacting the examinee to inform them of their dismissal was to call their hotel room between the hours of 6:00 and 10 P.M. the night before the exam. If you didn't receive a call by ten, then you could safely assume that you would be allowed to sit for the test.

"And I still need some time by myself to study," I told Blair. "I fail this, and you're out of a job, remember?"

"Not just me," she said.

Devin rolled back in just as Betty and Leticia had finished touching up my hair and make-up.

"This place is pretty sweet," he said, falling back onto one of the beds. "Maybe I'll even pick up golf while I'm here."

He reached for the television remote but Blair snatched it from his hand. "Can't you see we're working? Why don't you go back out there and find some girl like you usually do?"

"What do you think took me so long?" he said, staring evenly into her face. He looked over at me. "How you holding up?"

I shrugged. "Let's just get this done, please," I said to Blair. "I really do have a bunch of stuff to look over tonight."

I should have known saying that would only make everything take longer. I wound up spending an hour in front of the blue screen repeating the same three sentences over and over.

"This exam is a major milestone in my career. I have been working my entire life for this. I just don't know what I'll do if I don't pass it."

"Come on, Doc! Mean it! If you fail this thing, it's game over for you. *Show's* over. *Literally.* What are you going to do with your life? You're back to being nobody in a town full of more plastic surgeons than unemployed actors. Well, *almost.*" She glanced at Devin, who remained stone-faced.

"I wouldn't exactly call her a nobody," he said. "She *is* a surgeon. It's not like she's a pediatrician or something."

I'd been doing such a good job of keeping my guard up with him, but I couldn't help smiling at that.

"I think you're the last person in this room who gets opinions on nobodies," Blair snapped. "She's got everything at stake! In fact, say that. Say that you've got everything at stake."

"I've got everything at stake," I said.

"And what are you going to do if you fail it?"

Devin made faces at me from across the room, crossing his eyes, putting his thumbs in his ears and wiggling his fingers. Blair caught him and hissed, "Stop it!" She didn't have to worry. Laughing was about the farthest thing from my mind. Vomiting was more of a possibility.

"I might—" I started to say.

"Come on, it's not like the first time we've done this," Blair said. "Start with, 'If I fail this test…'"

"If I fail this test—"

Devin drew a line across his neck with his right index finger, stuck out his tongue and rolled his eyes backward.

"I am going to…kill myself?"

Blair stamped her foot, unable to make much of a sound on the carpeted floor. "You two better stop screwing around. And if you're going to threaten suicide, at least do it with conviction. And cry a little."

It was four-thirty. Less than two hours and I could get a phone call that would send me on my way home. What if one of those Haters-In-Charge decided to sabotage one of my case books—just rip out a few pages and tell me something was missing? No, they'd probably rather see me squirm to my death in person. My examiners undoubtedly had all kinds of torture in store for me tomorrow. What were their names again? Someone Carl something, and then a Smith from Minnesota. It would be useful to know what their specialties were. As soon as Blair and her minions left I was going to sit out on my non-smoking back patio and smoke and Google them all on my laptop.

"Hey, can I do one of those little speeches?" Devin said.

Blair spun around to look at him. "You're *volunteering* to work?"

Devin made a point of participating in the blue background interviews as infrequently as possible. Whenever Blair made him do one it always took at least ten takes because he would swear a bunch of times just to irritate her.

"I wasn't even going to ask you. But if we're going to spend the extra time you better not fuck it up. Go change your shirt so you don't look homeless and someone slap some make-up on this pretty boy's face and get him on up here."

I groaned inwardly. *Why the hell was he prolonging this?* He knew how stressed out I was, how I wanted everyone to clear out and leave me alone. What could he possibly have to say, anyway?

It never took them very long to get his face ready. He sat in front of the blue screen in a yellow alligator shirt Blair made him wear that I knew he hated.

"Rachel has worked very hard for this," he said. "She deserves to do well. I've never seen anyone work as hard as she does." He paused and looked straight at me with his next words: "I'm not going to wish her good luck because she doesn't need luck. She's smart and capable and ready for this. I know she's going to kill it." Even as it was digesting its own lining into multiple ulcers, my stomach did a flip-flop.

"How sweet," Blair said. "That's good. We'll keep it." She punched him on the shoulder. "It sounded so genuine. If I didn't know what a real-life ass you were I'd have gotten all choked up."

Then Blair had us switch places so she could get a few more good tearjerkers out of me. Just as we were wrapping it up, there was a knock on the door.

Blair arched an eyebrow. "Are you expecting someone?"

I shook my head. Who would I be expecting? Everyone that wanted to talk to me was already in the room. I had no friends out there.

"Hel*lo* there!" I heard a familiar voice sing out when Blair opened the door. I felt the blood drain from my face. What was *she* doing here? "Isn't this

Rachel Thomas' room?" Without waiting for an invitation, Jessica Bernholtz brushed past Blair to cross the room and give me a big sisterly hug.

"So how *are* you, Rachel? Oh, my God, can you believe we're actually here?"

Well, *I* can't believe that *you're* actually *here*, I wanted to say. *Like in my hotel room. Uninvited.*

"Hi, Jess," I said. "How are you?"

She seemed to suddenly become aware of the fact that I was sitting in front of an aqua blue screen with bright lights shining in my face and a crew of five people positioned around me. Her eyes widened. "Oh, I'm sooo sorry. Am I interrupting something? I just really wanted to get to see you and wish you luck—"

"I take it you two are close," Blair said.

"Oh, yes," Jessica reached over and shook Blair's hand while waving over at Devin with the other. "We've been studying for this together all year. I'm Jessica. Doctor Jessica Bernholtz."

I was satisfied to at least see Devin barely nod in return, looking even less interested in meeting her than when he had met me the first time.

But Blair was a different story. There was a weird flash of recognition on her face. "Nice to meet you in person."

'In person'?

Even Devin looked surprised.

"Well, Dr. Jessica Bernholtz," Blair said. "How would you like to sign a release and give us an interview?"

It was then that I noticed how Jessica was outfitted in a crisp red suit—a color that coincidentally contrasted just perfectly with the blue background. And how her hair and makeup were already *conveniently* camera-ready.

"Oh, I don't know." She glanced at her watch. "I guess I might have a minute or two."

"I don't get it," I said more to the air on the patio than to Devin, after the crew had packed up and everyone else was gone. "Why would she risk everything herself and come over here like that?"

I still couldn't believe what had just happened. Not only had Jessica waltzed into the middle of the shoot, but she had basically taken over with her own interview. She had answered Blair's questions, and then, without any prompting, she had gone on to describe the mechanisms of the test, the *grueling* preparation, how it was our *privilege* to be here, all the while speaking in her know-it-all, condescending voice as if she were telling a bedtime story that only she knew the ending to. The only satisfaction I got was when Blair told her to stop moving her hands around like she was conducting an orchestra and to lower them out of the frame.

I ashed into the now-empty twelve dollar macadamia nut can from the honor bar. From my perch on the edge of a lounge chair I had a clear view of the bedside phone through the sliding glass door. I'd be able to see the red light flash even if I missed the ring. How ironic. Actually sitting and watching a phone all night and willing it *not* to ring. They really knew how to torture us.

It was seven-thirty and Blair and the crew had cleared out roughly half an hour earlier, but not before getting several staged shots of my torment. Me sitting and staring at the phone. Me pacing back and forth in front of the phone. The phone on its own. I could only imagine the foreboding score that would be synchronized with the footage.

"What do you mean—risk everything?"

I lit another cigarette. "*She's* the one who told me how much trouble I was going to be in. For being on TV. So why would she get in front of a camera *now*?"

Get in front of it—and stay in front of it—*for over an hour.* She had sat and given the perfectly-poignant-yet-strong-career-woman interview that Blair had been trying to get out of me. And of course Blair had eaten it up, taken Jessica's card and practically promised her she was going to make her a regular on the show when we got back to L.A.

If it wasn't canceled. If I passed the test.

"That's easy. She probably figures by the time it gets aired your test will be long over, and it won't matter anymore."

So she wasn't so righteous after all. She was a hater just like everyone else.

Then I blurted out, "You don't think she's pretty, do you?"

Devin half-smiled and shook his head. "I really can't even remember what she looked like," he said.

"Well, she kind of has a weird body."

"What are you—still in high school?"

"Devin, for those of us who didn't become TV stars, high school is *never over*." He frowned. "You dope. What are you worrying about that shit for, anyway?"

Because that's the shit we women worry about. That's how we compete with each other. That's why I have a job.

"She's such a bitch," I muttered. "And she always knows fucking *every-thing*. Somehow she even knew about how I got in trouble at my old job that time with the insurance fraud."

Devin laughed. I'd told him about that once and he'd thought it was the funniest thing he'd ever heard. That I'd gotten in trouble for doing free lipo. "How'd she find out? Did she work there, too?"

"No! *She* never had to work in that shithole. Apparently it filtered down through the plastic surgery gossip grapevine." I sighed. "What a small fucking town."

"Are you sure about that?" He raised his eyebrows.

"What do you mean?"

"What I mean is, how do you know it wasn't the other way around?"

"What?"

"What if she's the one who found out and reported you to your boss?"

"What for? Back then I wasn't even on her radar."

"Well, she and Blair were like old buddies. She obviously talks to every-one. Just saying." Devin held up the stack of flash cards I had brought out onto the terrace. "Whatever. Who cares about her. You want me to do some of these with you?"

"No." I'd given up for now. I had already tried to go through a few on my own but I just felt like I was seeing the words and not really reading them.

"Oh, come on, Rach, what are you going to do—just sit and stare at the phone and smoke all night?"

"Until ten, yes. Those are my plans."

"At least we can get a movie. They've got some decent stuff On Demand."
I took a drag of my cigarette and continued staring at the phone.
"Well, then I'm taking off," Devin said. It sounded like a threat. If I wasn't
on the verge of a nervous breakdown I would have laughed. I could tell he was
shocked that I wasn't begging him to stay. But what might have been a sudden
mystery to him was just a simple equation. For once, Devin Breeze was not
the biggest thing in my life. He had been trumped by my board exam. And it
was driving him a little nuts. Figures that it would take me a near life crisis to
switch gears and play hard to get.

Once Devin was gone, my mind wandered back to what he'd said about
Jessica. It *was* an interesting perspective from an objective outsider's angle. But
it didn't make any sense. Why would she have cared what I was doing over the
hill, in a place that she once told me she "wouldn't even visit in a bullet-proof
SUV with bodyguards?" I wasn't a threat to her way back then.

"…*and I realized the case was already half done by another plastic surgeon…*"
What she'd said when I ran into her at the meeting. I could hear her voice in
my head as if her stupid face was right there in front of me.

Maybe she *had* seen me as a threat. Or she was smart enough to know that
I was blossoming into one. Because no matter where you put me, I was good
at my job.

And look where all my raw talent had gotten me. Boxed into my own little
corner of hell, chain smoking cigarettes and unable to enjoy the company of
the hottest guy I was ever going to meet in my life.

I burned through half the pack of cigarettes by the time the clock radio
on the night table displayed that it was 10:00 P.M. My chest was getting
sore enough that I didn't even feel like lighting another one. I confirmed
the time with my phone. I even called my personal hotel room voicemail in
case the phone had somehow malfunctioned and failed to ring. Nothing. No
messages.

I flopped back onto one of the beds. I was not overcome with the wash of
relief that I had expected. I just no longer felt fear. I didn't feel anything.

Except for one thing. There was something I needed to do. I just couldn't
remember what. Until I started wondering what else might be in that mini-bar,

and I started thinking about how Jake and I were punished for raiding the mini-bar in my aunt's hotel room when we were kids.

Jake. Maria. I hadn't spoken to either of them in a couple of days. Even though I thought we'd made amends, Jake hadn't been returning my calls lately. I had been way too busy to go out there and check on him, but I figured Maria had everything under control. Besides, it was only a few days. I'd be back soon enough.

My cell reception sucked so I used the landline to leave a message on Maria's voicemail. I wasn't even sure exactly what time it was in L.A. Didn't Arizona do something stupid like not go on Daylight Savings with the rest of the country? Figures they would have this stupid test in a stupid state like this.

I tried Jake's number as well, but he didn't answer. He must already be asleep. Fine. It wasn't like we never went a few days without talking to each other.

Eddie's stupid little-boy voice crept into my head: *"…I saw him at the beach…he's not looking so good…"*

Dammit. I couldn't take a chance that I might get a call from the Van Nuys Police that Jake was gallivanting barefoot and half-naked around the 7-Eleven parking lot while I was in the middle of this test. I managed to get a hold of Jenny, who promised to check on him tomorrow after her audition. (*Could I believe it, she actually had an audition tomorrow?!?*) So now at least that was under control.

Devin returned to find me staring at the ceiling.

"Well?" he said.

I shrugged. "Do you see me packing?"

"That's great, then!" He was visibly relieved.

"Not really. They're just delaying the torture."

He sat on the other bed. "I think you need to be a little more positive about this."

"What would you know about it?" I was amazed that it wasn't even difficult to look at him. It was about as arousing as a picture in a male cologne ad. "When was the last time *you* took a test? You didn't even go to college."

"How do you know?"

"I don't. Sorry." I felt my face flush. I hadn't meant to be mean. But what was *I* worrying about hurting *his* feelings for? What twilight zone was *this*? "I guess I just assumed."

"Well, you would be half-right," he admitted. "I was at a two-year school for a bit."

"And what happened?"

"What do you *think* happened?" He leaned back against his headboard, and stretched out his legs, resting them on the bed with his dirty feet and flip-flops dangling over the side. "I was visiting a friend in L.A. over spring break. I met a casting director who told me she could make me a star."

"Was that before or after you slept with her?"

"Ouch."

I could feel him trying to catch my eye and I felt a twinge—and that's all it was, just a twinge—of that powerless feeling coming back, so I turned my head and rolled away from him, facing the wall.

"I didn't sleep with her," he continued. "But if I'd had to I probably would. What would you have done?"

"What did she look like?"

"Ha! Isn't it what's on the inside that matters?"

"No, that's just in the movies," I said. "But everyone in the movies is good-looking, so it doesn't even make sense."

"You didn't answer my question," he persisted. He seemed happy that I was softening up. "What would *you* have done?"

"Sorry to disappoint you. No, I wouldn't sleep with her."

"Liar! For five million dollars?"

"You didn't get five million dollars."

"No, I didn't. But just suppose."

"What do you think I am, a lesbian hooker?" Even though he couldn't see it I was sure he could hear the smile on my face. It wasn't fair that he could win me over so easily, when I was trying so hard to be in such a state of torment.

The next thing I knew his hand was casually resting on my shoulder. I stiffened my body to stop the goose bumps that started the second he touched me.

257

"No," he said softly. "I don't think you're a hooker. I think you're a very smart and talented surgeon who is going to kick ass tomorrow on her board exam. Though I would like to discuss that lesbian thing later when you have more time." I felt his breath on the back of my neck, which I didn't mind. He never had bad breath, unlike most bachelors who have multiple permanent colonies of foul bacteria growing between their teeth because there's nobody around to instruct them on the basics of oral hygiene.

He was hovering so close, that I had this weird feeling that if I turned around he would start making out with me.

No way. I couldn't afford to let him fuck with my mind. Not tonight. And I was pissed to think that he would even try to, at a time like this, just because he might be bored.

"Thanks," I mumbled, forcing myself to keep my head planted in the pillow, concentrating on the ugly painting of a desert landscape on the wall in front of me.

He remained silent for a moment, then said, "Will it bother you if I turn on the TV?"

I felt the bed move with the shift in weight as he stood up. "No, that's fine." I planned to take an Ambien so I'd be able to sleep through a fire drill, if necessary. Though I did feel a stab of disappointment that he had given up so easily.

While Devin watched some action-packed thriller from his bed I tried unsuccessfully to look at a few more cards; the "zebras" that I wasn't one hundred percent sure about. The rare craniofacial syndromes. Transgender surgery. Congenital hand anomalies. But everything was just spilling out of my overstuffed brain. Besides, no matter how much I knew, they were going to get me to say something wrong enough to fail me, anyway. It was just going to be a long day of feeling like the dumbest, most useless plastic surgeon on the face of the earth.

I said goodnight to Devin.

"What time do you need to get up?" he said.

"Eight, I guess," I mumbled, already slipping into my Ambien-induced coma.

"You want me to wake you?"

"I set the alarm clock. Getting a wake-up call. But yeah, if I'm asleep, wake me." I can't remember if I said anything more, but I do remember willing myself not to dream about him. I needed my subconscious to organize everything in my brain for tomorrow. I tried to imagine the index cards. I wasn't going to let him distract me in my sleep either.

35

I had to be the first oral board exam candidate in the history of plastic surgery to show up in full hair and makeup and with my own camera crew. An hour before my first exam session I was ready to go—physically, that is—in a dark navy suit and simple black pumps. Although Blair hated it because she said it made me look like I was seven, I had been able to convince Letitia to style my hair in a ponytail. I have a habit of playing with the front strands when I'm nervous and I didn't want the examiners to mistake this for flirtation. There was folklore about a girl who got failed on the spot after she propositioned her examiner when she couldn't come up with the answer to a question. Supposedly, they never let her take the test again and eventually she wound up moving to some third-world country where she practiced primary care medicine. I wasn't sure how much of that story was really true but just hearing it was enough for me to stop Betty from getting over-aggressive with the eye makeup.

"Don't you want your eyes to pop?" she demanded when I snatched the heavy black liner away from her.

"They're not going to be able to get close enough where it'll even make a difference," I replied.

The Plastic Surgery Board couldn't keep the *Lipo Queen* crew out of the resort, but they were able to prevent it from entering the wing of hotel rooms they had reserved for administration of the test. The viewers were going to have to say good-bye to me fifteen minutes before my first test and if I hid at the other end of the hotel, I could pretend I was alone until 4:00 P.M., when my last session was over.

Devin had been sleeping when I'd left for hair and makeup, but he was gone by the time I stopped back at the room to drop off my phone. No electronic devices allowed. I would be showing up with only my hotel key card and a valid picture I.D. clutched in my sweaty palm. Another bit of folklore—someone once paid somebody smarter to take the test for them, and of course all involved got caught and lost their medical licenses.

My heart did sink a little when I found Devin's bed empty. I remembered him saying something about going golfing this morning, but the least he could have done was wish me luck before he left, especially after all of those heartfelt things he said last night. Another affirmation that he was basically full of shit.

But then he turned up at the poolside restaurant with Blair and the crew. He was still wearing the blue T-shirt he'd slept in and he had a little bed-head going on.

"Hey, Rach, you hungry?" He pointed at his half-eaten omelet.

I shook my head and I felt my focus blurring. It would be better if I could have just written him off as an asshole for the day. Blair was busy getting her B-roll of the other candidates already heading toward the examination rooms and just watching the sea of dark suits pass by already had my stomach in gymnastics. It was like a marching band minus the musical instruments. Except for the girls who couldn't seem to help themselves from stealing glances at Devin—they all stared straight ahead.

It was just as well that I didn't feel like eating because Blair filled my last few free moments with takes of me walking down the path toward my doom, barking at me the whole time:

"Look to the left." "A little to the right." "Slower." "Faster." "Purse your lips together." "Someone call Betty to get down here and touch up that eye make-up."

The minute hand of the clock hanging over the restaurant entrance finally clicked into place at the twelve. I was able to legitimately make my escape.

"I better go," I said.

Devin caught my eye and raised his brow and then I remembered something we'd talked about that night in between make-out sessions in the cab coming back from Guy Tanaday's house. I had asked him why dramatic shows like *Pacific Beach* always ended scenes with someone saying, "I better go," or "you better go," when if you think about it, nobody ever really says that in real life and just walks off like that. The same way they don't just show up at each other's houses unannounced and expect them to be home, or hang up at the end of a phone call without saying "good-bye."

Was he remembering it too? It was such a minute detail from what—for him—was a very insignificant evening of debauchery and yet... the way he smiled at me now made me think that he did.

"We'll see you back here at four," Blair reminded me for the fifth time, as if I might escape somewhere.

I couldn't feel my feet on the ground as I started walking. It was as if the sensory neurons below my waist had stopped firing so all of the energy could be directed toward my overloaded brain. At least the motor neurons down there were working. Somehow my legs carried me across the courtyard and up the stairs to the area of designated testing rooms. Although I certainly didn't want my posse anywhere near the exam rooms, I couldn't help thinking what an intense visual shot they were missing. The Board had blocked out a wing of the hotel that faced the golf course, away from the pool and restaurant so there would be minimal commotion and distraction. It was a quarter-of-a-mile long outdoor hallway with entrances to a row of about fifty rooms.

A small wooden desk chair sat to the right of the door to each room—like the kind you see in college lecture halls—and the twelve-thirty shift of test-takers had begun to fill the chairs. My room assignment was third from the end, so when I sat down and craned my neck slightly to the right I had a view of nearly the entire hallway. A candidate sat stiffly in each chair, and everyone looked nervously back and forth at each other. I stared straight ahead, trying to pretend I was invisible when I accidently caught the eye of the girl sitting to my immediate left. I recognized her from some of the meetings last year. I think she was from somewhere in New York and we had spoken a few times at the interviews. No surprise that now when she turned and saw me she seemed to actually glare, then look right through me.

I turned to the bearded guy on my right, who nodded curtly at me. I was about to flash a smile at him but he'd already turned his head away. Well, at least he'd acknowledged my existence. And hadn't anyone told him they didn't appreciate facial hair at these things, anyway?

I sat perfectly still, hands folded in my lap, staring straight ahead at the Spanish red brick roof and yellow stucco wall in front of me, and waited for my fate. It was so chillingly quiet that you could hear the pfffttt-pfttt noise of a hotel guest's flip-flops on the floor below us. The only other noise I heard was coming from inside my body—my own heart pounding away in my chest. Then, like violin players raising their bows in an orchestra, all of the exam room doors opened simultaneously. Instinctively I turned to my left and stood.

"Hello, Dr. Thomas," the man who opened the door greeted me. "I'm Dr. Walsh. Welcome." I'd heard it was super-formal like this.

"Hello, Dr. Walsh." I shook his hand. This must be my senior examiner. He was tall and bear-like, with thinning grey hair and horn-rimmed glasses. He had a surprisingly comforting expression in his face, as if he was having me over for dinner as a guest instead of to eat me alive.

"I imagine you're familiar with the layout of this part of the exam. The 'Unknowns.'" He handed me a binder. "The separate case photos are in here. You have ten minutes to look at them before we call you into the room." He smiled and closed the door.

I'm not sure what I had been expecting—(monsters jumping out from between the pages and attacking me?)—but when I flipped open the book, all I found myself staring at was a regular picture. Like so many I had seen before. It was a breast cancer patient with one missing breast and a radiated chest wall. That was easy. I started going through the drill in my head. What kind of cancer. How long ago. Family history. Is she a smoker. She needs a flap. I saw the big scar across the right upper quadrant of her abdomen. So she can't have a TRAM. Trying to fool me? I'd do a Lat. Blood supply Thoracodorsal. Type II muscle. Use a tissue expander underneath and what if it dies? Free Lat from the other side even though I've never done one in my life I could still talk myself blue in the face about it.

Next page. A profile of a four-year-old boy with a giant hairy nevus on the side of his face. Increased risk of malignancy—ten percent over his lifetime. Tissue expanders and serial excisions. Watch out for the facial nerve.

Next. Beautiful. There was the Cleft. Left Unilateral Complete. I could draw the Millard repair in my sleep. Lip at three months, palate at a year, speech therapy and palatoplasty later. Redo the lip and nose before he turns five and starts school so the other kids don't make fun of him.

Next. Spaghetti Wrist with missing skin and bone from a printing press accident. Debride. Flap. Try the Reverse Radial Forearm which of course they would kill so I could use a free flap. A Rectus or Radial forearm from the other side. Worst case scenario stick it in the groin.

Next. A Crushed Foot from a motorcycle accident with exposed bone and missing tissue—a Gustilo IIIB. Talk about local flaps but it was going to need a free flap. Stick with the Rectus even though it's a big, fat inelegant muscle. I can always talk about debulking it later. Ask about the sensation at the plantar aspect of the foot. Maybe a sensate flap? Could the Rectus be sensate? Gracilis could but it was too small and they'd kill it for sure. Shit. Okay, maybe they wouldn't ask.

And finally. The last one was a massive weight loss patient with skin hanging from her chin to her ankles. The pannus was red and inflamed. Treat with IV antibiotics. Panniculectomy purely for medical necessity. In the hospital. They'd give her a pulmonary embolus afterwards no doubt. Postoperative Lovenox. DVT prophylaxis. Staged excision for the rest of the skin.

I closed the book and snuck a look up and down the hallway. For as far as I could see, everyone else still had their heads bent over, studying the pictures. Maybe I needed to look at them again? I was up to the kid with the hairy nevus for the third time when I heard the door open behind me. Once more, all of the hotel room doors had opened in concert, and everyone sitting in the chairs stood up at the same time.

"Ready to join us?" Dr. Walsh said. "This is Dr. Owens."

The second examiner sat at the work desk, which had been turned around to make a table in the middle of the room. He stood up to shake my hand. This was the junior guy. He couldn't have been more than a few years older than me. He nodded hello, but didn't smile.

"Have a seat, Dr. Thomas," said Dr. Walsh.

As I did so he added, "Oh, and we need to see your ID."

Like many designer suits, mine had no real pockets and I had been carry-ing my driver's license and hotel key card around in such a death grip and for so long that I'd forgotten they were even there. The fingers of my right hand cramped as I uncurled them and the cards left long red indents in my sweaty palm.

"Hot out there, huh?" Dr. Walsh chuckled as he took my driver's license. "Well, it's you all right," he said and handed it back to me.

I felt the panic mounting. Did he mean me, *Lipo Queen?* Or was I read-ing too much into it? He could just be making a comment like, *yes, this is your driver's license, Dr. Rachel Thomas*, like he would to anybody else. Wasn't there, after all, a tiny possibility that he didn't know who I was? That maybe he was the only other person in the western hemisphere besides my mother who didn't have basic cable at home?

Oh, but one glance at the junior guy and it was obvious that he knew *exactly* who I was. I could see the calm, yet intense delight blazing from his eyes, like an animal that has finally trapped his prey and is going to fuck with it for a little while before he goes in for the kill. Like when Sushi catches a moth and then bats it around in the corner of the room on the floor with its wing torn, until he gets bored and just eats it.

This guy had probably found out he was going to get to torture me weeks ago and had been tuning in to *Lipo Queen* ever since, licking his lips and rub-bing his hands together, counting down until the feast.

Once the senior guy sat down, the junior guy took over.

"So, Doctor Thomas, you've had a chance to look at the pictures. We have six minutes for each case, and then there will be some time at the end for you to make any comments that you think you may have missed." His voice was hypernasal, like the caricature of an evil teacher in a children's movie. "If there is a subject that you are not familiar with, and you do not know the answer to the question—" He paused and seemed to almost sneer at me, letting the words linger in the air before he completed the sentence— "Then it is best if you just say you don't know, and we move on to the next one. Where you *might* know the answer. It is better to admit that you don't know something if it is out of your range of knowledge than to *pretend* that you know it. *Pretending* that you know something will not work in this arena."

I had heard that this might happen—that the junior guy could be over-obnoxious just to show off to the senior guy what an advanced genius he was.

"*This* is *real life*, after all."

I winced at the obvious intention of those last words and nodded.

"All right, then. Let's begin." He flipped open the book so we were all staring at the first picture—the breast cancer patient. "Go ahead. Will you please read the caption and then tell us your plan."

"'A forty-four year-old woman status post right-sided mastectomy and radiation, now presents to you seven years later for reconstruction,'" I read. I took a deep breath. I had to slow myself down because it was almost too easy. "First I would want to know about the type of cancer that she had—"

"Infiltrating ductal carcinoma," the junior guy shot back.

"And what her last mammogram showed on the other side—"

"Yeah, yeah, last mammogram was recent and normal. Nothing on the other side. What are you going to do?"

His abrupt interruptions took me off guard; for the past few months I had been practicing these answers in a vacuum by myself.

"I would…want to know if she was a smoker. If she has a family history—"

"Just forget all that. Everything's normal. She's ready for surgery. What are you going to do?" The junior tyrant leaned across the small desk till his face was nearly touching mine and demanded, "Dr. Thomas, what are you going to *do* for this forty-some-odd woman who is seven years status post mastectomy and radiation?"

Now *that* was some bad bachelor breath. The saliva spray that came with his "t's" hit my nose.

My train of thought was broken. Here it was. The personal persecution that I had been waiting for. The attack on me, the *Lipo Queen*, for exploiting the sacred field of plastic surgery and all that it stood for, for my own personal gain. But as I felt myself start to unravel, as I started to get all the answers that I had so carefully planned out while sitting outside the door five minutes ago jumbled together to the point where I was afraid I wouldn't be able to articulate them anymore, something somewhere else inside me snapped to attention. *Because there was something that felt extremely familiar about this situation that had nothing to do with plastic surgery.* It was just like one of my famous blue background soliloquies. This junior asshole sounded like Blair. Blair's job was to rile me up so she could get a juicy segment that Middle America would want to tune in to. This guy's job was to intimidate the shit out of me and see if I could still think and stand on my own two feet. *This should be nothing compared to what I had to do for Blair and Gloria every day.*

Everything this guy was asking me for was somewhere in my brain. It had to be after all those weeks—*months*—of cramming. I'd been doing surgery now for nearly one third of my life. And I'd been performing on a reality show for—what—a little over three months? So you're going to tell me that I could make it through three months of Blair yelling in my ear to be more captivating, three months of operating on camera with the risk of even my tiniest of mistakes being exposed to the world, three months of having out-of-my-league Devin Breeze dangled in front of my face…*that I could handle all of that without going crazy and that I couldn't handle this grotesque, greasy gremlin asking me a few stupid questions about things I already knew?*

I just had to rearrange things a bit. Play the game his way. I took another deep breath and fast-forwarded my planned answer to the part he was asking me for. I knew my voice was going to shake when I started talking, and I knew he would respond to that like a Great White in bloody waters, so I bought some time by answering him the same way Blair always made me answer her—starting with rephrasing the question—so that by the time I got to the important stuff, I would sound more sure of myself.

"What I would do with this forty—"—I caught myself in time from saying "some-odd" because that could come off as sarcastic—"year-old woman who is seven years status post mastectomy and radiation is an autologous tissue flap." It was working. My voice had leveled off and gained strength. I closed my eyes for a few seconds and pretended I was narrating while doing a case in the operating room to Blair and the crew. And by the time I opened them, without a hitch I had launched into why I would do a Lat, and not a TRAM because of the abdominal wall scar, and what the blood supply was. I batted away the questions he threw at me like tennis balls from one of those practice machines. When the senior guy sort of took over and started quizzing me about what kind of implant would I use, and what's the rupture rate, and what would I do about a capsular contracture, and don't implants cause autoimmune disease, I knew I was over the hump and I had won that question. The word on the street was that, despite the poker faces, you could estimate your success by the direction the questions were headed, and how the fictional patient was holding up. The road they took you down depended on your previous answers. If they were asking you fluffy questions about your favorite brand of implant it meant you had passed that case. If they knew you were full of shit they would let you dig yourself into a hole. And if you killed someone then you knew you'd really done something wrong.

I could tell the junior douchebag was trying to get me to kill the morbidly obese weight loss patient. After I told him what procedure I would do for her, he gave her a pulmonary embolus on the first post-op day. I skillfully avoided her demise by heparinizing her and rushing her to the spiral CT scanner at the first sign of tachycardia. Then he made her bleed and I had to take her back to the operating room on heparin. He even took me into the I.C.U. with her by screwing up her fluids and electrolytes, and giving her a flesh-eating streptococcal infection but I pulled her through with aggressive antibiotics and surgical debridement. It wasn't like I hadn't been through a few of those over at the Valley Hospital. He finally seemed to give up and let the wound heal and let me discharge her from the hospital, all the while keeping his face even and expressionless.

I could sense his frustration. He leaned in one more time across the table. "Okay, so let's go back to the surgery. That's all you want to do on her—a panniculectomy? Come on, that's it? Are you sure you wouldn't do any *liposuction* on her? Look at all that *fat* she's still got. I bet you could get a lot off. Make her look a lot better…Make a lot of money…*Hmmmm?*" He held up the book and shoved the picture under my nose, like he was trying to tempt me with a drug. What an idiot.

"I could…" I started to say, as if genuinely contemplating it and I saw his eyes light up. "But I wouldn't. It's not safe. This isn't a cosmetic case. She's too high a risk patient. Besides, Lipoplasty Task Force Guidelines are five liters max, and that wouldn't even make a dent in her. No pun intended."

"Okay." The senior guy grunted and seemed to suddenly come to life. He hadn't said a word for the last two cases, and I had been so busy with the junior guy jumping down my throat that I wouldn't have been able to tell you if he'd even been awake. "Doctor Thomas, we've got a few minutes left. Would you like to add anything to any of your responses before we conclude this session?"

I looked at the digital clock on the nightstand beneath the cactus print hanging on the wall. Were we really done? The senior guy handed the book back to me—practically having to forcefully yank it from the junior guy's hands—and I flipped through the pages, trying to recount everything I had said, and how each patient had fared. As I had predicted, the Reverse Radial Forearm died and I'd used a Free Radial Forearm from the other side and then that died, so I used a Free Rectus and then that died and finally I stuck it in the groin and they let it live. But none of the patients died.

"No, I don't think so," I said, and closed the book.

"Well, then," the senior guy said. Still not friendly, but not unfriendly. "Thank you. And good luck."

Just as I stepped back outside the junior guy called out, "Dr. Thomas."

I turned around.

"You might need this." He held up my hotel key card, which must have fallen on the floor. He handed it back to me. His face was softer now. He actually smiled. "Make sure to cut it up when you leave. I hear these things have all your credit card and personal information on them."

Now that I had the rhythm down, the examiners in the second session were less menacing, and more comical. Also, this time their sympathies were switched—it seemed to be the senior guy giving me the evil eye and grunting while the junior guy asked the questions with a benign, passive voice. This time around there was the Facelift, the Nose Job, the Scalp Wound (nearly identical to the one I had practiced with Devin). The coronal CT image of a mandible with bilateral rami fractures. Oh, *wait wait wait*…was that an NOE they had snuck in there? I'd never actually seen one but I recited the book answer as confidently as if I'd done hundreds —transnasal wiring and immediate cranial bone graft. There was a Dupuytren's contracture with a nodule, an abdominal hernia next to a permanent colostomy, and the final case—another Gustilo IIIB. This time it was a nasty open ankle fracture. I felt myself chill out a notch when we got to it since I'd already nailed one just like it in the first room, and I still hadn't had anybody die or lose a limb yet.

"So how would you cover it?" the junior guy said.

I used my standard bag of tricks. Nothing fancy. Just a good old beefy Rectus free flap. They killed it, of course. So I put a Latissimus on it.

"Why are you jumping directly to a free tissue transfer?" the senior guy grunted. "Aren't there any other options for the distal lower extremity?"

Not in the real world, I wanted to say. But clearly they wanted me to name them all anyway. I tried to visualize my "distal third leg wounds" flashcard. In the upper right hand corner I had listed a few less drastic options that sounded good on paper, but would never have worked in real life.

"Well, of course you have to acknowledge some of the more local options in the reconstructive ladder," I said. The senior guy grunted again and checked something off on the paper in front of him. I guess I must have hit the key word they'd been fishing for.

"And what might some of those be?" said the junior guy, his voice still indecipherably neutral.

"Well, uhh.." *Crap.* I hadn't spent a lot of time memorizing these because they weren't practical. Reading about them was just an academic exercise. When it came right down to it and you had a big ugly open ankle wound with exposed bone on a Border Jumper you just slapped a big fat Rectus or Latissimus on it and called it a day.

"You could do a..umm…Reverse Sural Flap."

"Really. Tell us about that one."

Now both of them stared at me with new intrigue, and it was the first time I felt myself slip back into panic mode. *Was I digging a hole? Was there even a Reverse Sural Flap?*

I pictured the sketch on my index card. Yes. There was. I was sure of it.

"Well, it's usually only about five by ten centimeters, and it's kind of thin, so I don't think it would be a good choice for this wound, especially with all that bone exposed—"

"Pretend it's big enough." The junior guy handed me the dreaded black marker. "Can you draw the flap for me?"

Again, not mean. Not nice. Neutral. This should be easy. They just wanted me to put my money where my mouth was. But when I covered the picture with the clear plastic overlay and raised the Sharpie in the air, I had a new dilemma.

The photograph was of the foot and ankle only. This particular flap started up somewhere in the middle of the calf. *How could I draw something that wasn't in the picture?*

Certainly he was aware that he had mistakenly commanded me to do the impossible. In another second he was going to say, "Oh, I'm sorry. Forget it." But he didn't. He just kept staring at me with his wide-eyed poker face.

"But…" I started to say. "It's not—"

"Just draw the flap."

Now the senior guy seemed to have perked up again. He leaned forward in his chair.

I looked down at the picture, then back up at the junior examiner. Was he bluffing? Did *he* even know where the Reverse Sural Flap came from? *Dammit, if I'd just taken five minutes to Google him.* What if he was just a nose guy and hadn't even been anywhere *near* a Reverse Sural Flap in the last five years?

"Okay then," the senior guy said. I had gotten enough of a feel for this room by now that I understood that once the senior guy opened his mouth the show was over. "If you can't draw it we need to move on."

Now, this wasn't fair. I knew where the fucking flap was. I shouldn't be penalized because they had the wrong picture.

"But, it starts above the ankle—" I started to say.

"'Above the ankle?'" the senior guy sneered.

"I mean, cephalad," I corrected myself. "Five centimeters cephalad to the lateral malleolus."

"So are you saying you can't draw it?"

"No, I can…" And then I did the only thing I could think of. With the Sharpie in one hand, I stuck out my own freshly shaved leg and I drew the long ellipse on the back of my calf where the flap would have come from. I cringed as I applied the permanent black marker to my skin, knowing that it was going to be a bitch to get off and in the process of removing it I was going to wreck my perfect airbrush tan.

When I looked back up again, both of my examiners were still expressionless. Or was that a smile on the senior guy's face?

"Are you sure?" he said.

I thought I was, but now I wasn't. Their blank faces made me feel the need to elaborate. I embellished the skin paddle with a dotted line, and little circles for the artery and vein. When they still didn't say anything I drew arrows for the arc of rotation. I looked back at my examiners, who may as well have been deaf mutes by the reactions they were giving me, and back down at my graffiti.

"You don't have another color, do you?" I asked deadpan. I knew we weren't supposed to make jokes but I couldn't help myself. It had suddenly become so crystal clear how idiotic this whole situation was. This time I was positive the senior guy was trying to keep from laughing.

He rested back in his armchair and held up the book. "Doctor Thomas, we have a few minutes if there's anything else you'd like to add."

Before I knew it I was back out into the bright sunlit afternoon, and once again I felt nothing. I couldn't remember anything except for drawing on my leg. Jesus. I glanced down at my artwork as I made my way down the stairwell to the ground floor. Of all the stories, I'd never heard of anyone having to draw on themselves. Were they just testing me to see how far I would go? What if it had been on my abdomen? Or better yet—on my chest? If I had been forced to unbutton my shirt to show them where the internal mammary perforators were would they have failed me on the spot for unprofessional conduct?

I had half an hour till my next and final session. It was enough time to stop down at the poolside bar and restaurant where everyone else went for their intermissions, but I just couldn't deal with Blair right now. I had to stay focused.

Oh, who was I kidding? It was Devin I was avoiding. After how nice he'd been to me lately and his heartfelt send-off this morning, I couldn't bear to wander back over there and find him chatting up one of his new poolside waitress friends. Not that that would have an impact on anything whatsoever—because, of course, we weren't really *together*—but still, I knew myself… and I knew how unglued it would make me. Better to stay living in my own little TV fantasy land until this whole sordid ordeal was over. I'd confront the true reality of my silly unrequited lust for him back in L.A. *After* I had become board-certified.

But now what to do for the next…umm—I glanced at a wall clock—*twenty-five minutes?*

I still had some cigarettes in my hotel room. And where, exactly, was that? I tried to get a handle on my surroundings. Everybody was filing past, down in the other direction toward the restaurant. I caught a few of my colleagues stealing looks at my leg but nobody actually said anything to me.

Which hotel wing was this? There was the golf course in front of me so my room should be up there, to the left, on the other side of that little hill. If I hustled I could probably make it up there in seven or eight minutes, leave in fifteen, and be back in plenty of time.

Thinking about smoking got me so excited that I imagined I could smell a cigarette burning. And as I rounded the corner up the hill I thought I could see the smoke. Could I be so emotionally traumatized that I was experiencing desert mirages?

Wait, no. That really was cigarette smoke. And someone was sitting on a giant rock about ten feet in front of me. It was a woman. She had her back to me and she was alone, well hidden by the hill from all of the action going on down below. When I got closer I saw that she was dressed in a dark suit nearly identical to mine, except the jacket was laid out next to her on the rock and the sleeves of her shirt were rolled up to her elbows.

My shoes made crunching sounds in the dry ground and she turned to see who was there, expertly concealing the cigarette below knee-level with her left hand.

It was Paula. Donarski's Paula. My replacement.

36

"Oh, hey," she said, exhaling a cloud of smoke. She shielded her eyes from the sun to look up at me. "How's it going?"

I gave her the expected response—a pained expression and a shrug.

"This thing really sucks, doesn't it?" She lifted her cigarette out of hiding and took a long drag. She saw the way I looked at it. "You want one?"

She made room for me on the rock. I wondered where she was going to get the cigarette since like me her suit jacket probably had no worthwhile pockets. Her hotel key card and driver's license sat in a neat pile next to her.

She retrieved a cigarette and a lighter from her right bra cup and handed them to me. Huh. She owned a lighter. She wasn't fooling around.

"Thanks," I said. The cigarette was still warm from being pressed against her skin. I wondered how many more she had in there. I lit the end of it and inhaled, savoring the comforting burn of the smoke against the walls of my trachea. It tasted perfect. "Marlboro?"

"Camel. Way better."

She was right. After a few drags I was able to lure myself back into my familiar state of cigarette-smoking calm.

"I'm Rachel," I finally said.

"I know who you are." She wasn't being bitchy, just matter-of-fact. She ground the butt end of hers out into the dirt and lit another one. "I've seen your show."

I immediately felt the need to apologize. "I know it's really stupid—"

"I like it. I'm Paula," she said. "What happened to your leg?"

She laughed when I told her the story.

"What a douchebag. He was totally fucking with you."

She offered me another cigarette and she started on her third. I was impressed.

"You sure?" I said. "Don't we have to be back pretty soon?"

"Relax. We have ten minutes. What'd you do with the NOE?"

"Just fixed it." I tried to remember but it was all a blur now. "They didn't bother me much about that one."

"Really? They gave mine a dural leak when I took the cranial bone graft. I had to call a neurosurgeon."

"Did they kill him?"

"No. They left him in the ICU on pressors. I think he was supposed to have meningitis. Those guys really are such a bunch of fuckers, you know?"

I nodded. She was *so* not what I had expected.

"It's fucking hot here," she said. "Why don't you take your jacket off?"

"I'm soaked underneath." I grimaced. "Major sweat stains."

She raised her arms in the air. There was not a single wet spot on her white silk shirt. "You don't Botox your pits?"

"No." Obviously I needed to start. I noticed the ring on her left hand and absent-mindedly asked if her husband was here.

"I'm not married," she said.

"But you're wearing a ring."

"The guys where I trained said if you're not married they're going to wonder what's wrong with you. So even if you're not married, they said wear a ring anyway."

"I hadn't heard that." *Fortunately.*

"I'm not even dating anyone. Ha. Now *your* boyfriend is cute. Did you really meet him on call in the E.R.?"

It was funny the way the tone of her voice changed when she said that—she suddenly sounded like a wistful schoolgirl, instead of the foul-mouthed, super-powered surgeon she had just been a minute ago.

I studied her face. Her skin was a little more weathered up close than I'd originally thought, and she really needed some help her with her hair. But even without a scratch of makeup on she was undeniably pretty.

I hesitated, then said: "Yes."

"Fuck, how come someone like that doesn't show up when *I'm* on call?"

"Yeah, it was...just lucky, I guess."

She took a deep drag. "*Sooo* lucky," she said as she exhaled.

"We should get back." I stubbed out my cigarette in the dirt.

"Yeah." Paula pulled a mini perfume bottle out of the left side of her bra. "Want some spray?"

I had prepared so intensely for my "case book" session that I knew there was nothing they could catch me on, yet I was still petrified going into it. But this time it had nothing to do with *Lipo Queen*. It was because this time it was about who I really was, and the way I practiced medicine and surgery. They would be criticizing me as me, Doctor Rachel Thomas, about real people I had treated and real decisions I had made. Whether I could have done better. Whether I should have *been* better.

My cases were straightforward: a mandible, two breast reconstructions, a breast reduction and a finger replant that had died. My examiners remained stone-faced, questioning me in a very calm, methodical manner. Nobody veered off on crazy tangents about liposuction. It went so smoothly that when we were finished, I almost said, "That's it?" They thanked me and shook my hand and wished me a good afternoon.

And then I was standing outside by the staircase again and I was done. It was ten minutes after four, less than twenty-four hours since I had started waiting by the phone, and it was over.

37

The next, and probably most time-honored tradition of this whole miserable process was that afterwards, everyone started drinking immediately. As the individual exams ended, the test-takers congregated down at the poolside bar, and proceeded to get as wasted as possible until the debriefing meeting at 9:00 P.M. in the Cactus Conference Room, at which time the results would be distributed in sealed envelopes.

By the time I got there, the bar was already packed with the rest of my colleagues, gathered around tables, sharing pitchers of margaritas and bowls of chips.

I was supposed to meet Blair and the crew down here, but I hesitated at the door. What if they weren't here yet and I was standing around and nobody else offered me a place to sit?

I had almost convinced myself that it would be better to go back to my room and wait for Blair to call and scream at me asking where the hell I was, didn't I know I was wasting valuable time and money, when I heard his voice.

"Rachel!"

At first I could only hear him. And the rest of what he said wasn't completely clear, but even above the din of the restaurant I recognized his voice. "Rachel!"

Now I saw him. He was across the room, wedged into the middle of a booth full of girls. They were the only patrons in the restaurant who were not wearing suits. Business suits, that is. They wore "barely there" bathing suits and appeared to be doing body shots off each other for the cameras. Devin stood up against the wall and waved his arms at me, then escaped over the back of the booth.

"Hey," he said when he reached me. "How was it?"

I felt my knees start to buckle. Not just because of the realization that I had made it through what had to be the most emotional torture I thought I would ever have to endure. Not just because Devin Breeze was standing so close to me. But because I could feel that he really did have some semblance of *genuine* concern. He really *cared*. Somebody really *cared* about *me*.

He hugged me and I literally felt myself go limp in his arms. After all of the sheer exhaustion and stress, it felt so good to have someone hold me, to physically support me and let all of that pent-up emotion just drain away. He was tan with the hint of a sunburn, and I could feel the heat of his skin through his thin cotton shirt. His arms felt strong across my back, and his hands felt better than I had let myself remember. I felt like even if I just collapsed he'd keep me standing.

"Let's get you something to eat," he said and, squeezing my hand, led me back to the table. "Have you eaten *anything* today? You must be starving."

I was sure that everyone around us was watching as we crossed the room together. I didn't even care that he was role-playing. I caught at least a few of my female colleagues stealing glances at him and whispering to each other. I stood a little straighter, and tried to stop limping in my heels.

Blair was too busy barking orders to the girls in the booth to even say "hello."

"Move over and let them in there. What's your name? No offense, but I don't want you in the shot. Your breasts are terrible. Can the other girl switch with you?"

Once it became clear that the show was no longer about them, the bathing beauties dispersed back out to poolside.

"We'll call you if we need you," Blair yelled after them. "Don't forget to sign the waivers." She turned back to Devin and me. "How did it go, Dr Thomas?" Without waiting for an answer she continued, "Okay, you guys We only have a couple of hours till results time, right? I want you to sit across from each other—here, like that—and hold hands. Breeze, talk to her, tell her how you've been pacing back and forth all day, how you haven't been able to eat—"

"How was it?" Devin said.

I took a swig from the drink that the P.A. handed me without even asking what it was. "It was...hard."

"But how do you think you did?"

"Breeze, are you listening to anything I'm saying? Drama! I need drama! Doctor Thomas, think you can drum up some tears for us? Tell him how you think you failed and the show will be cancelled and your whole life is ruined—"

"Shut up, Blair!" Devin yelled at her. He turned back to me. "Here, I brought you your phone." He pressed my cell into the palm of my hand. "It's been going off all day. Mostly Jenny, I think."

I glanced down and scrolled through the numbers, silently thankful that he hadn't tried to call any of them back. What an idiot I had been to leave my phone lying around and still on. I had taken Jake's name out a couple of months ago in case anyone from the set picked it up, but I recognized his number. He had called twice.

"Remember, these are your ratings too, Breeze," Blair said. "Someone get a mic on her."

"Hey, Rachel." I heard a voice above me. While the sound guy adjusted my mic, I peered over his head and saw Paula standing there. She had two other girls with her. And the bearded guy who'd been sitting next to me before the first exam.

She motioned toward our huge booth that was now empty except for Devin and myself. "Don't mean to intrude, but there's not a lot of free tables—"

"No, no, come on in," I said, almost too eagerly, letting the four of them slide in next to us.

"Fine," I heard Blair mutter. "We can do a group after-party instead." I saw her nod to the P.A. who started handing out drinks. "Make sure you get the waivers."

"Hey, you guys, this is Rachel," Paula said. The three of them murmured "hello" and their names, none of which I could catch over the dull background roar. The important thing was that they didn't seem to hate me.

"How about a round of tequila shots?" Devin said and I watched the girls swoon.

Historically, the test had a twenty-five percent failure rate. With the five of us sitting there, odds were that one of us would be back next year. But the two hours we had to kill until we got our final results were two hours suspended in time. Two hours in which nobody had yet failed, and anything was still possible.

Paula's friends were all from hospitals in the southeast, and I'd never met any of them before. I was surprised at how easily they signed the waivers.

"I had the shittiest week," one of them spoke up. She was from some remote town in West Virginia where she said she spent most of her time putting hands back together after farming injuries. "I had a five-finger replant on Tuesday." Appropriate sympathetic groans from the rest of the group.

"I had one of those once," the other girl said. "A guy stuck his hand in a tractor. Seriously, *nineteen* hours. And I'm a decent microsurgeon."

"Speaking of hands…" the bearded guy—who turned out to be from Alabama—said, "What did you guys do with the spaghetti wrist?"

We sat and went word for word over each exam case: what we'd said, what they'd said, and after three rounds of tequila shots the whole thing became totally hilarious.

And then it was just like old times. Bonding with colleagues, sharing stories and laughing at punch lines that would have been offensive to anyone who hadn't lived through the things that almost everyone in this restaurant had lived through just to get here. *This* was what I had really missed all of these months. I was part of the club again.

The highlight was when Paula started talking about the artwork on my leg and it seemed completely appropriate for me to stick it straight up in the air so everyone could see the Reverse Sural Flap diagrammed on the back of my calf.

But we couldn't make our party last forever. The restaurant gradually emptied out and it came time for all of us to start heading back up to the Cactus Conference Room. My stomach started burning holes in itself again, and as I glanced around the table I could tell that the rest of our new little clique felt the same way. It was time to be handed our fates. Even Devin had become sympathetically somber.

"Find me later," Paula said, giving me a quick hug before she left. "Good luck."

"You too." I had to stay behind and walk slowly with Devin so that the cameras could follow us back to the lobby and up the elevator. He kept his arm around me and even though I knew it was just for the show, I was glad that he was there.

We had to wait for one of the elevators to be empty so we could have a "moment together" alone inside on camera. I was the last to arrive. The "Q through Z" line was already snaking out the door and down the hallway when we got there.

The line moved too quickly. By the time I could see the "Q through Z" Woman behind the desk, a significant fraction of the group had already opened their envelopes and were heading toward the exit door. Most of them looked relieved and happy, some of them appeared grim, and some were expressionless.

Blair and the camera followed closely from my left side, and Devin's fingers pressed firmly around my right hand as I moved closer to the table where files of sealed white envelopes sat in front of the same women who had signed us in just less than two days before.

Now the line was moving *way* too fast. I was three away. I felt my entire body visibly shaking, and I swallowed against the waves of nausea that started to hit me. Before I could catch my breath I was standing at the box of filed letters with nobody in front of me, giving the "Q through Z" Woman my name.

Please, God, I prayed, even though I wasn't even exactly sure to which God I was praying. But isn't it funny how the minute we want something we start doing this barter thing in our heads—as if such a system is really an option? As if all we have to do is be willing to sacrifice one thing to get another? *I'll let Jake move into the condo with me next week. I'll give him my car (the Porsche was not a stick). I'll give up anything.* I felt Devin's fingers tighten around my own. *I'll give up on this stupid fantasy, even.*

The "Q through Z" Woman held my envelope out toward me and I let go of Devin's hand to reach for it.

As soon as I had the letter in my hand I knew that I had passed. It was thick. And wasn't that the rule? Like a college acceptance letter?

Still, my hands shook so much that I couldn't pull open the sealed flap fast enough. The contents dropped to the floor and when I scooped them up I scanned the top line of the first paragraph. *"Pleased to inform you"* was all I needed to see.

"You passed, didn't you?" Devin said.

"I passed! Oh my God, I passed!" I was jumping up and down and screaming. The "Q through Z" Woman smiled congratulations and then asked me to kindly move myself and my sideshow out of the way so the next person in line could be helped.

Somehow I was back outside in the cool desert evening air. I felt Devin squeezing my hand and his breath up against my ear: "I knew you could do it." There were lights and cameras and then I heard Blair yelling out stage directions and I felt Devin's lips on mine and then I knew this had to be the happiest moment in my life. *It can't possibly get any better than this,* I thought.

And honestly, it still hasn't.

38

Everybody started migrating in the same direction. We moved like a swarm of ants back to the bar by the pool. Somehow my feet carried me and when I got there someone handed me a shot of something. And then the next few hours were just one big happy blur. Everyone was talking at once and we had to yell at each other over the noise like you do at a fraternity party. It was too loud and crazy for Blair to get any kind of staged action, so she had to just give up and satisfy herself with B-roll of all the commotion.

There was another round of shots. Lemon drops this time. Then there was Paula with her cigarettes. Her friends were there. Now *my* new friends. *Everybody* was friends. When Jessica waltzed by with her husband and we congratulated each other I felt like even *she and I* could be friends.

Hours passed and the crowd thinned out until there were just about five or six of us left. It got down to me and my entourage and a group of married guys, all of whom were hell-bent on making the most of their weekend away from their families.

I don't remember much of what happened before one of them said, "How about a swim?" He was from the northeast and couldn't get over how warm he thought it was, when it really wasn't. It was Arizona at night.

"I say hot tub," said another guy, and he was already disrobing down to his briefs as he spoke. The other three followed suit, and pretty soon they were all sitting on the inside ledge of the Jacuzzi.

"You coming in?" It was the Alabama bearded guy from earlier.

"Unnhh, unnh," Devin said. "I'm not getting in a hot tub with a bunch of dudes." Even though it was still just B-roll, Blair had made him stick around within a tight radius all night. After all, how would it look to our viewers if he was off celebrating my victory with someone else?

"Well, *I* am," I said and watched Blair's eyes light up. *Here. I was going to give her some good TV.* A couple of the guys wolf-whistled while I shimmied out of my clothes, leaving only my bra and underwear on. I slid down into the warm water, up against the remaining vacant wall of the hot tub. One of the guys opened a bottle of champagne and I watched the cork fly up into the air and land somewhere in the pool. We passed it around and drank from the bottle and sucked the foam off the sides.

I was intoxicated, not just on alcohol but on how happy and…*free* I felt. I had done it. I had *won*. I had beat the boards and I had beat Blair. I was invincible. It didn't bother me that Devin and I hadn't talked since our momentous heart-stopping kiss outside the Cactus Conference Room. In fact it might not have even bothered me if he *did* go off and celebrate with someone else. I had freed myself from everyone, including him.

Besides, look at all this undivided male attention I was getting. So what if my admirers didn't all look like TV stars? The fact that they were all partially bald and partially fat and hairy-in-all-the-wrong-places didn't take away from my feeling like a Prom Queen.

And then, sitting there in my bra and underwear in the hot tub, submerged up to my chin with the water-jet churning and frothing against the back of my neck, I had this great epiphany. Maybe I was finally getting it. Maybe my mother had been wrong. Maybe you *didn't* have to be a model, or even just the most beautiful girl in the VIP lounge to feel desirable and sexy. Was "how you feel about yourself on the inside" really the thing that mattered most? Was that corny saying *not* complete bullshit?

Because at that moment I was feeling more desirable and sexy than I should have. I was certainly not at my external best. My spray tan was all but gone except for patches around my knees and elbows. I was sure my eye makeup was smudged down my cheeks. I felt frizzy tendrils of hair escaping around my face despite my attempt to pull it up and out of the way. I could feel the inch of soft fat that had started pooching out above my bikini line since I never had time to work out anymore, and it wasn't even bothering me.

"How do *you* do them, Rachel?" Somebody's voice broke through my hazy philosophical thoughts. "You go through the nipple?"

It was the D.C. guy. They were talking about breast augs. I felt the camera over my head zooming in and suddenly realized that there was a directional mic aimed at all of us.

"Yeah," I said. "Mostly."

He glanced at my chest. "Hey, so how come *you* don't have them?"

"Dude," Devin said. He had still adamantly refused to get into the hot tub and was sitting a few feet from us on a patio recliner. Though he wasn't reclining.

"Yeah," the Alabama guy said, ignoring him. "How do you sell them when you don't have them yourself?"

"I don't need them," I said. "From my neck to my belly button I look like I could be eighteen." And then, because I was so wasted, I felt it was important that I show everyone what I was talking about. "You want to see?"

Devin scowled and shook his head, but Blair motioned for the camera guy to stay on me.

"Sure," the three guys said practically in unison.

"Okay." I reached back to unstrap my bra underwater. "But no touching. Everyone stays where they are."

Once my bra was off I elevated myself up from the floor of the Jacuzzi just enough to be exposed down to my navel.

"Rachel, what the hell!" Devin said, throwing my shirt at me. He missed and it landed in the middle of the hot tub foam.

I could hear Blair's voice: "Keep the camera on her...we'll edit later...pan on the rest of them. Guys, keep your tongues hanging out...just like that..."

I wouldn't say they had their tongues hanging out. But they were definitely paying attention.

"Not bad," the Texas guy said. "Maybe younger than eighteen."

"Right?" I said. "It's like I'm stuck in Tanner Stage III."

"Maybe sixteen, even," said the D.C. guy.

"That's it. This is fucking disgusting," Devin said. He stood up and stormed off.

"This is good. This is good," Blair said. "Let him get really pissed." She turned to the camera guy. "Follow him."

"No, you know what?" Devin shouted over his shoulder as he disappeared down the path and into the darkness. "Can you for once not fucking follow me?"

"Sorry," one of the D.C. guys said. "Didn't mean to get you in trouble."

"In trouble?" I said. "My producer's thrilled."

"No, with your boyfriend."

"Oooohhhh." I laughed. "That's no big deal. Let him go. You want to hear something funny? I'm going to tell you a little secret—" But as I cupped my hand around his ear Blair yelled after Devin, "Hey Asswipe, come back here! We're not done!"

When he didn't answer, Blair turned to me. "Doc, go get him. He can't just march off like that unless I tell him to."

"She can't leave," the guy from D.C. said. He went to put his arm around me. "Not in the middle of the party."

"Hey, man," the Alabama guy said, nodding his head toward the camera. "Be careful."

"Of what?" The D.C. guy let go of me to wave toward the camera with both hands. "Who am I going to get in trouble with now? Hi Mom, Dad, Dr. Miles you motherfucker! You tried to bring me down and you lost, you four-foot tall midget motherfucker—"

"You have to delete that," I heard the Alabama guy tell Blair. "Or he's going to lose his job."

"Dr. Thomas, please go get Mr. Breeze before the sun comes up."

"Okay, okay." I hoisted myself up onto the cement patio, dreading the instant chill I got from the cold desert night air hitting my wet skin. I discretely dislodged a wedgie, and tried to wring my wet shirt out before I put it back on. The thin cotton stuck to me in patches.

"Don't be long," the Alabama guy drawled after me. "We'll save your seat for you."

Initially I couldn't see Devin—I only knew that he had bolted down the crunchy dirt pathway that led to our block of hotel rooms. The path was deserted, but it was well lit with gas lamps on either side, and once I turned the corner I spotted the glint of light off the back of his shiny blonde head.

"Hey!" I said. My voice sounded hoarse and faint and my throat ached from the celebratory yelling and smoking I'd been doing all night. When he didn't stop I thought he hadn't heard me so I called out again, but he still didn't turn around.

"Hey, come on!" I caught up to him but he didn't look at me. "Why'd you leave? We're having so much fun!"

"Does it look like *I'm* having fun?"

"Well, you don't have to ruin it for *me*!" It was fortunate that nobody had me on camera, stumbling and swerving along beside him. "This is my big night! What—it's too *boring* for you? Not *Hollywood* enough for you!"

I tripped over a rock in the middle of the path and landed in the dirt on my ass. Of course, with all that alcohol on board I didn't feel a thing.

"It's not my fault Blair chased all the hot girls away," I continued to yell from the ground. "Don't worry—I'm sure we can find someone up to par for you to have sex with later." When he still didn't even slow down I couldn't restrain myself from adding, "Maybe even someone who could help you keep it up."

I could barely see him up ahead but the sound of his footsteps halted.

"You bitch."

"*I'm* a bitch? Don't you think you're being kind of an asshole? Just because you're jealous—"

Finally he turned around.

"I'm not jealous."

"Oh, I get that you're not jealous of those *guys*. You're just jealous that for once you're not the center of attention and you can't deal with it." I don't think I really believed what I was saying but it sounded good.

"Riiight…"

"Maybe those guys actually find me attractive!" I continued. "Though I know that's probably a huge shocker to you."

"Rachel, what's your problem?" The overhead lights played off his head and his feet crunched on the gravel as he started moving back toward me.

"I think you know," I said.

"Know what?"

"What you said about me."

"And what was that, exactly?"

After surviving today, I felt liberated enough to say just about anything. Including what I had wanted to say to him since the day we met in Gloria's office.

"You said I wasn't hot."

By now Devin was standing over me. He looked down and although I knew he was trying to stay pissed I could tell it was hard for him to keep from laughing. Now that I was sitting still I was acutely aware of the icy night air, and the wet shirt plastered against my body wasn't helping. I started to shiver and my teeth began chattering, like one of those Halloween toys you wind up and let go on the floor.

"You think it's funny?" I chattered. "That you said I wasn't hot?"

"Well, right now you're not."

"No," I persisted. "What you said that day in Gloria's office."

"I have no idea what you're talking about." He kept staring evenly at me, then when I didn't move, he extended his arms to help me up.

Sitting on the ground was certainly getting old. The gravel had started to dig in and pinch the skin on the backs of my legs. I grabbed onto his hands and he pulled me into a standing position.

"You said it," I said through my chattering teeth. I'd come this far. I wasn't going to give up now. "At that first meeting."

"What the hell—how can you possibly remember anything I said back then? I don't think I even talked to you."

"No, you're right. You didn't talk to me. You talked to Russell. You told him I wasn't hot."

"You're nuts." He started rubbing the sides of my arms, trying to warm me up.

"I wasn't supposed to hear it," I said. "At least, I'm pretty sure I wasn't. But I did." I took a deep breath. "And it really hurt my feelings."

"Rachel." The way he looked directly into my eyes sent a shock of electricity through my body and suddenly I felt quite toasty. "You gotta know that's not true. Come on, you know how cute I think you are."

"It's not the same," I said. "You know what I mean."

"Jesus Christ…" Devin rubbed his eyes. "You know what? I think we're all just a little tired here. It's been a long day. And you need to stop drinking. Fuck Blair. I'm taking you back up to the room. You didn't happen to bring any of that I.V. stuff with you, did you?"

"I don't want to go back to the room." The thing was, I really just wanted to go back to the hot tub. Not just because I was freezing, but because I wasn't ready for the night with all of my admirers to be over. At the hot tub I was the prom queen. "And you still haven't told me why you were being such an asshole before."

He took a deep breath in as if he was really trying to say something, then stopped himself.

Maybe I needed a gentler approach. Blair would freak if I came back without him. "Come on, please… let's go back." I playfully took his hand.

"No." His voice was uncharacteristically firm.

"Devin, what's your problem?"

"*I* don't have a problem."

"Then why are you so mad?"

He looked down at the ground and then, while staring at his foot as he scuffed the edge of his flip-flop into the gravel, he said, "I don't like those guys looking at you like that."

"Like what?"

"Rach, you're naked."

"No, I'm not."

"You were."

"Just my boobs." I folded my arms across my chest. "They're just a bunch of geeky surgeons. It's not a big deal. They see them on the table all the time."

"That doesn't mean you have to show them yours."

"Devin, really. It's an anatomic part. It's not like I'm doing a striptease or something."

"It's just that…Oh, crap." He looked up at the sky and then back at me and sighed, his beautiful denim blue eyes narrowing. "I like you, Rachel."

"I know." I started chattering again. "You already told me that. I'm a 'cool girl.' Great. Now can we please go back so Blair doesn't get even more pissed? I need to get back in that hot tub. In case you can't tell, I'm freezing my ass off here."

"No. I mean, I like you. Like, *really* like you. A lot." The look in his eyes and the intensity with which he spoke immediately jolted me back to some semblance of sobriety.

"What?" Now I was cold, wet, sober…and confused. "You like me like… *how?*"

The way he kept looking at me—the depth of his eyes growing with every second, locking my gaze so I couldn't turn away and sending my insides into a tailspin—gave me my answer.

So then this couldn't be real life. This was my recurring Devin Breeze fantasy dream from five years ago, when I used to watch him on TV. Sometimes it took place on the set of *Pacific Beach*, somehow meshing with the fake storyline and making sense, or sometimes it took place in my own life. But it was always a dream. And no matter how vivid and real it seemed, I always woke up from it.

It had to be a dream. Oh, fuck, then did that mean passing the boards was part of the dream too? I must have fallen asleep in front of the TV in our hotel room. *Dammit.* I was going to wake up any minute with a crick in my neck and the lights still on and a spot of drool on the pillow. Devin's bed would be empty next to me because he would still be out gallivanting around from the night before and I would be about to face the whole damn test all over again.

I closed my eyes and willed myself to wake up, but when I opened them I was still standing on the dirt path. With Devin.

This really could not be happening. How could this be happening? *Suddenly, after all this time?* My poor overloaded brain was just fucking with me. It must have short-circuited after cramming so much bullshit plastic surgery information into each little neuron for so long. I wasn't going to be tricked that easily. I squeezed my eyes shut and opened them again.

"What are you doing?" he said. He was still there.

"No-nothing."

And I was still here.

"Do you have something in your eye?"

"No."

"Rachel, say something."

I stood motionless, rooted to the ground. That inhuman charisma of his enveloped my entire body as if I had just stepped into a warm bath.

I had to resist. I had to. I wasn't going there again. There had to be some crazy explanation for all of this.

"Tell me," I whispered in his ear. "What's going on, Devin? Did you just take some Ecstasy? I promise not to tell anyone—"

"What? No!" He pushed my hands away.

"Devin, what is wrong with you?"

"Forget it. Why even bother? You think I'm too stupid to say anything meaningful—if I do, I must be on drugs. You know what? Fuck you. What would I know, anyway? I didn't even go to college."

"Doctor Thomas, did you pass out over there? Are you okay?" That was Blair. "Do we need to send the cameras after you?"

"We're coming," Devin called out to them, then said to me, "Let's go. I'm taking you back. You shouldn't be out here in the dark alone. Especially dressed like that."

When we reached the pool area I saw that two of the guys were already gone. The only ones left were Blair, the crew and the bearded Alabama guy. I guess everyone wasn't as enamored of me as I had thought. Bearded Alabama was holding up my phone, which I had left wrapped in my skirt on one of the lounge chairs.

"It rang like five or six times," he said. "Same number, so I answered it. Some guy from the E.R. at the Valley Hospital?"

Ha! So *now* they needed my help in the E.R.?

Grabbing my phone, I turned to the camera guy. "Start rolling. I want this on the next episode."

"Hello, this is Dr. Thomas," I said, smirking at everyone around me. "I don't know why you're calling me. You must be new there. But unless you're living under a rock you ought to know that not only am I a board-certified plastic surgeon, but I'm a TV star. Maybe you've heard of me—*Lipo Queen*? Oh, and by the way, your shit hospital administration fired me over three months ago, so I can't come see anybody there in the E.R., anyway. You better call someone else."

"Rachel, it's Gary."

Gary? Gary was a friend of mine from med school who worked the night shift at the Valley Hospital E.R. Why was Gary calling me? He of all people was one of the first to know that I'd left that place.

"Oh, Gary, I'm sorry…" I said. "I'm just a little…drunk still…you know we just took the boards today and we've been celebrating…I passed, can you believe it, and we're still in Phoenix—"

"Rachel, your brother's here," he said.

"What? What do you mean?" My mind jumped to an image of Jake wandering around the hospital looking for me. "Why? He knows I don't work there anymore—"

"The paramedics brought him. His neighbor called when she couldn't get him to answer the door to take his dog back inside."

"But I just talked to him…a few days ago…he was fine—"

"Rachel, I think you need to come."

"But is…is he okay?"

"Just get here as soon as you can. Your mom is already on her way."

In what felt like slow motion, the phone dropped from my hand and bounced across the tile into the hot tub.

"What's going on?" Devin said.

"It's my brother," I said.

The camera was still rolling.

39

The next available flight back to L.A. wasn't until ten in the morning. Somehow Devin found a rental place open and got us a car and the two of us were heading west on the I-10 freeway at ninety miles an hour by 2:00 A.M. Alone. Without even our toothbrushes.

I smoked out the window of the passenger side the entire way. Cigarette after cigarette, burning every little bronchiole, blunting every coherent thought, pushing away all sensory input so that I couldn't even feel the vinyl seat of the rental car against the back of my legs.

We didn't speak to each other the entire way. We couldn't. There would have been too much to speak about. We stopped wordlessly once to fill up the tank, but I didn't even get out to pee. I was glad that my cell phone had fried from landing in the water. I didn't even try to dry it off. I was afraid I would get a call that I didn't want.

I vaguely wondered if we would get pulled over for going so fast. Devin didn't ask me for directions. He must have been following signs to the Emergency Room that I'd never noticed before. Or maybe he just remembered from the time he picked up the leeches.

It wasn't until he pulled the car up to the curb in front of the ambulance bay that he took my free nonsmoking hand in his and looked at me for the first time since we'd left Phoenix. I don't think anyone has ever looked at me like that in my life. It wasn't a look of sympathy. It wasn't pity. It was as if he was trying to feel what I felt.

The emergency room is always remarkably quiet in the morning. All of the chaos from the night before has been sorted out and the uninsured haven't yet started wandering in, using it as a private clinic. There's usually only one or two nurses working and by then the E.R. physician is sitting at the desk, finishing off the charts. Security is usually dozing off at his post by the waiting room door.

"Thom!" It was Jenny, standing out in the early morning shadows with Sam straining on his leash.

"Rachel, don't—" I heard Devin say and he grabbed my arm, but I yanked it back.

I knew before I was inside. I knew even before I saw the look on the desk clerk's face when the automated emergency room doors opened in front of us. I knew before I saw my mother cowered in the corner of the waiting room. Before my estranged father appeared out of nowhere with his latest girlfriend at his side. I knew like I knew I had passed the boards.

The doors to the Trauma Bay were closed.

"Is he there?" I said to my father, as if it wasn't the first time I had spoken to him in over a year.

"Rachel—" my mother started to say. I ignored her and kept moving toward the Trauma Bay.

There was Gary now, trying to block the door.

"Wait, Rachel," he said, but I shoved his arm away and pushed past him through the double swinging doors.

It was too late. *I* was too late.

The body was covered entirely with a white sheet, completely disconnected from all of the monitors, waiting to be transported down to the morgue.

I gently lifted the edge of the sheet up off Jake's face.

He looked the same. His eyes were closed. I touched his cheek and the skin was still warm. At least they hadn't put him in a body bag yet. They'd taken the ET tube out of his mouth. Except for the fact that he wasn't breathing, he looked like he could just be asleep.

I felt Gary's presence behind me. I heard his voice but only caught some of the words as he droned on about how sorry he was. How Jake had basically been like this since EMS brought him in. That they did ACLS for over an hour anyway but got nothing. How they found dangerously high levels of antipsychotic medication in his bloodstream. How it was nobody else's fault.

How this was a typical scenario. How schizophrenics often eventually stop taking their meds and become delusional and psychotic and suicidal and overdose. How it wasn't my fault that his doctor had called me with some "concerns" when Jake hadn't shown up for his last appointment, but that the call happened during some time when I had no cell reception and I never saw it. That it wasn't my fault that the doctor had also left a message at the hotel but I hadn't checked the landline voicemail since 10:00 P.M. the night before the test. That it wasn't my fault that that the other "emergency contacts" weren't responding either. That it wasn't my fault that psychiatrists don't treat potential emergencies with the immediate action that a surgeon does.

But it wasn't just the overdose. He'd actually lost a lot of blood. Gary peeled back the sheet and showed me Jake's wrists where he'd slashed himself. The trailer floor carpet had been soaked in blood when the EMT's got there, Gary said. At least a couple of liters.

All I could think was, *Jake, you idiot. How did you manage that?* People never die of slashed wrists. That's just something unhappy high school kids do on TV. The radial artery is too small. It clots off before you can get even close to bleeding out. Back in my General Surgery training we used to joke about all the unsuccessful wrist slashers that would come into the E.R. How there should be a course called, "Suicide: Getting It Right the First Time."

"He had high levels of salicylic acid," Gary was saying. "He must have known to take aspirin for a few days before to make it work."

"Rachel." It was Jenny. Her face was tear-stained and puffy. Nobody stopped her from bringing the dog through the doors. My parents stood behind her. This was probably the first time they'd been in the same room in about ten years.

"Rachel," Jenny repeated. "I went by there yesterday like you told me and he was sleeping. I swear, after my audition I went by there and he was sleeping. He was fine."

It wasn't her fault. There was no way for Jenny to know that that wasn't fine, for Jake to be sleeping in the middle of the day. She couldn't have known that Jake had such a regular sleep schedule when he was on his meds that it was impossible for him to take naps even if he wanted to. She couldn't have known that if he was napping during the day, something wasn't right.

"He's at peace," my mother said, as if she was wrapping everything up. My mother, who stood there in a yoga outfit with a bare abdomen.

I looked at my father. Except for his swollen eyes and the redness in his face, he looked the same to me as he had the last time I saw him. Which was probably about five years ago. The same as ten years ago. The same as when I was five and he lived in our garage tinkering around on his power tools, and only came out to eat dinner by himself after we were in bed. I grew up thinking that everybody's father lived in the garage.

I wanted to scream at him, "How do you get the right to cry about this? You haven't even been here!" Instead I just said: "Dad."

I let him hug me until I thought I was going to vomit. The reminiscent scent of his cologne made me nauseated and I pulled away.

An attendant brought chairs for us. We sat silently in a row next to Jake's body. My parents were both crying quietly and I felt like I should be too, but for some reason I couldn't find the tears. Maybe because part of me didn't find this entire scenario all that unexpected. As if somehow I knew this was going to happen, I just wasn't exactly sure when.

At some point someone brought us water, asked if we wanted something to eat. We refused both. We declined the presence of a pastor.

I must have fallen asleep sitting up. I was woken by the light touch of a few fingertips on my shoulder. It was Gary.

"I gotta get going, Rachel," he said. It was mid-morning, and I knew he'd stayed way past the end of his shift. My parents were both gone. "And I'm so sorry, but, we have to clear out the room. It's starting to get busy out there."

I didn't argue. I was actually relieved to have somebody kick me out because I wasn't sure how I was going to leave of my own volition.

The clerk handed me an envelope of paperwork.

"Your mother said you would take care of this," she said.

"Of course she did." I took it from her.

"I'm so sorry for your loss. No rush. Go home and get some rest. Then take a look at it. It's all about—"

"I know what it's about," I said.

Jenny drove the two of us back to the condo in my Porsche. It didn't occur to me to bitch her out about how she'd gotten her hands on the keys.

What *did* occur to me while we drove back over the hill to West Hollywood was that at some point during the morning Devin had disappeared. Without saying good-bye.

40

The next few weeks were a blur of nothingness intruded on by the logistics of daily living. I'd stopped operating long enough before the boards so that I didn't have anybody "cooking." Jenny told everyone I was out sick. I just stayed home and did my usual sitting and smoking routine, ashing into handmade tin foil ashtrays that I left all over my luxurious condo, some of which spilled onto the floor. The smell permeated everything.

I didn't even turn on the television. Jenny was in and out and tried to bring me food but all I wanted was more cigarettes. My phone actually came back to life but I shut it off. The thought of any external stimuli at all was unbearable, and the only way I could block it out was to keep inhaling on those Marlboro Reds.

The first conversation I remember having outside the hospital was in Gloria's office with her and Blair, discussing our damage-control strategy. I sat at the long table in the middle of the room, staring over the glass bowl of assorted beverages and out at the incredible view while the two of them walked and talked circles around me. I chain-smoked and ashed the cigarette end into an empty Diet Coke can. When I had first pulled out my pack of cigarettes Gloria looked at me as if she was going to tell me to put it away, then probably reconsidered since she was holding one herself.

"We'll figure it out," Blair was saying said to her. "It's not really that big of a deal—"

"Are you insane?" Gloria turned to me and frowned. "Sorry—I didn't mean...It's just...well...it's public information. I'm sure it's all over the internet by now." Gloria said.

"Someone at the hospital must have leaked it. Why doesn't your hospital have better security?" Blair said to me.

"It's not *my* hospital. And it's not 1990. Nobody had to 'leak' anything. Do you not remember all those other people around when I got the call? I'm pretty sure everyone had state-of-the-art social media access. Including your crew," I added. "How do you know it wasn't one of them?"

"Regardless," Gloria said. "The network is not happy. We need to figure this out."

"Figure what out?" I said. "Besides, I thought you said you *were* the network."

Blair shot me a look.

"I am. To a *point*. But I'm not a miracle worker. And what we have here is an utter catastrophe." Gloria leaned against one of the chairs and sucked on her cigarette, striking a pose that she'd probably practiced long and hard over the years to get what she wanted. Head tilted slightly up, back arched, butt out, right knee bent. As she did, I noticed that a small but visible amount of her muffin top had come back and was poking out from under her shirt over the top of her jeans. She leaned over and put her cigarette out in my Diet Coke can.

"It's not like we can't salvage this," Blair said. "We just need to think of a way—"

"I'm sorry," I said. "But shouldn't I be hearing things more along the lines of: 'We're sorry for your loss?'"

"Dollface, of course we're sorry," Gloria said. "We just wish we had... known about it...beforehand."

"Well, had I known my schizophrenic brother was going to go off his meds and then kill himself with an overdose I certainly would have given you guys a heads-up."

Neither of them even flinched. "What we meant," Blair said. "Is that we wish you had told us the truth. From the beginning."

"Would it have made a difference?" As I spoke, I stared past their faces and out the window at the horizon where the brown smog transitioned into blue sky.

"We could have...worked around it," Gloria said. "But now we've got this dead psychotic secret brother thing...and how do we spin that in the context of our fun little show?"

"It's more than just a '*fun little show*,'" Blair muttered. "I work my ass off on this 'fun little show.'" She then glanced down at her phone and started scrolling through the browser. "It's already bad: 'Lipo Queen—Just Trailer Park Trash Like Her Crazy Brother', 'Lipo Queen's Secret Life, Living in a Trailer Park—Is She Even a Plastic Surgeon at All?', 'Breeze's Friends Say Their Relationship is a Sham—"

"How did you get all that so fast?" Gloria was madly pushing the buttons on her Blackberry.

"I would think it would make things more interesting," I said. "My crazy brother who lives in a trailer park killed himself. What—is that too much reality for you?"

"We can't work it in quite like that." Gloria sighed. "Mental illness…it's just not…TV-friendly." She closed her eyes and grabbed her head with both hands as if she was experiencing a ruptured berry aneurysm. "And why did he have to be living in a trailer park, anyway? It's just—the *visual* of that—I mean—*a trailer park*. That's going to be impossible to undo.'"

"He had a thing about having his own four walls," I said.

"Wait! How about this!" Blair jumped in. "What if he was her *estranged* step-brother—your parents are divorced, right? So they're not really related, and she didn't even know him—" She stopped in mid-sentence as if waiting for Gloria's glowing affirmation. When she didn't get it, she started talking faster. "And he was a junkie and he overdosed. And we can do on-camera interviews with his 'friends' that didn't know how troubled he really was."

Gloria squinted her eyes. "Possible. It *is* much sexier. Like River Phoenix and the Viper Room."

"Right?!?" Blair nodded furiously. "And how many entertainment news documentaries did they get out of *that* one?"

"We can get a bunch of unknowns to talk. Maybe even a heartbroken woman. That'll distract everyone. We need a new storyline anyway. Since we have no idea what's going on with What's-his-name. Have you heard from Russell?"

Blair shook her head. "I left him three messages."

Gloria lit another cigarette. "You might be on to something. I'll talk to the network."

"No," I said.

"What?" Blair spoke as if I was interrupting their conversation.

"I said, 'no.' Jake is—was—my real brother. And he wasn't a heroin addict."

"*We* know that," Blair said. "But nobody else has to."

Gloria turned to me. "Dollface, it's going to kill your career. No pun intended. Everyone knows that all that bipolar, schizo stuff is genetic. I agree, neither is optimal, but if we have to choose, a drug addict is definitely the way to go."

"I'm not going to say those things about him." I looked at Gloria. "And I'm not going to let you say them, either."

Blair shook her head. "But a drug addict is *so* much better than a mental patient! I mean, drug addict—we can work with that, look at *Celebrity Rehab*—"

"He wasn't a 'mental patient,'" I said. "It's not his fault he *lived with* mental illness." I had learned in previous discussions with Jake's doctors that this was the politically correct terminology.

"Well, what we ultimately decide to call him is not your decision."

"I think it is."

"Do you want to lose the show?"

I remained silent.

"Doctor Thomas!" Blair's voice was higher and screechier than I had ever heard it get before. "Is that what you want? You want to lose the show over this? *Are* you as crazy as your brother?"

"Maybe I am," I said. "Maybe that's the whole problem."

Of course I didn't want to lose the show. *Lipo Queen* was my fame and fortune. And now that I had passed the boards I didn't have to worry any more about getting "in trouble." As the *Lipo Queen*, my career would have no boundaries.

As if she were reading my mind, Blair said, "You're really an idiot, you know. You're on the brink of having it all."

She was right. Before I'd left for Phoenix, Jenny had said we were booked out until Thanksgiving. By this time next year I'd probably be able to buy a house. Maybe even one of those on the bluff.

Blair sat down next to me. "You're still in shock." She took my hand. "Why don't you go home and rest…take a break for the next few days…give yourself some time to think about it."

"Shock is a physiologic state of distress of the human body," I said. "It means dangerously low blood pressure, usually brought on by severe infection or major blood loss. I'm not in shock."

"Whatever!" Blair said. "Look, do you want to lose everything?"

"I kind of already have," I said.

"Jesus, don't be so dramatic. We're trying to save your TV show."

"I want to save it too," I said. "But not that way."

"Well, it's the only way. What about Don?" Blair turned to Gloria. Don was Gloria's older-than-dirt husband, the president of the network, and everyone involved's God.

"Don is…angry." Gloria stood up. "He won't help me. He said it's my own fault for jumping into a project without enough background research."

"How much time do we have?" Blair said.

"The network is giving us until Friday."

It was Wednesday.

Gloria reached for the blazer she'd thrown over the back of her chair. "I have another meeting. I don't have a lot of time to dwell on something that's just about gone away. Too many other projects in the works. Rachel, best of luck to you."

"At least give her till Friday!" Blair said. "Why can't we let her think about it, call her on Friday?"

"You can call me on Friday," I said. "But my answer is going to be the same."

"How can you do this?" Blair burst out. "How can you do this to us?"

"I really don't have time for this. This meeting is over." Gloria's hand was on the door.

"What? You're going to let her destroy everything we've worked so hard for—"

"If that's what she wants—"

Blair snorted. "She doesn't know what she wants."

"She's a big girl." Gloria started down the hallway with Blair chasing after her.

"Gloria, wait, can you please at least try to talk to Don? Can't you talk to the network one more time? At least try?"

"I said, the network is done!" Gloria shouted at her. I'd seen her act a lot of ways before, including like she'd just done a few lines of coke. But this was the first time I'd ever seen her this angry. Then she yelled without turning around. "I'm sorry, Rachel, but plan to be out of the condo and the office by the end of next week. Blair will take care of the car."

Jenny was waiting for me in the Porsche at the curb on Sunset. She'd conveniently had an audition scheduled that morning so she was unavailable to help me face the wrath of my producers.

"How'd it go?" she said when I got in the car.

"They're cancelling the show. We have to be out of the office by the end of next week."

She nodded without looking at me. We were on our way to the Valley to clean out Jake's trailer.

"Is my mother there yet?"

"She said it's not that bad."

"Maria was there yesterday." I watched the line of cars ahead of us as each slowed and stopped at the freeway on-ramp light. "We can go in the carpool lane."

"Yeah, I always forget that."

"He hasn't even called me once."

"Who?" Jenny said. "Oh, you mean him. Well, why should he? I'm sure he already knew it was cancelled."

"I suppose." I hadn't told Jenny what had happened with Devin right before Gary's phone call. She would have just dismissed it: *Of course he hadn't meant a word of it…it was all for the show…he's an actor. How could I be so stupid as to take him seriously?* And I guess she would have been right.

Maria had done a good job of cleaning the trailer. There was no trace of a crime scene. It looked pretty much like I'd last seen it—when Jake and I had watched that first episode of *Lipo Queen* together on the couch. If the bloodstains were still there they were faint, and I didn't look for them. My mother was squatted on the middle of the floor in her yoga clothes, packing all of Jake's CD's into a box.

"What's this?" she said, holding up Jake's *US Weekly/People/Star Magazine* poster board *Lipo Queen* collage, unfinished and now warped from the heat.

Jenny got to work in the kitchen while I started going through his dresser. My mother had brought a stack of broken-down cardboard boxes that she'd probably had since I moved into my college dorm room over fifteen years ago. I reconstructed two of them with packing tape and then started with the top left drawer, trying not to look at anything that I was tossing in. When I hit the bottom drawer I came across my spare Audi key wrapped in the shrunken bright-patterned Tommy Bahama. It was the only piece of clothing I unfolded to look at. It was wrinkled, and there was a brown stain on the front pocket. I folded it back up and placed it in my purse.

"Rachel, can you give me a hand," Jenny called from the tiny corner kitchenette. "There's a lot of crap in here."

I went to help her while my mother continued to toil away in the living room area, boxing up videocassettes and dog toys.

Jenny handed me a stack of papers. "See if there's anything important. You know his stuff better than anyone."

I sat down at the table and started thumbing through the pile. It was mostly old mail, dating as far back as six months ago. Almost all of it was junk—catalogues, packs of coupons, credit card applications for me. There were five or six utility bills but they were just automatic pay statements; for the past year and a half the money had been taken electronically from my account. Then I came across what looked like a personal card in a blue envelope. It was addressed to me at my old Van Nuys apartment, and it was postmarked from June. It had the red "return to sender" stamp with the pointing index finger. The return address was Jake's.

I quietly tore open the envelope. Jenny's back was turned, and my mother was completely oblivious. I don't know why I didn't want either of them to see what I was doing. Maybe because so far here in the trailer, none of us had delved beneath the surface of what was going on, and I wanted to keep it that way. It was too painful for it to be any different.

I held the card under the table so I could read it without either of them seeing. The front had a glossy color photograph of a tabby cat that looked like

Sushi. On the inside was a note in Jake's shaky writing: "Dear Rachel, thank you for calling and talking to me every night. It keeps me from feeling lonely. Love, Jake"

There it was. The pain in the back of my throat, and the stinging at the corners of my eyes. Finally.

41

But as these things happen, the tragedy came and went. The chore of daily living continued as if nothing had happened and I had to figure out what I was going to do about work. According to Jenny, new patients were still calling. The landlord at the North Bedford address had graciously offered for me to stay if I could come up with the $20,000 a month rent on my own, but even if my business continued to thrive, that wasn't a remote possibility. I should have known that the only reason Gloria had been able to get me into that office so quickly was because it was too expensive for anybody but a network to rent it.

Meanwhile, Jenny had transferred our phone line to her cell and ran my virtual office from her car.

"I got it up on the website that you're board-certified," she said to me a week after we'd been kicked out. We were having our daily morning phone conversation about what I was going to do next. It always went in a circle and we would hang up without any kind of definitive plan besides the fact that I was going to have to do *something*.

"That's great." I leaned back on the couch and Sushi jumped out of the way. I had temporarily moved in with my mother. Miraculously, it wasn't going so miserably. Mostly because she was locked up in her room all the time doing yoga.

"Listen, Thom, I know you're not going to like this idea but Jessica Bernholtz called and she offered to let you sublease from her—"

"No."

"Just hear me out. It's the same building, it's easy for the patients. She said 5G a month and we have enough money to get us through till the end of the year, and she said she'll even drop the rent if we use her O.R.—"

"I said 'no.'"

"We could start tomorrow. And we wouldn't have to deal with a lease—"

"Jessica Bernholtz is never going to be my landlord," I said.

"Well, you're going to have to do something because you can't see these people in your mother's garage."

I sighed but didn't say anything.

"Thom, I need you back. Your patients need you. People want to see you. And there are a bunch of condolence messages on the website chat board. You should take a look. Some of them are really nice."

"I don't want to talk to anyone."

"The holidays are coming up. Everybody wants surgery. You know how it got at Ferraro's last year."

"Jenny, he hasn't called me once. Not even a text."

"You're not talking about Eddie."

I hadn't heard from oh-so-concerned-Eddie either, but there was no surprise there. It was like when he stood me up for that big gala. At least his behavior was consistent.

"No, I'm not."

There was an uncomfortably long pause and then she said what she said every time: "I'm really sorry, Thom. I know how much you liked him."

I stared up at the circles of water stains on the ceiling from all the times we had let the bath water overflow when we were kids. "It was stupid. I know. I'm just a regular girl. I should never have let myself get all caught up. It's just— I feel like we were really starting to connect—"

"Thom, you need to forget about him."

"Even if it was all just stupid, superficial bullshit…he could have at least called to see how I was doing. I mean, you would think…after everything that happened."

Jenny never knew how to answer me when we got to that part.

At least once a day I would almost call him. I certainly had a legitimate excuse. My brother had committed suicide. Wasn't that alone enough of a "get out of jail free" card for just about anything right now? Besides, he had been there *with* me when it happened. *He had driven me six hours to the hospital.*

Wouldn't it be appropriate for me to want to talk to him after that immeasurably bonding experience?

But each time I went to call him, I stopped myself. I was afraid of being sent to voicemail. Or worse, he would answer and be unfriendly. And then all of my above questions would be answered and that would be it. I had to face it—if he'd meant anything he said to me that night by the pool, I would have heard from him by now.

I missed Jake, and I felt guilty about not being there for him when he had needed me the most. I felt guilty for being alive when he wasn't. I felt guilty for allowing myself to think about anything else *but* Jake, and for missing Devin. But mostly I felt guilty—and this was the worst part—because I suspected—it was possible—*that I missed Devin more than I missed Jake.*

One afternoon about two weeks into it, my mother wandered out of her bedroom after a marathon yoga session. I was parked on the couch, a place where I spent the majority of my time those days. I could reach over and slide open the window to smoke without getting up.

"I just did four hours of yoga," my mother said, putting her hands on her hips and pinching her waist. "You should try it. It's great for the mind."

"Not today." Though pretty soon I was going to have to start doing something. I was starting to feel really fat but at the same time I couldn't imagine engaging in any form of exercise. Then I felt guilty for caring about the way I looked when Jake was dead.

I reached for my tin foil ashtray on the coffee table.

"I really wish you wouldn't smoke."

"Sorry." But as I struck the match it did occur to me that using yoga to shut things out was way more constructive than using cigarettes. I'd give her that.

She leaned over my shoulder. "What are you reading?"

Rhetorical question since I was thumbing through a tabloid.

When I didn't answer, she continued: "I don't find her attractive. She has a thick upper body. You know, Asians usually have thick upper bodies."

She was referring to one of the "best celeb bodies of the summer." It was an old tabloid.

"*I'd* take her 'thick upper body,' " I said. And as I glanced over at my mother standing there in her Lululemons, with her spindly legs and crepey skin and paint all over her shoes, I suddenly had the epiphany of a lifetime.

Was *she* comparing her*self* to the actress in the picture? My nearly seventy year-old mother was competing with a young, Photoshopped celebrity? At what age had her beauty worship turned to jealousy and bitterness? *And how had I never realized this before?*

I was so caught up in my "Aha" moment that her next question completely caught me off-guard. "I'm sorry you haven't heard from that boy."

"How do you know about him?"

"You're always on the phone, talking about him. And this is a small house with cheap, thin walls. I'm sorry that didn't work out."

I shrugged. "I wasn't pretty enough for him. It happens."

"Nonsense! You are a lovely girl—"

"Mom, stop with the bullshit. I know what I look like and so do you. He's completely out of my league."

"You're a plastic surgeon! Isn't he some has-been—"

"He can still get into any club in town with any girl he wants."

She made the huffing noise she makes when she's talking about some-one—or something—completely beneath her. "Those things are so unimport-ant. I refuse to talk about it with you."

"Well maybe if you hadn't talked about it the whole time I was growing up I wouldn't be so fucked up about it now."

"I have no idea what you mean. Don't roll your eyes at me."

"Jesus! Really, Mom? Look at what I *am*!"

"Rachel, what on earth are you talking about? Where is this coming from—"

"Where is this coming from? Are you fucking kidding me? It came from you! Why do you think I became a plastic surgeon in the first place?"

"You were always good with your hands. It had nothing to do with me. It was your idea."

"*My* idea. Yeah. Okay. It was all me. Are you sure you didn't whisper it into my ear while I was sleeping at night when I was a kid? Have you heard of the term, 'inception?' Did you see the movie?"

"You're sounding as crazy as your brother."

I was about to go into a rant about my great new discovery, how I'd suddenly realized that my life and even my career were somehow a product of my mother's demented value set, how my lack of self-esteem compounded with my lack of beauty—or what I interpreted to be my lack of beauty in her eyes—had driven me down this warped path to success, and yet to a place of such severe self-hatred.

And if it had been ten, or maybe even five years earlier, I would have ranted. I would have shared with her my groundbreaking revelation. That it could be possible that my career was my way of "owning" beauty, since my own beauty would never be good enough. That the seed of motivation she had planted in my childhood had become a winding, weedy, mess of self-torture. We would argue, we would cry and yell at each other, but in the end I'd finally make her understand that I was right. And she'd sit down and we'd discuss it ad nauseum. She'd apologize. We'd work on it together.

If it was five or ten years earlier, I would have tried. But I was adult enough now to understand her, and that she was too far along in life to understand anything new about *me*. There would be no enlightening her.

And even if I *could* push and push and push until she got it, how would that even help anyone if she *did* change? It was too late for her. And it was too late for Jake. But it wasn't too late for me. I didn't have to continue living a life measuring my self-worth by the size of my body parts. I'd just saved myself thousands of dollars and years in therapy. Breaking through to her, getting her to really understand how much she'd fucked me up, would just upset her. And I had been so busy feeling sorry for myself that I hadn't even considered how hard this whole morbid ordeal must be on her. What it would be like to lose a child.

I closed my eyes. "You're right. Forget it. I don't know what I'm saying. I'm really tired. I guess I'm just upset because they canceled the show."

"Oh, Rachel, I'm sorry."

"It's okay. It was pretty dumb, anyway."

"I didn't think it was dumb at all. What you did for those women was quite fantastic."

I was so surprised that I almost dropped my cigarette out the window. "You *watched* it?"

"Of course I watched it. Why do you think I got cable?" She went into the kitchen.

I stood up for the first time all day and followed her.

"What would you like for dinner? How does chicken sound?" She held up a cookbook that lay open on the counter. "This is a fat-free recipe. There is no fat in it at all. I never eat fat."

"I know, Mom."

"And yet…" Again, she pinched at her lower back, "I just can't seem to get rid of this. No matter what I do. Even after hours of exercise every day."

She couldn't be serious. She couldn't *really* be wanting to have this conversation with me right then.

"Mom—"

"I know, I know. I'm just trying to keep myself preoccupied, I guess." She opened the refrigerator door and started searching the shelves. Even though I couldn't see her face I could hear in her voice that she was trying to keep from crying.

I put out my cigarette in a half-filled dirty coffee mug and rested my hand on her shoulder. She was still sweaty.

"You want me to help you with it?" I said.

"You hate to cook." She sniffed. "You always hated it."

"Let me at least try."

She looked at me. Her eyes were red. I handed her a paper towel so she could wipe her nose.

"You can't smoke in here," she said.

"Okay," I said. I don't know why, but I didn't want to leave her alone.

42

Somehow without all of us ever being in the same room together, my parents and I managed to organize a time to scatter Jake's ashes. It was my idea to do it at his favorite place—off the bluff into the ocean in Malibu.

I arrived first with my mother. We met my father at the Zuma beach parking lot. He had driven down from Northern California alone. His girlfriend hadn't been especially interested in participating.

There was a dirt footpath that curved along the side of the cliff, separated from the houses by fences. The three of us trekked up the steep incline in single file. It took my parents less than three minutes to start arguing.

"I don't think we need to go that far," my father said, pointing to my mother, the star athlete, who was about ten yards ahead of us. She had taken Sam along and he was straining on his leash. "This is fine right here."

"Well, I think we should keep going," my mother yelled back at him.

"What's the point of walking all that way? And watch out for the horse droppings."

"The water's too shallow. We can't do it here. We can't scatter Jake on the *sand.*"

"There's water right there. I don't know why you have to make everything so difficult." My father was chewing gum. He always chewed gum.

"Can you guys please just stop arguing?" I said. "It's not like I'm asking you to move in together. We're walking up a hill."

"I agree," my mother said. "This needs to be as peaceful an experience as possible. For Jake's sake."

"Well, whatever we're going to do here, we need to do it soon," my father said. "This place is starting to get crowded."

"Don't be ridiculous," said my mother. "Who comes to the beach in the morning this time of year? It's freezing cold."

"Apparently, a lot of people," my father said.

We turned around to see what he was talking about. Usually he was just a complainer, but the parking lot *was* starting to fill up with cars, turning in from both directions on the Pacific Coast Highway.

What was this? The start of some stupid mid-winter 5K run? Or was it one of those cycling clubs with all the men in the creepy spandex outfits?

"Who are all these people?" my father said. "And why are they coming up here?"

That was the next weird thing. Everyone from the parking lot seemed to be headed toward the bluff. Toward us. In a very organized fashion. As if they had all been expecting to run into each other. As if they had been expecting *us.*

I watched as they waited patiently to get in line to walk up the path. The figures got closer and larger, and each one started to come into focus individually. Nobody was wearing spandex. And nobody had any numbers tied around their waists.

And then I heard my mother say: "Hey, isn't that the nutty scrub tech from your show? And your nurse?"

I looked at where she pointed and did a double take. She was right. At the head of the pack was Mateus, decked out in a fashionable yellow V-neck sweater that matched his shock of crazy highlighted blonde hair. A red and white scarf encircled his neck, the ends brushing around down to the waistband of his skintight black jeans. Next to him was Adeta, in an orange floral print gown with an actual train dragging behind her. She must have been wearing her fancy shoes, because she was hanging onto Mateus' arm like she needed crutches.

"Uh, oh. Look who's here," my mother said.

Once Mateus and Adeta rounded the corner and the view was clear again, I saw him too, and my heart involuntarily went into my throat. It was Devin. Looking just like he had the first time I saw him. In real life, that is. He was even wearing the same charcoal grey hoodie and faded Levi's. Only this time he didn't have a surly expression on his face. And he was coming toward me.

"Hey," he said when he reached me.

"Hey," I said. "How—"

"Jenny told me." He glanced down at his cell phone. "Speaking of, she said to tell you she's really sorry but she's running late. Something about the baby sitter." He looked behind him. "I hope you don't mind that I brought a few people along."

I tried to comprehend what was happening around me. I waved my hand at the crowd of people that congregated alongside the bluff, and streamed out of their cars into the parking lot. "But how did *they*—"

"I tweeted about it," he said proudly.

"*You* tweeted?" A laugh escaped from somewhere inside me. I'm pretty sure it was the first time I'd genuinely laughed since the boards.

"What? You think you're my only fan? I'll have you know, I've got ten thousand and twenty-two followers on Twitter."

"Devin, this is like the corny ending of one of those bad TV shows I watch."

He shrugged. "Sorry. That's all I know is bad TV. I just hope your family's okay with it."

I shook my head in disbelief as I watched my mother squeeze sideways along the path, greeting people and thanking them for coming, while my father just looked pissed as usual.

"I would hardly call us a family," I said. "But Jake would've gotten a kick out of it."

As people sidled by us to get to the wider area of the path and the top of the bluff, the sea of unknown faces morphed into ones that were recognizable and I realized that I knew almost all of them. There were patients of mine. There were colleagues. I saw Donarski. Paula. Jessica. *Eddie.* And even…

Blair and Gloria. Standing a few feet away from me. They'd both gone for the traditional head-to-toe funeral black. Gloria had a pair of large sunglasses on and a scarf around her neck that whipped slightly in the wind.

"The network wouldn't budge," she said. "I really am sorry."

"Dr. Thomas," Blair said. "We're sorry for your loss."

I nodded a "thank you." They each gave me a hug and continued past.

"Rach, c'mere." Devin took my hand and led me around the white picket fence that bordered the grassy backyard of the house behind us. It was the

Tudor style one. From the beach you couldn't see that the lawn had a lot of weeds growing in it and that the patio furniture was old and weathered. Up close, the beautiful beige and green striped lounge chair cushions were too dirty to sit on. There was no pool, either.

Devin bit his lower lip and looked away from me. "Rachel, I'm sorry I didn't call you. I owe you a big apology."

"What for?" I knew my voice was a little too high-pitched. Totally unconvincing. "Why would I expect you to call me?"

"Come on, you didn't think after what I said in Phoenix it was a little weird that I didn't call you?"

"To be honest, I wasn't thinking about you at all. I mean, I've had a lot going on these days."

"Huh." He kind of laughed and shook his head. "You must think I'm a serious asshole."

"I understand." I swallowed at the lump in my throat. "I really do."

"No, you don't." He shook his head again. "Rach, What I said that night… in Phoenix…by the pool…"

"What?" I said, even though I was afraid to ask. I didn't want to know any more.

"…I meant it…"

"It really wasn't just for the show…" I started to say.

No, that wasn't true. Of course I wanted to know. But only if…

"No," he said softly. "It wasn't."

"…Or to get into my pants?"

This time he really laughed. "*No!* For starters, I was trying to keep you from taking them off for all those other guys."

I looked around. Most of the people there—guests, I guess you could call them—were too busy networking with each other to notice the two of us talking. *Is there any city besides L.A. where people come to a funeral to network?*

"It was Russell," Devin continued. "He's the one who made me leave the hospital before the paps showed up. He told me it would be bad publicity for me. He didn't think I should have anything to do with you anymore."

"There were paparazzi there?" I said.

"Listen to you! A few. There are some pictures floating around on the Internet."

"He was just looking out for your best interest."

"No, he wasn't."

"They cancelled the show."

He nodded and motioned toward the growing crowd. "Looks like you still have a lot of fans, though."

His voice trailed off and it got quiet again. The dull ache that I had been fighting for the past few weeks started rising up again in the back of my throat, and I felt that stinging at the corners of my eyes.

"I wish you could have known my brother," I said. I tried to concentrate on the row of houses in front of me to steady my voice. I had never seen these houses so close up before. *One at a time, left to right, and starting over from the beginning. The Spanish style, the Tudor one where we were standing, the modern one, the Cape Cod...*"I used to take him here all the time. It was his favorite place. And then, there wasn't time to do it anymore. And now there really isn't."

Then I felt his arm around tightening around me.

"I know," he said. "Jenny told me everything."

He pulled me toward him and I pressed my face up against his chest, inhaling his familiar clean-boy scent. I could feel that his shirt was getting wet beneath my eyes, maybe even beneath my nose.

"I'm a bad person," I said.

"What happened isn't your fault."

"Yes it is. I ignored him."

"You weren't ignoring him. You were living your life."

"I wasn't taking care of him—I mean, I *was* taking care of him, but not like I should have been—"

"It wasn't your job to take care of him. You were his sister." He hugged me tightly and then it was impossible to stop the tears. Welling up in my eyes, rolling down my cheeks, soaking the thick cotton of Devin's hoodie. And I knew that I was crying not because Jake was dead, but because of the way he had had to live.

"He couldn't work," I said into Devin's chest. "But he had lots of hobbies. Music…and…snorkeling…I would bring him here and he'd go snorkeling in that freezing water. That fucking freezing water."

"Why don't you tell them about it, too?"

I looked past his shoulder at the crowd that filled the path to the bottom of the hill and spilled out into the parking lot. There had to be at least a hundred people there.

"What—you mean like make a speech or something?" I tried to suck back some of the snot that was dripping from my nose and wiped my face with the back of my hand. "Now *that* would be corny." I tried to laugh. "Like a *really* bad TV moment."

"The worst," he agreed. "But that's what people like, isn't it? Besides, seems like they're waiting for something."

"Maybe." I studied the crowd again. "If I do that Blair will want to kill herself because she doesn't have a camera with her."

"Well, there's a cliff right there for her." He caught my eye. "Sorry. I know. Too soon."

"Hey, *I* said it." I wiped my nose again. I could feel how swollen and red my eyes must have been, and I was sure that my mascara and eyeliner were pooled around down at my tear troughs by now. "I'm not exactly camera-ready."

"You always look hot," he said.

"And you're a great actor."

He put his hands on my shoulders. "Please don't make me have this conversation right now. Just go get this thing over with."

"Okay." I took a deep breath in and felt a ripping sensation in my chest. I really was time to cut back on the smoking. "Thanks."

Devin nodded. Then, just as I was about to duck around the fence again he grabbed my hand.

"Hey, Rach. What are you doing…I mean, after?"

I felt my heart instantly pick up speed. *Was it wrong to feel this way at a time like this?*

"You mean, after I scatter my dead brother's ashes into the Pacific Ocean with my fucked-up family in front of a bunch of random people?" I tilted my head to the side. "Actually, nothing."

"Cool." He nodded. "Okay, then, you want to maybe hang out or something? Maybe…go get something to eat?"

Here it was. The moment I had been waiting for. Devin Breeze was genuinely asking me out. All of his own volition. No cameras, no paycheck. The mere contemplation of the whole idea seemed so absurd at such a somber moment and yet, I couldn't really think of a practical reason to say 'no.'

"Well," I said. "I don't exactly have a reception planned for all these people so…sure."

"Good." He smiled and then he kissed me. It wasn't a hot and heavy makeout session. It was more of a sweet gesture, appropriately comforting from a Significant Other at a time of solemnity. I shivered at the brush of his unfairly full lips against mine, and I couldn't help thinking I was about to go on a date this afternoon with a guy who had better lips than me.

Which is okay because, after all, there are always fillers.

43

"Dr. Thomas. You're on time." Brenda didn't even try to hide the surprise in her voice when she returned to her desk and found me already seated in the waiting room at twelve forty-seven.

"Actually, I'm early," I said without looking up from the tabloid on my lap. It was an old one but all news to me.

"You might have a little bit of a wait. He's running behind."

"That's okay. I need to get caught up."

I was choosing for myself who I thought "wore it better." I didn't recognize the actress' names but the outfit definitely hung more elegantly on the one with the broad shoulders. Never underestimate the power of broad shoulders, especially on a woman.

"Can I get you any water or anything?" Brenda said from behind the desk.

"No, thanks," I said. "I'm good."

I thought she would leave me alone until Donarski was ready to see me but that wasn't the case. Instead, she came out from behind the reception area and sat down on the couch next to me. She rested her elbows on her knees and cupped her chin in her hands and leaned toward me.

"How are you doing, Dr. Thomas?" she said. "Are you okay?"

"Yes," I said. "I'm okay."

It was the truth. At least at that moment, on that day, I was okay. It had been almost a month since the ceremony for Jake, and while I definitely had my moments, I was, for the most part, back participating in the world. I had never had anyone close to me die before and I was learning that the loss didn't come and go all at once. It would be nice if that were the case, because then you could just check out for a couple of weeks, sit around at home and smoke a few packs of cigarettes and be done with it.

But nothing is ever simple. The aftershocks come suddenly, at uneven intervals, at odd times. I would think I was fine all day, and then it would creep up on me without warning—triggered by a song on the radio, something someone said during a case in the O.R., or even from nothing at all. The most confusing part was that sometimes I would forget that Jake was dead. We had spent so much time apart the last few months anyway that on a daily basis I didn't feel like all that much was missing. And then I would go to call him and I would remember.

"I heard you and your boyfriend got a new car," Brenda said. "I saw it online."

I sighed. Clearly she was not going to allow me to ignore her. I put down the magazine.

"Yes, he helped me get a new car."

"He is just darling, you know."

"Yeah, I know." Except actually, the day that we got the car was the first time he'd been a little less than darling. I had thought he'd seemed a little grouchy the whole time we were at the Audi dealership but I figured it was just the long hours he'd been putting in lately reading all those scripts that Russell kept sending him. I didn't understand I had done anything wrong until we were driving off the lot less than an hour after we'd arrived, and I had the signed loan contract in my hand.

By the time we were back on the freeway I asked him what his problem was.

He just sulked.

"Did I do something?"

"You're not supposed to act like you *want* the car," he said, staring straight ahead.

"But I wanted it. It's the same car as I had before."

"You don't *tell* them that. '*Oh my God! I love this car! It looks just like my old one! I have to have it!*'" he imitated me. "How can I negotiate a lower price for you when you act like that?"

"I had no idea," I said. *How would I? No one else had ever tried to take care of me like that before.*

"Besides," he added. "I don't like you speeding around in such a little car. You need to be driving something safer."

"Raquel."

Dr. Donarski stood in the open doorway. Two administrative types dressed in dark suits shook his hand and nodded at me on their way out.

"Dr. Donarski." I followed him into his office, and took a seat in the extra chair that I'd sat in so many times before, now the first time as a visitor.

"Thank you for coming." He sat across from me at his desk. "So, Raquel. How are things? I'm so sorry about your brother."

"Thanks."

"Busy?"

"You could say that."

"Too busy to take your old job back?"

I'd had a feeling it was going to be something like this. I'd heard through the grapevine that Paula had met some guy during the boards and within two weeks had picked up and followed him to San Francisco and taken a job at UCSF.

"Why would you want to give me my job back?" I said.

Dr. Donarski leaned toward me over the desk. He spoke with a smile and that familiar unmistakable glint in his eye.

"It seems that the administration is interested in starting a cosmetic surgery program."

"Really," I said.

"Really. And who better to run it than the 'Lipo Queen'?"

"I thought I was a liability. What made them change their minds?"

He cleared his throat. "Well, I would like to tell you otherwise but… Frankly, we've had a lot of people—patients—asking about you. Especially once they found out you used to work here."

"So, basically the suits here now see me as a cash cow."

"Yes, I believe that would be the correct expression."

"I don't want my old job back," I said. "I like working for myself." That wasn't entirely true. I liked not having to answer to anyone, but there were things I missed about the Valley Hospital. Not just the part about really helping underserved people, but the feeling of belonging somewhere, being a part of something bigger.

When I didn't say anything else he continued, "It wouldn't have to be full-time. You could still continue with your private practice. But they are offering a generous salary."

I thought about riding back from the Audi dealership with Devin, and did my best to keep a poker face. He was right. I needed to start negotiating.

"*How* generous?" I said.

"Oh man, turn that thing off," Devin moancd as I reached in the general direction of the alarm clock. I was still facedown on my pillow with my eyes closed, but I was able to feel around on the nightstand and hit the snooze button without knocking anything else over. I felt Sushi cross over me so he could jump to the windowsill above our heads.

"I need to clip his toenails," I said, opening my eyes. Our window faced west so there was no sunlight yet, but I could hear the rhythmic sound of waves crashing against the bluff. It must have been high tide.

"Mmmhmm…" Devin's arms were around me and he tried to pull me closer but I wriggled away, and almost tripped over Sam, who sat patiently at the foot of the bed. He never came too close when the cat was around. He was still wary of Sushi.

"No, sorry. I can't be late today," I said as I padded into the bathroom. "You've made me late every day this week. If I'm late today I have to buy lunch for everyone at the surgery center."

"So? I'll buy it for them. C'mere."

Of course I returned to the bed. I wondered how long it was going to take for the novelty to wear off. Or if it ever would.

He wrapped his arms tighter around me and started kissing the back of my neck.

"I'm just warning you," I said. "I don't have a lot of time."

"You know I can be quick."

"Don't you have to go to work?"

"We're off today. Just have a pre-pro meeting later up at Guy's house."

He'd officially moved into the rented beach house with me about a month earlier. I had been more curious than serious when I first called the number on the For Rent sign. But it turned out that I might be able to live up on this bluff after all. The owner wasn't asking for much. She was in a rush to do some documentary film on another continent, and she was more concerned about getting someone into the house to take care of it rather than making a pile of money. Devin's new movie had started filming out here in Malibu, and even after we were done moving my stuff in, he still almost never left. Finally, one day I told him he could no longer use my toothbrush and I gave him a drawer.

It was the smallest house on the street, but it was big enough for the two of us. There wasn't a pool but there was a fountain that we kept running all the time. And there was a small guest house with a window facing the ocean. Even though it had a kitchenette and a full bathroom, I could never bring myself to let anyone stay there. It was always empty.

When I finally returned to getting ready for work, it occurred to me that Devin wasn't having his "thirty percent" problem. In fact, as far as I could tell, there were no problems at all. *Interesting.*

I went back to the bed where he was still lying on his stomach, his eyes closed.

"Hey." I lightly traced his strikingly prominent cheekbone with my finger. "Are you going to start losing your hair now?"

He shrugged without opening his eyes. "Maybe. But I think it'll hold out till this movie's over and then I'm just a doctor in Guy's pilot. They're all bald from what I remember, anyway." He squeezed my leg. "Besides, I know this kind of hot plastic surgeon who can get me some hair plugs…"

"'*Just a doctor*!' You better watch it." I kissed the crown of his head and as I did, I caught a glimpse of the clock. "Crap. I really gotta go."

"What are you doing today?" he called over the stream of the shower.

"Breast reduction. On a fourteen-year old. True Juvenile Breast Hypertrophy."

"Oh, and Rach—" Devin said something else that I didn't hear after I closed the glass shower door so I opened it again.

"Yeah?"

"I forgot to tell you last night. *The Discovery Channel* called."

About The Author

Suzanne Edmonds (Dr. Suzanne Trott) is a board-certified plastic surgeon who specializes in breast and body contouring. She practices in Beverly Hills, California.

Edmonds lives in Los Angeles, California, with her husband. Her "Lipo Queen" shape wear line is the first shape wear designed by a female plastic surgeon who specializes in body contouring, and has truly become one of Hollywood's "best kept secrets." She wishes she could tell you who's wearing it. She blogs at www.lipoqueen.com, providing her readers with accurate, objective information regarding cosmetic procedures and treatments.